TATIA'S TATTOO

LINDA BRENDLE

TATIA'S TATTOO
Copyright © Linda Brendle

All rights reserved. 2018
Published in the United States by BookPros.
Library of Congress Cataloging-in-Publication.

Typeset by BookPros in conjunction with Lightning Source,
La Vergne, Tennessee. Printed in the United States
by Lightning Source on acid-free paper.
Set in Grotesque MT Std Regular.

ISBN: 978-1-945455-82-7
Ebook available.

Inasmuch as ye have done it
unto one of the least of these my brethren,
ye have done it unto me.

MATTHEW 25:40

In my Father's house are many mansions:
if it were not so, I would have told you.

JOHN 14:2

Come and go with me
to my Father's house
It's a big, big house
with lots and lots a room
A big, big table
with lots and lots of food
A big, big yard
where we can play football
A big, big house
It's my Father's house

BIG HOUSE BY AUDIO ADRENALINE

THIS BOOK IS DEDICATED
to all the Tatias who cannot tell their own stories
and to the One whose love is big enough for the least of these.

To Roxana —
Pray for the least of these. Blessings,
Linda Brendle

THE IDEA FOR TATIA'S TATTOO

was sparked by a presentation given at my church several years ago by a couple whose mission in life is to rescue children like Tatia. Since then, many people have encouraged, advised, listened, and participated in countless ways in bringing this story to life. I owe a huge debt of gratitude to all of them, with a special shout-out to a few extraordinary people who went above and beyond the call of family and friend.

During the initial phase, Jessica Schmeidler listened to my early thoughts and helped me give them shape. Christian Piatt, my son and fellow author, inspired the tattoo element that is so vital to the story. My church friend, Jeremy Case, allowed me to draw on his experience in law enforcement to add authenticity to the arrest and arraignment scenes. Sara Attaway, my cousin, shared her legal expertise for the CPS aspects of the story and the trial sequences.

After the manuscript was reasonably presentable, my amazing husband David, who waits patiently while I disappear into my keyboard, became my first beta reader. I watched his face anxiously for any reaction as he read and was gratified to see tears glistening in his eyes more than once. When he finished, he smiled at me and said, "This one will sell." Other beta readers were Sara Attaway, Maria Corley, Christi Palmer, and Lisa Moseley. My sister-in-law, Jo Lynn Robinson, not only read the manuscript but volunteered to do the line edit. Thank you all so much for your encouragement and constructive comments.

Thank you to Christian Piatt for his guidance and support through the process, to Brianna Snyder for the perfect cover and interior design, and to the rest of the amazing staff at BookPros who brought ***Tatia's Tattoo*** to life.

None of this could have been possible without those who supported the dream financially by contributing to my crowdfunding campaign.

Fay Robinson	Daryle Whitaker
Jason and Stacy Rolen	Donna Wheeler
Sandra Nickel	Jim Robinson
Sara Attaway	Sue Brown
Stella Larson	Betsy Stiles
Christian Piatt	Candis Taylor
JoLynn Robinson	Jodi Denning
Mary Kay Pumphrey	Peggy Chaney
Brianna Snyder	Unknown Donor
Christi Palmer	

For information about what you can do to help fight sex trafficking near you and around the world, visit these websites:

For the Silent https://www.forthesilent.org/
Our Father's Children https://www.ourfatherschildren.org/
Ink180 http://ink180.com/
Let My People Go http://www.lmpgnetwork.org/

CONTENTS

Preface - The Nightmare   11

FRIDAY

1	Off to Camp	15
2	Camp Memories and Family Good-Byes	21
3	Encounters with an Angel and a Biker	29
4	Welcome to Camp	31
5	The Darker Side of Eric	35
6	The Whirlwind of Camp Activities	43
7	Imagination Station	49
8	Happy Birthday to Everybody!	55
9	Birthday Dreams	59
10	The Real Nightmares	65
11	Statistics	73
12	After the Party	77
13	Long Sleeves	79
14	A New Identity	87
15	Suspicion	91
16	Preparations	93
17	Choices	97
18	Limited Options	105
19	On the Stroll...	109
20	...and in the Slammer	113
21	Court is in Session	119
22	Finding Mrs. G	123
23	Show Time	127
24	A Cry for Help	131
25	Loss and Gain	141
26	Help and Hope	143
27	There Is Still Light	147
28	Going Home	155
29	New Beginnings	161

SATURDAY

30	My Father's House	169
31	Taking the Tour	173
32	Decision Time	185
33	A Parable Comes to Life	189
34	Meeting Jesus	193
35	Celebrating a New Birth	195
36	Invitation to Camp	197
37	Meeting Jesse – Again	199
38	No Condemnation	203
39	Saying So Long, Not Good-Bye	207
40	Family Reunion	211
41	The Next Step	215
42	The Deposition	217
43	No Deals	221
44	An Unwelcome Encounter	223
45	Tatia's Story	227
46	Cindy's Story	233
47	Cross Examination	237
48	Tatia's Testimony	241
49	The Defense Rests	243
50	New Evidence	247
51	The Verdict Is In	251
52	Cindy Speaks	255
53	Tatia's Tattoo	263
54	The Sentence	267

SUNDAY

| 55 | Jesse's Surprise | 273 |

| Epilogue | | 281 |

PREFACE
THE NIGHTMARE

Tatia couldn't breathe. She could feel his weight on her chest, his hot breath on her face – and pain – she felt hot, searing pain running up the center of her body. Then, he rolled off of her, and she could breathe again, but she wasn't sure she wanted to. If she could hold her breath long enough, maybe she could go where Mama and Daddy went, to their Father's house. Suddenly, he grabbed her by the shoulder and jerked her off the bed into a standing position.

"Go clean yourself up. My friend will be here in fifteen minutes. Stop your bawling and freshen your make-up. You look like hell."

He turned to the bed to straighten the rumpled sheets. When he caught sight of the fresh bloodstains, he threw his hands in the air in exasperation.

"Was this really your first time?"

The only reply from the bathroom was the sound of running water and soft sniffling.

"I could have charged twice as much," he yelled.

Tatia woke with start as her alarm clock freed her from the nightmare she had re-lived for more than a decade. She turned off the alarm and slipped to her knees beside the bed, asking God to take away the horror of the dream and to replace it with His light. Basking in the love she felt in response to her prayer, she rose and picked up her partially packed suitcase from the floor. She placed it on the bed, ready for last-minutes toiletries, and headed for the shower. She had a plane to catch and girls to rescue.

FRIDAY

CHAPTER 1
OFF TO CAMP

Tatia heard a car horn emit two quick beeps, and she knew her ride to the airport had arrived. She stepped out onto the balcony of her second-floor apartment and waved to the gray-haired man who stood beside the open door of an almost brand-new Lexus.

"Hi, Henry," she called, waving and smiling as he looked up. "I'll be down in two minutes."

"No hurry, Miss," he said, returning her smile. "We have plenty of time, and the traffic is light this morning, or at least lighter than usual."

Tatia continued to smile as she closed and secured the sliding glass door. She was glad Henry had been available this morning. Her records at the executive car service she always used indicated that he was her preferred driver. She knew she could trust him to chat lovingly about his wife of nearly fifty years and his multiple children and grandchildren instead of hitting on her like some of the younger drivers.

She looked in the mirror and moved her arm into several positions to be sure her sleeve didn't pull up and expose her mark of shame. Satisfied, she took a quick pass through the bedroom and bathroom in case she had forgotten anything vital. She closed the quart-sized plastic bag that held all the cosmetics she would need for a week at camp and tucked it into a corner of her small rolling suitcase. Then, she grabbed the laptop and the loose-leaf notebook that lay waiting on the ottoman in front of her favorite chair, slipped them into her shoulder bag, and headed for the door. She wouldn't have time for work the next week, but she never liked to be completely out of touch – and she'd have time to review the notebook in the airport and on the plane. Before she shut and locked the door, she glanced around the tiny apartment that had been home since the previous year when the Justice for Victims of Trafficking Act had been passed and she had been asked to chair the Council on Human Trafficking. The flat wasn't much by Washington, D.C. standards, but as one of twelve trafficking victims whose job it was to advise policymakers, she wasn't exactly an insider anyway.

"Good morning, Henry," she greeted him again with a big smile. "Are you ready to roll?"

"Always ready to drive you wherever you need to go, Miss," he replied with a grin. "You make yourself comfortable, and I'll put your bag in the trunk." He took her suitcase, knowing she would want to keep her shoulder bag with her.

Once they were on the road, Henry began a now-familiar conversation. "Miss Robins, I don't understand why a successful lawyer like you continues to live in a cramped walk-up in this neighborhood. I'll bet you could find something much nicer if you looked around a bit."

"I'm sure I could, and it would be much more expensive. Then, I wouldn't be able to afford to have you drive me around, and that would be just too sad."

Henry sighed and continued. "I worry about you. This area isn't safe for a young, beautiful woman alone. You need a husband who will protect you."

"Henry, I know you care about me, and I appreciate it. But you know I'm waiting for God to choose a husband for me. Until He does, I have my guardian angels watching out for me."

"So, I guess I should mind my own business and let Him mind His and yours. In the meantime, I'll keep reminding Him that you need a good man in your life."

Tatia laughed and changed the subject. "Henry, I'll bet you can't guess where I'm going today."

"No, I can't. But since you're dressed in jeans and boots instead of a business suit, I'm guessing it's not a business trip."

"You're right. No business for the next ten days. I'm going to visit some old friends, and then I'm going to summer camp for a week."

"Summer camp, huh? My grandkids are each going to different camps this year."

With that, Henry began talking about his favorite subject: his family. Tatia settled back into her seat and half-listened while she thought about her first time at camp.

It was the summer of her twelfth birthday with nothing to look forward to but three months of Texas heat in a house crowded with too many foster kids and Josie, her pre-menopausal foster mom. Josie didn't really seem to like any of them, and she usually took her frustrations with her absentee, truck-driving husband out on the kids.

At least Tatia would be free of the incessant taunting of her classmates as they droned on about their hectic vacation schedules and the hardship of finding time for cheer camp, youth camp, and several other camps between trips to the beach, the mountains, and The Continent. Tatia had no idea what they meant by that last one, but she knew she was supposed to be impressed. She didn't bother to answer the snide questions about her summer plans, plans that consisted of remaining unnoticed and spending as much time as possible losing herself in a pile of books at the blissfully cool library.

Even those expectations were probably too high. Since she would be home from school, she would be noticed and subject to Josie's expectations. Josie didn't like being called by her first name, but she would never be "mama" to Tatia. She was more like the wicked stepmother in *Cinderella.* While she was finding relief at the mall or the movie theater, Tatia would probably be stuck in a house with a couple of ancient window units and a few box fans that did little to fight the triple digit temperatures. Instead of spending time in the library, she would be surrounded by sweaty, smelly kids with runny noses, dirty diapers, or both. At least they could all go outside and spray each other with the water hose to cool down and wash away some of the unpleasant odors.

The only break Tatia could count on was the weekly meeting with her social worker. It wasn't really Ms. Dunham's fault that their time together was spent checking on Tatia's situation and filling out reports. Even though Tatia was smart, pretty, and sweet, she had issues, issues that had kept her moving from foster home to foster home instead of finding the forever home she longed for. Most prospective parents wanted newborns or at least a toddler to rock and cuddle. The few who would consider an older child wanted one who would respond to overtures of love and tenderness instead of an emotionally unavailable little girl who rarely made eye contact and who resisted all efforts to break through her ironclad defenses. It didn't help that her files included accounts of frequent night terrors caused by recurring nightmares. Still, sometimes Ms. Dunham dropped the formalities and took her out for ice cream or shaved ice, and that was better than nothing.

With such low expectations, Tatia was totally shocked when, at one of their meetings, Ms. Dunham said, "Tatia, how would you like to go to camp this summer?"

"Yeah, right. Like Josie would let go of that kind of money."

Ms. Dunham smiled. "I know finances are tight right now, but this camp won't cost Josie anything."

"I don't know. I spend enough time during the school year with those snobs. I don't want to waste my summer with them, too." The regular kids made life miserable for the foster kids, so the thought of spending more time with them seemed almost unbearable

"You won't be with your classmates from school. This is a camp especially for kids in the foster system, so everybody will be more or less in the same situation."

"Ah, I see. It's one of those 'let's take care of the poor foster kids so we can feel better about ourselves' kind of things. And I suppose we spend most of our time in group counseling sessions spilling our guts to perfect strangers."

Ms. Dunham was accustomed to the defensive cynicism of her young clients, so she wasn't put off by Tatia's resistance. "No, as a matter of fact, there are no counseling sessions. If the campers want to talk to a staff member about something, that's okay, but the purpose of the camp is to have fun."

"Fun, huh? Like what?" Tatia's curiosity was piqued in spite of her best efforts to remain disinterested. By the time Ms. Dunham had given her a more detailed description of the camp facilities and activities, Tatia couldn't help feeling a little excited by the possibility, but after so many disappointments in her life, she was afraid, too. "Maybe, but Josie would never let me go. She needs me to help with the little kids."

"I've already mentioned it to her. She said if all the kids can go so she can have a week off, she's all for it."

"Oh, I see. So, I get stuck with the same bunch, just in a different location."

"No, Tatia. It's not like that. The campers are divided by age group, and each counselor has two campers for the week. You'll be paired with a girl your own age, and the two of you will get lots of one-on-one attention from a counselor who is already praying for you and looking forward to meeting you."

"I knew there was a catch. This is a church camp with lots of preaching and telling me what a failure I am. Right?"

"It is a faith-based camp, and there will be a couple of Bible stories each day, but the focus is on how special you are to God. And I guarantee you won't be bored with the praise and worship times. All I can say is you'd better take your dancing shoes."

"Really? The way you describe it, it sounds too good to be true."

"It's better. I'm probably not doing it justice. It's only five days. What have you got to lose. You might have some fun."

"Well, if you want to go to the trouble of getting it set up, I guess I could try it just this once." She tried to retain her cool demeanor, but Ms. Dunham was thrilled to see a spark of something in Tatia's eyes she hadn't seen before – hope.

"Miss Robins?" said Henry. "We're almost to your stop. Are you checking your bag or carrying on?"

Tatia knew his question was his diplomatic way of calling her out of her reverie. She had lost a bag once, and not wanting to repeat the experience, she had learned to pack lightly enough to meet the strictest carry-on limitations.

"Just drop me at the curb, Henry, and thanks for calling me back from La-La-Land."

He smiled at her in the rear-view mirror. "Anything for my favorite passenger. I hated to disturb you. You looked like you were enjoying your thoughts. Looking forward to your week at camp?"

"I am, Henry. It's an intense few days, but it is the most rewarding thing I've ever done. And I get to do it with some very special people."

"How special?" he asked mischievously.

"Henry, you're impossible."

She laughed as he stopped the car and moved quickly to the trunk to retrieve her bag. She was reaching for the door handle when her phone notified her that she had a text. She glanced at the screen and saw a selfie of Jesse in a do-rag and Harley T-shirt. The brief comment said, *Wanna race?*

She grinned and responded. *You nerd! I'll be in DFW before you make your first gas stop.*

So smart & beautiful! 1st gas stop already.

You cheated! Left early!

His reply began with a thumbs up symbol, and then he continued. *Making 500+ today. Stopping in Springfield, MO tonight. 400+ tomorrow. Breakfast Sunday?*

Deal!

She slipped the phone back into the side pocket on her shoulder bag and slid toward the car door which was now open. As she stood up, she looked up into Henry's grinning face.

"Very special, I think," he said knowingly.

Tatia felt the heat rise in her cheeks, but she couldn't help smiling back at him.

"Yes, I thought so," he said as he pulled out the handle of her suitcase and handed it to her. "I've already scheduled myself for your return. I'll be waiting in the cell phone lot when you touch down. Have fun."

"I will, Henry, and thanks."

CHAPTER 2
CAMP MEMORIES AND FAMILY GOOD-BYES

She made it through security in record time and, as always, Tatia breathed a prayer of thanks for Senator Porter's administrative assistant. After Tatia almost missed her first opportunity to testify before the Senate subcommittee that was reviewing the Trafficking Act, the efficient young woman from the Texas Senator's office walked her through the red tape of the TSA Pre-Checked Security System. Still, Tatia always arrived well before flight time, just in case.

Her frequent flyer status entitled her to lounge privileges, but since she didn't drink, smoke, or flirt, she preferred to spend her pre-flight time with the regular folks. She did, however, drink coffee, so she picked up a decaf mocha before heading toward her gate. She paid no attention to the glances and outright stares she attracted as she walked down the concourse with a long-legged stride, her shoulder-length blonde hair swinging in rhythm with the tap of her heels. Her thoughts were focused instead on the two campers she would meet for the first time in a couple of days. She felt the same mix of emotions she always felt before camp – the excitement of almost unlimited possibilities and the dread of the heartbreak that would come when, after being together twenty-four hours a day for five days, the week came to an end.

For now, however, she had a plane to catch, and she suddenly realized she was beyond where she would find hers. Relieved that she had no traveling companion to notice her lack of concentration, she quickly turned around and made her way back to the correct gate. The waiting area was almost empty, so she had her pick of seats. She chose one with a view of both the tarmac beyond the window and the desk where the gate agent would deal with irate passengers who were certain their situation was the most important on the planet. She smiled, looking forward to a week free of irate politicians who were even more certain than the passengers that their situations were the most important on the planet.

She settled back in her seat and pulled the purple notebook out of her shoulder bag. She sipped her coffee and flipped to the first page: "Royal Children's Camp, Counselor and Staff Manual, Preparing Yourself for Camp." The familiar pages were highlighted and the edges were tattered from years of use. She knew most of the material by heart, but going through it again helped refocus her mind from the outside world to the children. She skipped over a couple of pages and read the camp's mission statement. The last sentence was underlined, highlighted, and marked with a star in the margin: "We will create life-changing moments and extend loving hands to these children of abuse." She closed her eyes and whispered, "Help me create life-changing moments and loving memories for Carmella and Amanda."

Her thoughts were interrupted by the patter of little feet and the excited squeals of a dark-haired five-year-old with sparkling brown eyes. "Daddy," shouted the little girl, running to the window and pointing toward the runway at a plane that was just touching down. "Is that our airplane?"

A tall, handsome man with a suitcase in each hand followed her to the window and knelt beside her. "I don't know, Angel," he said with a loving smile as he pointed toward the area directly in front of where they were kneeling. "It might be. Our airplane will pull up right there, and when it's time to go, we'll walk through a tunnel and get on the plane."

A young woman joined the pair, putting her overnight case on the floor and kneeling on the other side of Angel. "Mommy, our airplane will park right there, and we'll walk through a tunnel. Daddy said!"

Tatia felt like an intruder, watching the little group share a family moment, but she couldn't look away. It wasn't a life-changing moment, but it was one of many moments that would accumulate into a lifetime of loving memories for Angel. Tatia's life might have been very different if there had been time for a few more family moments for her.

"My daddy died," said five-year-old Tatia.

"I know, sweetie," said the nice church lady. "Would you like another cookie?"

Tatia didn't want another cookie. She'd had three already and a plateful of chicken strips, macaroni and cheese, and mashed potatoes. She didn't want any more food. She wanted to talk about Daddy.

"He died over the seas somewhere. His car ran over a bomb, and he blew up. The preacher said he's in his father's house, but I saw him. He's in a box and his face looked all painted."

The church lady looked funny and her eyes got a little red.

"I'm so sorry, sweetie."

She hugged Tatia and went to see if anybody else wanted another cookie. Tatia looked for her mama. She couldn't find her, but she found her grandmother. She tried to climb up in her lap, but her grandmother pushed her away.

"Get down, Tatia. You're too big to be sitting in my lap. Besides, your shoes are dirty, and you'll ruin my dress."

Tatia looked down at her black, patent-leather shoes. They had always been her favorites, the ones she was only allowed to wear to church or parties. They had straps, and she liked the special socks that went with them, the white ones with the pink lace around the edges. Now the shoes were splattered with sand from the graveyard. Bits of grass and several stray burrs clung to the lace on her socks.

"Now, go outside and clean yourself up."

"Yes, ma'am," Tatia said as she shuffled toward the door.

"Pick up your feet when you walk, and don't slam the door on the way out."

Tatia concentrated on being sure her shoes cleared the floor each time she took a step, and she slipped outside as quietly as she could.

It was nice outside. The fellowship hall of the little country church was too warm, and there were so many people that it was hard to breathe. Everyone in town knew her daddy, and they all came to pay their respects to a local war hero. They also turned out for the lunch afterward – the ladies at the First Baptist Church were famous for their cooking.

Tatia walked on the curb that ran along the edge of the driveway that looped from the parking lot to the front door and back toward the street. She balanced carefully until she came to the intersection of the cement and the grass, and then she sat down. She began gingerly pulling the burrs from her socks and brushing away the sand and grass. When they were as clean as she could get them, she stood and shook the way she'd seen her friend's dog do after his bath, hoping to get rid of anything she missed.

"Tatia!"

She jumped when Aunt Sheila called her name. She had been so intent on her task she hadn't heard the door open. Sheila wasn't really her aunt, but she was Grandma's best friend and acted like a surrogate aunt sometimes.

"Yes, ma'am?" she said quickly.

"You'd better get in here. Your grandma has been looking everywhere for you."

Tatia sighed and hurried inside. No matter how hard she tried, it seemed like Grandma was always mad at her. Sometimes Tatia saw her whispering with Aunt Sheila and other ladies, and they all looked at her funny. One day she was outside playing, and she could hear what they were saying. She hadn't meant to listen, but the window was open, and Grandma had a pretty loud voice.

"Steve would never have married her if she hadn't been expecting Tatia. Sometimes I wonder if Steve is even her father, but he was determined to do the honorable thing. She and that baby ruined his life, and I'll never forgive either of them for that."

Tatia didn't know what all that meant, but she knew it wasn't good and that somehow it was her fault. Tatia wondered if Daddy liked it in his father's house. She wondered if he had to stay in that box or if he could get out and walk around. She didn't want to have to get her face all painted up and lie in a box, but if there was another way to get to where Daddy was, she'd sure like to go. She was still in Springdale, though, where he'd left her, and now Grandma was mad at her again. Mama was really sad, and tonight she would probably drink too much of that brown stuff that made her act funny. She wished her Daddy hadn't run over that bomb.

Tatia had put on her pajamas and had been playing on the floor for a long time, but Mama hadn't come in to help her say her prayers, tuck her in, and kiss her goodnight. She stood up, put all her dolls to bed, and kissed them. Then, clutching her favorite bear under her arm, she quietly opened her bedroom door. She peeked out into the hallway, and seeing no one, she tip-toed toward the living room and peered around the door jamb. Mama was lying down with one arm covering her eyes and the other hanging off the edge of the couch. She had a half-empty bottle of brown liquid clutched in her hand.

"Mama, I'm ready for bed."

"Honey, this one time can you be a big girl and put yourself to bed? Mama doesn't feel well."

Tatia could always tell when Mama had been drinking a lot. Her words got all fuzzy and mashed up together.

"But, Mama, aren't you going to help me with my prayers?"

"Why bother? He doesn't hear them anyway, or if He does, he ignores them. We prayed for your daddy every night, and look how that turned out."

Tatia was a little bit scared. She had never heard Mama's voice sound like it sounded now – like somebody else was using Mama's voice – like Mama wasn't really there.

"But, Mama..."

"Tatia, I can't! I have to think. I have to figure out what to do, how I'll feed you, where we'll live. I can't do this by myself!"

As Mama began to sob, tears escaped from Tatia's clear, blue eyes, rolling down her pink cheeks, dripping onto the blonde curls that fell across her shoulders as she stared at the floor. She thought about what she had heard outside the church before they left. Grandma was yelling at Mama.

"You think you're all set now, don't you? Well, I have an appointment with my lawyer tomorrow morning, and I will personally see to it that you and your daughter don't get a cent of my son's money, no survivor benefits, nothing. And that's my house you're living in. You have thirty days to be out."

"But where will we go?" Mama had asked. "How will we live?"

"You'll think of something. You managed to trap my son into marrying you. I'm sure there is a market somewhere for your skill set."

Tatia didn't understand what Grandma meant, but she knew it made Mama cry.

"Mama, please don't cry. You're not by yourself – I'm here. The preacher said Daddy is in his father's house. Maybe we can go live with him."

Mama's sobs gradually slowed down, and she finally spoke again, so quietly that Tatia almost couldn't hear her.

"Maybe." She was quiet for a minute or two. "Yes, maybe I can. You go on to bed now, honey. I'll be in to kiss you goodnight in a few minutes."

Clutching her bear to her chest, Tatia slowly went back to her room and climbed into bed. She lay very still, listening for Mama. She was half asleep when she finally heard footsteps headed toward the bathroom. She heard Mama open the medicine cabinet door and turn on the water. Tatia imagined her taking an aspirin – she did that sometimes when she drank a lot of that stuff. Then, she heard Mama coming toward her room. The door opened and Mama came over and sat on the edge of the bed.

"Are you still awake, Tatia."
"Yes, Mama."
"Give me a hug, sweetheart."
Tatia hugged her, and Mama squeezed her so tight she could hardly breathe. Then, she kissed her on top of the head and Tatia could feel Mama's tears dripping onto her hair. She almost giggled, but then Mama began to whisper, almost like she was talking to herself.

"Tatia, you are the best thing that ever happened to me. The only good thing I ever did was bring you into this world, and now I can't even take care of you. But you're so beautiful, so special – they'll grow to love you as much as I do. I miss you already."

"But I'm right here, Mama."

"Of course you are, my darling. I just hate to be away from you even when you're asleep. I love you more than anything. You know that, don't you?"

"Yes, Mama, I know – to the moon and back. And I love you, too."

Mama kissed her one more time and then tucked her in. She walked to the door and paused. Without turning around she spoke again, so quietly Tatia wasn't sure she heard right.

"I'm so sorry, Tatia. Good-bye."

When Tatia woke up the next morning, the sun was peeking through the cracks between the blinds. She stretched and listened for the familiar morning sounds of Mama taking a shower or fixing breakfast, but she heard nothing. She strained to hear the talk show Mama watched every morning, but there was nothing but silence. She sniffed for the smell of coffee, but that was missing, too. Maybe Mama was still in bed with a headache from the stuff she drank. Tatia would have to be very quiet this morning.

She slipped out of bed, dragging her bear and her blanket with her. She opened the door of her room as quietly as she could and tip-toed down the hall.

"Mama?" she whispered.

There was no answer – Mama must still be in bed. She went into the living room and saw Mama lying on the couch like she was last night – one arm was covering her eyes and the other one was hanging off, touching the floor. She wasn't holding the bottle, though. It was on the floor on its side with a little dribble of brown liquid forming a small puddle under its mouth. Tatia went over and carefully picked up the bottle, but she accidentally brushed Mama's hand. She froze, afraid Mama would wake up and be mad, but she didn't move. In fact, her hand was cold — really cold — and it felt kind of funny, not really like skin. Tatia put down the bottle and her bear and gently covered Mama with her blanket. Now she would get warm and feel better when she woke up. Tatia picked up her bear and laid him on Mama's tummy. That was sure to make Mama smile when she woke up. Then, Tatia picked up the bottle and took it into the kitchen to throw it away.

She was getting hungry, so she pulled a juice box out of the refrigerator and a Pop Tart out of the cabinet. She sat down at the kitchen table to eat so she wouldn't make a mess. When she was finished, she threw away her trash and went into her room to get dressed. She stayed there and played for a while, but she checked on Mama every once in a while to see if she was awake yet. She wasn't. After a long while, Tatia was growing bored playing by herself, so she ventured all the way into the living room.

"Mama," she whispered. When she got no response, she spoke a little louder. "Mama, it's time to wake up."

She put her hand on Mama's cheek. Her face was really cold, and Tatia was getting a little scared. She patted Mama's cheek, but nothing happened. Then, she laid her head on Mama's chest. Sometimes she went to sleep that way at night while Mama watched TV. She liked the sound of Mama's heart beating and of her breath going in and out. Now she heard nothing. Tears began to form in the corners of her eyes, and she grabbed Mama's shoulders and shook her gently.

"Mama, please wake up. I'm scared. Please wake up."

She didn't know what to do. Then she remembered what Mama taught her about the telephone.

"Tatia, if anything bad ever happens and you need help, just pick up the handset and hit this button that has a "1" on it. I have it programmed to automatically dial some nice people who will come and help you."

Tatia, picked up the handset and pushed the button. In a minute she heard a nice lady talking.

"911. What's your emergency, please?"

Tatia began to cry. "My mama won't wake up, and she's really cold."

"What's your name, sweetheart? And how old are you?"

"My name is Tatia and I'm five years old."

"Is anyone else in the house with you?"
"No, just Mama."
"Okay, Tatia. You did the right thing. Don't hang up the phone. I'm sending someone to help you."

The calm voice on the phone had a soothing effect on Tatia, and her tears began to dry.

"Tatia, is your door locked?"
"Yes, ma'am."
"Can you unlock it?"
"If I stand on a stool."
"Okay. Go get your stool and unlock the door so the helpers can get in."

Tatia did as she was told. While she was putting the stool back, she heard sirens. Then, she went back and picked up the phone.

"Okay. I did it."
"That's great, Tatia. The helpers should be there any minute."

Tatia took the phone and went back to the couch where she sat on the floor. Her bear had fallen off Mama's chest, so she picked him up with her free hand and hugged him to her own chest.

"Mama," she said quietly. "The helpers will be here in a minute. They'll help you and make you warm." Her tears were flowing again. "Dear God, please don't let Mama be dead. Please don't make her be in a box like Daddy."

CHAPTER 3

CONVERSATIONS WITH AN ANGEL AND A BIKER

"Are you sad?" said a little voice.

It took Tatia a minute to realize that the voice wasn't in her head but was coming from Angel who was standing in front of her, staring up into her face. She smiled at Angel, wiping away the wetness from her cheeks.

"No, Sweetheart. I was thinking about a time when I was sad, but I'm happy now."

"Me, too!" said Angel, rocking from one foot to the other. "I'm going on an airplane to see my grandma."

"I'll bet she's happy about that, too," said Tatia.

"Yeah. Are you going to see your grandma and make her happy?"

"No, sweetie. My grandma is with Jesus now, and I'm sure she's happy there."

"Yeah, Jesus makes people happy. I gotta go now." Angel turned toward where her parents were sitting.

As Angel skipped away, Tatia thought about her grandmother. She did the right thing and took Tatia into her home – she always did the right thing – but she never grew to love her granddaughter. Maybe it was because her heart was broken over the loss of her only son, or maybe she was filled with the guilt of her daughter-in-law's suicide. Regardless of the reason, she rarely spoke to Tatia or even looked at her. She stopped going to church and eventually withdrew into the safety of her bedroom where she surrounded herself with photo albums and memories.

One day a neighbor dropped a bag of groceries on the way from the car to the house. A careless grocery clerk had put a half-gallon of orange juice in the same sack with a bag of cereal. The heavy juice landed on the cereal, and the bag burst, scattering toasted O's across the driveway and the lawn. The frustrated homeowner hurried into the house and returned with a broom and dustpan, hoping to sweep up the mess before she had a mass of ants to deal with. She was shocked when she saw a dirty and unkempt five-year-old girl kneeling on the driveway, stuffing handfuls of cereal into her mouth as fast as she could.

The neighbor brought Tatia inside and sat her down at the table with a real bowl of cereal, a piece of toast, and a glass of milk. Then she began making phone calls. Within hours Grandma had been taken away in an ambulance, and since she had no other living relatives, Tatia became a ward of the State, one more homeless child in the foster system.

Tatia's phone simultaneously vibrated and chimed, jarring her out of the past. She looked up, surprised at the crowd that was now packed into the waiting area and the line that was beginning to form in front of the tunnel entrance. Then, she looked down at her phone and smiled at Jesse's latest text.

Are you there yet?
Still at the gate, she typed.
Better get going, Girl. I'm halfway there!
Ha! That ancient hog probably isn't out of Ohio yet.
Did you pack your boots?
No room. Wearing them. Should be in sandals. You better have a good reason!
Maybe. Maybe not! You'll see!

Tatia had been ignoring the annoying announcements of the gate agent, but the words "Boarding all rows" finally caught her attention.

Final boarding call. Gotta go! she typed quickly.
See you Sunday!

She flashed him an emoticon smile, set her phone on silent, and stuffed it into her pocket. She felt it vibrate as she handed her boarding pass to the agent. She rolled her bag down the jetway, and when she stopped behind the line of people waiting to board, she pulled her phone out and glanced at the screen. The little round face blowing a heart-shaped kiss made her own heart skip a beat, but she shook her head as if shooing away a buzzing pest. *If only she had met Jesse before she met Eric*, she thought. Setting her phone on airplane mode, she slipped it into her shoulder bag and tried to shift her thoughts from Jesse to the two pre-teen girls who were waiting for her in Texas.

CHAPTER 4

WELCOME TO CAMP

Tatia inched down the aisle of the MD-88 behind a tangle of arms, legs, and luggage wheels as the late-boarding passengers vied for limited overhead bin space. Her nose told her that at least one of her fellow passengers had opted for a heavy spritz of cologne in lieu of a shower, and she was grateful when she realized she was passing rather than sitting by the offender. The aroma of brewing coffee soon overpowered the unpleasant smell as Tatia moved back toward the galley. Her travel agent usually arranged seats closer to the front of the plane, but apparently the Dallas-Ft. Worth area was a popular destination this time of year. Thankfully, though, her seat was by the window on the two-seat side of the plane so she would only disrupt one person if she needed to move around during the flight.

By some miracle, Tatia found a vacant spot where her suitcase fit with a minimum of shoving, and she slid into 29E just as the stewardess began to encourage the stragglers to take their seats. Her traveling companion for the next two and a half hours was already plugged into the tunes she had stored on her phone, so Tatia pulled out her notebook before sliding her shoulder bag under the seat in front of her.

She had received the resource notebook the second time she went to Royal Children's Camp, that time as Deborah Grochowsky's staff assistant. The neatly typed pages, organized into sections by printed dividers, belied the emotions behind the words – words that attempted to prepare the volunteer camp workers for the intensity of the feelings they would experience as they encountered innocent victims of childhood abuse and sought to impact their lives with the love and acceptance they wanted and needed.

When she opened the purple vinyl cover, her eyes fell on the two index cards in the inside pocket. After her first year as a counselor instead of a staff assistant or teen helper, Tatia was allowed to forego the training weekend with the understanding that she would review the notebook on her own. Each spring, she received any material revisions along with two cards, one for each girl she would fall in love with during their week together. The cards contained scant information – first name, age, and pertinent information. Notations might include *New, *Bed Wetter, *Runner, or *Night Terrors, and almost all of them included *Meds. This year, both her girls were on medications, and one was new, but neither had other issues. One was eleven years old, and the other was twelve. She preferred to work with the older girls, always hoping she might create life-changing moments and somehow save them from making the mistakes she had made.

She whispered a prayer for the two precious children whose lives had been reduced to words on cards, praying that by this time next week they would both know how special they were to God and to her. She thought about Monday when each child would step off the bus, timidly looking around for an unfamiliar face and a welcome sign with his or her name, indicating that, at least for the next five days, she belonged. She smiled as she thought of the signs she had made over the years, signs on neon-colored poster board lettered with sparkly letters cut from sheets of adhesive foam, all supported on stir sticks from the paint store.

These silly signs represented so much to these who had so little, and that's why the entire staff jumped around like crazy people as the buses approached, yelling and waving signs, anxious to see the fearful expressions melt into relieved smiles as the thought registered, *Oh, that's my name!* That's also why she was flying in a day earlier than absolutely necessary – so she could spend a couple of hours in the middle of piles of art supplies, cutting out sparkly letters.

Tatia thought back to the summer Ms. Dunham had arranged for her to go to camp. The day they left, she and her foster siblings were so excited and full of chatter that even Josie's threats of making them stay home if they didn't settle down couldn't dampen their spirits. However, as soon they climbed aboard the bus and confronted a sea of tense, wide-eyed faces, their smiles faded, and they froze in place until Tatia pushed them all toward the back where they squeezed together onto two seats across the aisle from each other.

By the time they reached the camp, the younger ones were whimpering and begging to go home. Then, they noticed a commotion in front of them as the other children crowded close to the windows in spite of admonitions from the adult riders to stay seated.

"Look! Look!" they shouted excitedly as they pointed and pressed their noses to the glass.

WELCOME TO CAMP

Curious, Tatia and her crew moved to the right side of the bus and craned their necks to see what had sparked life into everyone. What they saw was a large group of people from teens on up, all smiling and jumping, waving their arms or signs, laughing and shouting. The signs had names in large letters, and some of the letters were sparkly.

"Look! Shelby! That's my name!!" shouted one excited little girl.

"Yes, campers," said one of the adults. She had given up trying to keep them in their seats, and she seemed as excited as the people outside. "All this excitement is for you, to welcome you to camp. As soon as the bus stops, gather up anything you brought on the bus with you. When you get off the bus, there will be camp grandparents, aunts, and uncles to help you look for a sign with your name. The person who is holding that sign will be your counselor for the week. Your counselor will take you to lunch and then help you find the rest of your luggage. Welcome to Royal Children's Camp. Get ready to have fun!"

As she finished speaking, the bus lurched to a halt, gently tossing everyone against the seat in front of them. No one seemed to mind, though, as the sense of excitement spread. Tatia herded her little group toward the door, making sure nothing had been left behind. She was halfway down the aisle when she felt a tug on her shorts. She turned to see her youngest charge, looking scared and smearing tears across her cheeks with the backs of her hands.

"Tatia," she wailed. "how will I find my name? I can't read."

"It's okay," Tatia said, kneeling beside her and picking up the ragged, stained blanket she had dropped on the floor. "I'll help you."

"How about I help her," she heard someone say. "And how about you go find your counselor and start having a good time."

Tatia looked up into a pair of twinkling gray eyes that were so full of life and joy that she couldn't help smiling back. "Well, that's very nice, but..."

"I know. Your mom told you to watch out for the little ones, right?"

"Yeah."

"But that's not your job this week. Your job is to be a kid and have fun."

"But you're a kid," she said, still a little bit unsure.

"Well, yeah, but I'm sixteen, and I'm one of the teen helpers. My name is Jesse. See. It says so right here," he said, showing her the badge he wore on a lanyard around his neck. Then, he smiled and held out his hand. Reassured by his easy-going manner and the small heart and cross tattoo on the inside of his forearm, she took his hand, and he pulled her to her feet.

"Thanks. My name's Tatia, and this is Kaley."

"Hi, Kaley," he said, squatting down by the five-year-old who, by this time, had her thumb in her mouth and the corner of her blanket lying against the side of her face. "I'm Jesse, and I can read. Can I help you find your name while Tatia goes and finds hers?"

Kaley stared at him silently for a few seconds before nodding and putting her free hand in his.

"Do you have anything on the bus besides your blanket," he asked her. She continued to stare at him seriously as she slowly shook her head. "Okay, let's go," he said as he led her toward the front of the bus. After a few steps he stopped and looked back at Tatia. "The counselors for the older kids are over there," he said pointing past the driver. "Have a great week. See ya' around."

By the time she did a final check to be sure she wasn't leaving anything, Jesse and Kaley were gone. She smiled to herself, thinking that she liked his eyes and his smile. He was almost as cute at Eric.

CHAPTER 5
THE DARKER SIDE OF ERIC

Tatia looked up when the flight attendant began her pre-flight announcements. She was one of those who tried to be entertaining in order to maintain the attention of her passengers, but it was still the same information Tatia had heard on the hundreds of flights she had been on in the last few years. She turned her attention back to the section of her notebook dealing with signs of neglect and various kinds of abuse. She recognized some of her former campers as she re-read the now familiar pages, and she also recognized some aspects of her younger self.

While Tatia had not been actively abused, the neglect she suffered in the home of her emotionally unstable grandmother and later, in over-crowded foster homes, left her vulnerable. By the time she was in middle school, she was beautiful in a sensually innocent way that child predators dream of. She suffered from the low sense of self-worth that comes when a child's basic need for food, shelter, protection, or love goes unfulfilled. She craved positive personal attention, but she didn't know how to get it, so she was often alone.

Tatia was supposed to ride the bus to and from school, but she hated it. It wasn't too bad in the morning, because hers was the first stop. She could sit in the front seat, and no one dared to taunt or torment her within earshot of the driver. When she rode in the afternoon, though, the kids whose last class was closer to the bus stop filled the front seats before she boarded the bus, and she was forced to sit toward the back. No one sat with her, but the more popular girls surrounded her, throwing out the passive-aggressive verbal torture that was the plight of the foster kids.

The first day of school wasn't too bad, but after that, once the rest of the student body had identified the foster kids, life was pretty unpleasant. So, Tatia sat on the front seat in the morning, and she walked home every afternoon. It wasn't difficult. With the promise of doing extra chores when she made it home, she talked Josie into signing a note giving her permission to ride home with a friend she didn't really know after book club meetings she never attended. She was such a good student that nobody questioned the truth of her claims, and she came to enjoy the quiet solitude of the mile walk between the torture of school and the chaos of home. Then, she met Eric.

On a beautiful day in early March, one of those rare spring days in Texas when the air promised new life and the trees were tinged with green, he came into her life. As she walked down the shoulder of the road with the light breeze playing with her curls, she was almost happy until she heard a car coming from behind, slowing down as it approached. She picked up her pace a bit and focused on the path ahead of her, determined not to let this intruder spoil her last few minutes of peace before the bedlam of the evening began. However, as the shiny fender of the sporty red convertible entered her peripheral vision, she couldn't keep from sneaking a peek.

"Excuse me," said the driver. "I just realized I'm almost out of gas, and I'm new in town. Is there a gas station down this direction?"

Tatia kept walking but slowed a bit, matching her stride to the slow roll of his vehicle. Without looking at him, she replied, "No, not for about twenty miles. Make a u-turn and turn right at the stoplight. There are two stations in the next block."

"OK. Thanks."

"No problem," she said, beginning to pick up her pace again.

"I hope you don't mind my saying this, but you have beautiful hair."

Surprised, she stopped and turned her head to look at him. She struggled to keep her mouth from falling open – he was the most startlingly handsome man she had ever seen, except on the covers of the romance novels Josie liked to read. He had it all – the square jaw, full lips, dimples, smoldering eyes, black hair, and one stray curl that had escaped onto his forehead to keep him from being absolutely perfect. She felt what she was sure was the monster blush of all times reddening her cheeks as he flashed her a perfect smile.

"Anyway," he said, waving and stepping on the gas, "thanks again."

Before she could find her voice, he had made his u-turn and was gone. "Real cool, Tatia," she said as she continued her walk toward home. "Mr. Perfect pays you a compliment, and you can't say thanks, you're welcome, or even have a nice day. Not that it matters. I'll never see him again."

She did, though. The next day she saw him on the same road, driving in the opposite direction. He smiled and waved, and she almost smiled before ducking her head. The following day, his flashy ride was at the four-way stop a couple of blocks from the school, and the day after, he came out of the post office as she was walking by on the other side of the street. Each time, he smiled and waved, and each time, she became a little braver, finally returning his greeting with a smile and wave of her own.

Then, it was the weekend, and she didn't see him for two days. When Monday came, she found herself hoping to catch a glimpse of him as she walked out of the library. What she saw was her handsome stranger sitting in one of two chairs just outside the door, twirling a single dandelion between his fingers. She didn't actually see him at first – she was reading the cover blurb of the book she had just checked out.

"Hi there," he said.

She jumped, let out a little screech, and dropped her book. "You scared me," she stammered, leaning back against the door jamb with one hand on her chest.

"I'm so sorry," he said, picking up the book and handing it to her.

"It's okay. I just wasn't expecting to see anyone. Nobody sits in those chairs – usually," she replied with a breathless giggle.

"Well, I just saw this first color of spring," he said, holding out the flower, "and I thought of you the first time I saw you walking along the road last week."

This time she managed a real smile as she accepted the flower. "Thank you. That's really sweet."

"No problem, right? I gotta run, but since we seem to run in the same areas, I'll probably be seeing you."

"Okay," she said, still looking at the rather wilted flower. "It's pretty."

"Like you. I wish it could be a bouquet of roses," he said as he walked toward the parking lot. Then, he turned back. "By the way, my name's Eric. What's yours?"

"Tatia."

"A beautiful name for a beautiful lady," said Eric, getting into his car and driving away.

Tatia slowly sank into one of the chairs as she watched him drive away. Her head was spinning from the unfamiliar feeling of being the focus of so much attention and so many compliments. "Beautiful? Me?" she whispered. "A lady?" Then she let out a self-deprecating laugh. "He's not perfect after all. He needs glasses!"

Still shaking her head slightly, she shifted her backpack into a more comfortable position and turned her thoughts toward home and the reality of her world.

After their encounter at the library, Tatia and Eric saw each other almost every day after school. Some days he would wait for her outside the library, and they would sit in the two chairs on the porch and talk. Other days they would walk to the tiny city park that was three blocks away and sit together on a bench and watch the squirrels. Sometimes he would pass her as she walked along the county road toward home, and he would do a quick u-turn and pull over to the shoulder of the road. At first, she would lean on the edge of the door, but as she became more comfortable with him, she would sit in the car while they talked.

Tatia looked forward to their little encounters. It never occurred to her to wonder why Eric was always around when other adults she knew were still at work. All she knew was that he seemed interested in her and in what was going on in her life, even if it was just a science project that was due or a snotty group of girls in the cafeteria. He really listened to what she had to say, and he made her feel special. He also brought her little gifts from time to time. At first he brought silly things, like the dandelion or the fortune cookie from his take-out lunch. As they became better acquainted, he brought gifts that were small but significant in their meaning – a pink gel pen because pink was her favorite color or a tube of cherry flavored lip balm because one of the brats at home had stolen hers.

After a few weeks, on a particularly warm day in April, Eric took another step in their friendship. He had the top down on his Corvette, and Tatia was sitting in the passenger seat, telling him about the latest antics of her crazy math teacher. "Hey," he said when she paused in her story, "I'd give my right arm for a cherry limeade right now. How about you?"

"I don't know," she hesitated. "I don't have any money with me."

"No problem. It's happy hour – my treat."

"Okay, sure. I just can't stay very long. Josie gets really mad when I'm late and she has to deal with the kids."

"We'll leave in plenty of time, and I'll drop you off at the end of your street so you don't have far to walk."

After that, he often waited for her in his car a block or two from the library, and she hopped in with no hesitation for a breezy, top-down ride to run an errand with him or into town for ice cream or a shaved ice. The gifts came more often, and if not exactly extravagant, at least a little bigger and more expensive. One day he brought her a T-shirt featuring her favorite band.

"Oh, Eric! You shouldn't have," she said excitedly.

"But I wanted you to have it."

"Thank you so much. But how will I explain this to Josie?"

"Do what my mom used to do. Hide it in the back of your closet for a few weeks before you wear it. Then, if she asks where you got it, just say 'This old thing? I've had it for a long time, but it was stuck in the back of the closet.'"

Tatia laughed, still admiring the shirt. "That would probably work. I do all the laundry anyway, so she doesn't really know what we have. And it wouldn't really be a lie, would it?"

"Of course not. Besides, you'll look great in that shirt. But then you look good in anything you wear."

"Oh, you're always saying that."

"That's because it's true. You really are beautiful." he said, reaching over and playing with a couple of curls that had escaped from her ponytail.

The touching was something else that had increased. At first they didn't touch at all. When they started walking to the park or along the roadside together, he would sometimes bump her playfully with his elbow or sometimes even with his hip. Then, if he had a special gift for her, he would make her close her eyes and hold out her hand. He would sandwich her hand between his with the gift between their palms, and when she opened her eyes, he would reveal the surprise by opening his hand as if he were opening the lid of a treasure chest. She didn't really notice the progression until she began riding in the car with him. When she made him laugh, he would sometimes grab her playfully by the back of the neck or pat her on the leg, and when they went for ice cream, he sometimes sat on the same side of the booth with her, really close so their legs touched, almost like a real boyfriend. She never felt uncomfortable, though – well, almost never – and if she withdrew even a little bit, he backed off, so she felt safe.

There was one time, though, when she saw a side of him she didn't like very much. It was early June, right after school was over. As an end-of-school present, he had given her a prepaid cell phone so she could get in touch with him when she could manage to get out of the house. This particular day, she called to see if he was free. He was, so she told Josie she was meeting Ms. Dunham for a special session about what to expect at camp and how to handle the new situations she would encounter. Tatia said she would walk into town, and Ms. Dunham would pick her up there so Josie wouldn't have to drive her. After the T-shirt incident, it had become easier to stretch the truth or outright lie, especially if it meant spending time with Eric. She missed their daily visits after school, and she was pretty sure he did, too. She was really excited to see him and tell him her big news about camp.

Eric picked her up at the four-way stop in front of the courthouse and headed toward her favorite ice cream shop in Cameron, a nearby town where they were less likely to run into anyone who knew her. She was almost bubbling over and wanted to tell him about camp in the car, but she also wanted to have his full attention so she could watch his reaction as she told him about all the exciting things she would be doing. Unfortunately, he didn't share her enthusiasm.

"Camp? Why would you want to go to camp?" he almost shouted, his face darkening in a way that made her draw back and drop her eyes. He saw her reaction and took a deep breath and continued in a calmer tone of voice. "I mean, I thought we had a good thing going here. Why would you want to go hang out with a bunch of kids?"

"I thought you'd be excited for me," she said, still looking down. "I don't get to do much in the summer. I have to lie to Josie to get out long enough to see you. At camp someone else will be looking after the kids and all I'll have to worry about is me. Besides, it's only five days."

"I know," he said, covering her small hand with his larger one. "I guess I'm just afraid some other guy will steal your heart if I'm not around to protect my interests." He laughed self-consciously and pulled his hand back. "Pretty pathetic, huh?"

She smiled and put her hand on his arm. "I think it's sweet. Nobody has ever been jealous over me before."

He returned her smile and relaxed back into his seat. "Okay. Let's start all over. Tell me about camp."

She chattered on for five minutes, telling him everything Ms. Dunham had told her – about the swimming, the crafts, the princess tea, and the birthday party. "One of the fun things is that camp is the week before my real birthday. It will be the first birthday party I've ever had. Oh, I probably had them before...you know...but I don't remember them."

"Hey, when is your birthday?"

"June 30."

"Tell you what. When you get back, you and I will have a real birthday party, one you don't have to share with a camp full of other kids."

"Really?" she asked with wide-eyed wonder.

"Really," he said. "Be thinking of some way you can get away for a whole evening. We'll go out to dinner at a fancy restaurant – do it up right."

"That sounds awesome," she said quietly as if she was afraid to believe it.

"Wait a minute," he said. "This isn't one of those Bible-thumping camps where they fill your head with God and Jesus and all that stuff, is it?"

"Ms. Dunham said it's a Christian camp. We have Chapel and sing songs, but there's no pressure. She said the main point is to let kids like me have fun and be kids for a few days. I don't know about the God part, but the fun part sounds like Heaven to me."

"Okay, I guess," he said. "As long as you don't decide to be a nun or something and forget all about me."

"Right. Like that's gonna happen," she said as she turned her attention back to her ice cream.

CHAPTER 6

THE WHIRLWIND OF CAMP ACTIVITIES

"Would you like something to drink?" asked the flight attendant.

Tatia sighed, realizing she had been staring at the page dealing with signs of neglect and abuse since takeoff. She closed the notebook, slipped it into the small space between her hip and the armrest, and lowered her tray table. "Yes, I'll have orange juice and a glass of water, please." She would have liked another cup of coffee, but she couldn't handle the instant decaf the airlines served. Her seat mate asked for black coffee, and the flight attendant turned back to her cart to fill their requests after handing them each a napkin and a bag of pretzels.

While she sipped her juice, Tatia thought about all the camps she had attended – the first one as a camper and ten more as a staff volunteer. The preparation for the last nine, when she had reviewed the study material on her own, had all been the same. She tried to re-read the text, and every year she became lost in the memory of those early years. She pulled out the notebook again, careful not to knock over either of her glasses, and opened it to the section called "Been There, Done That." She read through it quickly, reminding herself that her own experiences could be an asset as long as she used them to help her understand her campers, focusing on the uniqueness of each child and not projecting her story onto any of them. Then, she slid the notebook that she could quote by rote into the seat pocket in front of her and settled back to remember.

After Jesse and Kaley disappeared, Tatia looked around and realized all her other siblings were gone, too, so she resumed her trek toward the front of the bus. As soon as her feet touched the ground, an older woman who must have been one of the grandmothers offered her a wide smile and held out her hand and said, "Hi, welcome to camp! I'm Ellie."

Tatia responded with a tentative smile and took her hand. Ellie gently covered Tatia's hand with her other one and gazed into her eyes with a look that said *it's okay, you're safe here.* With her mouth, she said, "What's your name, honey?"

Tatia responded first to the look, and she felt some of the tension leave her tight shoulders. "Tatia," she said, responding to the question.

"Okay, Tatia," said Ellie, tucking her hand protectively into the crook of her elbow, "let's go find your counselor."

They didn't have far to go. As they rounded the front of the bus, they almost collided with a short, middle-aged woman wearing a lop-sided smile and a wide-brimmed straw hat. She was holding up a neon yellow sign with *TATIA* spelled out in hot pink bubble letters.

Ellie looked at Tatia and grinned. "Looks like we found her."

The woman smiled even wider. "Tatia?" she asked.

Tatia nodded shyly.

The woman gave her a warm, camp-regulation side hug and said, "Hi! I'm Betty, your counselor for the week. I'm so excited to finally meet you. And this is Michelle." She indicated a girl about Tatia's age but slightly taller and heavier. She had a mass of braids, caught up on top of her head and cascading down one side. She had a sweet smile and one perfect dimple. "The three of us are going to be a team this week, and we're going to have lots of fun."

Michelle and Tatia said a timid "Hi" to each other while Betty struggled with the three lanyards that were twisted around her neck. "Here," she said, holding out the welcome signs to the girls. "Hang on to these while I get your name tags untangled." When she finally straightened out the mess and put the name tag around Tatia's neck, it was much more than a cord and a little piece of plastic. It was a promise that, at least for the next few days, somebody knew who she was and that somebody cared.

The first thing on the agenda was lunch, followed by rest time. Nobody really rested though; there was way too much to see and do. The counselors helped their campers dig through the piles of luggage to find the suitcases, backpacks, or plastic bags that contained the clothes and other personal belongings they had brought from home. Tatia and Michelle had no problems locating their bags, and Betty was soon herding them toward the dorm they would call home for the week. A steady stream of humanity funneled into the main doorway before splitting, boys and men to the hallway on the right, girls and women to the left. The stream continued to diminish as people found their rooms. Betty and her girls continued all the way to the last door on the left. Then, they stopped as they were confronted once again with the preparation that had been made for their arrival.

The door to the room was covered with names – lots of names – and Tatia wondered just how big that room was. First, though, she scanned the door until she found her own name. She reached out and traced the letters with her finger as if to make certain that somebody really had been expecting her.

"Hey, what's the holdup!" someone shouted from further back in the hallway.

"Come on, girls," said Betty. "Let's get on into the room so we can get settled and get ready to go swimming."

"Swimming! Yeah!" said both girls as they pushed the door open. They almost stopped short again, but Betty urged them to keep moving.

"We're all the way in the far corner," she said.

The room was small and ugly – no more than twenty feet by thirty feet with a concrete floor, cinder block walls, and a ceiling covered with insulation held in place by chicken wire. It was furnished with nine sets of bunk beds lined up against both walls with barely a foot of clearance between beds. A narrow aisle, approximately four feet wide, ran down the center of the room. Still, it had been transformed into a wonderland by counselors armed with strings of lights, crepe paper streamers, balloons, posters, and signs. The girls gaped at all the decorations, almost stumbling over campers who had arrived before them and were already trying to find places to stow their belongings.

Tatia squealed with delight when she reached the end of the room and saw the small sign on the last bunk – TATIA'S BED. "I've never slept in a bunk bed before, and I get the top one!"

Michelle seemed a bit disappointed that she had a lower bunk, but she took it in stride. "I had the top bunk last year. Just be sure you don't step on me if you have to get up and go to the bathroom in the middle of the night."

Both girls giggled, and Betty hoped their good start would continue throughout the week. She set to work helping the girls find places for their bags and checking to see if they had swimsuits, flip flops, and towels for their trip to the pool. She discovered that Tatia needed a T-shirt to wear over her swimsuit since her two-piece suit didn't meet the camp dress code. Both girls needed sheets, and Betty thought they might need socks later in the week, but she'd worry about that later. The first priority right now was to get the girls to the pool for the swim test.

There were two choices for swimming – the pool and the pond. Non-swimmers and the more timid kids stayed in the pool that was about five feet at the deep end. This was a great place for volleyball games, floating toys, and water gun fights. The swimmers and more adventurous went to the pond, a deeper and more natural body of water with a big slide, a trapeze, and a zip line. Both girls passed the test and were awarded a red wrist band which gave them access to the pond and the pool, with an accompanying counselor, of course. They spent forty-five minutes in the pond, squealing, splashing, sliding, and having the kind of carefree fun that was too often lacking from their lives.

Lights out was at nine o'clock. By the time Tatia donned her pajamas, brushed her teeth and climbed into her bunk, she had made a pillowcase and a bookmark using a real sewing machine, learned several new songs and watched a funny skit in Chapel, eaten dinner and played games with new friends, picked up a handful of notes from her counselor and camp grandparents from her personal camp mailbox, and had a devotional and bedtime prayers with her counselor. As she snuggled down in the sleeping bag Betty had brought her from the camp store, her head was spinning with new memories. She played each one through her mind like a video, trying to decide which was her favorite, and she finally settled on the song they sang in Chapel called "Big House." It was exactly what she pictured when she thought about her Mama and Daddy being in their Father's house. She lay in the darkness, listening to the sounds of the other girls settling down for the night, and drifted off to sleep singing to herself:

Come and go with me to my Father's house. It's a big, big house with lots and lots of room; a big, big table with lots and lots of food; a big, big yard where we can play football; a big, big house. It's my Father's house.

She was so exhausted each night from the blur of activity that she had the nightmare about Mama and Daddy in their boxes only once. Even the morning after waking up in tears in the middle of the night, she was excited to see what the day held. Throughout the week, she built a keepsake box with a real hammer, she had her first root beer float ever, and she played on a huge homemade Slip-and-Slide. She attended a royal princess tea party dressed in a beautiful ball gown, and at the camp variety show she performed a rap recitation of the books of the Bible with the other girls from her cabin. Her two favorite activities, though, were Imagination Station where she met Mrs. G and Everybody's Birthday Party where she really met Jesse.

CHAPTER 7
IMAGINATION STATION

On Wednesday, Tatia's group finished lunch and went to the camp post office to check for any new messages. After reading her three notes, Michelle plopped down next to Betty on a bench and asked the most common question at camp: "What do we do next?"

Betty consulted the schedule on the back of her name tag before she answered. "We have forty-five minutes before we're scheduled for Imagination Station. Let's go to the patio. We'll be right next to the Station, and there are three crafts to choose from."

Both girls had time to make a spin-art picture, and while they were drying, another teen helper showed them how to weave a key chain with multi-colored strands of plastic. Betty stood back and smiled as she watched her giggling campers continue to forget their problems and enjoy a normal childhood for a few days. When the girls each had about a three-inch start on their chains, Betty glanced at her watch.

"Okay, ladies! It's time for Imagination Station. Let me put your chains in my bag and let's move in that direction."

"But what about our pictures?" wailed Michelle, who was a bit of a drama queen.

"They need a few more minutes to dry. We'll pick them up on the way back to the cabin to change for swimming."

"Okay," said Tatia, handing over her project. "What is Imagination Station anyway?"

"It's a little hard to explain," said her counselor. "You'll see for yourself in just a minute."

The trio followed several other campers into the large room that normally served as the dining hall. The tables had been pushed back against the walls, and some of the chairs had been arranged in a circle at one end of the room. On the raised platform on the other end of the room, a Cheval mirror stood in front of a lone chair. The space between was filled with several hanging racks filled with fancy dresses, uniforms of various first responders, jerseys from a number of sports teams, and a selection of super hero costumes. There were also several tables loaded with shoes, purses, jewelry, and all sorts of accessories.

The counselors took seats and settled back with looks of anticipation on their faces, eager to see what their children would discover about themselves in the next few minutes. The curious campers were greeted by a tall, solid woman with shoulder-length salt-and-pepper hair, deep brown eyes, and an enthusiastic smile that put the girls at ease.

"Good afternoon, ladies!" she said. "My name is long and hard to pronounce, so you can call me Mrs. G. I'm sure you've seen me around, helping out here and there, but my favorite part of camp is Imagination Station where, for a few minutes, you are all encouraged to let your minds run free and imagine all the opportunities that are open to you in the years ahead. Does that sound like fun?"

Some of the girls, especially those who had been at camp before, nodded enthusiastically, but others like Tatia looked skeptical. Mrs. G continued.

"How many of you have ever played 'dress up'?" she asked. A couple of the girls raised their hands while the rest shook their heads. "Well, now is your chance. I want each of you to pick out an outfit, complete with accessories, that represents something you might like to be in the future. After you get dressed, our photographers are waiting to take your pictures, and then I will visit with each of you for a few minutes in front of my Magic Mirror. Sound good?"

She was greeted by a chorus of excited agreements, and the small herd of children flowed by her as she stood out of the way. However, Tatia hung back, reluctant to join in the fun. She half-heartedly fingered a few of the costumes while Michelle donned a slinky black dress that was slit up one side, and Jane, another girl from their room, held up a pink satin dress, announcing that she wanted to dress like Jennifer Lopez. Mrs. G watched Tatia and recognized the symptoms of an imagination that had been crushed by too much hurt and too many disappointments.

"Hi, Tatia," she said gently. "Is there someone in your life that you admire – someone you would like to be like one of these days?"

"I don't know," Tatia almost whispered.

"Well," encouraged Mrs. G. "Is there someone on TV or the movies that you like?"

"No, I really don't want to be famous."

"That's okay. How about a special teacher or a doctor – someone who has helped you or been especially kind to you?"

A small smile tugged at the corners of Tatia's mouth. "There was this one lady I met several times when Mama died and then when Grandma got sick. She was the only one who really paid attention to me and asked me what I wanted. Not that it mattered much since nobody wanted me anyway. I think she was a lawyer."

"A lawyer! I think you'd be a great lawyer, and I have just the outfit."

Mrs. G helped Tatia find a tailored dress and a pair of black pumps. Both were a little big, but the enthusiasm of all the other girls was infectious.

"I like it," said Tatia with a shy smile. "I'll look for a scarf or something to use for a belt, and it will be fine."

"Great!" said Mrs. G. "I'm sure you'll find the perfect accessories, and I'll see you in front of the Magic Mirror in a few minutes."

She left Tatia browsing through the jewelry and purses, and she began calling the girls to the platform one at a time. She sat in the chair and positioned each camper in front of the mirror and asked them what they saw. With gentle questions and suggestions, she encouraged them to see beyond the hurt and abuse in their past and see the truth of who they were and of the possibilities that lay ahead of them.

Tatia found a black purse that, with a little imagination, could pass as a briefcase, and a gold chain necklace that added the perfect touch of conservative bling. While she waited to be called by Mrs. G, she watched Michelle prance around and pose for the photographer as if she had been modeling all her life. Tatia found her know-it-all attitude a little irritating, but she couldn't help but envy her confidence. While she waited for one of the photographers to be free, she continued to watch as Michelle took her place in front of the mirror. Tatia was surprised when the self-assured, I-can-do-everything tween refused to look in the mirror. Suddenly, she was a timid little girl with no sense of self. In a flash of insight, Tatia realized that, in spite of outward appearances, Michelle didn't believe she was worth anything at all.

"May I take your picture?" said one of the photographers, rousing Tatia from her thoughts.

"I guess so," she said.

Her first poses looked like she was having a driver's license photo or a mug shot taken, but with a little encouragement, she loosened up a bit and let her beautiful smile and her personality shine through. When her turn in front of the mirror came, she was surprised at how mature and poised she looked. As she imagined herself standing in a courtroom, Mrs. G talked about her underlying confidence and how her strength would see her through even the hard times.

When her time in front of the mirror was over, Tatia reluctantly stepped down from the platform. Before she went to take off her lawyer garb, she stopped and turned back.

"Thank you, Mrs. G. I think if I ever do this again, I'd like to dress up like you."

Mrs. G didn't respond immediately, but Tatia could see tears shining in her eyes as she swallowed hard. Then she found her voice and said, "I'd be honored, Tatia."

After she carefully hung the dress back on the rack and returned her accessories to the table, Tatia went and sat next to Betty, who was wiping her eyes, and Michelle, who was uncharacteristically quiet.

"You both looked wonderful," said Betty. "How did you feel when you looked in the mirror?"

"I was surprised," said Michelle in a tiny voice. "I really looked pretty good."

"Yes, you did," said Betty, giving her shoulders a quick squeeze. "Really beautiful. And how about you, Tatia? Were you surprised?"

Tatia ducked her head and covered a smile with her hand. "Yeah, kinda," she answered. "I mean, I looked serious – like someone who could really make a difference."

Betty gave her a hug and wiped her eyes again, and then Mrs. G joined the group. Once again, she spoke with each girl individually. She talked briefly about her impressions of each one of them, and she gave them a stone with a single word painted on the front and a Scripture reference painted on the back. When she came to Tatia, she once again mentioned the inner strength she saw in her. The stone she gave her said "strength," and on the back, it said "Phil. 4:13."

"Do you know what that verse says?" Betty asked her as Mrs. G moved on to the next girl. Tatia shook her head, and Betty told her. "I can do all things through Christ which strengtheneth me."

Tatia turned the stone over and over in her hand as those words turned over in her mind. She didn't understand what they meant, and she certainly didn't feel strong. When Betty announced it was time to go on to the next activity, Michelle was out the door first, as usual, and Tatia brought up the rear. She was almost out the door when she heard Mrs. G call her name.

"Tatia, I'm not supposed to do this, but I want you to have this." She handed Tatia a card with her name and phone number on it. "I have a feeling that you're on the edge of some kind of trouble. I'd like you to keep this with you, and if you ever need help, give me a call."

"Okay," Tatia said, slipping the card into her pocket. "Thanks."

CHAPTER 8
HAPPY BIRTHDAY TO EVERYBODY!

After dinner that night, there was a huge party for the whole camp with popcorn, cotton candy, snow cones, bounce houses, a climbing wall, and face painting. Campers were running everywhere, trying to see and do everything at once, and the counselors were hard pressed to follow the rule of knowing where both their campers were at all times. The boundaries of the party area had been clearly marked to make the counselors' job a little easier.

Tatia drifted around close to the edges, close enough to feel the excitement without being overwhelmed by the confusion. She was fascinated with the face painting, more accurately with Jesse who was one of the painters. She had seen him several times throughout the week, and he would always smile and wave, and sometimes he would stop and ask if she was having a good time and if she needed anything. She looked forward to their little encounters, almost like when she first began to run into Eric. It wasn't the same thing, though. Eric was almost like a real boyfriend, and he was taking her on a real date when she returned home.

"Hey," Jesse shouted, calling her back to the real world. "Are you going to let me paint your face or not?"

She laughed self-consciously, a little embarrassed at having been caught daydreaming. "Sure, why not," she said, and walked over to his table.

"What'll it be, Ma'am?" he said in a very bad southern drawl. "Fairy? Butterfly? Unicorn?"

"I'll have the butterfly." She watched him clean his brushes and prepare his paints for a minute before she continued. "You're not from around here, are you?"

"No, I'm from the Chicago area. How did you know?"

"Let's just say your accent could use some work."

"You mean you didn't take me for a native Texan," he said as he began to apply paint to her cheek. "I'm crushed!"

"That tickles," she said when he began to fill in the wings.

"Don't giggle or I might smear this wing up onto your nose."
Of course, she giggled, and he had to do a little bit of repair work.
"How did you end up in Texas?" she asked.
"I'll talk. You listen – and be still!"

She clamped her lips together, and it was his turn to laugh. "That's better," he said sternly. "I came here for the camp. Last year was my first year as a staff member, and I loved it so much that I saved my money all year so I could spend the summer going around the country to as many camps as possible."

She started to open her mouth, but he put his finger to her lips before she could say anything. "Don't speak," he said. "In addition to being a talented face painter, I can read minds. You want to know how a bum—I mean student—like me can make that kind of money. After school and on weekends I work for the best tattoo artist in Chicago. I clean his shop and do whatever needs to be done. The pay's not bad, and if I'm real helpful, all the artists share their tips with me. And besides that, he's teaching me the trade." He sat back a minute and admired his work. Then he handed her a mirror and said, "So, what do you think?"

She gazed at the blue and silver butterfly that looked as if it could take flight at any moment. "It's perfect, Jesse. You really are talented."

"Aw shucks, Ma'am," he drawled.

"Just not with accents!" she laughed. "Did it hurt?"

"What?"

"That," she said, pointing to the tattoo on his forearm.

"Oh that. Yeah, a little."

"Would you paint one on me? I mean, there's nobody waiting in line or anything."

"Sure," he said. He quickly decorated her right forearm with a stylized cross inside a heart.

She watched him work, fascinated by the way he knew just how to get the effect he wanted with only a few strokes of the brush. "I used to go to church before...well, a long time ago. But I don't go any more."

He paused a moment, still holding her hand, and looked into her eyes. "It's okay, Tatia. God understands."

She felt as if she could sit there and talk with him forever, but everyone was beginning to move toward the Chapel.

"Looks like it's time for the big birthday dance," he said as he put the finishing touches on his design. "Try not to get it against anything for a couple of minutes until it's good and dry."

"Thanks! It looks great. Maybe someday I'll get a real one like yours."

"Maybe. Now, go dance the night way. Happy Birthday, Tatia."

"Thanks, Jesse."

CHAPTER 9
BIRTHDAY DREAMS

Tatia woke up and stretched, trying to hold onto the dream that was slipping away as the sun slipped over her windowsill and threw a bright ray across the foot of her bed. For the second time in the week since camp she had dreamed about sitting and talking with Jesse instead of her usual dreams of death and loneliness. She thought about pulling the sheet up over her head and trying to return to that happy place, but suddenly, she remembered what day it was. It was Saturday, June 30, and she was twelve years old today. Not only that, it was the day of her first real date.

She jumped out of bed, pulled on a pair of shorts and a tank top, and went to work. She completed her chores before anyone else in the house was awake, and then, she started on Josie's chores. Her plan was to be sure everyone's work was done so Josie would have no excuse to keep her home for the evening. As far as Josie knew, today was a normal Saturday except that Tatia had been invited to a birthday party. She was sure her records included her date of birth, but she was also sure that Josie didn't know or care that the birthday was hers. She was also sure that Josie didn't need to know that the party was for two, her and Eric. The plan was for Tatia to meet Eric in front of the library around 5:00 pm. That would leave plenty of time for Eric to spring all his surprises before Tatia's 10:00 pm curfew.

Motivated as she was, Tatia worked quickly and efficiently. Still, the time dragged, and she thought 5:00 pm would never come. Finally, though, all the chores were done, the kids were bathed, fed, and settled in front of their favorite movie. She took a quick shower, carefully curled her hair, and dressed in jeans and the pink T-shirt Eric had given her. He had told her not to worry about what she wore, because his gift to her would be a new outfit he had chosen especially for her. She hoped it would be as pretty as the dresses she had worn at camp. He had also promised her a real dinner date at a nice restaurant. She hoped she would know which fork to use.

When she arrived at the library, she was excited and relieved to see the red Corvette in the lot and Eric leaning against the trunk.

Based on her life experience, she was afraid he wouldn't show up, and she would end up hiding in a gas station restroom until it was time to go home. She shouldn't have worried, though. He was there, just like he said, and she just knew tonight would be the best night of her life.

As she approached the car, he straightened up and greeted her with a brotherly hug and a kiss on the cheek. "Happy Birthday, sweetheart. You look beautiful."

"Thanks. You look great, too."

He was wearing black slacks, a black shirt, and highly polished black loafers. To Tatia, he looked simply elegant. In a move she had seen only on TV and in the movies, he offered her his arm.

"Your carriage awaits, Miss."

Giggling, she took his arm as he escorted her around the car, opened the door, and handed her into her seat.

"We're going to dinner in Cameron so we won't run into anyone you know. The last thing I want is to cause you problems at home."

"You're always so good to me."

He smiled and patted her hand. "I rented a room close to the restaurant so you can change before dinner and then back into your jeans before you go home. We'll have to figure out a way for you to take the dress home later."

"It sounds like you have everything planned perfectly."

He laughed. "I read a lot of magazines."

Tatia smiled and thought that Eric must be the most perfect man in the world. She couldn't remember any fancy hotels in Cameron, but she had only been there once or twice. She tried to imagine where he had rented a room as they entered the city limits. There were lots of motels on the south side of town, some that were fairly nice, at least according to the ads on TV. Some, though, were not so nice, with names that were not meant to be remembered, as if the owners were ashamed of the dirty, run-down conditions of their businesses. She was shaken when Eric pulled into one of these. It was painted a sickly yellow color with a stripe of lime green around the middle like a wide belt that held the building together. The windows in one section were boarded up, and the rest were too dirty to see inside. She turned her head toward the window, hoping Eric wouldn't see the distress on her face. She didn't want to embarrass him if this was all he could afford after paying for everything else.

She tried to put a smile on her face as he came around and opened the car door, again offering his arm and escorting her to a door that sported a tarnished number "12". Some of her doubts weakened as she wondered if he had asked for this room in honor of her birthday. Then, when he opened it, her remaining misgivings disappeared.

The room was alight with scented candles, and spread out on the bed was the most beautiful dress she had ever seen. Instead of little-girl pink, it was a black satin, strapless dress under a lace overlay with a scooped neckline and elbow-length sleeves. The flared skirt looked like it would hit her about mid-thigh, and there were just enough sequins scattered across it to give off a nice shimmer when she walked. On the floor, a pair of silver sandals with kitten heels sparkled in the candlelight. The ensemble was the perfect combination of elegance and innocence so she would look grown-up without looking like she was playing dress up.

She picked up the dress, held it against herself, and twirled around the room a couple of times.

"You like it?" asked Eric.

"Oh, yes!" she gushed, running over and hugging him around the waist. "It's perfect."

"Careful," he said, pushing her away gently. "You don't want to get it all wrinkled before you even try it on. Now, I know a blonde in a black dress can be a little tricky, so I asked Cindy to help you put on a little make-up – just enough so you don't look washed out. I hope you don't mind."

She did mind a little bit. He had never said anything about her looking washed out before. In fact, he usually said she had such natural beauty that she didn't need make-up. Still, he was working so hard to make it a really special evening, and she didn't want to do anything to spoil it. "Sure, that would be okay, I guess. But I don't have any make-up or anything."

"That's okay. I had her pick up some stuff when she bought the dress."

Tatia felt another little twinge. She bought the dress? He had made her think he had picked out everything himself. She busied herself with straightening out the dress on the bed so he wouldn't see the disappointment on her face. She heard him open the door to a connecting room.

"Hey, Cindy!" he yelled. "Get your butt in here with that make-up, and don't be all day about it."

Tatia couldn't believe the harsh edge in his voice. She had never heard him speak any way other than gently – except when he found out she was going to camp. Before she could really think about it, she heard a female voice coming from the next room.

"Keep your shirt on. I'm coming."

Eric met Cindy at the door and put his face down within inches of hers. "What did you say?" he hissed between clenched teeth.

Tatia glanced around and saw the fear in Cindy's eyes. She looked down quickly before he looked in her direction.

"I-I-I said sure, Eric. Right away," Cindy stammered.

"That's what I thought you said."

Cindy edged by Eric, keeping her eyes down to avoid his glare. She hurried over to Tatia and picked up the dress. "Come on, honey. Let's go in the bathroom where there's more light."

Tatia picked up the shoes and followed Cindy. Just before she reached the bathroom, she looked back toward the connecting door where she caught a glimpse of Eric in the other room, pacing and smoking a cigarette. She had never seen him smoke before.

Cindy was a dark-haired girl in her late teens. She had olive skin, hazel eyes, and ample curves barely covered by a red silk kimono. She set to work with a small collection of tubes and bottles. The brush across her cheeks reminded Tatia of Jesse's paint-filled brushes the week before, and for a few seconds, she almost wished she was back at camp. Then, she looked at the dress and thought of dinner with Eric. *I need to chill out,* she thought. *After all, everybody has a bad moment now and then.*

Cindy was putting the finishing touches on her lipstick when Eric approached the bathroom. "Hey, gorgeous. Are you almost ready?"

Tatia saw a flash of resentment in Cindy's eyes, but she stifled it and answered with a smile in her voice. "Almost done. Give us a couple more minutes and we'll call you in for the big reveal."

"Okay, but don't take too long. We don't want to miss our reservations."

Tatia was relieved to hear the gentleness back in his voice, and her heart skipped a beat as her excitement returned. "Do I look okay?" she asked shyly.

"Oh, honey, you look good enough to...Well, let's just say you look beautiful. I think I'll just sweep all those blonde curls up off your neck in a clip, and we'll be ready for the dress."

Within five minutes, Tatia was dressed, perfumed, and standing in front of Eric, waiting for his reaction. It was everything she had hoped for. He whistled appreciatively, took her hand and twirled her around before pulling her into his arms and dancing around the room with her – all this while telling her again and again how beautiful, gorgeous, and stunning she looked.

"The only thing missing is – this!" he said as he dramatically pulled a small velvet box out of his pocket. He opened it to reveal a silver heart-shaped locket with a tiny diamond in the center.

Tatia gasped, and reached out a shaking finger to touch the sparkling gem as if to reassure herself that it was real. "Oh, Eric. I can't believe this is all for me."

"Believe it," he said, taking the locket out of the box. "Now turn around so I can put this on you, and let's go eat dinner."

CHAPTER 10
THE REAL NIGHTMARES

The restaurant was beyond anything Tatia had imagined. Eric pulled up in front of what looked like a turn-of-the-century mansion. Three attendants dressed in black pants, white shirts, and red vests surrounded the car. One opened his door, another opened hers, and the third drove the car to an unseen and supposedly safe place. A uniformed doorman ushered them through the entrance, and a *maître d'* in a black tuxedo signaled to a black-suited waiter who ushered them to an intimate table for two by a corner window overlooking an atrium with a lighted fountain.

After seating Tatia on her side of the table, the waiter took the fan-folded napkin out of the stemmed glass in front of her and ceremoniously placed it in her lap. He repeated the performance on Eric's side of the table and then handed him a menu. Tatia wanted to laugh with delight at everything she saw, but everyone else seemed to be so serious that she struggled to keep a straight face.

"I assume you will order for the lady," he said.

"Yes, if that's okay with the lady," he said, looking at Tatia with a straight face but with a mischievous twinkle in his eye.

"Sure," she said, ducking her head and putting her hand over her mouth.

"And would you care to begin with a cocktail?" asked the waiter.

"Why not. Would the lady care for a sweet drink or a salty one?"

"Sweet," she said, barely stifling a giggle.

"The lady will have a Faux Bellini, and I'll have a Double Martini."

"Very good," replied the waiter. Before he left to order their drinks, he waved over a busboy who filled their water glasses. After both men were gone, Tatia broke into a fit of giggles that made Eric chuckle in spite of himself.

"What's so funny," he asked when she had composed herself a bit.

"I'm used to ordering food through a speaker mounted on a pole and picking it up from a window. If it takes more than a couple of minutes, the other kids start whining, and Josie starts yelling. We've been here at least ten minutes, we've seen seven people, and we haven't even ordered our food yet. I just didn't know places like this existed except in the movies."

"Well, as you can see, they do exist, and you deserve to be waited on hand and foot every day of your life."

The waiter brought their drinks, and Tatia gasped with delight when she saw her sparkling drink in a champagne flute. The waiter disappeared and Eric lifted his glass and said, "A toast to the birthday girl. May you always be as happy and radiant as you are tonight."

She smiled and blushed, touching her glass to his before she took a sip. She closed her eyes as she held the icy liquid in her mouth, savoring the delicate peach flavor. When she finally swallowed, she opened her eyes and said, "That is the best thing I ever tasted in my life!"

Eric grinned and said, "Hmmm. Now the pressure is on to pick the perfect meal to live up to that beginning." He picked up the menu, but before he opened it, he looked at her and smiled. "I know that you like ice cream, but what else do you like?"

"Hamburgers, spaghetti, pizza."

"Unfortunately, none of those is on the menu. Do you like prime rib?"

"You mean like barbeque ribs?"

"No, this is more like roast."

"Like pot roast?"

"Well, not really. I guess you could say it's like a really tender steak, and it's usually pretty rare."

"Oh, gross! You mean like bloody?"

"Okay. Maybe not prime rib. Do you like chicken?"

"Sure."

"How about ham and Swiss cheese?"

"Uh-huh."

"Okay. Now for dessert. Cherries or bananas?"

"Bananas."

"Got it."

The waiter returned as asked, "Are you ready to order, sir?"

"Yes. The lady will have the Chicken Cordon Bleu, Lyonnais Potatoes, and Green Beans Almandine. I'll have the Prime Rib, medium rare, and I'll have the same sides as the lady. And we'll have Bananas Foster for dessert."

"Very good. And would you like another round of cocktails, or would you like to see the wine list?"

"Bring the lady a sparkling water, and send over the wine steward?"

"Yes, sir. Right away."

After the waiter walked away, Tatia took the last sip of her drink and said shyly, "That was really good. I wouldn't mind having another one."

"You don't need another one," Eric said in a less than kind tone of voice. When he saw the surprise on Tatia's face, he softened his expression and his tone and placed his hand gently over hers. "Unless you really want one, of course. After all, it is your birthday. I just thought all you beautiful women were always counting your calories."

She brightened a bit when he called her a beautiful woman. "Oh, no. I don't want another one. I usually drink water with dinner anyway."

The waiter brought her sparkling water, and when the wine steward arrived, he and Eric had a conversation, most of which she didn't understand. From what she gathered, he ordered a bottle of wine to go with his dinner. That worried her a little bit. She still remembered how her mother had acted when she drank too much.

When the food came, she sat and stared at her plate without picking up her fork. "Is something wrong with your food?" Eric asked.

"No, it's just almost too pretty to eat."

"Yeah," Eric laughed, a little too loudly. "At these prices we should probably have it bronzed and put in a display case. But don't worry about that. Go ahead. Enjoy!"

He poured himself a glass of wine. It was his second one. When the wine steward had brought the bottle to the table, Tatia had wondered if he and Eric would go through the little ceremony she had seen at some of the other tables. They didn't. The steward had pulled out the cork and held it out to Eric, but he had waved it away, and when he had poured a little in the glass for Eric to try, Eric had snapped at him, "Cut the fancy nonsense and just pour the wine."

The steward had raised an eyebrow and said, "The Merlot is best when it is allowed to breathe for a few minutes."

"Well, it can breathe in the glass. Just pour it."

Tatia had noticed a couple of people at other tables looking their way and snickering, and she had been a little embarrassed for Eric. She wondered if maybe he didn't know how it was supposed to be done or if it was because of the double martini. She didn't want to make him feel bad so she turned her attention to the fountain in the atrium and pretended she didn't know anything was amiss.

Once she tasted her food and discovered how delicious it was, she didn't pay much attention to anything else for a few minutes. When she finally looked up, Eric was leaning back in his chair, staring at her with a look she didn't understand but that made her uncomfortable. It reminded her of a look she had once seen on a dog's face when he was stalking a squirrel.

"What?" she asked. "Do I have something stuck in my teeth?"

"No, you're perfect. Almost too perfect to share."

"What do you mean? I met some friends at camp, but nobody special or anything," she said. An image of Jesse's easy-going grin flashed through her mind, but she pushed it aside and focused on Eric. "You haven't touched your prime rib. Don't you like it?"

Eric shook his head slightly and grunted under his breath. Then he emptied the bottle into his glass. "I guess I'm on more of a liquid diet tonight. Go ahead. Finish your dinner."

She took a few more bites before carefully placing her knife and fork across her plate at an angle the way she had seen the lady at the next table do when she finished. "I'm finished. I want to save room for the dessert you ordered. What did you call it? Bananas Foster?"

Eric looked irritated. "Yeah, I forgot." He looked at his watch. "I hope they don't take too long. I was kinda hoping to have dessert at the motel." Tatia didn't understand what he meant, but the way he looked at her when he said it made her skin crawl.

He finally attracted the waiter's attention and let him know they were ready for dessert. When the busboy had cleared the dishes, a man in a chef's hat and a white jacket rolled a little cart over to their table. On it was what looked like a little camp stove surrounded by a variety of bowls and bottles and two tulip glasses filled with vanilla ice cream. He smiled at Tatia and, as he began to peel and slice the bananas, he asked, "Have you had Bananas Foster before?"

"No," she said, her eyes sparkling with excitement. "I never even heard of it before tonight."

"It's really quite simple," he said, "I melt some butter and caramelize some brown sugar with some secret ingredients. If I told you what they were, I'd have to kill you." He winked good naturedly, she giggled like the twelve year old she was. "Then I sizzle the bananas a few seconds, and then I do this." He poured a little dark rum into the skillet and tilted the pan until the flame touched the sauce and the alcohol erupted into a geyser of blue flame. Tatia gasped and clapped with delight as he extinguished the flame and spooned his creation over the ice cream. He topped each glass with a swirl of whipped cream and a sprinkle of shaved chocolate before he presented one to each of them with a flourish.

"This is better than a dozen birthday cakes!" Tatia cried.

"Is this your birthday?" asked the chef.

"Yes," she said.

"Then you must accept these," he said, plucking two perfect red roses from the vase on an unoccupied table and wrapping a napkin around the stems in a graceful swirl, "as a token of our appreciation for spending your special day with us." He presented the small bouquet to her with a courtly bow, and she blushed with pleasure.

"Thank you. I never got flowers before."

The chef turned to Eric and said, "Treasure these special moments. They grow up all too fast."

"Faster than you might think," said Eric with a slight slur.

Tatia was too busy with her dessert to notice Eric's suggestive wink or the dark look that passed over the chef's face before he hurried away with his cart.

Eric paid the bill, and he and Tatia ran the gauntlet of attendants to get out the door and retrieve his car. He had a little trouble getting the car in gear after he fired up the engine, and he narrowly missed a tree as they wound down the driveway toward the street. Tatia wished he hadn't had that after dinner drink while she was finishing her dessert.

Once he was on the highway, driving more or less straight in his lane, he picked up his phone and said, "Hey, Siri, play Tatia's album."

"You picked out songs for me?" she asked in surprise. She really didn't like the oldies music he listened to, but it made her feel special that he had set up an album for her. Still, when she heard the lyrics of the first song, she wasn't so sure. It said something about a little girl and a man who wasn't supposed to be alone with her, and it made her feel kinda creepy like when he made the comment about dessert at the motel. That song was followed by one that was even worse. At one point the gravelly voice sang about loosening her pretty French gown, and Eric put his hand on her back and began playing with her zipper pull. Finally, there was a line about letting him come inside, and Eric put his hand on her leg and began inching her skirt up.

She sat up as straight as she could, clamped her knees together tightly, and brushed her skirt as if to remove stray crumbs left from dinner but in reality brushing off the encroaching hand. "You know,

Eric," she said. "This has been the best night of my night, but all the excitement has worn me out. Maybe you should just take me straight home."

"Oh, honey, don't be a party pooper," he slurred. "It's a long time till your curfew, and you need to change back into your jeans. Besides, I need you to do me a favor."

"What kind of favor?" she asked, suspicious but relieved that he had put his roving hand back on the wheel.

"No big deal. It's just that, with all the money I've been spending on you lately, all the gifts and taking you places, especially tonight, I'm a little short on cash. I have this friend who's rolling in dough. He's in town on business, and he's lonely. I told him about you, and he's dying to meet you. All you have to do spend a few minutes with him."

He pulled into the motel parking lot, stopped the car, and turned toward her, giving her a look that made her feel as if he could see right through her clothes.

"I know you know how to be nice to a man. Right?"

"No, I don't know what you're talking about," she said as tears began to form in the corner of her eyes.

"Sure you do, Tatia," he said, leaning toward her as she backed against the car door. "You just let him kiss you a little bit, like this," he continued, kissing her on the neck.

"Stop it, Eric," she cried, pushing him away. The tobacco and alcohol on his breath repulsed her, and she couldn't imagine how she ever found him attractive. "I just want to go home."

"Why you ungrateful little tease," he shouted. He hit her seat belt release, jerked open his door, and stormed around the car. Tatia tried to lock him out, but before she could find the button, he jerked her door open and pulled her out by the arm. Her roses fell forgotten to the asphalt as he dragged her toward the room.

"You want to go home, huh?"

He fumbled the door open and flung her inside where she stumbled and sprawled on the floor. The candles were gone and even in the dim light of the lamp on the nightstand, she was aware that the interior shabbiness matched the exterior perfectly. Without the distraction of her perfect dress, she could see the faded bedspread and the chipped veneer on the furniture that was edged with cigarette burns.

"Do you know what will happen if I take you home now?" Eric continued. "I'll tell Josie what you were doing all those afternoons after school – sneaking off to meet an older man, going riding with him in his fancy sports car, going who knows where and doing who knows what."

"But..but..nothing happened. We didn't do anything wrong!" she cried.

"Do you think she'll believe that when she sees all the gifts I've given you?" he sneered, contorting his handsome face into something ugly and vile. "Do you think she'll believe I gave you all those things out of the goodness of my heart?"

Defeated, Tatia stared down at the carpet and watched her tears add another dark stain to the collection that was already there – and that's when her real nightmares began.

CHAPTER 11
STATISTICS

Eric stomped over to the connecting door and flung it open. "Cindy," he yelled, "Get in here!"

"I'm with a client!"

"Well, hurry it up," he replied as he slammed the door.

Three minutes later, Cindy came through the door. She didn't look happy. "What was that all about? Thanks to the interruption, he didn't even leave a tip."

Eric grabbed the front of her robe and pulled her up close enough for her to smell what he had for dinner. "Watch your mouth! You can be replaced, you know."

"Okay, okay. I'm just trying to keep the customers happy. What did you need anyway?"

"I need you to get Tatia ready for her nine o'clock. She's in the bathroom bawling – and she'll need something to wear."

Cindy scanned the room quickly, not missing the rumpled, stained sheets and the torn dress lying on the floor. "Been sampling the merchandise, huh?" she smirked, scurrying back to her room before he could swing the fist he raised threateningly.

"One day you'll push me too far!" he yelled as he kicked a small silver sandal across the floor and stormed out the door into the parking lot.

Cindy peeked back into the room a minute later and, seeing that the coast was clear, she came in carrying her make-up bag and a robin's-egg-blue baby-doll nightie. She knocked gently on the bathroom door and called out quietly.

"Hey, honey. It's me – Cindy. Can I come in?"

The door opened slowly, and Tatia, sobbing and wrapped in a towel, threw herself into Cindy's arms. "Oh, Cindy. Why did he do that to me? I thought he cared about me. And when he says I have to be nice to his friend, he doesn't mean...that, does he? I wish I was dead!"

Cindy, definitely not the motherly type, patted Tatia's back awkwardly, making what she hoped were soothing, calming sounds. "Don't cry, baby. He's just like that sometimes, especially when he drinks. His friend won't be so bad. He's gettin' old, and he'll be done and gone before you know it."

Her reassurances didn't help. Tatia drew back in horror. "NO! I won't do it. He can't make me."

"Honey, you don't want to cross him. He can get real nasty when he doesn't get what he wants." She had moved closer to Tatia and encouraged her sit down on the toilet seat. While she dabbed at Tatia's smeared make-up, her robe fell open revealing a huge bruise on her thigh. Tatia reached out a tentative finger and touched the purplish mark that looked strangely like a hand.

"Did he do that to you?"

"Yeah, but I probably deserved it. I can get pretty mouthy in case you hadn't already noticed."

The color drained out of Tatia's face as her eyes fell on the sheer nightie and she realized the hopelessness of her situation. "Do I have to wear that?"

"Honey, I know it's not as fancy as that little black number, but it will look sensational on you – much better than it does on me. The blue will really bring out your eyes. Now slip it on and then I'll see if I can straighten your hair a bit."

Tatia did as she was told, moving mechanically and keeping her back to the mirror. At the same time, Cindy unwrapped one of the plastic glasses on the bathroom counter and filled it with water. She pulled a small bottle out of her pocket and shook a tiny pill into her hand. She broke it in half, popped half of it in her mouth and held the other half out to Tatia along with the water.

"Here ya' go. This is just a little something to take the edge off." Tatia started to object, but Cindy shushed her and continued. "It's just a mild sedative, nothing that's gonna hurt you. It'll just help you deal with everything. It's a lot for a kid your age. How old are you anyway?"

Tatia took the pill and washed it down with a swallow of water. "Twelve. Today's my birthday," Tatia said almost too quietly for Cindy to hear.

Cindy's face flushed, first with anger and then with tears that threatened to spill over her carefully-lined lids. Then, she visibly pulled her emotional armor back in place and produced a small tube from the other pocket.

"Here, take this. Rub it around, you know, down there. It'll kind of numb that area so it doesn't hurt so much. All the new girls use it."

"All the girls?" Tatia asked, eyes wide with disbelief. "You mean there are more?"

"Oh, yeah! Eric has a stable of a couple dozen fillies. You're the finest one he's brought in so far, though." She knew she'd said too much when Tatia's eyes became glistening pools, putting her freshly applied make-up at risk. "Now, now, don't you worry yourself about any of that. Like I said, I let my mouth run away with me sometimes. Just take a deep breath and think how happy Eric will be with you after his friend leaves."

Cindy went over to the bed and began straightening the disheveled sheets.

"Cindy?"

"Yeah, honey."

"I don't know what to do."

Cindy made a strange noise – something between a sob and a laugh. "Don't worry about that. He'll know, and he'll tell you what he wants you to do. And don't be afraid of this one. He's pretty easy to please."

A soft knock at the door made both girls freeze in place, looking into each other's faces. Cindy saw the terror in Tatia's eyes, so she winked and said, "Relax and enjoy the ride. You look stunning, and you'll be amazed at the power you have. See ya' later." Before Tatia could reply, Cindy scooted through the connecting door and closed it quietly behind her.

As that door closed, the front door opened a few inches, and a soft voice said, "May I come in?"

Tatia relaxed a little bit when she heard Eric's voice, but she tensed and stared at the floor as he approached her. She flinched slightly as he reached out and put his index finger under her chin.

"Tatia?" he said tentatively.

He sounded like the Eric she thought she knew, so she allowed him to lift her face until she was looking into his eyes. "I am so sorry I hurt you before. The last thing I want to do is see you unhappy or in pain. You believe that, don't you?"

She wanted to lash out at him, demanding that he take her home immediately, but she remembered the fear in Cindy's eyes and the bruise on her leg. There was also a part of her that wanted to believe him, to go back to the way they were yesterday, so she nodded her head and let him draw her into a tender embrace. She laid her head on his chest and felt the vibrations of his voice as he continued to talk.

"This is hard for me, too, you know. I can hardly stand the thought of you with another man, and if there was any other way, I'd take it. But after he's gone, things will go back to the way they were. Okay?"

She nodded, and he lifted her face again, stared into her eyes for what seemed like an eternity, and brushed her lips lightly with his. The moment was exactly the birthday kiss she had imagined, except that she was in a borrowed nightie instead of her beautiful new dress, and she was about to become one more statistic in the sex-trafficking industry in a small Texas town.

CHAPTER 12
AFTER THE PARTY

With the help of the pill Cindy had given her, and the ability she had developed through the years of disassociating her mind from reality, Tatia made it through the next half hour, but in spite of Eric's reassurance, her life never went back to the way it was.

After her first client left, she took another hot shower and put on her jeans and pink T-shirt while crying for her lost childhood. She wiped the steam off the mirror and stared at the face that no longer looked familiar. The hair was still blonde, but the blue eyes looked flat, lifeless, and so very tired. She wanted nothing more than to go to sleep and wake up yesterday when she was eleven and innocent. Instead, she walked over to the corner, staying as far away from the bed as she could, and sat down in the single plastic chair next to a tiny table. Whatever Cindy had given her was making it hard for her to focus, so she crossed her arms on the table and laid her head down.

She didn't know how long she stayed like that, but the next thing she knew, Eric was shaking her gently by the shoulder. "Tatia, wake up, honey. I have to get you home before Josie calls the cops."

She was groggy and disoriented, but when she caught a glimpse of the rumpled bed, she recoiled, both from Eric's touch and from the memory of what had happened. She jumped up and spun away from him, putting the chair between them. However, the sudden movement made her light-headed, and she clutched the back of the chair to keep from falling.

"Are you okay?" said Eric, reaching out a hand to steady her. Then, he put a finger under her chin and tilted her head up until he could look into her slightly dilated pupils. "Are you on something?"

"Just half a pill Cindy gave me," she said, slurring slightly.

His eyes darkened in anger, and he struggled to keep his tone level. "Don't ever take anything Cindy gives you. Do you hear me?" She nodded, her eyes wide with fear. "Good. I don't need another druggy on my hands. Now, get your stuff, and let's go."

They rode in silence until they were three blocks from her house. He pulled over to the side of the road and turned to face her. "You did real good tonight, Tatia. My friend really liked you."

She stared at her hands and remained silent. He slid his arm gently around her shoulders, pulled her to him, and kissed her hair. "I really am sorry that I hurt you before. I shouldn't drink that much, especially when you look so good." He kissed her temple. "Hey, beautiful, are you still my girl?"

She tried to resist, but she wanted to believe him. She nodded her head slowly and looked up at him, searching his eyes for the reassurance she so badly needed. He laid his free hand against her face and kissed her gently. "I love you, Tatia. You believe that, don't you?"

She nodded and laid her head on his shoulder, surrendering what little was left of her will to his manipulation. He hugged her tightly to him as he checked his watch over her shoulder. He brushed another kiss against her hair and whispered, "I could sit here like this all night, but you'd better get on home."

"Okay," she said, pulling away and avoiding his eyes. She opened the door and stood on the side of the road, watching while he made a quick u-turn, flashed a smile, and sped away, leaving her more empty and alone than she had been since her mama died.

CHAPTER 13
LONG SLEEVES

Tatia survived the rest of the weekend and avoided Josie's questions and most of her regular chores by saying she had a stomach virus. When Monday rolled around, she wished for school so she could avoid closer scrutiny, but she offered to take the kids to the park instead, knowing that Josie would stay home. She dragged herself behind the noisy herd, making half-hearted attempts to keep the little ones out of the road. She drifted through the next hour or so, pushing swings, spotting budding gymnasts, and examining scraped knees but feeling more isolated and out of place than ever. When the complaints about being tired, thirsty, or hungry began, she asked the next oldest foster sibling if she would take the kids home.

"While you do what?" snapped Macy who was always spoiling for a fight. "Go shopping or sneak off to the DQ by yourself?"

Tatia sighed, lacking the energy to think of a smart comeback. "No, Macy. I want to go to the library and check out a book. You can come with me and bring all of them along if you like."

Macy wrinkled her nose as she always did at any mention of books. "No thanks! Come on kids. Our resident genius is going to the library, and we're going home for a delicious lunch of mac and cheese or peanut butter and jelly sandwiches."

When Tatia began her solitary walk toward the library, she felt a small sense of relief until she saw Eric's car parked in front of it. She tried to walk past as if she didn't see him, but he opened his door, stood up, and leaned against the car as if nothing had happened.

"Hi, gorgeous!" he called.

"Hi, Eric," she said softly, looking at him in spite of herself. Why did he have to be so good looking!

"I was passing through and saw you with the kids. I was hoping you'd stop by here. Have you got time to go for an ice cream?"

She hesitated for a moment, but the need to be with someone with whom she didn't have to put on a front was too strong.

"Sure," she sighed. "Let me run in and grab a book so I don't have to answer questions when I get home."

She came out a few minutes later with two books under her arm and climbed into the car. He began chatting as soon as she had fastened her seat belt and kept up a steady stream of chatter until their ice cream was almost gone and they were parked on an isolated side road on the way to her house. He popped the last bite of cone into his mouth and wiped his hands on a napkin. Then, he reached into his pocket and pulled out a twenty dollar bill. He placed it on Tatia's lap while she scraped the last bits of cookies and cream off the bottom of her cup.

"What's that for?" she asked, licking her spoon.

"I forgot to give it to you the other night. My friend enjoyed himself so much he gave me a little extra for you. Buy yourself something special."

Tatia looked at the bill as if it were something vile. "I don't want it," she said.

"Why not?" he asked. "Are you too good to take money for making somebody feel good?"

"It's not that, Eric. You said I wouldn't have to do it ever again. I just want to forget that it ever happened."

"Did I say that? Well, that was before I knew how good you would be and how much my friend would like you. Do you know how much he liked you?" he asked, leaning close and whispering in her ear. "He liked you so much he wants to see you again tomorrow night."

"No, Eric!" she cried out in horror, turning to look at him. She saw the anger flash in his eyes, and fear flared in her stomach.

"Don't you tell me no," he snarled. He put his arm around her shoulders and pulled her roughly toward him until they were almost nose to nose. He slid his hand slowly from her shoulder toward her neck and began to squeeze her trapezius muscle gently. "You're my girl now, and my girls do what I tell them when I tell them. Understand?" She nodded, and her eyes began to water as he gradually increased the pressure. "I don't want to have to treat you like I do Cindy, and I sure don't want to tell Josie and your social worker what you were doing Saturday night when you were supposed to be at a birthday party."

"Eric, you're hurting me!"

He gave her muscle one last painful twist before releasing his hold. "Now," he said, with a predatory smile, "take your gift and put it in your pocket and be grateful I didn't keep it. I'll need you to meet me here at eleven o'clock tomorrow night. Josie and the rug rats should be asleep by then, so you can sneak out. I'll have you back before they wake up, and you can sleep in Wednesday morning."

Before the week was over, Tatia had met two more of Eric's friends, and by the end of July, he had stopped calling them friends and had begun referring to them as clients. She was soon working two or three nights a week which wasn't a problem since everyone was asleep before she slipped out. However, she was also working several hours on Saturday, so she had become adept at inventing excuses.

At first she was afraid Josie would question her about the mysterious new friends she met at the mall every week, but Tatia began using part of her tip money to pay Macy to watch the kids. Macy loved to shop, and as long as the money kept coming, she asked no questions – and as long as Tatia's chores were done before she left, Josie didn't seem to care either.

Tatia hated her new life, but she learned quickly not to express her feelings. One Saturday shortly before school started back, Eric dropped in between clients to see how she was doing, and she announced that she was going home and that she was not coming back.

"Oh, really!" he sneered as she turned her back on him and headed for the bathroom, intending to change out of her "working clothes" and back into her jeans and T-shirt. His fist hit her just below the shoulder blades, knocking the breath out of her and throwing her to the floor. Before she could recover, he removed the crocodile belt from the waist of his custom-tailored slacks and beat her with it until he could see the red welts across her back through the sheer fabric of her blouse. While she lay on the floor in a pool of tears and sweat, he slipped the belt back into place and made a big show of composing himself.

"Let's get one thing straight. You are mine, and you will do whatever I tell you to do with whoever I tell you and whenever I tell you. Do you understand?"

When she didn't respond, he grabbed her by the shoulder, flipped her over on her back, and leaned down so close she could smell the liquor on his breath. "I said, 'Do you understand?'"

She nodded.

"And don't get any ideas about running away from me. I found you once, and I know how to find you again. In fact, it may be time to make sure you know who you belong to."

He pulled his cell phone out of his pocket and hit Cindy's speed dial. "Hey Cindy, make yourself useful. Tatia needs a little ointment on her back, so get over to her room and see what you can do. Contact her next client and send him to Cheri...I don't care what she was planning. Now she's planning to take care of another client. And when you get that set up, get hold of the Ink Guy and see if he can do a rush job this afternoon. Tell him there's a big tip in it for him if he can be finished by six o'clock."

He disconnected, slid the phone back into his pocket, and turned his attention back to Tatia who was now lying on her side with her eyes closed and her knees pulled up to her chest. He kicked the bottom of her foot to get her attention, and she looked up at him through swollen, bloodshot eyes.

"Now that we understand each other, I'm giving you the rest of the afternoon off. But I don't want you to leave this room until I tell you to."

"Okay," she whispered.

"Cindy is coming in shortly to check on your back, and then a guy is coming in to give you a tattoo."

"A tattoo?" her eyes widened. "But I don't..." She stopped when she saw the anger in his eyes.

"That's better. You're learning."

A light tap on the door drew his attention. "Yeah?"

"It's me," called Cindy.

"Well, what are you standing out there for?"

The door opened and Cindy came in carrying a small first aid kit. Even in the dim light, Tatia could see that her right eye was swollen and discolored and her jaw was somewhat puffy. Eric grabbed her by the back of the neck in what might have seemed like an affectionate grip except for the grimace on Cindy's face.

"Now Cindy here is a slow learner," he said, giving her a less than gentle shake, "aren't you, Cindy?"

"Yes, Eric," she said without looking at him.

"Okay," he said, loosening his hold on Cindy. "Looks like we're good here. You two have your instructions, and I have work to do."

He slammed his way out the door, and Cindy knelt on the floor next to Tatia. "Honey, are you okay?"

In answer, Tatia began to sob quietly.

"Can you stand up?"

Tatia rolled over onto her hands and knees and then sat back on her heels. "I'm a little light headed."

"That's just the adrenaline. It'll go away. Come on, hold onto my arm, and we'll get you over to the bed."

With a gentleness she had learned from experience, Cindy removed Tatia's blouse and inspected the welts on her back. "The good news is he didn't break the skin, so you won't have to worry about your clothes sticking to you. You're going to be bruised and sore, though, and it's gonna be hard to wear a bra for a few days."

She dumped the ice bucket into the sink and filled it the rest of the way with water, using a hand towel to make a cold compress. Tatia gasped when she laid it on her back.

"I know it's cold, but it will keep the swelling down and numb the pain some. Lie still. I'm gonna run back to my room and get you one of my T-shirts to wear home. It'll be more comfortable than that little skin-tight number you wore over here. Do you want me to get you a downer while I'm at it?"

"No, I'm okay."

"Are you sure? You might need it when you get the tat. This guy is pretty good, but it still stings a lot."

"I'll bet it does, but I don't like the way they make me feel."

"Okay. I'll be right back."

Tatia lay still, trying not to think or feel until she heard the door open again. Cindy came in with a soda in one hand, a T-shirt draped over her arm, and a plastic grocery sack in the other hand. She set her open soda on the night stand and flopped down on the other side of the bed.

"Here's a shirt for you," she said, laying it on the pillow next to Tatia's head. It was long-sleeved turquoise shirt with a sparkly appliqué of a butterfly on the front. Tatia was relieved to see it wasn't one of her heavy metal shirts. Cindy continued as she emptied the grocery bag. "I brought a soda for you. I put a little something extra in mine, but I didn't think you'd want that. I also brought chips and cookies. Since we have some time off, we might as well make a party of it, right?"

Tatia managed a wan smile and said, "Cindy, you're a good friend."

"Aw shucks," Cindy teased, but Tatia could see she was pleased. "I think that cold pack has been on long enough. Let me smooth on a little topical ointment. I don't know if it will help, but it won't hurt. Then you can put on the shirt and join the party."

A few minutes later, the two were sitting cross-legged on the bed giggling like the teenagers they were, sharing jokes and stories and trying to forget the reality of their lives for a few minutes. At one point, Tatia pushed the sleeves of her shirt up – again. It was too big to begin with, and she was used to wearing short sleeves or tank tops.

"Cindy," she asked, "why do you always wear long sleeves?"

Cindy looked at her for a minute and then sighed. She slowly pulled up her sleeve to reveal her own mark of shame. Tears slid down Tatia's cheeks as she reached out and touched the imbedded ink, not wanting to believe it was real.

"Cindy, why do we have to get tattoos?"

"Well, you know how they brand cows?"

"Yeah."

"It's kinda like that."

The party was pretty much over after that. Cindy continued to sip her spiked soda, while Tatia scrubbed her face, put on her jeans, and put the rest of her belongings in her backpack. She wanted to be ready when Eric released her. She had just finished and sat down on the bed when there was a tap on the door. Cindy stood up and threw her empty can in the trash can.

"I'll get it on my way out. I gotta get back to work."

"I thought you had the afternoon off."

"Yeah, I'm not seeing any clients, but I have money to account for and stuff like that."

"Okay." Tatia didn't want her to go. She had felt almost normal for a little while. "Thanks for everything."

Cindy stopped with her hand on the doorknob and looked back at Tatia. "Any time, kiddo." She opened the door and spoke to the visitor on her way out. "Hi, you know what to do. Here's what he wants," she said, handing him a small slip of paper.

Tatia heard her steps fading as she walked away and down the stairs, and a large, muscular man stepped through the door. He had an equipment bag over his shoulder, a folding stool under one arm, and what looked like a wooden TV table under the other. She could see why he was called the Ink Guy. Every inch of visible skin was covered with a tattoo of some kind. In spite of the circumstances, she was fascinated with the variety of pictures that decorated his arms, chest, face, and even his bald head. "Hi," she said in a small voice.

"Hello, Miss," he replied in a gentle tone that surprised her. "You know why I'm here, right?"

"Yes."

"Have you ever had a tattoo?" he asked.

"No."

"Well, try to relax and enjoy the experience. I've been on both sides of a tattoo machine – a lot – so I know what I'm doing. The design we'll be doing today is simple, so it won't take too long, and since there's only one color, it's a one-step process. We won't have to come back and do any fill-in."

Tatia couldn't help but smile at his obviously practiced patter designed to put her at ease and distract her from the reality that he was about to mark her like the many slaves who had been marked before her. He set his table down beside the bed and slid his bag off his shoulder onto it. He pulled out a bottle and a hand towel and handed them to her. "This is antiseptic hand wash. Use it to wash both hands and all the way up to your elbows. And use my towel to dry off, not the one from the motel."

She did as she was told, and when she came back in he was sitting on his stool beside the table, wiping down the surface with an antiseptic wipe. He looked up at her and smiled in a reassuring way. "Lie down on this side of the bed and get comfortable. I'm going to lay your arm on this little table, and I want you to be as relaxed as possible."

"I'll need to lie on my side. My back is..." she hesitated, looking for words to explain.

He looked at her with sadness and understanding. "You do whatever you need to do to get through this. I'm flexible."

After she settled into a relatively comfortable position, she extended her arm onto the table, and he sprayed something on it that tingled a little bit. "I've sprayed your arm with a topical anesthetic that will ease some of the discomfort," he said. "I'll give it a few minutes to take effect, and then I'll wipe it with some alcohol to further clean the area where I'll be working. Now, close your eyes and think pleasant thoughts while I get my equipment ready, and then we'll get started."

She watched his face while he worked, trying to identify various tattoos and trying to understand the look of hurt she saw in his eyes. "I used to have a friend who liked tattoos."

"Yeah?" he said, glancing up with a half smile. "What happened?"

"Oh, that was before, you know. I'll probably never see him again."

He stopped and looked into her eyes. "Miss, sometimes we do what we have to do to survive. We do what we're told, when we're told, and where we're told. But they can't take what's inside us unless we let them. I sense a strong spirit in you. Don't let them break that spirit."

She continued to watch his face and examine his tattoos, carefully avoiding looking down at her arm. She never did know his name, but he did his job quickly and efficiently and with relatively little pain. When he was finished, he wiped it once more with alcohol, apologizing for the sting. He applied some over-the-counter triple antibiotic ointment and taped a sterile gauze pad over the new tattoo.

"This ointment will keep it from getting infected, and the gauze is just in case it seeps a little. You can remove it in twelve to eighteen hours and then apply this ointment a couple of times a day for the next week, just to be sure. If you do decide to put a new bandage on it, be sure the adhesive doesn't touch the ink. As it heals, it may itch and peel a bit. Some moisturizing lotion might help. Any questions?"

She shook her head and took the tube of ointment he gave her. She pulled her sleeve down over the bandage, and she knew it would be a long time before she wore a tank top again.

CHAPTER 14
A NEW IDENTITY

The next time Tatia saw Eric after the beating, he was attentive and as sweet to her as if nothing had happened. First, he took her to the mall where he bought her a pair of high-heeled, knee-high boots and a sassy mini dress. Then, they visited the cosmetics department at one of the anchor stores where he seemed to know several of the girls behind the counter.

"Hi, Eric," cooed a gorgeous redhead named Kitty. "What can I do for you today?" she asked suggestively.

"Kitty, this is Tatia. It's time to get rid of the little girl look and go with something more sophisticated," he explained. "She also has a new outfit. I'd appreciate it if you'd show her to one of your dressing rooms where she can change. I'll be back in thirty minutes to pick her up." With that, he spun on his heels and walked out, leaving Tatia standing alone in the middle of the aisle looking confused.

"Don't worry, honey," said Kitty. "You're in expert hands. Have a seat on that stool while I pull a few samples together."

For the next few minutes, Kitty skillfully applied a light-weight foundation, translucent powder, blush, and a staggering array of eye make-up. Some of the brushes tickled, and Tatia thought again of the butterfly Jesse had painted on her cheek a few short months ago. She pushed the thought away, though, as Kitty looked at her curiously and dabbed a tear away from the corner of her eye.

At each step, Kitty explained what she was doing so Tatia would be able to duplicate the look on her own later. When she was satisfied with the results, she released Tatia's blonde curls from the ponytail she wore and fluffed them with her hands until they fell softly around her face. She surveyed her work and smiled.

"Good! Now, let's go get you dressed."

When Eric returned a few minutes later, he whistled appreciatively and said, "Now that's what I'm talking about. Thanks, Kitty. Put it on my bill."

"Don't worry," she grinned. "I will."

Tatia followed him through the mall and out to the parking lot, glancing in the windows at a reflection she hardly recognized.

"Thanks for the new look, Eric," she said as she climbed into the car.

"You'll earn it," he said without looking at her.

Yeah, that's what I figured, she thought to herself.

Instead of driving straight to the motel, he pulled into an old strip center and stopped in front of a narrow establishment with a neon sign that said "Coffee Shop" in the window. She followed him in and was surprised at the trendy-looking interior. There were three small tables and a comfortable seating area in the corner by the window. A well-equipped serving bar was tucked into the back corner, and the tantalizing aroma of fresh-roasted coffee beans filled the air.

"Hi, Eric," greeted the barista behind the counter. "What'll it be?"

"A double espresso for me and a decaf mocha for the lady – as soon as she returns from the ladies' room."

"Coming right up, Eric. Miss, the restroom is just past the bar on the right. Ignore the sign on the left stall and use that one."

Tatia followed instructions without question, assuming she was about to pay for her afternoon at the mall. She found the restroom and walked in, expecting to find a client waiting for her. Instead, the room was unoccupied. The left stall sported an out-of-order sign, so Tatia opened the door and peeked in. As she stepped inside, she heard a buzzer sound somewhere behind the side wall, and the wall swung away, revealing a hidden room.

"You must be Tatia," said a voice from the darkness in the corner. "Come on in and have a seat."

She wasn't sure what she was stepping into, but she did as she was told and sat down on the small stool that was a few feet in front of what looked like a camera. The voice and the man who owned it stepped behind what really was a camera, made a few adjustments, and said "Smile." She smiled and was momentarily blinded by a flash. "Okay. That'll do. Go enjoy your coffee, and I'll have this out in a few minutes."

Totally confused, she retraced her steps into the coffee shop and made her way toward the seating area in the corner. Eric was sitting on a latte-colored leather sofa, talking with a distinguished looking older man who was in a matching chair that was set at a right angle to the sofa. The older man rose as she approached, and she smiled, wondering if this was her next client.

"Tatia," said Eric, "this is Joseph. Joseph, Tatia."

"Hello, Joseph."

"It's nice to meet you, Tatia."

A NEW IDENTITY

Eric patted the sofa next to him. "Have a seat," he said. "Have you ever had a decaf mocha?"

"No."

He picked up a steaming cup from the table and handed it to her. "Let me know what you think."

She sipped the chocolaty liquid and smiled. "It's delicious. Thanks, Eric."

He patted her on the leg in a proprietary manner. "Enjoy," he said as he resumed his chat with the man who was sitting in the chair beside him.

Tatia could tell they were talking business, so she tried to shut them out. She occupied herself with her new favorite drink and with enjoying a few more minutes without having to sell her body.

She had just finished her mocha and was wondering what was next when the barista walked out to the table. "Excuse me, Miss. I believe you dropped this in the restroom." He held out a small laminated card, and Tatia took it from him.

"Thanks," she said as she looked down and saw a picture of herself staring back at her. She realized she was holding a Texas driver's license that said her name was Kaitlyn Golden and that she was nineteen years old. She looked at Eric with a question in her eyes.

He glanced at her and said, "Put that in your purse and try not to be so careless with it."

"Sure, Eric."

"Come on. Play time's over," he said, standing and shaking hands with Joseph. She followed Eric to the car, thinking about the difference between this afternoon and the last time she had been with him. She was learning that the more money she made for him and the more compliant she was, the better he would treat her. She knew there was no way out, at least in the foreseeable future, so she made up her mind to smile and pretend to welcome each new customer.

CHAPTER 15

SUSPICION

School started the week after Tatia's makeover, and her double life began to take even more of a toll. She was so tired during the day that, even though she didn't actually fall asleep, her class participation suffered, she missed assignments, and her grades were well below previous years. She managed to cover the interim reports of failing grades by forging Josie's signature, but she hadn't come up with a plan to avoid showing her report card when the other kids came home with theirs.

Her Saturday excuses were wearing thin, too. She had become lax in doing her chores, Macy had begun to whine about babysitting so often, and Josie had become suspicious. She was growing tired of taking up the slack, and she started asking questions that were hard to answer.

On a Wednesday morning after a very late night, Tatia woke up late and was rushing out without breakfast when Josie blocked the door. "Cade had an interesting story at breakfast this morning," she said.

Cade was her five-year-old foster brother, and Tatia's heart jumped into her throat as she wondered what he might have said. "He loves making up interesting stories," she said. "I'm really running late this morning. Can you tell me about it when I get home?"

"You can spare a minute. Cade said he got up to go to the bathroom, and he heard something in your room. He peeked in the door and saw a burglar climbing in your window. What do you have to say about that?"

"He probably had a dream. That's all."

"I thought of that, but I went out and checked around your window. Your window screen was on the ground propped up against the side of the house, and there were lots of footprints in the flowerbed under it."

Tatia's heart was beating faster as she searched for a plausible answer. "I haven't been sleeping well lately. The nightmares have come back. Sometimes when I wake up and have trouble going back to sleep, I go for a walk."

"And you climb out the window to go for your nightly walks?"

"I don't want to wake the kids. You know they leave their doors open. Now, I really have to go or I'll be late for first period."

"Okay," Josie said, stepping out of the way. "But you'd better not be lying to me. If I find out you've been sneaking out to see some boy or letting one come into your room, I'll tell Ms. Dunham to find another placement for you."

"I'm not seeing a boy, Josie. I promise," said Tatia as she made a mad dash for the bus.

She made it to the corner just in time and fell breathlessly into her seat just as the bus pulled away from the stop. She pulled her cell phone out of her backpack and dashed off a text to Eric.

I need to talk to you after school. Josie suspects.

He hadn't been meeting her after school for the last several weeks and hadn't been picking her up for work himself. He had explained that business was so good that managing it was taking more time. Tatia knew what kind of managing he had been doing, because she had seen him squiring around a hot new brunette. She didn't really mind. Her fantasy of his being her Prince Charming had faded the day he stood over her with his belt in hand. With his attention focused elsewhere, she was less likely to experience a repeat performance.

He had also explained that the extra business was bringing in extra money that had allowed him to purchase a late model Beemer and hire a driver to pick her up. She rather enjoyed being chauffeured around. If she was alone in the back seat, she sometimes had time for a quick nap. Some days, though, when there were lots of clients, they made several stops to pick up other girls, and it was almost like a party until they arrived in Cameron and the driver began dropping them off at various motels. After an evening of dealing with the reality of their lives, the ride home was much less festive.

In spite of his busy schedule, Eric still checked on Tatia regularly, and he always told her she could contact him any time she needed him. Apparently, he meant it. By the time she arrived at school, he had responded.

How about a decaf mocha?

She sent him a thumbs up emoticon and slipped the phone into her backpack.

CHAPTER 16

PREPARATIONS

Tatia was a little disappointed to see the Beemer parked at the library and the driver, Zach, leaning against the back door, but she had learned to limit her expectations. "Afternoon, Miss Tatia," he said. "How was school?"

She held out her hand and waggled it back and forth.

He laughed. "That good, huh?"

"Yeah," she said as he opened the door. She smiled when she saw Eric sitting inside holding out a large decaf mocha. "But I think it just got better."

She slid in as the door closed, dropped her backpack on the floor, fastened her seat belt, and took the cup from Eric. "Thanks, I needed this!" She took a sip and settled back contentedly in her seat. She was learning to enjoy the simple things.

Zach started the engine and looked at Eric in the rear-view mirror. "Where to, Boss?"

"Just drive around – and put on your headphones."

"You got it," Zach answered with a grin. He slipped on a pair of wireless headphones and cranked up the music so loud that Tatia could hear the bass line in the back seat.

"Trouble at home, huh?" asked Eric.

"Trouble everywhere," she said, and she explained what was going on.

"Hmmm," he said when she had finished. "I hadn't planned on doing this for another few months, but it may be time for a road trip."

"A road trip? You're not going to leave me here to handle this all by myself, are you?"

"Now, would I do that to my best girl?" he said, leaning over and kissing her lightly. "No, I'm thinking you and me – and maybe two or three of the other girls – might head up to Las Vegas for a little R & R. How does that sound?"

"It sounds like fun, but won't things just be worse when we get back?"

"They'll be a lot different, but I don't think they'll be worse," he explained. "I'm talking about making a complete break – leaving

Josie and school and all that kid stuff behind."

"I don't know, Eric. Being a runaway is not a good thing when you're a foster kid."

"But you're not a kid anymore," he said, holding her face gently in his hand. "You're Kaitlyn Golden, nineteen-year-old woman of the world. I mean, have you ever traveled, ever been anywhere outside of Texas?"

"No," she admitted. "It would be fun to see a little bit of the world. Do you think we could see the Grand Canyon?"

"I don't see why not!"

"Well, if we're going to do this, it needs to be soon. Report cards are due next week, and then it's gonna hit the fan."

"Okay. You have a couple of clients tomorrow night. Just slip a few extra changes of clothes into your backpack, and you just don't go home."

Tatia drew in a shaky breath and blew it out. "Okay. Let's do it!"

Eric slipped his arm around her shoulders and pulled her as close as he could without strangling her with her shoulder harness. "That's my girl!" he said, giving her a squeeze. Always ready for adventure, right?"

She laid her head on his shoulder, enjoying the momentary tenderness in spite a nagging feeling that this might be more of a disaster than an adventure. His attention was short-lived, though, and after a minute, he released her dismissively and said, "Well, babe, I gotta get back to work." He leaned up and tapped Zach on the shoulder. Zach lifted up his headphone on one side and turned his head toward Eric without taking his eyes off the road.

"Drop Tatia at the usual spot, then head back into Cameron."

Zach nodded and dropped the headphone back into place.

Tatia finished her mocha while Eric focused on his phone. When the car stopped, she hopped out before Zach had time to come around and open the door. "Bye, Eric. See you tomorrow night."

"Sure, babe," he said absently. "I'll send the car at the usual time."

She picked up her backpack and trudged home, wondering how big a mistake she was making. She knew that after tomorrow night she would be basically homeless, sharing an apartment with several of the other girls, depending on the good will of the man who had stolen what was left of her childhood. Still, sometimes he was totally loving and generous, more than anyone since her mother and father. As long as she did what he told her, she would be fine – at least that's what she told herself.

Tatia arrived home well before dinner, much to Josie's surprise. She worked hard, catching up on the cleaning and laundry she had neglected recently. While she waited for the dryer to finish, she helped Josie with dinner, and afterward, she helped the younger kids with their baths, read them a story, and put them to bed. When all the clothes were folded and put away, she went to say goodnight to Josie.

"It's good to have the old Tatia back," said Josie as she gave Tatia an awkward hug. "I hated to come down on you like that this morning, but sometimes all of us need a little wake-up call."

"Yeah," said Tatia. "I'm sorry I've been such a pain."

Josie smiled. "I understand. Sleep well, and if you don't, come wake me and we'll have some hot chocolate or something."

"Thanks. Good night," Tatia said, knowing Josie really didn't understand. No one did. She also knew how Josie was if she was awakened in the middle of the night. She'd rather deal with the nightmares.

She went into her room and closed the door. She sat down on the bed and looked around, taking a mental inventory of her possessions. After tomorrow night, everything she owned would fit in her backpack – along with the small collection of "work clothes" that Cindy kept in her apartment. She would leave everything else behind and hope that Josie would pass on anything worth saving to the younger girls.

She began to sort through her clothes, putting the ones she would take into a single drawer. She looked through her small collection of stuffed animals and decided to leave them all behind with her childhood. She had few other toys – two dolls and a few games, none of which she would need where she was going. Finally, she sat down at her tiny desk and went through the drawers. She took out the spiral notebook she had used as a journal since Ms. Dunham had suggested it the year before along with the pink gel pen Eric had give her a lifetime ago. She also grabbed a blank spiral and a couple of extra pens. She was about to close the drawer when she caught sight of the box that held her keepsakes from camp.

She carried the box to the bed where she spent the next half hour reliving what she was sure would be the last happy time of her life. She reread all the notes from her counselor and from camp aunts, uncles, and grandparents. She admired the bookmark she had made and the key chain she had woven. She spent most of her time looking through the photo album her counselor had put together using the many pictures the camp photographers had snapped during the week. Tears began to run down her face and drip off her chin when she looked at the picture of herself dressed in her business outfit, trying to imagine what it would be like to be a famous lawyer on her way to the trial of the century. She closed the album, not wanting to be reminded of how far she was from that dream.

She put the album back in the box with the intention of leaving it behind with all the memories. Then her hand brushed against something hard, and she saw the smooth rock with the word "Strength" painted on it. She smiled through the tears as she remembered Mrs. G's words when she gave it to her – "I see strength in you." – the same words the Ink Guy has said to her. She picked up the stone and saw Mrs. G's card underneath. She remembered Mrs. G telling her that she could call any time she was in trouble. This certainly qualified, but she doubted that even Mrs. G could solve this problem. Still, there was something inside her that said there was still hope, and she realized she wasn't ready to cut all ties to her past. Instead of putting it back in the desk, she put the box in the drawer with the clothes she planned to take.

All she had left to pack were her toiletries which she would put in at the last minute, so she was as ready as she could be. She took a quick shower and crawled into bed, wondering where she would sleep the following night.

CHAPTER 17

CHOICES

Tatia was exhausted when she arrived at the rendezvous point a few minutes before midnight the following night. She hadn't slept well, and her last day of school had been emotionally draining. The hours dragged as she went through the motions of a normal evening that was anything but normal. When it was finally time to go, all she wanted to do was stretch out on the bed and sleep. Instead, she peeked into the kids' rooms, blew them silent kisses, and slipped out the window one last time. She walked along an off-road nature trail to avoid running into a late-night patrol car, and she waited in the trees where she wouldn't be seen by any passing cars. The sounds of the night made her nervous, and she was relieved when the Beemer pulled up shortly after she reached her hiding place.

Zach jumped out as soon as the car came to a stop. "Evenin', Miss Tatia, I mean Miss Kaitlyn. Eric said I need to use your new name," he said, wearing a characteristic grin on his face and a pair of wireless headphones around his neck.

Tatia's shoulders drooped, and she looked back the way she had come. It seemed she was leaving more behind than she had realized. She was leaving what little was left of herself behind and becoming whatever Eric wanted her to be.

"Miss Kaitlyn, we really need to get moving," said Zach.

"I'm sorry," she said, handing him her backpack.

He popped the trunk and stowed it among several bags of various descriptions. She was startled to see that her boots and the blue canvas shopping bag that held her work clothes were there.

"Zach," she said. "You usually leave my work clothes at the motel after you check me in for the night. Why did you bring it with you?"

"I'll let the girls explain that to you. Right now, Mr. Eric is in a hurry to get on the road." He opened the back door and closed it behind her once she was seated beside Kaycee and Belinda, two of Eric's other girls. Eric was in the front passenger seat, isolated from the rest of the passengers by a black satin eyeshade and a pair of wireless headphones. Zach slid into the driver's seat, positioned his own headphones, and headed for the highway.

"What's going on?" whispered Tatia. "I was supposed to have two clients tonight."

Kaycee, a tiny girl with straight black hair and almond shaped eyes, whispered back. "Eric got a tip that the cops were gonna raid several of the motels tonight, so he cancelled all the appointments. We've been hanging out at the coffee shop for an hour or so waiting until time to meet you."

"What about Cindy and the other girls?"

"They're getting a night off, too, except for Cindy, of course. She'll spend all night dealing with irate customers and trying to find safe places to set the girls up and get the cash flowing again. Eric hates downtime when he's not making money. That's why he's hibernating. He's in a really bad mood."

Tatia was quiet for a few minutes, mulling over what she had just heard. Then she said, almost to herself, "I still don't understand why Eric brought my work clothes."

Belinda, who was a few years older than the other two, spoke up in the tone of a senior speaking to an inexperienced freshman. "You haven't been on a road trip before, have you?"

"No, but Eric said we'd head up to Las Vegas for a little R & R," said Tatia, a little defensively. "He said we might even do some sight-seeing, like the Grand Canyon or something."

Belinda put her hand over her mouth to stifle a giggle. "Honey, the only sights you'll be seeing are the ceilings of some different motels and maybe the inside of some truck sleepers. We're not on a road trip – we're on the circuit." With that, she closed her eyes, pulled a sweat jacket over her shoulders like a blanket, and leaned her head against the window.

"Don't let her get to you," whispered Kaycee, leaning close to Tatia. "She's just got her panties in a twist because she's not queen bee anymore."

"What do you mean?"

"Well, if you hadn't noticed, Eric specializes in really young girls. Once you're past thirteen or fourteen, a lot of our customers don't want you. Belinda is seventeen. I wouldn't be surprised if Eric doesn't trade her to another stable."

"But what about Cindy? She's almost twenty."

"Cindy's special. I don't mean like she and Eric are in love or anything, but she was his first girl, so I think he keeps her around for sentimental reasons. She also knows his business better than he does. She keeps track of his clients, the appointments, the girls

– all that kind of stuff."

As it turned out, Belinda was right. When Eric woke up, he plugged his laptop and his wireless card into the accessory plugs and accessed the Internet. Tatia learned later what he was doing.

First, he contacted a nearby motel known to be friendly to the trade where he booked a room for each of them. Then, he went to one of several underground websites that specialize in advertising the services of prostitutes on the move. He posted the ages and vital stats of the girls along with their availability, and within an hour, they were all booked for four solid hours – three to four clients an hour. After their work was done, the girls had time for a shower and a few hours sleep before they grabbed a quick breakfast and hit the road again.

The next two nights they didn't bother with a motel. Instead, Eric put out the word that they would be at a well-known truck stop around midnight. Again, all three girls were busy for several hours, moving in the shadows at the back of the parking lot from one truck to another. The nights at the truck stops were the worst, because they slept in the car while they traveled to the next destination. Eric wouldn't even allow them to shower in the truck stops because of the cops that often dropped in for coffee and a bite to eat. On those nights, the smell of sweat, unwashed bodies, and stale cigarette smoke clung to all of them and kept Tatia awake until she finally passed out from exhaustion.

In the wee hours of Sunday morning, after leaving another truck stop behind, Tatia was sitting in a cloud of second-hand smoke, wondering how long it took to develop lung problems. When Kaycee offered her a cigarette, she accepted it out of boredom and self defense. It made her cough, and she hated the way it tasted, but it gave her something to do. Kaycee and Belinda agreed that she looked more sophisticated and a bit sexy when she smoked, so at the next stop, she bought a pack of her own along with a disposable lighter.

Later in the morning, they finally drove into Las Vegas. The girls gawked and oohed and aahed as they rolled slowly past one glitzy hotel after another, but Eric told Zach to keep driving. Finally, he directed the driver into the parking lot of a motel that was off the Strip. It was far from five stars but was still better than many they had seen. While Zach went in to register and get room keys, Eric turned toward the back seat.

"Okay, time for a little break. It's 9:00 now. Go take a shower and get some rest. Meet me back here at 3:00 this afternoon, and we'll go on a little outing. Dress casual."

The girls each had a separate room, so they knew they'd be entertaining clients later, but they were too tired to care. Tatia took a hot shower and crawled into bed with her hair still wet. She set the alarm on her cell phone and immediately fell into a restless sleep – and a new nightmare.

She fought to free herself from the arms that grasped her, crying out silently for Mama. Mama didn't come, though. She was lying in a box with Daddy, both of them cold and lifeless, staring up at her with painted faces that melted into a pile of ashes while Eric grabbed at her, pulling her through the door of a shabby motel room filled with men waiting in line beside a bed covered with dirty, rumpled sheets. They chanted her name again and again as she struggled toward a persistent ringing sound just outside the door.

The fog of sleep thinned slightly – enough for Tatia to realize the ringing was her alarm and that the restraint she felt was from the sheets that were tangled around her and not Eric's arms. She groped for her phone and raised one eyelid far enough to peek at the time. She groaned when she saw that it was already 2:30. Still exhausted, her body aching from the abuse she had endured the last three nights, she wanted nothing more than to close her eyes and sink into the oblivion of sleep. She feared the nightmares that waited there, though, and she feared Eric's anger if she didn't show up as ordered, so she dragged herself out of the snarled bedclothes and headed for the bathroom.

At two minutes before 3:00, Tatia trudged across the parking lot toward Belinda and Kaycee who looked somewhat refreshed as they leaned against the car, chatting and waiting for Eric to arrive. They fell silent as they saw Tatia, and Belinda eyed her with a sneer.

"Hey, girl! You look like something I scooped out of my cat's litter box. You having trouble keeping up the pace?"

Kaycee shushed her quietly. "Hush, Belinda. You know Eric doesn't like it when you rag on the other girls. Besides, Tatia's not an old pro like you."

Belinda scowled at her emphasis on the word "old," but Kaycee ignored her and turned her attention to Tatia. "What's the matter, girlfriend? Didn't you get any sleep?"

"Not so much," she said, stifling a yawn. "Too many dreams."

"If Cindy were here, she could fix that," said Belinda with a raised eyebrow.

"Right," said Kaycee, "and then she'd need something to wake up, and on and on."

"Don't be so self-righteous. I've seen you pop a few uppers and downers in your time."

Before the conversation turned into a real scrap, Eric and Zach showed up and jumped into the car. The two girls glared at each other as they slid into the back seat, and Tatia followed silently, ignoring them both and leaning her head against the window.

Eric directed Zach to a nearby shopping mall – not one of the fancy ones for tourists but one that looked as if it was frequented by the locals. When Zach had parked, Eric pulled out his money clip and gave each one of them, including Zach, two hundred dollars.

"You've worked hard. I have a meeting, so go have some fun. You, too, Zach. I'll drive myself. Stay together or split up, whatever you want. Just be back at this entrance at 6:00 pm. We'll go have some dinner before we go back to the motel. Don't make me wait – we're booked solid tonight."

Belinda and Kaycee, drawn back together by the prospect of spending money, immediately began planning new outfits. Kaycee asked Tatia if she wanted to come with them, but she shook her head. "I don't think so. I'm going to look for a bookstore."

Nobody asked Zach, but he walked beside Tatia as she headed for the entrance. "I don't care much for clothes, so I think I'll tag along with you if that's okay."

"Sure, Zach," she said, brightening up a little. "I'd enjoy the company."

"So you like to read, huh?" he asked.

"Yes, I usually take a book or two everywhere I go. But when Eric told me about this trip, I didn't realize we'd be spending so much time in the car and, well, indoors. I didn't bring anything to read, and I don't sleep very well in the car, so there's nothing to do but smoke – and I don't like cigarettes much."

"Yeah," he laughed. "Reading is much better for your health." They walked in silence for a few minutes, looking in the windows and watching the other shoppers. Then, Zach broke the silence. "Hey, I have an idea. Have you ever used one of those e-readers?"

"No, I haven't, but that's a great idea."

"I think some of them even light up so you can read in the dark."

She was energized, now that she had a goal. They found a map of the mall and located an electronics store one floor up and a few stores down on the right. She found a helpful salesman, and while he was showing her the options, Zach entertained himself by testing out all the latest headphones. She settled for a simple backlit reader so she would have as much left over as possible for e-books. The salesman helped her buy a couple of books and then helped her set up a gift card online with her extra money. All she had to do when she finished the books she had was choose another title.

When she was finished, she found Zach comparing the pictures on a line of TVs. "I'm all set and ready to read," she said holding up her bag. "We have over an hour left. Now we need to spend your money."

"No," he said, suddenly seeming a little shy. "I'm saving for an engagement ring. With what Eric gave me today, I'm almost there."

"Well congratulations," said Tatia. "She's a very lucky lady."

"No, I'm the lucky one," he said.

"So, how about the food court. I know Eric said we were going to dinner, but spending money makes me hungry."

"Sounds good. I could use a snack."

They found the food court without too much trouble, and he bought a slice of pepperoni while she ordered a cup of non-fat strawberry frozen yogurt. While they ate, they chatted about books they had read and places they would like to travel. When they finished, they disposed of their trash and strolled toward the entrance, as comfortable in each other's company as if they had known each other forever.

They reached the parking lot before any of the others, so they found a bench and sat down. She reached in her purse, pulled out a pack of cigarettes, and offered him one.

"No, thanks. I don't smoke," he said.

"But you have a pack right there in your shirt pocket."

"Yes, I do, but have you ever seen me smoke one?"

She thought for a moment before answering. "Now that you mention it, no I haven't."

"I carry them because Eric expects me to have them in case he runs out. I don't like the taste of them, and I don't like how I smell after I've smoked them."

"Yeah, me too. In fact, I had never smoked until this trip, but Belinda and Kaycee said I look good smoking."

"Tatia, you're a beautiful young lady, and you look good regardless of what you're doing. But I personally don't find a smoking woman particularly attractive."

Tatia's cheeks colored at the unexpected compliment. "Thanks for the kind words and the good advice." She looked at the cigarettes and put them back in her purse. "You're right, of course. I don't seem to have much choice about what I do for a living, but I have decided not to drink or do drugs. I guess I can do without this vice, too. Maybe I'll keep these just in case Eric runs out."

They laughed as Belinda and Kaycee ran up behind them, giggling breathlessly, and Eric screeched to a stop in front of them and beeped the horn.

"Well," said Zach, standing up. "Duty calls."

"Yeah," Tatia sighed. "No rest for the wicked."

CHAPTER 18
LIMITED OPTIONS

Eric took everyone to dinner at an Italian restaurant – nothing like where he had taken Tatia for her birthday, but the food was good, and it was a nice way to spend another few minutes feeling like a normal teenager. After dinner, Eric allowed Zach to drive down the Strip so they could see all the lights at night, but there was no time to stop. He had a full schedule of clients lined up for each girl, so they left the lights behind and spent the next several hours at the motel.

Tatia had been too tired to pay much attention to her assigned room earlier, but as she glanced around now, she noted that it was almost identical to every room she'd been in since she left Josie's. As it turned out, it looked like every room on the way back to Texas, too – and like the rooms where Cindy had set up shop back in Cameron.

Tatia read a lot on the return trip, mostly in the car, but sometimes in the few minutes between clients. She had learned to separate herself mentally and emotionally from situations she couldn't deal with, but she also discovered a new ability to withdraw into the world of her books while with her clients. It was a healthier method of getting through the night than the chemicals used by most of the other girls.

The reality of her new life was all too real, though. One morning shortly after the trip, she was between books, so she accepted Cindy's invitation to go shoe shopping. Tatia was saving for a leather jacket she had seen at the mall, so she watched as her friend picked out a pair of fancy cross trainers and some evening sandals with spiked heels. As Cindy paid for shoes, Tatia knew they would join the many other pairs in the top of her closet, but she was glad to see Cindy look almost happy for a little while. They left the store, chatting about where to have lunch, when Cindy stopped dead still and stared at Tatia.

"Are you on the pill?" she asked urgently.

"No," said Tatia, surprised by the sudden subject change. "But after that first night, Eric told me to make sure the guys use a condom. You know that, Cindy. You keep me supplied."

"I know, but those things don't always work," she said, dialing her cell phone. "Yes, I'll hold," she said impatiently. Looking back at Tatia, she went on. "Eric usually takes care of this part of it. He's got a special deal worked out with the doc. I can't believe he forgot – but he sure throws a fit if one of the girls gets pregnant. Last time it happened I thought he was gonna kill her – like it was her fault. Anyway..." she held up her hand while she listened to someone on the other end of the phone.

"Yes, this is Cindy, Eric Hall's administrative assistant. I need to talk with the doctor. Yes, I'll hold."

Later that afternoon, before Tatia's first client was scheduled, she stood in the alley behind the doctor's office as Cindy knocked on the door. A short, pudgy man in a lab coat opened the door, and Cindy introduced him as Dr. Simmons. He shook hands with Tatia, and as his eyes slid slowly down her body, she sighed inwardly as she realized her 8:00 o'clock wasn't going to be her first client of the day after all.

When Tatia wasn't working, she shared a room with Cindy in the two-bedroom apartment they both shared with Kaycee and Belinda. In the past, Cindy had an apartment by herself or sometimes with one roommate. However, she managed to incur Eric's wrath more often lately, and while she was recovering from his expressions of that wrath, she comforted herself with junk food and spiked sodas. The evidence of Eric's abuse and her overindulgence made her less popular with the clients, and her decreased production meant she lost the privilege of upgraded living quarters.

Tatia felt sorry for Cindy, but she was glad to be her roommate. Cindy had a laptop that she used to keep track of the business, and when she wasn't busy, she let Tatia use it. Tatia had learned about email at the library, so at first she would check to see if anyone was trying to contact her. She received a few messages from Ms. Dunham asking where she was and if she was okay, but when she didn't respond, even those emails stopped. Instead of focusing on an empty inbox, she surfed the Internet, looking for new sources for free e-books and reading about different authors on Goodreads and other sites devoted to the written word.

Sometimes she looked over Cindy's shoulder while she was working, and she asked questions about the word and data processing programs she was using. Cindy didn't seem to mind, and she even let Tatia do some elementary data entry from time to time.

The other girls were not nearly as companionable. They bickered and whined about real or imaginary violations of their limited personal space, and they argued over who worked the hardest and who Eric loved more. In spite of repeated hints and a few outright requests, they continued to smoke inside and to clutter the apartment with dirty clothes, crumpled fast food wrappers, and empty liquor bottles. Tatia worked harder to stay in Eric's good graces, hoping he would relent and allow her to have her own place with Cindy as a roommate.

The majority of her time, though, was not spent in the apartment but rather in one of the many sleazy motel rooms where she worked. Since he had taken on a couple of new girls, Eric had expanded his underground advertising and his client base. Now that she was always available, he sometimes booked Tatia for ten to twelve hours straight, often selling her to over a hundred men a month.

At first she thought a lot about the time she spent with Eric before her birthday, and hoped that once he had built his finances back up, things would go back to the way they were. She had been disappointed that their first road trip had been a working one with others along instead of a romantic trip for two, but she still wanted to believe that maybe one day he would take her away. Then, one night after a particularly difficult client, she was washing up when Eric came bursting into the room. As she leaned over the sink, he grabbed her by the hair and flung her back into the room where she hit the edge of the bed and slid down onto the floor.

"Eric, what..." she began, looking up at him in confusion.

"Shut up," he said, backhanding her across the mouth. "Your last customer was very unhappy with you," he continued in a threatening voice. "I don't like unhappy customers."

"Neither do I, Eric. They don't tip."

"And did he tip you?" he asked stepping closer and sliding his belt out of its loops.

"No," she said, her eyes wide with fear.

"He didn't pay either," said Eric.

By the time he left the room, she was so badly beaten that she couldn't work for several days. Eric took her tips for the next several months to make up for the lost income, but there was no way for her to recover her lost dreams.

CHAPTER 19
ON THE STROLL...

The first time she was arrested, she was sporting a dark, shoulder-length pageboy. A new client had requested a brunette, so Eric had purchased a wig for her. The client must have been pleased, because he left her a nice tip. After he left, she went into the bathroom to freshen up and make sure her hair was on straight. She didn't really like the look. The darker color made her face look harsh and angular, and the darker make-up Cindy had told her to use looked overdone. Still, if the client was happy, Eric was happy – and if Eric was happy, so was she.

Eric had said she was booked almost solid for the next several hours, so she was surprised when her phone rang. When she was working, she set it to let only calls from Eric come through, and he never called her while she was entertaining clients.

"Hello?" she said, wondering what she had done wrong now.

"Hey, Tatia," Eric said in a pleasant tone. "How'd the guy like you as brunette?"

Tatia relaxed a bit, hoping she wasn't in trouble after all. "He liked it. He left me an extra twenty bucks."

"Good job. I'll split the tip with you."

Tatia started to protest, but she knew better. At least he was only taking half. "Thanks, Eric."

"No problem, kiddo. Hey, you had a couple of cancellations and a couple of unfilled time slots, so your next client won't be there for an hour or so."

Tatia breathed a silent sigh of relief and thought about the book she had just downloaded today. She always carried her reader with her, just in case, and she felt a rush of hopeful excitement at the prospect of some free time to read. Her hopes were short lived, though, as Eric continued.

"I want you to go out and see if you can scout up a quick walk-in or two, if you know what I mean."

"Sure, Eric," she said, careful to keep the disappointment out of her voice.

"Just be sure to be ready when your next client gets there at 1:30."

"OK."

"Great! Love ya, babe!"

She hated going on the stroll. It was scary enough when Eric pre-screened the clients on-line, but it terrified her to pick up strangers on the street. Not as much as facing Eric's anger terrified her, though, so she slid into the clingy red dress and the knee-high black boots she had worn to work. She checked her hair and make-up one last time, grabbed her hot pink phone clutch, and slid her room key card into the pocket next to her fake ID. Then, she hit "Messages," Cindy's number, and her frequently used emoticons.

After one of the other girls had been mugged in an alley off the stroll the month before, Cindy had made up some special icons. One showed a screaming girl by a car; another showed the same screaming girl sitting on a bed, and the third showed a policeman. The idea was that, in case one of the girls had a problem, all she had to do was hit the appropriate emoticon, send it to Cindy, and she would send help. They hadn't really talked about what would happen if Cindy was working, but Eric didn't want them texting him. Even though Tatia had not run into trouble yet, she wanted to be as prepared as possible. Satisfied that she had covered all her bases, she snapped the gaudy rhinestone clasp closed, stepped out the door, and began the two-block walk to the area where prostitutes and their clients often connected.

Tatia sauntered casually down the sidewalk with the hip-swaying gait Cindy had taught her, the one that was guaranteed to attract attention. As she walked, she thought about her new book. She often browsed through the shelves at the library when she had time, making notes of books she might want to download. Recently, she had come across *Redeeming Love* by Francine Winters and was instantly captivated. The cover blurb said it was about a girl who was sold into prostitution as a child but later found redemption in the love of God and the love of a godly man. It sounded like a fairy tale, but Tatia couldn't resist finding out how the author imagined such a miracle might happen.

She was so deep in thought that she was startled when she heard a pleasant male voice say, "Hey there."

"Oh," she said, catching her breath as her hand flew up to her chest. "I didn't hear you drive up."

One of the reasons this area was so popular with the trade was that the one-way street allowed the drivers to talk to the girls without having to shout across the car or across an oncoming lane of traffic. Tatia recovered her composure and continued to walk slowly forward while offering the driver what she hoped was an inviting smile. He looked to be in his mid-thirties with sandy brown hair that looked as if he ran his hands through it a lot. He also had friendly eyes that crinkled a little bit at the corners when he returned her smile timidly.

"I'm sorry if I scared you," he said, allowing the car to drift along beside her. "I thought maybe you were looking for some company. Maybe I made a mistake."

"No, you're not wrong. I was feeling kinda lonely, so I thought I'd take a walk." She walked over to the car and leaned into the window. Cindy had taught her that, too. "What did you have in mind?"

"Ummm, I-I-I," he stuttered. "I'm kinda new at this."

He certainly wasn't like a lot of the guys she saw cruising around, acting tough and trying to look cool. Tatia smiled, thinking he might be one of the not-so-bad ones. "Tell you what. I have a room a couple of blocks over. Do you want to come over and have a drink?"

"Sure," he said, sounding relieved. "That sounds nice."

Tatia walked around to the passenger's side and stepped into the car, making sure the hem of her dress slid up provocatively. She buckled herself in and gave him directions to the motel. She told him where to park, led the way to her door, unlocked it, and invited him in.

"By the way," she said, closing the door behind them, "my name's Kaitlyn. I don't really have anything to offer you to drink except a soda from the machine outside."

"Hi, Kaitlyn. I'm Kevin. I'm not really thirsty anyway," he said, looking down at the floor.

Tatia chuckled at his innocence. She sat down on the edge of the bed and crossed her long legs.

"Then what do you want, Kevin?" she asked. Knowing the clock was ticking and Eric was expecting results, she began to make suggestions and quote prices. Suddenly, the person in front of her transformed from a timid, insecure mouse into a strong, confident man on a mission, a man she instinctively knew was a cop.

"Crap!" she said under her breath. Her phone clutch was still in her hand, so she flipped open the clasp, touched the third icon, and hit send. "Eric's gonna kill me."

CHAPTER 20

...AND IN THE SLAMMER

The man reached into his hip pocket and pulled out his wallet. He popped it open with one smooth, practiced move, exposing his badge and confirming Tatia's worst fears.

"Kevin Adams, Cameron PD. You're under arrest for prostitution. Stand up and turn around with your hands behind your back."

As he began reciting her rights, he pulled some flex-cuffs out of his pocket. He hated the things, because if you tightened them too much, you had to cut them off and start over before your detainee ended up with blue hands. The metal ones tended to rattle at the wrong time, though, so he made do.

"Do you understand these rights as I've told them to you?" he asked as he tested the cuffs to make sure he hadn't made them too loose.

"Yes," said Tatia in a voice so quiet it was almost drowned out by the buzz of her cell phone. "Can I take my phone?"

"You can't handle it in the car, and you know you can't keep it when they put you in a cell."

"Oh," she replied with tears in her voice.

"First time?" he asked with his voice softening a little.

"Yes."

He picked up the phone and slid it into his pocket. "They'll give it back to you when you're released."

Tatia nodded, biting her lip and struggling to control the fear of what would happen when she was released. Eric had no patience with girls who cost him time and money by getting arrested. Officer Adams held her arm securely but not roughly as he directed her back to his car, and he was careful not to bump her head when he helped her into the back seat. She knew Eric would not be so gentle.

While he drove to the station, Tatia saw him glancing at her in the rearview mirror every now and then. Finally, he spoke.

"What's your last name, Kaitlyn?"

"Golden," she answered.

"How old are you."

She did a quick mental calculation, making sure her answer matched her ID. "Twenty," she said.

"Shame," he said. "If you were, say, sixteen or seventeen, this would be a lot easier for you – especially if you told me where to find the guy you texted back in the room."

"Oh, that," she said. "That was just my roommate letting her know that I wouldn't be home tonight."

"Ahh," he said cynically. "I thought it might be your pimp."

"No, I don't have a manager. I'm on my own – just making a little spending money," she said, trying to sound much more blasé than she felt.

Both driver and passenger were silent for the rest of the trip. Adams pulled into a parking lot where he pulled in between two patrol cars. He helped Tatia out and guided her up the steps into the station and past the front desk where an officer was talking on the phone with his feet up on the desk.

"Slow night, huh?" said Adams.

"Yeah. Looks like you got a live one."

"Uh-huh. Is Anderson here?"

"Yeah, she's taking a break. We don't have a houseful, but there are a few ahead of you."

Tatia's eyes were wide with apprehension as the reality of her situation played out in front of her. "Where are you taking me?" she whispered to Kevin.

He lowered his voice so only she could hear. "To a holding cell where you'll stay until we're ready to complete the booking process. Then you'll be moved to a pre-arraignment cell where you'll stay until the judge gets here and gets started tomorrow morning."

"Tomorrow?" she said with tears puddling and threatening to spillover.

"It won't be too bad. I type slow, and the night's half over anyway."

"You still have my phone, right?"

"Right here," he said, patting his pocket.

The holding cell was down the hall from the front desk, but Tatia wished it was miles further. The small barred room was bare except for four metal benches bolted to the wall and the floor, a sink against the back wall, and an exposed toilet next to it. Women were lying on two of the benches with their faces turned toward the wall, and a third was sitting on another. None of them paid any attention as Kevin and Tatia approached. The officer who was sitting outside the cell at a tiny desk, however, gave her a thorough inspection.

"Hey, Adams! Looks like you caught a new one tonight. I haven't seen her around here before."

"Be nice, Hill. She's never been inside before."

"Yeah, first time but probably not the last. You know the drill – sign her in." He shoved a clip board toward Kevin and continued his inspection of Tatia. Kevin wrote down her name, his name as the arresting officer, and the time.

"Okay, Hill. Get your lazy butt out of that chair and open the door so we can get on with this."

While Hill unlocked the door, Kevin pulled a utility knife out of his pocket and used it to remove the cuffs from Tatia's wrists. She rubbed her wrists, not because they hurt, but because she couldn't believe she had actually been handcuffed. Hill swung the door open, she took a couple of steps inside, and stopped, frozen in place.

"This might take a little while," said Kevin. "There are three ahead of you, but Officer Anderson will come get you and finish the process as soon as she can."

About ten minutes later, Tatia moved toward the remaining vacant bench when she realized her toes were going numb from standing in four-inch heels. She sat on the edge of the bench, just enough to take the pressure off her feet, and stared at her hands to avoid making eye contact with anyone.

Tatia didn't know how long she had been sitting there when she heard a female voice call out a name. She looked up long enough to watch Officer Anderson collect one of the other women and take her back down the hall. Anderson didn't look nearly as nice as Kevin. In fact, the tall, husky brunette had a scowling mouth and an intense look that scared Tatia. She scooted back against the wall, tucked her feet under her, and wrapped her arms around herself, trying to keep from trembling.

She must have dozed off, because the next thing she knew, Anderson was calling her name. She stumbled to the door, trying to clear the sleep out of her head, and followed the officer to another room where she was instructed to sit down in the chair beside the desk. Anderson tapped on her keyboard for a few minutes, then, she began to ask Tanya some simple questions.

"Full name?"

Tatia caught herself before she gave her real name. "Kaitlyn Golden."

She made it through the rest of the questions, stumbling only slightly over her date of birth. She gave Cindy as her contact person, and she answered the medical questions easily since she had always been healthy. Before she printed the completed form, Anderson asked three more questions.

"Do you understand that you are being booked on a charge of Prostitution, a Class B misdemeanor?"

"Yes," replied Tatia quietly.

"Were your rights read to you, and do you understand those rights?"

"Yes," she whispered, thinking that the only rights she had were the ones Eric said she had.

"Would you like to make a phone call?"

"Yes, please."

Anderson dialed the number Tatia gave her and then handed the phone to her. Tatia listened hopefully to several rings, but her face fell as the voice mail activated. She listened to the familiar message before leaving one of her own. "Cindy, I hope you got my text. I'm at the Cameron PD, and court starts in less than an hour. Please come get me!"

The sound of Tatia's voice was covered by the chatter of the printer next to Anderson's desk. The officer took the phone back from Tatia and reached into her desk drawer, pulling out an ink pad and another form. As if she was grabbing another implement off her desk, she grabbed Tatia's hand and began rolling her fingers, first across the ink and then across the form. While she worked, Tatia asked her first question.

"Will I be searched?"

The hint of a smile tugged at one corner of the officer's mouth. Without looking up, she replied. "Not that a full-body search would be all that new to you, but no. I don't think you could hide anything under that dress. Besides," she said, looking at her watch. "It's less than an hour until court convenes. We won't even have time to put you into one of our lovely orange jumpsuits."

Anderson directed Tatia to an area with a backdrop that reminded Tatia of the back of the closet door where her mother measured her every few months to see how much she had grown. It was the first time she could remember being glad her mother was dead – at least she didn't have to see what her daughter had become.

"Face the camera and hold this in front of you," said Anderson as she handed her a slate with her name and a series of numbers on it. After snapping a front view and a profile shot, Anderson directed Tatia back to her desk. "Have a seat while I get your inmate ID."

She came back in a few minutes with a strip of plastic that contained Tatia's ID number, her name, her mug shot, and a bar code. As Anderson fastened the bracelet around Tatia's wrist, she caught a glimpse of Tatia's tattoo peeking out from under her three-quarter-length sleeve. She pushed the sleeve up a little and made a clucking sound with her tongue.

"Looks like you already have an ID. I thought Officer Adams said you were a solo act."

Tatia pulled her sleeve down, folded her arms across her chest so the tattoo was well hidden, and exercised her right to remain silent.

CHAPTER 21
COURT IS IN SESSION

By the time Officer Anderson had dotted all her *i*s and crossed all her *t*s, it was 7:30 am, only half an hour before court was called into session. Anderson proved she wasn't as hard-shelled as she seemed by taking Tatia to the restroom. Even though she made Tatia leave the stall door open, it was at least more private than the open toilet in the cell. When she came out of the stall, Tatia took a minute to straighten her auburn wig and wipe away the mascara and eye liner that had smeared during the night.

After they left the restroom, Anderson handed Tatia a bottle of water and a breakfast bar before taking her to a waiting room outside the courtroom. She ushered Tatia into the room, and Tatia saw a uniformed officer, the three women she had shared a cell with the night before, and several orange-clad men she didn't recognized. She sat on the back row in the only chair with a vacant seat next to it.

A few minutes later, a door on the other side of the room opened, and another uniformed man stepped in and said, "Show time, kiddies." Some of the others in the room seemed to know the drill, so Tatia followed their lead. She stood quietly and fell into line behind the closest person to her. She saw a trash can in the corner and dropped her half empty bottle of water and her barely touched bar into it. She had watched the officer growl at one of the men who tried to go through the door without emptying his hands. She knew she needed to eat something, but she decided the breakfast provided by the county wasn't worth fighting for.

Tatia had never seen a courtroom except on TV, and if she hadn't been so scared, she would have been impressed. As it was, she hardly noticed her surroundings. Instead, she kept her head down and followed the person in front of her until she stopped, and then she sat down. Still keeping her head down, she stood up when the judge entered the room and sat back down when everyone else did.

She peeked around the courtroom behind her, hoping to see a familiar face. There were several men and women dressed in business suits who she assumed were lawyers, and there were others who looked more like friends and family, but she didn't recognize a single person. Her heart began to pound so hard that she was sure everyone around her could hear it, and she was finding it hard to catch her breath. Maybe Eric was so mad at her that he was going to leave her on her own.

While she envisioned herself dressed in orange and staring at the world through iron bars, the bailiff called the first case, and a man in the front row stepped out of his seat and into the aisle. One of the suited men from the other side of the room met him in the middle, and they both went forward. The man was charged with DUI, and it soon became obvious that this was not his first appearance. It also became obvious to Tatia that the judge was not the ogre she had imagined he would be. There was no yelling or harsh criticism – except for the usual court room rhetoric, of course – and Tatia began to calm down a bit.

She still peeked over her shoulder every few minutes to see if help had arrived, but at least she could breathe. Finally, after the fourth or fifth case, the door opened quietly, and a nicely dressed man who looked vaguely familiar walked in. She was trying to remember where she had seen him when Cindy walked in right behind him, and then she remembered. He was Joseph, the man from the coffee shop. He must be a lawyer, Eric's lawyer and now hers. Cindy saw her and gave her a big grin and a thumbs up, and Tatia smiled for the first time in many hours.

She turned back toward the front and relaxed back into her seat, realizing for the first time how really tense she had been. For a few minutes she focused on each part of her body, consciously tensing and then releasing the muscles, trying to relieve some of the soreness of spending most of the night sitting on a cold metal bench. Once she was as relaxed as she was going to be under the circumstances, she became aware of a gnawing in her stomach and tried to remember how long it had been since she had last eaten. She was wondering if she could talk Joseph into stopping for a bite to eat when she heard the bailiff call out another name.

"Kaitlyn Golden."

She realized that she was the only inmate left and that everyone was staring at her. She jumped up, banging into the chair in front of her, and hurried into the aisle where Joseph was waiting for her with an indulgent smile. He leaned slightly toward her as he led her toward the judge and said in a voice so low she had to strain to hear.

"Don't be nervous. You'll plead guilty and this will be over in a couple of minutes."

His confidence was contagious, and she found the courage to raise her eyes long enough to glance at the judge. He had his eyes focused on the paperwork in front of him, so she let her gaze wander over what she could see of him behind the massive, polished-wood desk. He was a pleasant looking man – for someone who held her future in his hands. She guessed him to be in his mid to late forties and probably medium height and weight. He had a pair of black-rimmed reading glasses perched on the end of his nose, and he took them off when he lifted his eyes from her file and looked at her. She was accustomed to being visually assessed by men, but she was shocked to see the compassion and sadness in his eyes. His face hardened a bit as he looked over at Joseph.

"Well, Mr. Pittman, it looks like you have a new client," he said with an edge of disapproval in his voice.

Joseph nodded. "Yes, Judge Wellman."

The judge turned back to Tatia. "Miss Golden, it says here that you're twenty. Is that correct?"

"Yes, Your Honor."

"Hmmm," he sighed. "You are being charged with prostitution. You understand that, right?" He was all business now.

"Yes, Your Honor."

"And how do you plead?"

She hesitated for a moment and looked up at Joseph. He nodded encouragingly.

"Guilty, Your Honor," she said quietly.

"All right. A preliminary hearing will be set for two weeks from today. Since this is your first offense, bail is set at $500. Mr. Pittman, you know the drill."

"Yes, your Honor," said Joseph. "We'll see the clerk."

He turned to leave, and Tatia followed his lead. She stopped when the judge called her name.

"Miss Golden?"

She turned back. "Yes, Your Honor?"

"After we get this matter settled, I don't want to see you in my court room again."

"No, Your Honor."

Tatia ducked her head and hurried after Joseph who was walking toward one of two small desks to the left of the judge. She knew from Court TV that the woman at the first desk who was tapping keys on what looked like a narrow typewriter was the court reporter, so the other one must be the clerk Joseph mentioned. She listened long enough to realize he was taking care of the details of her bail. Then, she tuned out, exhausted from fear, adrenaline, lack of sleep, and lack of food. She moved through the next few minutes in a kind of robotic haze, following instructions as if on automatic pilot.

The next thing she knew, Tatia was walking down the hallway in the courthouse toward the door. Her cell phone was in her right hand, and Cindy was hanging onto her left arm, chattering non-stop. Cindy's talking was sometimes irritating, but today it was beautiful.

"Thank you for coming to get me," said Tatia, pulling her arm free and giving Cindy an awkward hug.

"No problem, kid," said Cindy, returning the hug. "Now let's get out of here."

The two friends had taken only a couple of steps toward the door when Tatia stopped, staring at a woman who was picking up her personal belongings after having passed through security on her way into the building.

"Hi, Mrs. Grochowsky," said the security officer. "I thought court was finished for the day"

"I'm not here for that, Charles. I have a pre-trial meeting about one of my girls."

"Gotcha. Hey, what kind of name is Grochowsky anyway?"

"Russian I think," she said with a chuckle. "My husband asked his grandfather about it one time, and the old guy said, 'We are Americans. That's all you need to know.'"

"Then why didn't he Americanize the name?"

"My husband asked him that, too. He said, 'We're not that American.'"

The officer laughed and shook his head. "Well, it certainly is a mouthful."

"Yes, it is. That's why most people call me Mrs. G."

Cindy turned and looked at her friend. "Hey, girlfriend, what's up?" When there was no response, she gently shook her by the shoulder. "Tatia?"

At the sound of the name, Mrs. G looked up, and she and Tatia locked eyes. "Tatia?" she asked.

Tatia ducked her head and hurried out the door.

CHAPTER 22
FINDING MRS. G

The disembodied voice of the pilot broke into her thoughts. "Ladies and Gentlemen, we're beginning our initial descent into the DFW area..."

Tatia couldn't believe she had been lost in the past for almost three hours. She looked at the notebook she had intended to review and smiled. She should have known she would be much too excited about seeing Mrs. G to concentrate. She retrieved the book from the seat pocket, slipped it back into her bag, and let herself drift back into memories of the woman who had been such a big part of her life.

After Tatia's first encounter with the law, Eric slapped her around a bit – not so badly that she couldn't work but enough to remind her of the total control he had over her life. As if to reinforce that fact, Eric worked her even harder. He said she had to pay him back for the fine he paid when she went back to court, and she also had to make up for the time she lost when she was in jail and in court. Some weekends, especially when there was a convention in the area, he set her up in a motel close to the meeting site and scheduled her non-stop for days on end. Those days, along with the hours she had spent in the jail cell and seated in the courtroom with other inmates, further chipped away at the fantasy that refused to die completely – that one day soon Eric would realize he really loved her, and they would go away and start a new life together.

Her only retreat was her e-books, but as she became more entangled in the ugliness that was her life, it became harder for her to find solace in the stories that had become so important to her. She no longer identified with the romantic heroines who were saved by the love of a good man. Instead, she pictured herself as the irredeemably fallen woman, destined to live out her life in seedy motels and dark alleys. Still, as she paced the worn carpet in one of those seedy motels, she wished she had not left her tablet in the apartment. Her next client wasn't scheduled for another forty-five minutes, the pizza Eric had dropped off earlier was cold and soggy, and the TV didn't work.

In frustration she threw open the drawer of the one scratched and chipped nightstand, hoping to find something to keep her from dwelling on the hopelessness of her life. She saw a five-year-old phone book and a Gideon Bible. She stared at the book for a moment, feeling unworthy to even touch it while at the same time feeling drawn to it. Finally, she picked it up, sat down on the bed, and opened it slowly. She had been given a Bible at camp, but with everything that had happened since then, she had rarely looked at it. Besides, since it didn't fit in her memory box, she had left it at Josie's. Now, as she flipped through the pages and read a sentence here and there, she wished she knew more about where to find specific verses.

Just when she was about to give up, she came across the book of Jeremiah, and that struck a familiar chord. The Bible studies at camp had been focused on a verse in that book. She remembered her counselor showing her how to find the chapters and verses, so she turned the pages until she found Chapter 29, verse 11.

For I know the thoughts that I think toward you, saith the Lord, thoughts of peace, and not of evil, to give you an expected end.

The version the camp teacher had used talked about plans in place of thoughts. He had said that this promise was made to the Hebrew people but that the principle still applied today. She wondered what plans God had for her – surely He had not planned for her to be where she was. The teacher had said God's plans for her would give her hope and a future, but this life she was living seemed hopeless with a future of pain and loneliness. Maybe she had wandered so far from God's plans that He had forgotten her.

The natural beauty that Eric had once praised in her had devolved into a sallow complexion from little exposure to the sun and circles under her eye caused by lack of sleep. Her diet and her appetite were so poor that her cheeks were sunken and her clothes, except for the spandex outfits Eric bought for her, hung loosely on her too-slim body. The naturally blonde curls that once drove her crazy now hung dry and lifeless, and the deep blue eyes that once dominated her pretty face were now dull and faded.

She sometimes wondered if anyone from her former life would recognize her or if they even remembered or missed her, but she was terrified by the possibility of running into someone who knew her before. She was haunted by the look in Mrs. G's eyes when they saw each other in the courthouse. At first there was a question, as if she wasn't quite sure who she was seeing. Then, there was a mixture of emotions – initial surprise and excitement that quickly turned to sadness, and much more. Tatia had looked away quickly, not wanting to see the disappointment, disgust, revulsion, and horror she imagined Mrs. G must have felt at seeing her dressed like a prostitute and wearing an inmate's ID around her wrist. She felt those same emotions when she looked at herself in the mirror.

Still, Tatia couldn't forget the look of excitement – Mrs. G seemed glad to see her. She glanced at her watch and realized it was almost time for her next client to arrive, but as she prepared for his arrival, she thought about the box of special things she brought with her when she left Josie's house and promised herself that she would dig it out if Eric ever let her go back to her apartment. She hoped she still had the card Mrs. G had given her with her phone number on it – just in case.

CHAPTER 23

SHOW TIME

It was three in the morning when Tatia returned to the apartment she now shared with Cindy. Tatia had worked hard enough that, when Eric needed a place for two new girls, he moved them in with Kaycee and Belinda and allowed Tatia and Cindy to get a place of their own. Tatia was exhausted, but she lay in bed, unable to sleep as the words of Jeremiah and thoughts of Mrs. G swirled around in her mind. Finally, she crawled out of bed, turned on her bedside lamp, and quietly opened the door of her closet, trying not to wake Cindy in the next room. She scanned the shelf above her hanging clothes and tried to remember where she had stored her camp keepsake box. After a couple of minutes, she spotted a corner of the hidden box and retrieved it by using the handle of an umbrella that was hanging over the end of one of the rods.

Unlike the night before she left Josie's house, she didn't spend a lot of time with her mementos. She opened it reluctantly as if she was afraid the happy memories would damage the protective wall she had built around her heart. She focused on finding Mrs. G's card, and when she did, she quickly closed the box.

She sat down cross-legged on the bed and stared at the handwritten phone number on back of the card. After almost running into each other at the courthouse, Tatia wondered if Mrs. G would even take a call from her if she had the nerve to make one. She was thinking of throwing the card away when she realized she had never looked at the front. She turned it over and was stunned by what she saw. In elegant black script on a slick, white background she read:

Deborah Grochowsky, Attorney-At-Law

That explained why she was at the courthouse. Smiling to herself cynically, Tatia thought, *Maybe if it meant a new client, she'd take my call after all.* She grabbed her phone off the nightstand and entered the number simply under Mrs. G. Then she returned the card to the box and the box to the shelf, turned off the light, and went to sleep.

Tatia didn't think about Mrs. G again for a while – Eric kept her too busy. She was arrested a couple of times, but she always had her phone ready to send the alarm, and Joseph was always in the courtroom the next morning. So far, she had avoided serving any jail time. Her fines were growing with each incident, though, and it took her longer to pay Eric back. Then, one weekend in June, Eric came over to the apartment to have a planning session with Cindy. Cindy was sitting at the kitchen table with her laptop in front of her, and Eric was lying on the couch looking through the Guide section of the weekend newspaper. Tatia was putting together some snacks in the kitchen.

"There's a couple of concerts coming up in the next few weeks," said Eric. "Be sure you get rooms booked close to the venues, and schedule those two Goth chicks to cover it."

"I got it, Eric," said Cindy, rolling her eyes and smacking her gum.

He picked up a candle from the coffee table and threw it at her, narrowly missing her head and knocking over a bowl of chips Tatia had just set on the bar.

"Watch where you're putting that stuff, kid," he yelled at Tatia. Then he turned on Cindy. "And you, chubbo, don't go getting smart with me. The only reason you're on the computer instead of the mattresses is because nobody wants your fat butt. You can be out on the streets before dark if you're not careful."

"Sorry, Eric," she said, keeping her head down so he couldn't see the anger flashing in her eyes.

"And get rid of that gum. You look like a fat cow chewing her cud."

Eric was engrossed in his paper again and didn't see the flush on Cindy's face as she began to rise from her chair. Tatia saw it, though, and hurried over with a beer in each hand. She placed one on the table in front of Cindy, turning slightly so her back was to Eric.

"Please don't," she mouthed. The tension between Cindy and Eric had increased dramatically in the last few months, and she didn't want to witness the explosion that was seething just under the surface. She pulled a napkin out of her pocket and held it close to Cindy's mouth the way her mother used to do before she went into her Sunday school class. Cindy looked at the napkin as if Tatia had offered her a used tissue. After a few seconds that seemed much longer, she relaxed back into her chair and spit her gum into the napkin. Tatia smiled and winked at Cindy, slipped the wadded up napkin into her pocket, and delivered the second beer to Eric before returning to the kitchen.

"Hey," said Eric, making both girls jump. "The Gun and Knife Show is coming to the convention center in a couple of weeks. We need all the girls lined up to work that. You like that one, don't you, kid – all those good ole country boys?"

"Sure, Eric," said Tatia. "But I was hoping I could get a day or two off that weekend."

"Days off!" he scoffed. "What do you think this is – the government!"

"No, it's just that it's my birthday," she said quietly.

"Your birthday, huh? You mean our anniversary, don't you? What's it been now, two years?"

"Three," she said with an inaudible sigh.

"That long? Time flies when you're having fun!" he said, laughing at his own joke.

She placed the bowl of rescued chips and another of peanuts down in front of him, and he grabbed her by the wrist and pulled her into his lap. He rubbed her back and nuzzled her neck while she looked away and bit her lower lip. "Anyway, no. I especially need my best girl that weekend."

"Uh, if I can interrupt," said Cindy sarcastically, "I've touched base with several of our usual contacts, and most of the rooms are already booked."

"That's not possible," said Eric, releasing his hold on Tatia and pushing her up and away. "I pay those pukes a lot of money. They always have vacancies for me. Check again."

Cindy's fingers flew across the keys for a few minutes, and then she sat back, shaking her head. "Apparently, some other dudes offered a higher percentage. I did find one place – the guy that moved into that place a block over from the north parking lot of the convention center. You know – the one that had all the storm damage. He fixed it up some and opened a month or so ago. He hasn't built up any contacts, and he has six rooms he can let us have."

"You know I don't like to put all the girls together. The law is out in force at these things, and I don't need everybody getting picked up in a vice sweep."

"That looks like the only choice at this point unless we go further across town."

Eric threw the paper on the floor and stood up, glaring at Cindy. "And why didn't you reserve rooms earlier?" he growled. "Am I the only one around here who can read a newspaper?"

Tatia could see the resentment on Cindy's face. She also saw Eric's clinched fists and knew what would happen if Cindy responded in her characteristic mocking tone. Tatia thought fast and knocked her glass of soda into the sink. It landed in a crash of ice cubes and broken glass, but it had its intended effect. Cindy and Eric both jumped and turned to stare at her. Even though it was her glass and her apartment, Eric began to yell and Tatia began to apologize.

"You clumsy idiot! What kind of mess have you made now?"

"I'm sorry, Eric. It was a glass that didn't match anything anyway, and it all landed in the sink. I'll get it cleaned up in no time."

"Yeah," he said, turning back toward Cindy, "and you'd better clean up the motel mess. Go ahead and book those six rooms, but tell him they have to be as far apart as possible." He walked over to her and leaned down until his nose almost touched hers. When he spoke again, his voice was inaudible to Tatia, but what he said made the color drain from Cindy's face.

CHAPTER 24

A CRY FOR HELP

The weekend of the Gun and Knife Show was pretty much business as usual. The main difference was that the room Tatia was in smelled strongly of paint instead of cigarette smoke, the carpet stains were faded from a recent shampoo, and the bed linens looked relatively new. It wasn't exactly a birthday bonus, but Tatia was learning to look for any ray of light in her abysmal existence. She often remembered the "strength" rock Mrs. G had given her and the strong spirit the tattoo guy had seen in her. She had watched an unending string of degenerates and Eric's continual abuse suck the life out of several of the girls until they gave up hope and disappeared into a haze of drugs and alcohol, dead in spirit and simply waiting for the body to follow. She was determined not to follow that path. She sat down on the bedspread and lay back, taking pleasure in a clean work area, at least until her first client arrived.

She must have drifted off for a few minutes, because she was still lying on the bed when she heard a knock at the door. She jumped up, glanced at the clock on the nightstand, and saw that it was time for her first client. She swore under her breath, kicked her chic travel bag into a corner and dropped her small but expensive purse into the dresser drawer. The tote was a gift from Eric a year or so before, after he had dislocated her shoulder. It was perfect for carrying the things she needed to get her through a night of work. The purse didn't really go with her skintight mini dress and barely-there sandals, but it was also a gift – this one to make up for a couple of broken ribs. She quickly turned down the bed, turned off all but the bathroom light, and rubbed her fingers under her eyes to remove any smeared mascara. Ready or not, it was time to meet the first customer of the night. As events developed, he was also her last customer.

She opened the door, and a muscular hulk dressed in camo and combat boots with a cigar dangling from his mouth swaggered past her, turned, and struck a Hollywood he-man pose. His eyes explored her body in a way that made her want to bolt out the door. Instead, she struck a provocative pose of her own, taking control of the situation immediately before this gorilla decided he was the boss.

"See anything you like, big guy?" she purred.

Her aggressive attitude seemed to strip away some of his bravado, revealing some of the insecurity underneath. "Oh, yeah!" he said, forcing the words past a dry throat.

"Oh, good," she said with a flirty giggle that would have gagged her if she hadn't practiced it so often. "Now, let's get a little bit of business out of the way, and I'll show you some more." She had learned that the more she could tantalize them with verbal and visual foreplay, the briefer the actual physical encounter was likely to be.

"First things first," she said, taking a step closer and leaning into him without actually touching him. Even in her spiked heels, she came only to his shoulder, so she tilted her face up strategically so her breath would brush his neck.

"Let's get rid of this before we accidentally set something on fire. It's going to be hot enough in here without that." She reached up with her thumb and forefinger and took hold of the cigar that was barely hanging onto his slack lower lip. She turned and glided to the still open door where she threw the evil-smelling piece of tobacco into the parking lot. She closed the door and leaned against it, fixing him with a sultry gaze.

"Now, I believe Cindy gave you the price when you booked the appointment, right?" He nodded mechanically without taking his eyes off her. "Good, let's get that out of the way so we can concentrate on having fun."

He fished his wallet out of his back pocket, pulled out a wad of bills, and held them out to her. She took them, again managing to avoid any actual contact, and deposited them into her purse in the dresser. Now she had to earn that money, so she approached him and, making contact for the first time, she place the finger tips of one hand on his chest and pushed him gently into a sitting position on the bed. With the grace of a dancer, she lifted one leg and placed the sole of her strappy sandal on his knee. As she unbuckled the shoe, she watched his eyes closely so she could judge his reaction, making sure she wasn't crossing that dangerous line from enticing to teasing. Suddenly his gaze jerked from her leg to the window behind her. He stood up so quickly she almost landed on the floor. At the last minute, though, she recovered her balance and spun around to see what he was seeing.

What she saw made her swear for the second time that evening. Red and blue lights were flashing in the parking lot, and she became aware of the sound of shouting voices and crashing doors all around her. She ran for her cell phone which was in the drawer next to her purse. Because of her unscheduled nap, she hadn't set up the alarm message. She had just clicked the icon and "Send" when the door flew open and an authoritative voice shouted, "Freeze! Police!"

Tatia slipped the phone into the purse, and in one smooth move, she raised her hands slowly to show that they were empty and also to allow the chain-link and leather strap to slide onto her shoulder. Then, she turned toward the door. A look of recognition passed over her face as she watched the cop with the friendly eyes struggle with her would-be client, trying to cuff and Mirandize him while he protested his innocence and demanded his money back, all at the same time. She relaxed her arms a bit, and with a mocking smile, she spoke.

"Well, Officer Adams, we meet again."

He ignored her for a moment while he turned the macho man over to another cop for transport. Then, he turned his attention to Tatia. When he focused in on her, the weary look on his face was replaced by a small smile tinged with sadness.

"Miss Golden I believe. I had hoped, after our last encounter, that you would find another line of work."

"And yet, here I am," she bantered, trying to hide her dread of the next few hours and even more of what would happen when she went back home and faced Eric.

"Yeah, well, let's get on with it," he said, all business now. "I've got a lot of folks to process and a ton of paperwork to do."

"No more Mr. Nice Guy, huh?" she sighed. "I don't guess you could leave my hands loose or cuff them in front. I have a bad shoulder."

"No, sorry. But I'll try not to hurt you too much. You don't seem dangerous to me."

"Cool. And to save time, I'll do the Miranda thing while you do the cuffs." She launched into a loose but accurate version of her rights, and by the time she reached the part where she asked herself if she understood her rights, Adams was laughing along with her.

"Ok. Enough horseplay. Miss Golden, you're under arrest for prostitution. Do you understand these rights as they've been explained to you?"

"Yes," she said, and she began walking toward the door. Adams caught up with her and took hold of her arm just before she stepped outside. He almost ran into her when she stopped dead in her tracks and looked around in amazement. There were a dozen cop cars with lights flashing and almost as many transport vans filling quickly with a wide variety of men and a lot of girls, most too young to be called women.

"What the...?" She stopped, speechless at what was happening around her. She craned her head around and looked up at the second floor balcony behind her. All the doors were standing open, and a small army of police officers was leading people in varying states of undress toward the stairs. "At least we still had our clothes on," she said to herself. Then, she turned back to Adams. "How many?"

"All of them," he said.

"All...? Wait, you don't mean... A set-up! This whole thing was a set-up. Eric is gonna kill her! Oh, Cindy."

Adams guided Tatia through the chaos and helped her into the van that was already half-full of girls. Then, he went back to work. Tatia slid onto a bench next to Ginger, one of the girls that belonged to another pimp named Daniel. Tatia had met her on the stroll a couple of times. The two exchanged a few words and then sat in silence until the van was full and the doors were closed. During the fifteen-minute trip to the station, several of the girls began chatting about what had happened and what lay ahead, but Tatia remained withdrawn, thinking about what kind of God would have planned this life for her.

When the van stopped and the doors were opened, the girls were directed to get out and were then herded into the waiting room of the Cameron Police Station. Cameron was a small town, and the station was not equipped to handle the large number of people who had been rounded up in the sting. The waiting room was a gallery of the arrested – all the chairs were full, and people were lined up on any available wall space, spilling over into the hallways leading back to the holding cells and the office space. Many of the prisoners were yelling and cursing – protesting their innocence, pleading that their handcuffs be removed, insisting on making a phone call, or demanding to see their lawyer. Stressed-out officers worked quickly to bring order to the chaos – taking names, confiscating personal property, and moving prisoners to holding cells or interrogation rooms where they would await booking by their arresting officers.

Tatia leaned quietly against a wall next to a water fountain, trying to be as invisible as possible. She had heard horror stories of riots that broke out in situations like this one, and she didn't want to do anything to make herself a target. Her arms had fallen asleep by the time a female officer from a nearby town approached her with a clipboard and what looked like a large nail clipper.

"I don't suppose you have any idea who arrested you," said the weary young woman without much hope in her voice.

"Sure," said Tatia. "It was Officer Adams."

The officer looked up with a knowing looking. "Yeah, I guess Adams is pretty memorable."

Tatia gave her a small smile that didn't reach her eyes. "He and I have had a previous encounter."

"Whatever. That makes it easier anyway."

It took only a couple of minutes for her to take Tatia's name and contact information and lead her down the hall to a door that said "Interrogation 1." The door stood open – Tatia assumed for ventilation since the room appeared to be filled well beyond the legal occupancy limit. Another out-of-town officer was posted just outside the door, and he was also holding a clip board.

"This one is Kaitlyn Golden. Arresting officer is Adams," said the first officer as she used the clippers to release Tatia's wrists.

The second one noted the information and then turned to Tatia. "Squeeze in wherever you can. Another few and we'll have to start stacking 'em two deep."

Conversation in the room stopped when Tatia stepped through the door, and every eye in the room turned her way to inspect the newcomer. She stood in the doorway for a few seconds and gazed around the room, trying to figure out where she could settle without causing too much of a commotion. The chances didn't look good. The three chairs were taken, and the occupants wore expressions that dared anyone to try and unseat them. Half a dozen more young women sat on the table and looked equally possessive. All four corners were occupied by girls who were sitting on the floor, and empty wall space was at a premium. She was about to sink to the floor where she stood when she heard a hiss slightly behind and to her left.

"Psst! Kate, over here."

Tatia turned and saw Ginger leaning against the wall just inside the door. She scooted over a few inches, causing the girl next to her to grumble, but she just rolled her eyes and patted the small empty space beside her. Tatia gratefully stepped over next to Ginger as the conversations in the room resumed.

"Thanks," whispered Tatia. "I owe you."

The girls talked for a few minutes and then fell into an uneasy quiet as each one contemplated what was to come next. Tatia's feet were killing her, so she slid down the wall and sat, hugging her knees to her chest in order to take up as little space as possible. She rested her head on her knees and tried to summon the strength Mrs. G had talked about. One or two other girls were stuffed into the room, and occasionally a name was called. Then, one of the girls was escorted down the hall. After each departure, the remaining occupants would rearrange themselves, like birds on a wire, to fill in the empty space. The room was almost empty when Ginger's name was called.

"Well, maybe I'll see you in a holding cell a little later," she said to Tatia as an officer led her away.

It was probably twenty minutes later when a weary-looking Officer Adams appeared at the door and called Tatia's working name. She rose to her feet, trying unsuccessfully not to show how stiff she was from hours on the cement floor.

"Whoever planned this should be shot," he muttered. "We should have done this in the high school gym or something."

He directed Tatia to the metal folding chair next to his desk and plopped down into a saggy office chair behind it. He glanced over at the small printer on the corner of his desk, immediately swore under his breath, and stood up again.

"I forgot to pick up a new ink cartridge on my way back," he growled. He looked at Tatia as if it were her fault. "I don't even have any more cuffs to secure you to the chair," he continued accusingly. "If you move a muscle while I'm gone, I will hunt you down. Got it?"

Tatia nodded, wide-eyed and a little unnerved by a side of Adams that she had not seen before. She jumped a little when she heard another hiss, this time from across the aisle.

"Hey, Kate!" Ginger said in a stage whisper.

Tatia looked around and saw Ginger sitting on the other side of the desk next to the one where she was sitting. She tried to smile at the other girl, but the result was more of a grimace

Ginger didn't seem to notice, and it was obvious that she had something she wanted to tell Tatia.

"You're with Eric, aren't you?"

"Yes," Tatia replied.

"Well, I hope you have someone else to call. I don't think he'll be showing up tonight."

"Oh, he'll be here," said Tatia, "unless he's busy smoothing the ruffled feathers of the clients who missed their appointments because of the bust. If he can't make it, he'll send Joseph, our lawyer."

"I don't think so," Ginger went on. The friendliness she exhibited before seemed to have been replaced by a slightly sadistic delight at having some juicy gossip to share. "I heard that he's in jail."

Tatia's eyes widened. "What for? Promoting or something like that?"

"No! Aggravated assault!"

"Assault!" cried Tatia in disbelief. "But Eric wouldn't hurt anyone."

"Oh really," said Ginger, eyeing the fading bruise that peeked out from under Tatia's mini-skirt.

Tatia pulled at the hem, trying unsuccessfully to cover the bruise while avoiding Ginger's eyes. "Who do they say he assaulted?" she asked.

"I don't know her name. It's that fat chick – you know, the one who is, like, his secretary or something," she said. "They say he beat her up pretty bad," she continued quietly. Her gleeful attitude was replaced by one that could almost pass for genuine concern.

"No!" cried Tatia. "That sounds like Cindy, my roommate. It can't be her!"

"Maybe not," Ginger said, looking over her shoulder. She saw her officer returning, so she added quickly. "Anyway, your lawyer is probably tied up with Eric, so you'd better call somebody else. Or let me know, and I'll see if Daniel will take you on."

Ginger suddenly became aware of a large officer looming behind her, so she straightened up and stared straight ahead. He moved around in front of her and leaned over with one hand on the back of her chair and one on the desk. His face was so close to hers that little drops of spit sprayed her face as he talked. "Having a little chit-chat are we, ladies?" He didn't wait for an answer. "Well, knock it off!"

When he sat down, he turned away from Ginger to pull some forms out of his drawer. She stuck her tongue out at him, then, she looked to see if Tatia had seen her act of defiance. However, Tatia was too lost in what she had just heard to even notice. She felt the strength she had gathered earlier drain away, and when Adams returned, he noticed that Tatia looked distracted and pale.

"Are you okay?" he asked. "Are you feeling sick?"

"What? Oh, no. I'm okay. I...I... Is it too late to make a phone call?"

"What's the matter?" he said, a bit sarcastically. "Roommate didn't respond to your 911 text?"

When Tatia didn't respond, he looked over at her. Her head was down, and a curtain of blonde hair obscured her face, but he could see tears dripping unheeded into her lap and making a dark stain on her dress.

"Here," he said more gently as he picked up the cordless phone from his desk and held it out to her. "Make your call."

Without raising her head, she replied softly. "I don't know the number. It's in my cell phone."

He sighed and turned to his computer. "What's the name?" he asked. "I'll see if I can find it on-line."

"I can't remember her real name. I just remember Mrs. G."

"Mrs. G?" he said in surprise. "You mean Deborah Grochowsky?"

Tatia raised her head with a surprised look of her own. "You know Mrs. G?

Adams nodded his head with a smile. "Everybody around here knows Mrs. G. I think I've got her number right here."

He flipped through his Rolodex until he found the right card. He dialed the number and held the phone to his ear.

"Mrs. Grochowsky? This is Kevin Adams from the Cameron Police Department. I have a friend of yours here, Kaitlyn Golden, who would like to speak with you."

He listened a moment and then cut his eyes over at Tatia. "Oh, you don't, huh? Well, she seems to know you...Okay. Here she is."

He handed the phone to Tatia, and this time, she took it. When she spoke, Adams could barely hear her. "Hello...Mrs. G, you may not remember me. This is Tatia from camp a few years ago...Yes, ma'am. That was me. I didn't speak to you because I was ashamed... Yes, ma'am, I want you to be my lawyer, but I don't know how I'll pay you...Yes, ma'am. I have a few dollars in my purse...Really? You'd do it for just a dollar? I..."

At this point, Tatia began to sob. Adams took the phone from her and handed her a box of tissues.

"Mrs. G, she's having a little trouble talking right now... Uh-huh...Uh-huh...okay." He put the phone on speaker before continuing. "Kaitlyn, Mrs. G wants to talk to both of us for a minute."

Tatia wiped her eyes and nodded. "Okay."

"Tatia," Mrs. G's voice sounded hollow and thin coming through the speaker. "I want you to tell Officer Adams your real name."

"Tatia. Tatia Robins."

"And tell him how old you are, Tatia."

"Sixteen my next birthday."

"And when was your last birthday?" asked Mrs. G knowingly.

Tatia sighed. "Yesterday."

"Well, dear, we'll have to celebrate later. Now, are you doing what you're doing on your own, or are you working for someone?" When Tatia hesitated, Mrs. G prompted. "Tatia, you have to trust me on this. You need to be completely honest in your answers."

"Okay. I work for Eric."

"Eric!" growled Adams. "That son of a..."

"Officer Adams!" Mrs. G broke in. "We can discuss him at another time." Adams clamped his mouth shut noisily, and Tatia could see the back of his neck turning red.

"Tatia, do you know what 'duress' means?" asked Mrs. G.

"Sort of."

"It means that a person is doing something against their will because they are being threatened or forced into it. Does that describe your working relationship with Eric?"

"Yes," she whispered.

"Okay, Officer Adams, you heard my initial interview with my client. I will be there in two hours or less. Since we are dealing with a juvenile here, I expect her to be segregated from the general population."

"I understand. We're short on space tonight, but I'll find a spot for her, even if I have to find another chair to set beside my desk."

CHAPTER 25
LOSS AND GAIN

Tatia was moved from the chair beside Officer Adams' desk into the Chief's office. The Chief himself was helping with the booking process, but his office had been declared off limits. Adams decided to ask forgiveness later rather than permission now as he settled Mrs. G's newest client into a reasonably comfortable guest chair. Before he headed back to the chaos, he stopped in the doorway, intending to repeat his earlier warning of staying put or else. Maybe it was because he now knew her real age and situation, or maybe it was because her hair was in disarray and her face was streaked with mascara and tears, but his words and his tone would have made him a laughing stock if any of his buddies had heard him.

"Hey, don't go anywhere. Remember, you're still under arrest."

Tatia gave him a weak smile before she responded. "I won't. Is it okay if I lie down on the floor? I'm really tired."

"Sure. I'll come get you when Mrs. G gets here."

She watched him pull the door almost closed and walk back to his desk. He sat down and looked back at her through the small windows next to the Chief's door. He smiled and made the popular "I'm-watching-you" sign – pointing two fingers at his eyes and then back at her. She almost smiled but couldn't quite manage it. Then, she looked around the Chief's office. The office was small, so it didn't take long. A well-used oak desk and a matching credenza took up half the floor space. The other half was filled with the two guest chairs, a couple of file cabinets, and a bookcase stuffed with books and a few family photos. Tatia walked over and looked at the pictures of a woman and two laughing children. The woman reminded her of her own mother, and the children made her wonder. If things had been different, would she have had a brother or a sister? Her emotions were already raw, and looking at the happy family broke through the last of her fragile defenses. She sank to the thin, institutional carpet, curled up with her face hidden in the curve of her arm, and wept for the happy little girl she had once been.

Tatia drifted into a troubled sleep, rousing some time later when she heard voices right outside the door of the Chief's office.

She raised her head and peered with sleep-blurred eyes through the pane of glass in the top half of the door. She saw Mrs. G talking with Officer Adams, and she sat up, rubbing her eyes with the soggy tissue she was still clutching in her hand. Her attorney was speaking softly, and Tatia strained to make out the words.

"So what's her situation as you understand it?" Mrs. G asked.

"Cindy Landers who we believe is Kaitlyn's roommate..."

Mrs. G interrupted. "I believe you mean Tatia's roommate."

"Right. Sorry. Tatia's roommate was beaten by Eric Hall. He was arrested and charged with aggravated assault. Cindy died from her injuries about an hour ago, and he has now been charged with manslaughter. Tatia is charged with simple prostitution for now, but..."

He stopped, and both he and Mrs. G turned toward the office where Tatia had begun to whimper, a low moan that quickly grew in volume and pitch to a blood-curdling scream.

"No! No! Nooooooooooo!" she wailed. "She can't be dead! No! It's not true!"

Mrs. G ran in and pulled Tatia into her arms – or she tried to. Tatia struggled against her, striking out blindly, still screaming her disbelief. The older woman took hold of Tatia's shoulders, ignoring the small fists that continued to try to ward off the unbearable truth of another tragic loss. Mrs. G gently shook Tatia while constantly calling her name. The movement and the sound finally broke through, and Tatia froze, looking around as if she didn't know where she was. Then, her eyes widened as reality broke through, and she began to sob, falling into Mrs. G's waiting arms. Adams stood back, looking on helplessly.

"What can I do?" he asked.

"Bring me a damp towel and a bottle of water. Also, some peanut butter crackers or something."

Tatia's sobs slowly quieted, but her shoulders continued to shudder, and her breath came in silent gasps. As she calmed, she began to stiffen in Mrs. G's embrace. From experience, Mrs. G knew that, while some girls in Tatia's situation craved the comforting touch of a trusted guardian, others rejected any touch at all. When she felt Tatia was past the worst of the hysteria, she gradually released her and guided her to sit in one of the chairs.

"You're safe, Tatia," she said gently, handing her the towel Adams had brought. "I'll take care of you now."

CHAPTER 26

HELP AND HOPE

Tatia wiped her face and hands with the damp cloth and then opened the bottle of water. After drinking half of it and eating a couple of the crackers, some of the color came back into her face. She looked up at Mrs. G and wrinkled her nose.

"I could really use a shower," she said, "and a change of clothes," she continued, looking down at her disheveled working-girl outfit.

"I can't help you there," said Mrs. G, glad to see a little bit of life creeping back into her new client. "This is all I have to offer right now."

She reached into the tote bag she had brought in with her and pulled out a small plastic bag filled with travel-sized toiletry items. She handed it to Tatia and pointed to a small door in the corner that Tatia had missed in her earlier survey.

"I don't think the Chief would mind if you used his private restroom to freshen up. Since you're still in custody, I can't let you close the door, but I'll close the office door and sit over here to give you as much privacy as possible."

Tatia's eyes began to fill up again as she looked down at the bag. "Thank you for being so nice," she said in a shaky voice. Then, she spun around quickly and walked into the restroom.

Mrs. G pulled out her laptop and began pulling up and filling in legal forms. She could hear Tatia sniffling and blowing her nose followed by the sound of running water as Tatia tried to regain a little bit of control over herself. The attorney focused on her work until she heard her client's footsteps and the sound of her sitting down in the other chair. She saved her work to a thumb drive, and then she dropped it into her jacket pocket before shutting down her computer and returning it to the tote. She looked at Tatia and smiled at the incongruity of the picture in front of her. She was still dressed in the form-fitting mini dress and sexy sandals she had worn to work, but she had washed her face clean of all make-up and brushed her hair into a softly waving ponytail. Mrs. G resisted the urge to put her arm around her shoulders in a protective hug and instead gave her a smile that was business-like but comforting at the same time.

"Tatia, we need to talk a little business now. Okay?"

"Okay," she replied with a slight tremor in her lower lip.

"You want me to be your attorney and represent you in your current arrest and any other legal matters that might arise from it. Is that correct?"

"Yes, ma'am."

"Good. Since you're a minor, I'll pull your records that show you have been a ward of the state and then petition the court to appoint me as your lawyer." She saw a look of dismay on Tatia's face. "What's wrong?" she asked.

"Do you have to pull my records?"

"Yes. If we don't do that, they will continue to treat you as an adult, and we don't want that."

"Will I have to go back into foster care?"

"Let's take one step at a time. I don't have time to go into a long explanation, but I'm doing everything I can to make this come out in a way that you'll be happy with. Do you think you can trust me on that for now?"

Tatia nodded, still not convinced.

Mrs. G continued, "Now, this next part is going to be hard for you to talk about, so take a deep breath and draw on that inner strength I know you have."

Tatia drew a shaky breath and angrily brushed away a tear that had slipped down her cheek without permission. She squared her shoulders and said, "Okay. I'm ready."

Mrs. G had to swallow the lump in her own throat before she continued. "I think you heard Officer Adams and me talking about the arrest of Eric Hall."

Tatia nodded, not trusting her voice.

"You worked for Eric, right?"

She nodded again.

"How long have you been with him?"

"Three years," she whispered.

This time it was Mrs. G who brushed a tear off her face. "Were you with him willingly?"

Tatia shook her head.

"Okay. First, let's talk about your situation. The charges will probably be dropped because you're underage and were acting under duress. Under the circumstances, we can probably even go back and get your previous record expunged."

Tatia was beginning to look hopeful. "That's good, isn't it?"

"Yes. It means your record will be wiped clean, like it never happened, and that's very good.

"There's another thing I want to talk to you about. The police have been trying for years to get a conviction on one of the..." She looked as if she had something nasty in her mouth. "...one of the men who run the prostitution business in Cameron, but even when they make an arrest, none of the girls will testify against them, so they go free. If you agree to testify against Eric, they might charge him with aggravated promotion of prostitution, compelling prostitution, and maybe a few other things thrown in."

"If I did that, Eric would kill me."

"Kill you? Has Eric hurt you before?"

"Well, it was usually my fault."

"Did he do that?" Mrs. G asked, pointing to the fading bruise on her leg.

Tatia nodded silently.

"Tatia, no one should hurt you like that, no matter what you do. If you decide to testify against Eric, he will probably go to jail for a very long time. Even if he doesn't, Mr. G and I can keep you safe. It's what we do."

"What about the charge for what he did to Cindy?"

"That would be added to the prostitution charges and make his sentence even longer. Did he hurt her, too?"

"Yes. She was his first girl, and she didn't like it when he started adding other girls so they argued a lot. He hit her a lot."

"Would you be willing to testify about that if the judge asked you to?"

Tatia thought about it a minute and then nodded. "Yes, I'd do that for Cindy."

"You're brave as well as strong, Tatia. I have some phone calls to make and some paperwork to do. I'm going to try to get the judge to meet with us in chambers so you don't have to appear in open court. I'll be back to get you, but it may be a while. Do you need anything before I go?"

"No," Tatia said, pointing to the small side table between their chairs. "I still have some water and crackers – and I have a bathroom and a floor to sleep on. I've made do with a lot less."

CHAPTER 27
THERE IS STILL LIGHT

Tatia was asleep on the floor again when Mrs. G returned. Remembering her client's apparent aversion to being touched, Mrs. G spoke to her softly.

"Tatia, it's time to wake up."

Tatia must not have been sleeping deeply, because she almost immediately opened her eyes and looked around. Her look of confusion was quickly replaced by a look of misery as she remembered where she was and why.

"Okay," she said without looking at Mrs. G. She stood up, brushed herself off, and picked up the sandals she had slipped off before she lay down. Finally, she took a deep breath and looked up. "I guess I'm ready. What happens now?"

"We're going to see the judge."

"If we're going into court, I'd better put my shoes on, huh?" Tatia sounded as if wearing shoes was the last thing she wanted to do.

"No, we're seeing him in chambers, so I don't think the judge will mind bare feet. In fact, as your lawyer, I think I'd advise it. Come on, he's finishing up the last few cases, but we don't want to keep him waiting."

"Why do you advise bare feet?" Tatia asked as she trailed Mrs. G through the squad room carrying her shoes in her hand.

"You have a very confident, mature attitude about you. I'm sure it's the defense you've built up to survive what you've been through. But it will be good to let Judge Wellman see you as vulnerable – the innocent teen under that hard shell."

Tatia's laugh was anything but mirthful. "Innocent? Right." The two were silent as they left the squad room and entered a hallway that earlier had been crowded with belligerent arrestees and stressed-out cops. Now it was quieter with only an occasional officer or lawyer hurrying from one room to another. Suddenly, Tatia stopped and looked at Mrs. G.

"Did you say Wellman? I think that was the judge the first time I was arrested. He said he didn't want to see me in his courtroom again. He'll probably be upset whether I have on shoes or not."

"When he hears your story, he'll be upset alright, but not at you." She resumed walking and motioned for Tatia to keep up.

"Why are we seeing him in chambers anyway?"

"Speaking of chambers, here we are." Mrs. G knocked on a dark paneled door with a brass plate etched with the words *The Honorable Edward L. Wellman*.

The door was opened by a clean-cut young man in his early twenties. "You must be Mrs. Grochowsky," he said, trying not to stare at Tatia. "I'm William, Judge Wellman's clerk. He usually calls a recess about this time, so he'll be with you shortly." He showed them into a small sitting area in a pleasant but not luxurious office. The room was paneled with the same dark color as the door, and it was furnished with what looked like living room and office furniture from a "rooms-are-us" kind of store. Mrs. G sat on one end of a striped love seat and Tatia joined her, looking stiff and uncomfortable with her shoes held awkwardly in her lap.

"Can I get you something to drink?" asked William. "Coffee or maybe a bottle of water?"

Mrs. G raised her eyebrows and looked at Tatia for her answer. Tatia shook her head slightly, so Mrs. G looked back at William and smiled. "Nothing right now, William. Thank you."

"Okay. Just let me know if you change your mind. I'm going to step back into the courtroom now. Ms. Delaney is in court this morning along with the ADA, so she'll be in with the Judge."

After he left, Mrs. G tried to put Tatia at ease. She opened the top of her tote and held it out toward the girl. "Why don't you drop your shoes in here for now – and for goodness sake, try to relax. The worst is over."

"I hope so," replied Tatia as she handed over the shoes and sat back a little. "Who is Ms. Delaney?"

"Elizabeth Delaney is the district attorney, and I didn't finish explaining why we're meeting in chambers, did I? Normally, the Assistant DA handles the vice cases, especially the misdemeanors. But with the volume of arrests last night, Elizabeth was working along with everyone else within three counties. I had a chance to visit with her for a few minutes last night, and I briefed her on your situation. Because you're underage and coerced, she agreed to drop the charges."

Tatia's eyes widened, and the tiny spark of hope Mrs. G had seen earlier grew a little brighter. "Really?"

"Yes, and she also agreed to ask the Judge to see us in here so we could handle the juvenile part of your case. Normally, that would be done by a separate judge, but in a small town like this, Judge Wellman deals with just about everything."

Tatia's shoulders sagged, and she stared down at her hands that were twisting together in her lap. "So I'll probably end up in juvie detention," she said with no hint of the hope she had shown a moment before.

"Oh, no!" Mrs. G resisted the urge to reach out and pat Tatia's hands. "Nothing like that. I've petitioned to be appointed as your attorney, to represent you in any legal matters we have to go through. I've also petitioned to be granted temporary custody of you until you get your bearings and we have a chance to look at your options."

"Temporary custody?" Tatia was confused.

"Yes. Mr. G and I are licensed foster parents."

"You mean you're going to be my lawyer and my guardian?"

"Yes. Sounds like a conflict of interest, doesn't it? It might be if someone wanted to pursue it, but so far, no one has. That small town thing again."

Tatia shook her head as if she couldn't believe what she was hearing. "Is that all?"

"Almost. After the Judge has made his rulings – all in our favor, I'm sure – Elizabeth wants to talk with you about being a witness against Eric."

Tatia was sitting quietly, wondering about plans and God and if He was involved in what was happening to her, when the door to the courtroom swung open and Judge Wellman breezed in, unzipping his robe. He was followed closely by William, the court reporter, and a woman Tatia assumed was Elizabeth Delaney. The judge slipped out of his robe and hung it on the hook that was mounted on a door to either a storage closet or a private restroom. He sat down in the leather chair behind his desk, put on the same black-framed reading glasses Tatia remembered, and flipped open the file folder that was lying on his desk. While he studied it, William took up a position by the courtroom door, and the court reporter busied herself setting up her steno writer across the room on the small table that had been provided for her use. Tatia and Mrs. G rose from their seats and stood behind the loveseat, facing the judge's desk. Ms. Delaney joined them. She turned slightly toward Tatia, smiled, and spoke softly.

"You must be Tatia. I'm Elizabeth Delaney, and I'm looking forward to working with you."

Tatia returned her smile and nodded, afraid to speak without specific permission. Ms. Delaney was shorter than Tatia, but since she wore shoes and Tatia didn't, the DA was able to look her straight in the eyes. She looked to be in her mid-to-late thirties, and her sandy brown hair was cut in a shoulder-length bob. Her eyes looked tired from her long night of work, but there was an openness in them that immediately put Tatia at ease.

"Ladies," said the Judge, "if you will take your seats, we'll begin."

There were two matching chairs and an odd one that had been brought in for the occasion, all facing Wellman. The two attorneys took the outside positions, seating Tatia in the center chair directly in front of the Judge. She was as uncomfortable as if she were on an empty stage with a spotlight shining on her, especially when he removed his glasses and studied her for a moment. There was a look of recognition in his eyes along with a look of confusion. He looked back at the file, flipping back to the front page, and the confusion left his face. He turned his attention back to Tatia and spoke to her in a voice that was business-like but not unkind.

"Your name is Tatia Robins. Is that correct?"

"Yes, Sir...I mean, Your Honor."

"I believe you met Ms. Delaney just now, and you already know Mrs. Grochowsky. How did you meet her?"

"She was working at camp when I was eleven, and she gave me her card in case I ever needed her."

"So you called her and asked her to represent you?"

"Yes, Your Honor," she said, glancing over at Mrs. G.

"And why did you call her instead of your parents or another relative?"

"Daddy and Mama died when I was five," she said in a flat voice, "and I'm not sure what happened to Grandma after they put her in a nursing home."

He picked up a pen, signed a paper in the file, and moved it over to the side.

"Mrs. Grochowsky, I've signed the order appointing you as Miss Robins's attorney. William will make a copy for your records when we're finished here."

"It says here that yesterday was your birthday." He referred back to the file. "Your fifteenth, I believe. Is that right?"

"Yes, Your Honor."

"You've been in my courtroom before, haven't you?"

Tatia nodded, looking down at her lap.

"At that time you were Kaitlyn Golden and, as I recall, around twenty years old."

She nodded again.

"You must share your secret for not only stopping but reversing the aging process."

She looked up, startled at the slight hint of amusement in his voice. She remained quiet, but she visibly relaxed a tiny bit – at least until he looked at the file again and turned serious.

"I see you're one of Eric Hall's girls. How did that happen?"

She told him how she had met Eric and about her twelfth birthday dinner. "Then he took me back to the motel. He said it was so I could change clothes, but he raped me. After that, he said if I wasn't nice to his friends, he'd tell my foster mother what I did and I'd go to jail."

She paused and looked up from the small scuffed spot on the front of the judge's desk that she had been staring at. His face was red, and his jaw muscles were tense. "And he controlled you with violence and threats?"

She slid her hand over the exposed bruise on her leg. "Yes, Sir."

"And he branded you?"

Her face turned red as she realized that her sleeve had crept up, revealing her tattoo. She tugged at her sleeve as she nodded with tears filling her eyes. "Yes, and he said if I ran away, he'd go after my foster sisters."

"Okay, Ms. Delaney," he said as he signed another form. "I'm signing the order to dismiss charges. That leaves one more – a request from Mrs. G for placement." He looked up and spoke directly to Tatia. "What that means is that, even after almost three years, you are still a legal ward of the State, but Child Protective Services is requesting that you be placed temporarily with the Grochowskys who are licensed foster parents. Is that what you want, Tatia?"

Tatia nodded, wiping the tears that were now spilling over.

"So ordered," he said as he signed the last form and handed all of them to William. "Now, if you ladies will excuse me, I'm going to get back to the other guests of the county. Ms. Delaney, I believe you asked to use my office for a few minutes after we finished. That's fine. When you come back into court, William will come in and close up." Then, he turned to Tatia.

"Miss Robins, the last time we met, I probably said something like 'I don't want to see you in my courtroom again,' didn't I?"

"Yes. I'm sorry, Your Honor."

"Yes, I'm sorry, too. But I believe in God, and I believe He has given you an excellent opportunity here. Take advantage of it."

"Yes, Your Honor. I will."

Wellman stood, grabbed his robe off the hook, and slipped it on as he headed for the door. The three women stood when he did, and as soon as he was out the door, the two attorneys sandwiched Tatia into a group hug. Mrs. G broke away quickly and apologized to Tatia.

"I'm sorry. I know you're not comfortable with such nonsense, but I'm just really excited for you."

"It's okay. I'm excited, too – I think."

"It is a lot to take in all at once, isn't it," said Ms. Delaney. "If you're up to it, I'd like to talk with you for just a few more minutes."

"Okay. Mrs. G told me you want to talk to me about testifying against Eric."

"That's right. Let's move over to the comfortable furniture."

Once again, Tatia and Mrs. G sat on the love seat, and the DA took the chair closest to her prospective witness.

"Tatia, we have been trying for years to break up the human trafficking that goes on in this town, but up to now, we've never found anyone willing to testify against those who make it happen. If you will tell a jury what you just told Judge Wellman, we can send Eric Hall to jail on statutory rape and several other serious charges. Deborah said you were willing to do that. Is that right?"

Tatia was feeling intimidated by everything that had just happened, so she looked at Mrs. G for reassurance. "Will you be there with me?" she asked.

"Yes. You won't need an attorney, but I will be there as your friend and whatever else we work out between now and then. You won't have to go through this alone. I promise.

Tatia turned back to the DA. "Okay, I'll do it."

"Deborah also said you had seen Eric abuse Cindy."

The tears rushed back into her eyes, and she swallowed hard. "Yes, all the time. They had a kind of love-hate thing, and he took a lot of stuff out on her."

"Did he also threaten her?"

"Uh-huh. Sometimes."

"How about this last time?"

"Well, he was mad that we had to all be in the same motel. He likes to spread us out, just in case of something like what happened. He told her that nothing had better go wrong."

Elizabeth smiled and sat back in her chair. "If you will tell that to a jury, we should have no problem in getting several convictions."

"Like I told Mrs. G, I'll do that for Cindy. But I don't have to do it today, do I? I'm really tired."

"Of course not, it may be months before it goes to trial. I have to get back in the courtroom now anyway, so you two head on home and get some rest."

The two older women hugged and promised to keep in touch, and Elizabeth disappeared. Mrs. G picked up the copies William had silently left on the table. After checking to see if she had left anything, she stepped into the hallway. Tatia followed her silently, dazed and exhausted by the turmoil she had experienced. Mrs. G led her back to the lobby of the police department where she stopped at the front desk. She presented all the pertinent paperwork to the officer on duty.

"Good morning, Officer," she said with a smile. "It is still morning, isn't it?"

The officer returned her smile. "Morning, Mrs. G. Yep, it's still morning, but just barely."

Tatia looked out the windows and was surprised to see the bright Texas sun shining outside. She felt as if she had been trapped for days in an eternal state of darkness where the sun would never shine again. She was also surprised to see people going about their business as if nothing unusual had happened while her world was being changed forever. She continued to stare out the window until Mrs. G's voice broke into her thoughts.

"Tatia, here's the envelope with your personal belongings in it. Let's check to be sure everything is still here before we leave."

Tatia opened the envelope, and after a cursory glance, she declared that nothing was missing. She signed a form and followed Mrs. G out onto the sidewalk.

"Do you want to put on your shoes?"

"No. I'm too tired to walk in those heels. Besides, Texas girls can walk barefoot on any surface."

"Right!" Mrs. G. smiled. "How about a late breakfast before we head for home?"

Tatia made a scornful noise that might have been a laugh. "I'm not exactly dressed for polite society in Cameron."

Mrs. G smiled. "Yes, I guess you're right. How about we drive through the Golden Arches and eat on the road."

"I guess that would be okay." Tatia looked at Mrs. G quizzically.

"Why are you doing all this?"

"Do you remember the verse you studied at camp the summer you were there?"

"The one in Jeremiah about God having a plan for us?"

It was Mrs. G's turn to look surprised. "I'm glad you remembered. Well, God's plan for me was to act as a rescue agent for some people He calls 'the least of these.' This time, it was you who needed to be rescued."

"I don't know. I think I'm beyond rescue."

"Nonsense. No one is beyond God's love," she said, beginning to walk down the sidewalk away from the police department. "Now, let's get going. I'm hungry."

Tatia followed her. "Where are we going anyway?"

"Remember? We talked about this before we saw the Judge. He gave me and Mr. G temporary custody of you, so you're going home with me for now."

"I don't want to be any more trouble. You've already done so much."

"I have a big house, so it's no trouble. In fact, I have several other girls staying with me already, so the more the merrier."

Tatia smiled. It was her first real smile in quite a while. She began to sing softly, "A big, big house..." She cut her eyes up at Mrs. G.

She smiled back and continued with the next line, "with lots and lots of room." She raised her hand like a conductor, and as she brought it down, the unusual pair continued down the road singing, "a big, big table, with lots and lots of food..."

CHAPTER 28
GOING HOME

The flight attendant jarred Tatia out of her reverie once more. "Excuse me, Miss. Please raise your seat. We're about to land."

After Tatia had complied with FAA rules, she looked out the window at the familiar terminals and runways of DFW. Her stomach growled, and she wondered if that little barbeque place was still open. One of her foster placements was in Farmers Branch, and the barbecue her foster father sometimes picked up on the way home from work was the only good thing about that house.

The pilot set the big jet down gently on the runway, and Tatia pulled her shoulder bag out from under the seat in front of her and made sure everything was back in its place. Her seat mate removed her ear buds and prepared her own belongings, and as soon as the plane came to a stop at the gate, she popped up out of her seat. She was quite small, probably not more than five feet tall, and Tatia smiled at the vision of her trying to retrieve her bag from the overhead.

"Can I help you get your carry-on?" she asked.

The girl smiled gratefully. "Would you mind?"

"Not at all."

It was the first time they had spoken to each other since Tatia excused herself while climbing into her seat. After accepting her bag and thanking Tatia, the other girl immediately immersed herself in social media, so Tatia took her own phone off airplane mode. Based on the multiple dings and chimes, Tatia could tell that she had several texts and emails.

The emails could wait, but she looked at the texts. She had three from Jesse – two at gas stops and one at a scenic overlook. Predictably, each one included an update of his progress along with a taunt about his surprise and a ridiculous selfie. Also predictably, she laughed at all of them. She had a text from Mrs. G, too, saying she was waiting in the terminal close-in parking lot. She replied to Mrs. G that she was on the ground and should be at the curb in five minutes. Then, she snapped a quick selfie and sent it to Jesse along with a note that said, *I'm in Texas. If you stop every 5 minutes, you'll never make it!* The aisle began to clear, so she pocketed her phone and steeled herself for the Texas summer heat.

Once she cleared the jetway, Tatia picked up her pace, anxious to be reunited with the woman who had given her so much. She was almost trotting as she approached the exit. When the doors slid open and she saw Mrs. G's welcoming smile, she ran into her open arms.

"Yay!" celebrated Mrs. G, wrapping Tatia into a bear hug. "I picked the right door. I'm so glad to see you, sweetie!"

"Me, too!" said Tatia, clinging to her. "I'm so glad to be home, Mama. I've missed your hugs!"

"That's because you won't let anyone hug you but me," teased Mrs. G.

"Only because your hugs are the best. You have the spiritual gift of hugs!"

The two women laughed and finally separated. Mrs. G looked at Tatia's suitcase which she had left several feet behind. "Do you need any help with anything?"

"No, I got it," she said, grabbing the handle and pulling the bag behind her as she followed Mrs. G across the street and into the parking lot. "And thanks for ordering the triple-digit temperature for me!"

Mrs. G laughed. "What do you mean? It's only 96. Besides, you'd be more comfortable if you'd wear something besides boots and a long-sleeved shirt."

Tatia looked self-consciously at her forearm and said, "You know I don't do short sleeves, and I'm wearing the boots because they wouldn't fit in my suitcase. Jesse said I needed to bring them for a surprise he has for me."

"Jesse, huh? So you're still hanging out with that reprobate?" teased Mrs. G.

"Yeah, I am. I haven't actually seen him in person but once since last year at camp, but we keep in touch regularly." Her phone notified her of an incoming text as if to prove her statement.

Mrs. G didn't miss the special smile on Tatia's face when she mentioned him. "You like him a lot, don't you?"

"I do. He's very...unique. Have you heard about his new ministry?"

"No, why don't you tell me in the car. Here we are," she said, pointing to a late model, dark blue CR-V.

Tatia whistled. "Fancy new ride! What happened to Betsy?"

"Not brand new – 46,000 miles. But old Betsy had over 300,000 miles when she gave up the ghost last winter."

"Poor Betsy! I'll miss her."

Tatia put her bags into the back and went around to the passenger seat. As they fastened their seat belts, Mrs. G asked her, "Are you hungry?"

"Starving!"

"Barbeque?"

"Absolutely!"

"And then a stop for materials for welcome signs and gifts for your girls, right?"

"You got it."

"Okay," said Mrs. G as she put the car in reverse. "Now you can tell me about Jesse's new ministry."

"Well, besides the fact that he loves the Lord more than anything, there are three things that define Jesse. First, he's been working with inner-city youth for several years. Second, he's a very talented artist, and third, he really likes tattoos. Now he has found a way to combine those things. In working with former gang members, he learned that their gang tats cause them a lot of problems – prospective employers are hesitant to hire them, police are suspicious of them, and sometimes they become targets for their old gangs or rival gangs. He really wanted to use his gifts for God, so he began offering free cover-up tats – you know – to conceal the gang markings. He expected a moderate response, but he's done over three hundred in the first six months. Isn't that awesome?"

"Yes, it is. It just proves that God can use us wherever we are if we just make ourselves available."

"Right."

The two women continued to chatter throughout the drive to Farmers Branch, lunch, and shopping. By the time they headed for the Refuge, Tatia was feeling the effects of her early morning. She settled back in her seat, intending to catch a few winks if she could, but instead, memories of the first time Mrs. G drove her home came flooding back.

As the last notes of their impromptu duet died away, Tatia's energy seemed to drain away with them. By the time they reached the parking lot, she was drooping and almost sullen.

Mrs. G had dealt with enough girls that the she wasn't surprised or upset by the emotional roller coaster. She had become sensitive to the needs of her young victims, always maintaining a positive attitude and trying to provide a sense of stability that had been missing from their lives. She remained quiet until she found her car.

"This is Betsy," she said as she unlocked a new, white CR-V that was still sporting dealer tags. "She's the first brand new vehicle we've ever had."

Tatia slid into the passenger seat and fastened her seat belt, trying to hide her surprise. Somehow she had expected an attorney, even one from small town East Texas, to drive something a bit fancier than an SUV. Still, it was comfortable, and she breathed a sigh of relief at being out of the police station. She let her eyes drift closed for a moment, and suddenly, Mrs. G was touching her shoulder.

"Tatia, what would you like to eat."

Tatia opened her eyes slowly, trying to figure out where she was. When she saw the fast-food menu outside Mrs. G's window, the fog lifted slightly and her stomach growled.

"I'll have a Quarter Pounder with cheese, fries, and a large lemonade," she said hesitantly. "Is that too much?"

"No, that's perfect. I'll have the same thing."

She pulled up to the speaker and passed the order on to the disembodied voice that crackled out at her. As she eased up to the pay window, Tatia slid down in the seat, and covered the side of her face with her hand. Mrs. G had seen that move before. She picked up their food and pulled into an empty parking space.

"Old client?" she asked as she handed Tatia her drink.

"Yeah," answered Tatia. "The guy behind the register – the fat one with the bad complexion – one of my regulars. Creep!"

"I'm sorry, Tatia. That won't be happening much from now on. Our place is about two hours west of here. We're out in the country, so we don't have any close neighbors, and we do our shopping anywhere but Cameron just so our girls won't run into old acquaintances." She wanted to say more, but she knew she had to earn Tatia's trust before she could give the kind of advice she wanted to.

Tatia nibbled at her food in silence and finally wrapped her half-eaten burger and put it back in the bag. She sat for a while, gazing out the window at the passing countryside. Then, she retrieved the envelope with her personal belongings from the back seat where she had pitched it. She pulled out her cell phone and turned it on. The notification dings and chimes played a tune as hours of texts and voice mails were pulled in from cyberspace. She looked at a couple of them and groaned in disgust. She opened her window and was about to throw the offending phone out when Mrs. G saw what she was doing.

"Wait!"

Tatia stopped and looked at her with a question in her eyes.

"I'm thrilled that you are so willing to make a break with your old life, but that might contain evidence that could be used against Eric. Would you mind if I keep it for now? If there's nothing on it we can use, we'll have a phone trashing party later. Okay?"

Tatia held the phone for another minute and then shrugged. "Sure. Okay."

"Just drop it into my tote back there on the floor."

Tatia ran the window back up and dropped the phone in the bag. Then, she went back to staring out the window.

CHAPTER 29
NEW BEGINNINGS

Tatia was growing curious about exactly where they were going. It looked like they were in the middle of nowhere – no businesses, no houses, nothing but trees and cows. Then Mrs. G turned into a driveway and stopped at a black wrought-iron gate with a sign across the top that said "Refuge." There was a key pad mounted on a post on the left side of the driveway, but Mrs. G hit a button on an opener that was clipped to her visor, and the gate swung open. Tatia liked what she saw so far. At least Eric would have to climb over the fence if he was released from jail and came after her.

As the car proceeded along the curving drive, she saw a large white sign. Mrs. G paused long enough for Tatia to read what it said:

REFUGE
In the name of Jesus
we welcome
the least of these.

Tatia remembered what Mrs. G had said about rescuing the least of these, but she still didn't know what that meant. While she was still pondering, they rounded another curve and saw a large wooden cross on the right side of the driveway. What kind of place was this anyway? Was she being taken to a convent or some kind of religious cult hideaway? Before Tatia could think much more about it, the most beautiful house she had ever seen came into view. It looked like the pictures she had seen of plantation homes, complete with a wide columned porch with rocking chairs and a swing. It was white with black trim and shuttered windows across the second floor.

The driveway ended in a loop that ran by a white picket fence surrounding a flower garden that filled the space between the fence and the porch. Mrs. G stopped in front of the gate, and Tatia followed her hostess/attorney/guardian up the steps and through the large front door that featured a leaded-glass transom and side panels. She felt as if she had stepped across the threshold into a Civil War movie set. She stood on polished wood floors surrounded by soft blue walls that soared two stories to a ceiling that supported a sparkling crystal chandelier. On her right was an ornate entrance table under a gold-framed mirror. On her left was a large dining room with a table that looked as if it would seat at least fourteen. In front of her, a wooden staircase rose and curved to the right. She could almost hear the swish of hooped skirts as the southern belles descended to meet their beaus. The entry hall continued beside the staircase, and that's where Mrs. G went.

"Come on back, Tatia, and I'll see if one of the girls is available to get you settled in."

Tatia followed her slowly into the brightly lit room. She could tell that it was a huge space, but before she could take in any details, she stopped short to avoid running into Mrs. G.

"Oh, Ashlie. I'm glad you're here," she said, turning to a girl who was curled up in a comfortable chair reading a book.

"Hi, Mrs. G." She stood up and gave the older woman a hug. "I'm working on an assignment for English Lit."

"Good! You're almost finished with that course, aren't you?"

"Yep. Once I finish this paper, I'll take the final."

"That's great! Are you at a place where you can take a little break? I'd like you to meet Tatia. She's going to be staying with us for a few days." She turned back to Tatia and continued her introduction. "Tatia, this is Ashlie."

Ashlie offered her hand and a smile that included her eyes as well as her mouth. "Welcome, Tatia. I'm glad to meet you."

Tatia held out a limp hand and pulled it back almost too quickly to be polite. "Thanks. Me, too," she said without meeting Ashlie's eyes.

"Tatia, you didn't eat much of your lunch. Do you want something to eat or drink?" Mrs. G turned to Tatia with a question in her eyes. Tatia shook her head, so she continued. "Okay. I have a little work to do in the office, and I want to shower and change clothes before dinner. Ashlie, would you mind helping her get settled in? Just show her around, help her choose a bedroom, get her some clothes and some PJs for tonight – you know the routine."

"Yes, ma'am. My pleasure," responded Ashlie, and Tatia believed she really meant it.

Ashlie went to the refrigerator and took out two bottles of water. She handed one to Tatia and said, "Just in case."

Tatia took the water and followed Ashlie up the stairs. The landing at the top was bigger than Tatia's room in the apartment she and Cindy had shared. It was furnished with a couch, a rocking chair, and a couple of occasional tables. Tatia was feeling exhausted after the emotional turmoil she had been through, and she was tempted to tell Ashlie she would just curl up on the couch for a nap. Then a realization hit her. She didn't have to entertain any clients tonight, so she could go to bed like a normal person. The thought made tears spring into her eyes, and she blinked furiously trying to keep them from spilling over. Ashlie noticed her struggle and offered a sympathetic smile.

"Oh, sweetie. It's okay. Go ahead and cry if you need to. I bawled the whole first week I was here."

Tatia lost the battle and laughed and sobbed at the same time. Ashlie grabbed a couple of tissues from a box on one of the occasional tables and handed them to Tatia before proceeding down the hall. Tatia followed, wiping her eyes and nose as she walked.

"We have some private rooms and some shared rooms. Please feel free to correct me, but I'm thinking you'd rather be in a room by yourself to begin with," said Ashlie.

"Yeah," said Tatia. "I don't know anybody, and besides, I'm pretty restless at night. I don't want to keep anyone awake."

"Nightmares?"

Tatia nodded.

"I used to have those, too, but not anymore. I think we have the perfect room for you," Ashlie said, opening a door off the hallway and flipping a switch that turned on a lamp on the nightstand. "This is the Blue Room. You can't see it right now since the drapes are closed, but it has a great view of the back of the property." She walked across the room, opened another door, and flipped another light switch revealing a small bathroom. "This is your private bath. Will this work?"

"You're right! It's perfect," said Tatia. She stood still, frozen in place, afraid that if she moved, she'd wake up.

Ashlie smiled knowingly. "You look about my size — a six?"

"Uh-huh."

"Okay, and shoe and bra sizes?"

"Seven and 34B."

"I'll be right back. Make yourself at home."

Tatia took a step, and when she didn't wake up, she ventured over to the bed. It was a colonial four-poster covered with a silvery blue comforter and skirted with blue flowered fabric that matched the drapes. Coordinating pillows were scattered across the head of the bed, and an old trunk draped with a crocheted runner sat at the foot. She turned to take in the antique wardrobe and the oak table and chair that completed the most beautiful room she had ever been in. She sat down on the edge of the bed, overwhelmed and exhausted, and dropped the sandals she had retrieved from Mrs. G's tote in a tangle on the floor. She looked up when Ashlie knocked on the door, confusion once again showing in her eyes.

"House rules," Ashlie explained. "We're not allowed to lock our doors – that's to discourage us from trying to do drugs or something stupid like that – but no one can come into your room without your permission. Is it okay if I come in?"

"Oh sure. Come on in."

"Here's a change of clothes and some pajamas to get you started. You look pretty beat, so I went ahead and picked out some things for you. If you'd rather choose your own stuff, I can show you where we keep the emergency stash."

"I'm sure whatever you picked will be fine," she said, looking at the small pile. She saw a pair of pink and gray patterned pajama pants paired with a pink tank top. There was also a pair of jeans, a teal T-shirt, a pair of teal and black running shoes, a pair of teal socks, and white panties and bra. "The only thing is, I usually wear long sleeves, because..."

"Because you have one of these?" said Ashlie, revealing the tattoo on the inside of her forearm. Tatia nodded. "It's okay," Ashlie continued. "Most of us have one so it's no big deal around here. We'll get something to cover it when you go out. For now, the hot water is all yours. At this time of day, everyone is up and doing their thing so you can shower as long as you like. If you want to take a nap, that's cool. Dinner is at 6:00, so come on down whenever you feel like it – or if you sleep straight through till morning, Mrs. G puts on an awesome breakfast. That's at 7:00. Do you have any questions, or is there anything else you'd like to see?" When Tatia shook her head, Ashlie continued. "Anything else before I get out of here?"

"Well," Tatia said quietly, "I don't have a toothbrush or anything." She had realized when they were halfway to the Refuge that she had left her little toiletry kit in the Chief's bathroom.

"Duh!" said Ashlie, rolling her eyes and hitting herself in the forehead with the heel of her hand. "Here." She held out a blue gift bag that was still in her other hand. "Here's a toothbrush, toothpaste, brush, shampoo, all that stuff. It should be everything you need until Mrs. G can take you shopping. If I forgot anything, give a yell. My room is right across the hall. I'll be in it or downstairs in the great room working on this research project. Now, I really am leaving. Get some rest."

"Thanks, Ashlie," said Tatia, feeling the sting of tears behind her eyelids again.

"My pleasure," said Ashlie, pulling the door closed behind her.

Tatia continued to sit on the bed for a few minutes, looking alternately around the room and at the pile of items that represented a new life for her. She finally stood up wearily and caught a glimpse of herself in the mirror. She stared at the clingy red dress she was wearing. Eric had long since abandoned the sweet and innocent look of three years ago in favor of short hems, low necklines, and sultry eyes. She had learned to totally rock the look, but that afternoon, since she had scrubbed her face and pulled her hair back out of her eyes at the courthouse, the dress looked totally out of place.

She continued to watch as the girl in the mirror slowly unzipped her dress and let it fall to the floor. She stepped out of it and picked it up along with the shoes that lay beside the bed. She grabbed the gift bag and headed into the bathroom where she set the bag on the counter and stuffed the dress and shoes into the trash can. She added her lacy black underwear to the trash before she stepped into a hot shower where she cried for Eric and Cindy and also for herself.

Fifteen minutes later, she emerged from the bathroom, wrapped in a towel and a cloud of steam. Except for the world-weary pain in her eyes, she looked like any normal teenager as she sat on the edge of the bed and stared again at the stack of clothes. She had intended to go downstairs and look around a little before dinner, but exhaustion was catching up with her. All she wanted to do was lie down, so she pulled on the pajamas.

The pants were a little loose, but the drawstring waist held them up, and the roomy comfort felt luxurious after years of spandex and tight jeans. She pulled back the comforter and smiled when she saw silvery blue sheets bordered with blue flowers. She crawled into the bed that smelled of lavender and lilacs and marveled at how her life had changed in the last few hours. She thought of all the rooms she had seen since she arrived and wondered how many she had yet to see. She also thought of the big tables in both the dining room and the kitchen, and she wondered about the food. She fell asleep singing under her breath: *a big, big house with lots and lots of room; a big, big table with lots and lots of food.*

She roused some time later, wondering what time it was. She

could hear laughter and happy chatter from downstairs, and the tantalizing smells of dinner drifted under her door. She thought about going downstairs to meet some of the other girls, but before she could put her thoughts into action, sleep pulled her back into its arms. After several more hours, she danced around edges of consciousness for a moment or two, but sensing that everyone in the house had joined her in sleep, she slipped back into the most peaceful rest she had experienced since her twelfth birthday.

Tatia roused when Mrs. G pushed the remote to open the gate.

"Lots of memories, huh?" said Mrs. G.

"Yes, a lifetime of them," replied Tatia. "I have a question about one of them. That first night I had a dream – at least I think it was a dream. I thought my mama came into my room, knelt and prayed by my bed, kissed my forehead, and then left. Was that you?"

"Yes, it was. I prayed for all my girls every night, and I still do."

SATURDAY

CHAPTER 30

MY FATHER'S HOUSE

Saturday morning, Tatia woke up early from a milder version of the full-blown nightmare she had suffered the night before she left Washington. She dressed quietly and went out to walk around the property. Mr. and Mrs. G were still asleep, a luxury they occasionally allowed themselves now that they had no live-in guests, so Tatia had the path all to herself. She talked with God while she walked the circuit twice, and the second time around, she walked through the wrought iron arch that was covered with what she now knew was Asian Jasmine. She had also learned that the bushes on either side of the arch, the ones that were covered with tiny red and white flowers and smelled like lilac and honeysuckle, had the unusual name of Hot Lips Salvia. She sat down on the bench beside the path, and as she did every year, she remembered the first time she had visited this place.

The next morning, Tatia woke up wondering where she was. Instead of lying in a tangle of dingy sheets smelling of stale smoke and sweat, she was lying under a flowered comforter that smelled fresh and clean and on sheets that were equally clean and that matched the comforter. Memories of the day before came rushing back, and she wondered if it was really true – that Cindy was really gone, that Eric was in jail for murder, and that she really didn't have to entertain any clients today.

She slipped out of bed and carefully opened her bedroom door a crack, trying not to make any noise. She needn't have worried. There was so much chatter, laughter, and clattering of dishes going on downstairs that no one would have heard her anyway. The sounds of joy, along with the delicious smells of breakfast in the making, drew her out into the hall and down the stairs. As she neared the last step, Ashlie looked up and saw her peeking over the banister and into the kitchen.

"Look who's up," she shouted happily. "Tatia, come on in and meet everyone."

She headed for the stairs, but Tatia backed up a riser or two.

"I should go back to my room and get dressed first," she said, suddenly very unsure of herself.

"No, no, you're fine. Mr. G has already eaten and gone out to till a new section in the garden. It's just us girls, and most of us are still in our PJs, too." Ashlie walked to the foot of the stairs and held out her hand encouragingly. Tatia hesitated a moment before taking Ashlie's hand and following her into the kitchen and the beginning of a new life.

Mrs. G had brought her into the kitchen the day before, but Tatia had only glanced around before Ashlie took her upstairs. She hadn't realized what a huge, multi-purpose room it was. The kitchen was to her left and was separated from the eating area by a massive island that served as a work counter on one side and extra seating on the other. Mrs. G was busy at the antique-looking stove while half a dozen girls swirled around the room in what looked to Tatia like barely-organized chaos. Still, it looked as if everyone knew what she was doing, and breakfast was slowly coming together.

Mrs. G turned and saw the two girls coming into the room and greeted them with a wide smile. "Good morning, Tatia. I hope you're room is okay. Were you comfortable last night?"

"Yes, ma'am," Tatia replied quietly. "It's great. I've never had a room that nice."

"Good. I'm glad you like it. Girls, say hello and then get back to work. You can introduce yourselves once we sit down to eat. Right now, let's get it all on the table."

After a ragged chorus of friendly greetings, everyone, including Ashlie, went back to their assigned duties. That gave Tatia a few minutes to look around the room. Directly in front of her was a large table with a bench on one side, three chairs on the other, and a chair on each end. Ashlie, who had been setting the table when she saw Tatia on the stairs, was finishing her job.

"Mrs. G, where do you want Tatia to sit?" she asked.

Mrs. G continued transferring a mass of scrambled eggs from a skillet to a large crockery bowl. "Madison, you can sit in Mr. G's place this morning, and Tatia can take your place on the bench. When we finish breakfast, we'll add a leaf so we can put a fourth chair for Madison on the other side. We wouldn't want Mr. G to have to sit at the bar."

"Hey," crowed Madison, "I'm moving up in the seating order!"

One of the girls whose name Tatia didn't yet know threw a dish towel at Madison and said, "You'll be sitting outside with the dog if you don't finish pouring the juice."

"I didn't know we had a dog," quipped Madison.

Tatia smiled as the banter and the work continued. She also liked the thought that a special place was being prepared for her. She looked to her right where there was a large seating area with three couches arranged around a fireplace. There were also several smaller seating areas – a small writing desk and chair behind the couch nearest the kitchen, two comfortable chairs with a small table and a reading lamp between them against the inside wall, and next to the windows were four chairs around a game table.

As amazing as the rest of the room was, though, the windows were the best thing about it. They reached from ceiling to floor and stretched from one end of the room to the other. Double French doors opened onto a covered veranda that extended across the back of the house and was furnished with a dozen white wooden rocking chairs. Beyond the house was an in-ground hot tub that was big enough for all the girls and several more. Tatia could almost picture herself sitting in one of the chairs or in the hot tub, gazing out at the largest expanse of green grass she had ever seen. The lawn was bordered by trees and what looked like a path of some sort, and there was a building in a far corner that looked like a tiny church.

She walked over to the windows and placed the fingers of one hand tentatively against the glass as if to be sure that the scene beyond it was real and not simply an illusion. Mrs. G walked up quietly beside her and said, "What do you think, Tatia?"

Tatia looked up and grinned. "I think you have a big, big house with lots and lots of room."

Mrs. G returned her grin. "And a big, big table with lots and lots of food – which is getting cold. Come on, let's eat."

Tatia hung back a little, unsure of which seat was hers. Ashlie was sitting on the end of the bench. She poked the girl next to her with her elbow and said, "Scoot over, you two. Let Tatia sit on the end next to me."

Tatia gratefully slid into the empty space and put her napkin in her lap. She jumped slightly when Ashlie began tapping her spoon on her glass, and smiled a little as the girl who was obviously a leader among the group cleared her throat and straightened her posture as if in preparation of offering a formal toast at a wedding.

"Ladies," she said, "last night Tatia told me she never wore short sleeves. I explained that around here, it's safe to relax and let it all hang out – within house limits, of course."

She looked at Madison and raised an eyebrow at the large

girl who was wearing a low-cut top that revealed ample cleavage. Several of the girls giggled, and Madison smiled back at Ashlie.

"You're just jealous, girl!" she teased.

"As I was saying," Ashlie continued, "Tatia is a little self-conscious, so I want you to all show her that she's not alone."

Madison pulled the neck of her T-shirt a little lower to expose what looked like a gang emblem on the inside of her right breast. Another girl whose name Tatia had not learned stood up, turned around, and lowered her house pants just low enough to show the stylized name of her former pimp centered between the dimples on her butt. The rest of the girls extended their arms so she could see marks between their wrists and elbows – marks very similar to her own. Tatia could feel the heat rise in her face and tears filled her eyes at the touching display.

After everyone was seated again, Ashlie reached over and took her hand. Tatia looked up with a question in her eyes, and Ashlie whispered to her, "We hold hands when we say grace." Tatia realized that Mrs. G who was sitting at the end of the table to her left was holding out her hand expectantly. Tatia hesitantly placed her hand in Mrs. G's and bowed her head.

After everyone said "Amen," chaos once again reigned as bowls and platters were passed and flatware clinked against crockery. While they dished out their food, Ashlie continued to speak quietly to Tatia. "I heard what you and Mrs. G were saying before. I just thought I'd tell you that, even though we have a big, big yard, we don't play football – we play volleyball sometimes, though."

Tatia burst out laughing, releasing any remaining tension she felt. "Instead of Refuge," she said, "you should call this place My Father's House!"

CHAPTER 31

TAKING THE TOUR

After breakfast, all the girls went about their chores, but Tatia gravitated toward Mrs. G because she didn't know what else to do. Mrs. G took care of her uncertainty quickly enough. "Tatia, why don't you run up to your room and get dressed. I'll go brush my teeth and take my vitamins. Then, we'll meet back here, and I'll show you around. We only skimmed the surface yesterday. I'll give you a real tour this morning."

Tatia's cheeks hurt from grinning so much, but she couldn't keep the smile from her face. "That sounds great! I'll be right back."

Five minutes later, she hurried back into the kitchen dressed in jeans that didn't fit like a second skin and tennis shoes that were not at all sexy but made her feel like she wanted to run somewhere or climb something. Mrs. G turned and gave her a quick visual inspection.

"Now that's the Tatia I remember from camp, and you look like you're ready for some walking."

"Yes, ma'am. Ready to see this amazing place."

"Okay, then," Mrs. G said, smiling at Tatia's enthusiasm. "Our first stop will be at what I call the brains of our operation. "Actually, it's our ministry center."

"Ministry? You mean like missionaries and stuff?" asked Tatia.

"Sort of, but not exactly. Most people think of a ministry as being the work of a minister or a pastor, and a lot of people would call an organization like ours an agency. I like to think of our ministry as a combination of both – an agency with a spiritual mission."

"Mission, but not missionaries? Now I'm confused."

"I mean our mission as in our purpose. Our purpose is to find people who have lost their way or have been pushed aside in life and to help them get back on track. The name of our ministry is The Least of These."

"The Least of These? That's on your welcome sign, and you said it last night. What does it mean?"

"That's a good question, Tatia. During His time on earth, Jesus taught in parables, or stories. One that is recorded in the Bible is about a king who called his subjects together and passed out rewards. He complimented a group of his subjects because he said they fed him when he was hungry, gave him water when he was thirsty, took him in when he was a stranger, clothed him when he was naked, took care of him when he was sick, and visited him when he was in prison. Then he gave them a reward – but they were confused because they didn't remember helping him when he was in need. He said to them, 'Inasmuch as ye have done it unto one of the least of these my brethren, ye have done it unto me.' Does that make sense?"

"Yeah, I think I get it. He's talking about people like me who don't have anyone else to help them, right?"

"Exactly! Now let me show you what we do in here."

The large room had several cubicles along one side and across the back wall. Each cubicle was furnished with a metal desk, a task chair, a phone, and a computer. The other side of the room was lined with file cabinets and shelves stacked high with books, T-shirts, bags, and bracelets. In the center of the room was a large work table that was set up as a shipping center. Against the front wall were a copier and a shelf that contained office supplies. Jillian and Felicia were in two of the cubicles, and two ladies Tatia didn't recognize were taking items off the shelves and packing them in boxes.

Mrs. G explained that Jillian, the girl with the tattoo on her back, was their webmaster and that she spent an hour or two a day in the office taking care of the website. The other girls spent two to four hours a week in the office responding to both on-line and snail mail inquiries and prayer requests. They also processed orders for books and other merchandise, and they let the outside volunteer organizer know how many work hours would be needed each week. Mrs. G went on to explain that a paid bookkeeper came into the office three days a week to prepare deposits, pay bills, and take care of anything the girls couldn't handle. The fourth cubicle was unused at the moment but was available in case of future need.

Tatia was fascinated that all this busy-ness was housed behind the columned front porch, but she was curious about one thing. "So, do you sell enough books and stuff to cover all the costs, or do you do that phone solicitation thing?"

Mrs. G smiled. "You have a lot of good questions, Tatia. We are what's called a non-profit which means all the money we receive goes back into the organization. We don't solicit donations. We have a link on the website to accept them, but that's because we had so many inquiries about how to donate. And the purpose of the books and merchandise is to educate the public about the problems we address. We pretty much break even on the sales, and the donations cover the office costs. The rest of our funds come from investment income from an endowment fund."

"What's that?"

"The short answer is that, years ago when Mr. G and I started this ministry, we rescued the daughter of a very wealthy man. He showed his gratitude by setting up an endowment fund – a kind of bank account. He put so much money in it that we can support the ministry with the interest income without ever touching the original money."

"Wow!" said Tatia, her eyes wide. "How'd you learn all that stuff? You must be really smart."

Mrs. G laughed. "Not really. When we first started, we had no idea what we were doing. Mr. G decided from the beginning he wanted to handle the operations and leave the business to me. I began educating myself by taking some business courses. Later we found it hard to find lawyers who really understood our mission, so I added some law courses, and the next thing I knew, I had a law degree."

Tatia shook her head in wonder. "I knew you were a lawyer, but I didn't know you were involved in so many other things, too."

"I like to keep busy. Now, let's move on or we won't finish our tour before time to prepare lunch."

The next stop was a much smaller room adjacent to the business center. In it were four computer desks with what looked to Tatia like state-of-the-art desktop computers, a file cabinet, and shelves containing a variety of text and reference books as well as more than enough school supplies for all the current residents and several more. Two of the desks were occupied – one by Kensey, who was wearing headphones and watching an on-line lecture, and one by Ashlie, who was writing on what Tatia assumed was the paper she mentioned the night before.

"This is our classroom. Our girls are enrolled in a home school program. They work independently under my supervision as well as that of Mr. G and a volunteer teacher who comes in a couple of evenings a week. Kensey graduated last month and is now taking her first college course. Ashlie is finishing her last high school class, and after she completes it and passes her final exam, we'll have a graduation ceremony and present her with a diploma."

Mrs. G continued as they walked toward the other side of the house. "If you decide to stay with us for a while, you might want to consider continuing your education before you decide what you want to do with your life."

Tatia was quiet, mulling over what she had seen and heard. Mrs. G could see that there was skepticism in her eyes, but she could also see that her new guest was intrigued by the idea. She led Tatia through the kitchen and opened a door off the living area. Tatia admired the large cherry wood desk, the matching credenza behind it, and the bookshelves that covered most of the available wall space. A very large flat-screen monitor sat in the middle of the desk, and a variety of electronic equipment she couldn't identify sat on the credenza. Every surface was covered with books, papers, framed photographs, figurines, and other memorabilia, but there was a sense of organization that kept the room from feeling cluttered. Like every other room in the house, this one smelled faintly of a combination of flowers and spices that was pleasant without being overpowering.

"This is my office," Mrs. G explained. "This is where I write, study, and sometimes come to hide from the chaos."

"What do you write?" Tatia asked as she idly gazed around the room.

"Articles for our website, letters, curriculums for our training courses, books."

Tatia's eyes snapped around to Mrs. G's face. "You write books, too? Is there anything you can't do?"

Mrs. G laughed. "There are lots of things I can't do, and I couldn't do any of it without God's help. Now, are your shoes comfortable enough to do a little walking?"

"Sure. They fit perfectly."

"Good. Let's go outside for a while."

They walked past the hot tub, and Mrs. G explained that anyone could use it when they had some free time, but it was used most often in the evening when several people could relax together and chat about their day. From there, they walked on to a large area that looked like a large sandbox except for the net bisecting it.

"The girls like beach volleyball, so we brought in a load of sand. Do you play?"

"No. I was never into sports when I was in school, and of course, lately..." Her voice trailed off into what could have been an uncomfortable silence, but Mrs. G smoothly picked up the thread.

"There hasn't been time. I know. Well, we work hard here, but we make time to play. We have other outdoor games. We have all kinds of balls, bean bag toss, ladder ball, horse shoes, croquet, you name it."

Tatia smiled gratefully. "Sounds fun."

The garden was beyond the game area. Tatia had expected a small plot with a few spindly plants, but what she saw was almost an acre of row after row of thriving vegetables, most of which she couldn't identify. She did recognize the tomatoes and peppers, but she didn't recognize the man halfway down the row who was tying up some drooping tomato vines. He was dressed in a long-sleeved shirt, worn jeans, and scuffed work boots; and a pair of stained leather gloves was stuffed into his back pocket. His face was mostly hidden by the wide brim of his straw hat, but his hands and neck had the rough, tanned look of a man who had spent a lot of time in the sun.

"How's it going?" shouted Mrs. G.

The man looked up and grinned. "Great! Looks like we'll have a prize-winning crop this year. I see a salsa-canning party in our future."

"You make your own salsa?" asked Tatia incredulously.

"Sure," said Mrs. G "We also make all kinds of pickles, jam, relish. Our goal is to can and freeze enough vegetables to last through the whole year. We've come close, but we haven't made it yet."

"This may be the year, though," said the man. He had joined them at the end of the row. He had removed his hat and was holding it in one hand while he ran the other through his matted, sand-colored hair. He had a nice smile that made his eyes crinkle at the corner, but Tatia glanced away uneasily. He opened his mouth as if to say something, and he lowered the hand from his hair, wiping it on his jeans as if to clean it a bit before offering to shake hands. Before he did, though, Mrs. G caught his eye. She shook her head slightly, and he withdrew his hand and hooked his thumb in his belt loop.

"Tatia," she said, "this is my husband, Mr. G. He would rather work outside than anything else, so that's what we let him do. You'll see him at meal time and Bible study and when you work in the garden. Other than that, he's like Big Foot – rumored to exist and occasional sightings reported." The corner of Tatia's mouth twitched, but Mrs. G wasn't sure if it was a grin or a grimace. "Honey, this is Tatia. I'm showing her around, and I'm hoping she'll want to stay with us for a while."

"Hi, Tatia," he said. "It's nice to meet you."

"Hi," she replied without looking at him.

Mr. and Mrs. G exchanged knowing smiles, and he kissed her on the cheek. "Back to work," he said. "See you for lunch."

Mrs. G waved and stepped onto the walking path Tatia had seen from the window. She fell into step beside Mrs. G, visibly relieved to be moving away from Mr. G.

"Does everybody have to work in the garden?" Tatia asked.

"Not unless they want to. I noticed that Terrie and Stephanie were out there today. They would both prefer to pull weeds than mop floors any day! But I'll explain more about work assignments later in the tour. For now, let me explain about the path."

The path was covered with something that looked like a combination of coarse sand and fine gravel, and it was lined on both sides with stones of all different sizes and shapes. Mrs. G explained that shortly after the first group of girls came to live with them, some of the more energetic ones challenged each other to walk a mile at least three times a week.

"It became an obsession with some of the girls," she said, "a healthy alternative to the nocturnal life they had come from where they rarely saw the sun and were constantly exposed to substances that were anything but healthy. They asked Mr. G if he could make them a walking path, so he measured out a quarter mile trail that makes a wide loop around the house. At first, he mowed the path a little shorter than the rest of the grass, but before long, the persistent pounding of feet wore the grass completely away. As the path became more defined, some of the girls began picking up rocks, especially after Mr. G turned them up when he tilled the garden, and lining the path with them. It has become an ongoing project. Some friends of the ministry donated the material to surface the path – others have donated yard art, metal sculptures, birdhouses, all the things you see along the path. We've created flower beds, an herb garden, and a rock garden. And there are always more plans on the drawing board. See anything you like?"

"I like the bird houses. In that one area on the side of the house, I counted fifteen bird houses before I lost count, and I didn't even try to count the feeders. Your birdseed bill must be huge!"

"We do go through a lot of seed, but it's not too bad. The local feed store sells it to us at their cost."

"Why would they do that?" Tatia asked.

"Because they believe in what we do here. They believe that every girl should have a home where she is safe and that she should have the chance to be something other than a slave to another person's greed and lust."

Tatia was quiet for a few steps before asking quietly. "Is that why he does it, too?"

"Who?" asked Mrs. G.

"Your husband, Mr. G. Is that why he works so hard? I mean, this path took a lot of work, and that garden looks like a full-time job. Most men I've know won't do anything unless they're getting something out of it."

Mrs. G smiled. "Oh, yes! My husband has a heart as big as Texas, and it breaks every time he hears another story like yours. If I didn't make him rest, he'd work until he dropped to provide for all of you and to keep you safe."

Tatia could hear the passion in Mrs. G's voice, and she stopped and turned toward her. "Am I really safe here? Eric has bosses. What if they come looking for me?"

Mrs. G looked into Tatia's eyes and tried her best to reassure her. "Sweetheart, we have spent years learning how to make sure our girls are safe. We have the law on our side, both man's law and God's law. If anything or anyone ever makes you feel unsafe, you tell me or Mr. G, and we will take care of it. Our calling is to make girls like you safe so you can grow into the women God created you to be."

"It's been a long time since I felt safe," said Tatia as she turned and began walking again. She looked away toward a bunch of broken crockery and colored glass balls artfully arranged in a bed of gravel, but not before Mrs. G saw tears sparkling on her lashes. Mrs. G smiled, knowing the ground was being softened and seeds were being planted in another young heart.

They walked around the front of the house and along the other side until Tatia could see the little church-like building she had spotted out the window before breakfast. "What's that?" she asked, pointing toward the tiny structure with the steeply pitched roof.

"That's the chapel. That's the highlight of the tour."

The main path continued to the right behind the back yard, but another trail went straight, through a wrought iron arch covered with unfamiliar vines that still had a few yellow flowers left from their spring bloom. Flanking the arch were matching plants that gave off a heavenly smell and sported delicate red and white flowers. As they walked through the arch, Mrs. G walked over to a bench on the left side of the path and sat down. Tatia stopped and gazed around.

"Go ahead," said Mrs. G. "There's a lot to see in this little garden area. I think I'll sit right here and rest my feet. Give a shout if you have questions, and when you're ready, we'll go into the chapel together."

Tatia wandered over to her right first, because she knew she was going to have questions about the left side of the path. On the one side was a collection of statues and memorabilia similar to what she had seen along much of the path. The main difference was that most of the pieces seemed related to the chapel, and most of them were damaged. A stone bench that resembled a small pew had a large chip out of the back. A ceramic angel with a broken foot that had been glued back on was seated on a tree stump. Tatia's favorite was a tall, thin bird house that looked very much like the chapel. It was mounted on an old treadle-style sewing machine table, and although she couldn't find the flaw, she was sure it had one.

When she couldn't stand the suspense any longer, she finally walked over to Mrs. G and pointed to the other side of the path. "Okay, I think you're going to have to explain this to me."

Mrs. G smiled and stood, walking around the bench and stepping off the path with Tatia. "What does it look like?"

"It looks like the shape of a cross laid out on the ground with a mailbox and a basket of rocks at the bottom. But what's it for?"

The cross shape was approximately twelve feet long and six feet wide. It was covered with the same sand and gravel mixture that was on the path, and it was also outlined with rocks.

The mailbox was a standard rural model mounted on a four-by-four and anchored in a bucket of cement. Sitting on the ground in front of it was a large wire basket filled with large, smooth river rocks. Tatia had noticed that there were a few similar rocks scattered around the interior surface of the cross.

"Open the mailbox," encouraged Mrs. G, "and tell me what you see."

Tatia did as she was told. "It's a Tupperware box."

"Take it out and see what's in it."

"There are two Bibles and two black markers."

"Okay. Put them back and I'll explain." When Tatia had finished, she walked over and stood by Mrs. G, staring at the cross. Mrs. G continued, "Paul tells us in the book of Colossians that God took our sins and nailed them to the cross with Jesus. There are many other places in the Bible where we are told to give our burdens and troubles to God. Many of us ask God to forgive us for our sins, but we continue to carry the guilt of those sins with us. Or we take our cares to Him in prayer, and then when we get up off our knees, we pick up our cares and continue to carry them with us. Do you understand what I mean?"

"Kind of, I guess."

"That's okay. It's been a while since you were involved in regular Bible study, but I know you're a smart girl. You'll get the hang of it soon enough. Anyway, the whole idea of this area is to give us a visual reminder to leave our guilt and cares with the Lord. When something is bothering you, come down here and tell God about it. The Bibles are there so you can read and meditate on His Word while you're here. Then, before you go, pick a rock, write whatever you want to leave at the cross on the bottom, and leave it here. Later, when you start to fret again, you can remind yourself that you left that particular worry at the cross."

"Does that really work?"

"There's no magic to it, but it's a little like baptism or Communion – an outward sign of an inward grace. All I can say is that it has worked for me."

"I don't think you have enough rocks for all the bad things I've done. Besides, I wouldn't want to write them down and leave them out in the open for other people to see."

"Well, first of all, this place is covered with rocks, and more surface every time it rains. Second, there's one real rule. Under no circumstances is anyone allowed to pick up a stone and turn it over to see what's on the other side."

"I guess that might make a difference." She looked pointedly at Mrs. G and raised one eyebrow. "Might!"

Mrs. G laughed and said, "Tatia, you make me laugh. Now, let me tell you about the chapel and then ask you a couple of questions before it's time to go fix lunch."

Tatia was a little wary about questions, but she was curious about this odd structure. It was only about eight feet wide, but with its peaked roof, it was at least twice that high. The main building was built of vertical white wooden planks, and it had a raised porch of stained wood. The paneled door was stained oak, and the upper half was stained glass. A cross was mounted on the wall to the left of the door. The basic structure of the cross had been constructed of one-by-fours. A straight, thin branch had been stripped of its bark and highly polished before being mounted on the crosspiece. Then, a length of twisted wire with a loop on either end had been mounted on the upright. The effect was compelling and a little disturbing.

Mrs. G touched the cross affectionately and then stood and looked at the stained glass for a moment before beginning. "We call this The Chapel the Village Built, and sometimes we call it the

Broken Chapel. Several years ago there was a lot of talk about how it takes a village to raise a child. That means that a mother and a father need lot of help from friends and family if they are going to be successful parents. After we started this ministry, it didn't take long for us to realize that we needed a lot of help from a lot of people to successfully rescue young women from a life they had been forced into. We also felt like God wanted us to build a chapel on the grounds, but we didn't want it to be a slick, new building built by a contractor who would look at it like any other job. We wanted it to be special and meaningful.

"For the next year or two, we discussed the project with lots of friends and supporters of the ministry, and a lot of them seemed to catch the vision. People began to ask what they could do to help, and others sent or brought us things they thought we might use. Eventually, the vision solidified into a plan to take materials that had been cast aside or broken and to recreate them into something beautiful, just like the girls we rescue."

Mrs. G was looking at the chapel with a look that Tatia struggled to understand. She made up her mind to listen closely and to try and see at least this small corner of the world through her eyes.

"Come up on the porch with me, Tatia, and look up at the overhang." Tatia looked up and saw that the underside of the overhang was lined with weathered boards. "That lumber came from an old fence that was being torn down. This door had no window when it was given to us by a friend, and another friend asked if she could make a window to go in it. When she was putting in the piece just above the cross, it broke, so she replaced it with a dove flying upward. Did you know that the Holy Spirit is represented by a dove in the Bible? And do you see this line of solder on this arm of the cross? This piece cracked while she was putting it in, and she decided to leave it as a representation of the broken people our ministry serves."

She opened the door, and she and Tatia stepped inside. The small room was furnished with small pews that seated two or three at most, and the walls were decorated with a collection of artwork that Tatia was sure had an interesting backstory. The most interesting piece by far was the table at the front of the room. Tatia walked forward and touched it gently with the tips of her fingers. "Tell me about this," she said.

The table was long and narrow, and it had been covered with what looked like mosaic tiles, but closer inspection revealed broken pieces of china, porcelain, ceramic, and pottery. Embedded here and there were identifiable pieces – a bird without wings, the handle of a coffee cup, the face of a watch.

"I let it be known that I needed a table or something for the front," explained Mrs. G. One of our volunteers found an old sofa table at a garage sale for two dollars. She brought it to me with apologies, saying she didn't think it could be saved. But another volunteer saw the potential and asked to be allowed to work on it. She sent out a call for small broken items that represented something special to the donor. She got what she asked for and so much more. Pieces poured in, and with them came notes and letters telling the story behind the items. Now, look what she did on top."

Tatia moved closer and saw the word "BROKEN" spelled out with letters cut from stained glass. Under the letters were key words cut from the notes that accompanied the items. It was so beautiful she was once more brought to the brink of tears.

"So," said Mrs. G quietly. "What do you think of the chapel?"

Tatia thought for a minutes and said, "I think it makes me feel like I'm not so alone after all."

CHAPTER 32

DECISION TIME

Mrs. G went outside and sat down on the bench. Tatia gave one last look around and followed her, sitting nervously on the edge of the bench next to her. "Now what?" she asked, twisting her hands together and staring at her shoes.

"Well, we'll have to take care of some legal issues, like where you're going to live. I know you mentioned your parents and your grandmother, but do you have any other family?"

"Not that I know of. Like I told the judge, Daddy was killed in the service, and Mama...died soon after that. I stayed with Grandma for a while, but she was sick and they put her in a home or something. I don't know what happened to her after I was put in foster care."

"Was Grandma your mother's mom or your dad's?"

"Daddy's. She was a widow, and Mama's parents died when she was little."

"Do you have any aunts or uncles?"

"No, they were both only children." She looked up at Mrs. G. "Will I have to go back to foster care?"

Mrs. G smiled and tried to offer reassurance without doing what came naturally which was to enfold the bewildered girl in a big hug. "Technically, you're already in foster care, but right now it's a temporary emergency placement. I'll be in touch with CPS about a more permanent placement for you, and the courts will make the final decision."

Tatia's head sank down until her elbows were resting on her knees and her face was cupped in her hands. She drew in a shaky breath and let out a sigh full of all of the anxiety she was feeling.

Mrs. G hurried on. "Before you get all upset, remember what I told you yesterday. Mr. G and I are foster parents. All the girls here are in our care except Kensey. Last year we went to court, and she's now an emancipated minor."

Tatia raised her head, eyes widened and her mouth open. "Are you saying that I could..."

Mrs. G interrupted, "Stay here? Probably, if you're sure that's what you want. At your age, the judge will take your desires into consideration. Before you make up your mind, let me outline the house rules. No tobacco, alcohol, or drugs ever! No tolerance on that one. No boyfriends until, well, until I say so, and no visitors without prior approval.

"No free rides – everybody pitches in. As part of the school curriculum, each girl makes a life plan with short-term and long-term goals, and the plans are reviewed at least twice a year. Oh, and when a new girl moves in, we ask her to sign a covenant with all of us that she will stay at least six months, regardless of how hard it is." She paused for a minute or two before continuing. "So, what do you think? Would you like to stay with us for a while?"

The tears that had threatened all morning were spilling over onto Tatia's cheeks. She was staring at her shoes again and nodding her head.

"Is that a yes?" asked Mrs. G.

"Yes, I want to stay."

"Good," Mrs. G said, patting Tatia's shoulder in a non-threatening way. "Now, what kind of chores do you like to do?"

Tatia pulled herself together, wiped her face with her hands, and dried her hands on her jeans. "I took care of the kids and did most of the housework when I was with Josie, so I can do any household chores. My favorite part was cooking."

"Really," said Mrs. G with increased interest. "What kind of things did you cook?"

"Oh, you know. Kids' food – hot dogs, hamburgers, fries, mac and cheese, spaghetti, tacos. I can do other stuff if I have enough time and the ingredients, but Josie pretty much bought the same things every week."

"That's interesting," said Mrs. G. "Sally, who graduated and got a job a couple of months ago, liked to help me in the kitchen, but now that she's gone, I'm pretty much on my own. How would you like to be my assistant?"

Tatia ducked her head to hide her smile. "Yeah, I guess that would be pretty cool."

"Okay, then it's settled. Speaking of the kitchen, we'd better head that way before the hungry mob descends and finds an empty table." She stood up and began to walk toward the house, and Tatia followed closely.

"So," Mrs. G continued as they walked, "how are your office skills?"

"Worthless," Tatia said, scuffing her shoes on the path. "I was doing pretty well in school until I met Eric. Then, my grades dropped, and after...well, you know... I just dropped out. I'm probably better with toilets and dishes."

"Wait a minute," said Mrs. G. "Didn't you have a smart phone?"

"Uh-huh."

"Do you know how to use it – I mean, other than just to make phone calls?"

"Sure, I guess so."

"Do you have any other electronics?"

"Yeah, or at least I did. Who knows what happened to my stuff when I didn't come back?"

"But you've only been gone one night, and since your apartment is now a crime scene, it should be taped off."

Tatia looked up with a sardonic smile. "Do you really think a little tape will stop anyone who really wants to get in? In my world, if you're not there to protect what's yours, it's fair game. And with Cindy gone..." Her voice cracked and she didn't say any more.

"Tough life, huh?"

"Yeah, I guess."

"So back to the electronics, what else did you have?"

"A laptop, a tablet, an MP3 player, and an e-reader. Eric bought me stuff sometimes, especially after he'd knocked me around some."

"Did that happen often? I mean, did he knock you around often?"

"Not as much as some other managers. And I usually deserved it. I knew the rules, but sometimes I pushed the limits."

Mrs. G turned on her suddenly. "Let's get something straight, Tatia. Nobody – not you, not your friends, not anyone – deserves to be knocked around. Not ever. Not for any reason."

Tatia was shocked at the anger in Mrs. G's voice, and she took a step back from her. Mrs. G realized how her rant had come out, and her hands flew up to cover her mouth. "Oh Tatia," she said as she slowly lowered her hands. "I'm so sorry. I'm not angry at you. It's just...when I think about sweet young women like you being exploited and mistreated by that, that, that trash..." She spit out the word and blew out her breath. She shook her head and turned back toward the house. Calmer now, she continued. "Did you use all your electronics, or were they more or less trophies that gathered dust?"

"Oh, I used them. I surfed the net and shopped. I downloaded lots of music, and watched movies. And I read a lot."

"Do you know how to use any of the office programs – word processing or data management?"

"No, nothing like that. I can type well enough to send an email, but I don't know how to write a fancy business letter. And Cindy showed me how to do simple spreadsheets so I could help her keep up with which girls were producing the most revenue and all that, but I don't know anything about databases or real bookkeeping."

Mrs. G smiled and said, "It sounds to me as if you know a lot more than you give yourself credit for. I think we can find you some work to do in the ministry center, and after you get settled in, we'll have you take some tests so we can find out where you should be in school and lay out a plan for you."

They had reached the veranda, and Mrs. G stopped and turned to look back toward the garden. "We have a few more minutes before we have to start lunch. Do you have any questions?"

"Yeah, but..." Tatia looked around, avoiding Mrs. G's eyes.

"It's okay. You can ask me anything. Just spit it out."

She took a deep breath and looked up with pleading eyes. "Do you really think I can change my life?"

"Not by yourself, you can't," Mrs. G responded, once again resisting the urge to gather the vulnerable young girl in her arms. "But there's a verse in the Bible that says 'I can do all things through Christ who gives me strength.'"

Tatia dropped her gaze. "Jesus wouldn't want anything to do with someone like me."

"Oh, you'd be surprised who Jesus liked to hang out with."

Tatia looked up again with a puzzled look on her face. "Tell me again – why are you doing all this?"

"Because it's what Jesus taught us to do."

CHAPTER 33

A PARABLE COMES TO LIFE

A hummingbird buzzed Tatia's head and brought her back to the present. She had work to do before camp the next day, but she wanted to make one more stop before she went back into the house. She stood up and walked toward the chapel where she first met the One who really changed her life.

When Mrs. G had first showed her the chapel, Tatia had thought it was very interesting and beautiful in a unique way, but she hadn't thought much more about it. She also hadn't thought much about the sealed envelope Mrs. G had left on her pillow one morning a few days later while she was doing her chores.

The day before, Mrs. G had announced that the case worker who had visited earlier in the week had approved the Grochowskys' application to make Tatia an official part of their foster family. All that was need was for Judge Wellman to rubber stamp her recommendation, and Tatia's placement would be permanent.

Later that evening, after the family celebration had dwindled down, Mrs. G had given Tatia her own informal assessment – telling her how proud she was of how quickly Tatia had settled into her studies and how well she was fitting in with the other girls. She had said she loved seeing Tatia change and blossom before her eyes, and then the plain white envelope appeared. These words were printed on it: "When you're ready for a real change, take this to the Chapel and read it."

One Saturday morning a few weeks after her arrival, Tatia was pretty much alone in the house. Mrs. G had taken all the girls shopping, but Tatia wanted to save her money for a new tablet. She decided to stay home and work on a research paper she wanted to finish so she could move on to the next module in her schoolwork. She finished it around eleven o'clock, and since she had finished all her chores the day before, she had almost an hour before getting lunch on the table for Mr. G and the small crew of volunteers that was helping him in the garden that day. She trotted up the stairs to her room, intending to retrieve the book she was reading and spend the next hour in one of the rocking chairs on the veranda. However, as she reached for the book, her eyes fell on the envelope.

It was smudged from frequent handling and close examination –Tatia had held it up to the light, but it was security tinted, and she couldn't see a thing. She had felt it thoroughly, but it didn't feel like there was anything in it but a single sheet of paper. She had even examined the seal to see if there was any way to sneak a peek – no luck.

Instead of the book, she picked up the envelope and sat on the edge of the bed staring at the words she knew by memory. *Is this the day,* she thought? *Am I ready for a real change?*

After staying home the first Sunday, she had begun attending church with Mr. & Mrs. G and several of the girls. She enjoyed the music, the prayers, the sermons, and especially the discussions afterward around the lunch table. She wasn't crazy about all the shaking hands and hugging during the meet-and-greet time, but she had learned to avoid most of the physical contact by moving quickly from person to person with a smile and a wave. What she hadn't learned to avoid was the feeling she experienced at the end of every service when the pastor offered an opportunity for anyone who wanted to respond in any way to come forward. She felt as if something or someone inside her head and chest was urging her to do something. One morning, the pastor said that if anyone was feeling a tugging in her heart, it was probably the Holy Spirit drawing her to God. He described her feeling so accurately that she felt as if she were on display, and he was talking directly to her. She had tried to brush it off as an emotional reaction to the situation and not anything spiritual. Now here she was, alone in the house after writing a non-emotional civics paper, feeling that now familiar sense of unrest. *Maybe I'm ready.*

She stood slowly, still staring at the envelope. Then, she walked deliberately down the stairs, made a u-turn through the kitchen, and continued out the back door. She stopped for a moment on the veranda and surveyed the lawn and all that lay beyond it. When she could no longer avoid it, she turned her gaze on the chapel and began to walk in that direction. As she drew closer, her stride became more quick and resolute until she was almost running. She stepped up onto the small porch and reached for the knob. She hesitated and looked at the stained-glass window in the door. Mrs. G said the dove rising from the top of the cross represented the Holy Spirit. She paused for another moment and whispered, "Are you really calling me?" Then she opened the door and went in.

The air conditioner wasn't on, and the air seemed a little stale, so Tatia left the door open. Still, she felt as if she had somehow entered a sacred place, and she slipped off her shoes. She took a couple of steps and stopped in front of the drawing of Jesus washing Peter's feet. In the Bible study the night before, Mr. G had read several passages that said Jesus was the Son of God. She wondered how it would feel to have the Son of God kneeling at your feet. From there, she moved toward the mosaic table at the front. She reached out and traced the stained-glass letters with her forefinger.

When she could delay no longer, she sat down on the nearest pew and took hold of the envelope with both hands. She turned it over and slipped a fingernail under the edge of the flap. The glue loosened a little, then stuck fast, and the envelope began to tear. In frustration, she ripped it the rest of the way open and pulled out a single sheet of paper. Tatia couldn't believe it. She had expected something deep and insightful. Instead, all it said was:

John 8:1-11
Read it out loud.
Yes, even you!

Tatia sighed with exasperation. "This is ridiculous!" she said out loud. Still, experience had taught her that Mrs. G never did anything without a purpose, so she retrieved one of the Bibles from the stack that was artfully arranged on one side of the table and returned to her seat. She was still learning her way around the Scriptures, so it took her a few minutes to find the passage. When she located it, she began to read to herself. After a couple of verses, she realized that she was familiar with the story. Jesus was teaching in the temple, and some of the Jewish big shots who were always trying to trap Him dragged a woman into the Temple and set her down in front of him. She had been caught in a compromising position, and the law said she should be stoned. They asked Jesus what He thought.

Tatia stopped reading and looked up, lost in thought. *Yeah, I guess I know who I am in this story.* She continued to read silently. Jesus squatted down and doodled in the dirt with His finger. Then he said that whoever had never sinned should throw the first rock. Then, He went back to His doodling. The big shots all dropped their rocks and left, and it was just the two of them – the woman sitting in the center of the courtyard and Jesus squatted down in front of her. At this point, Tatia's mouth fell open.

"Wait," she said audibly. "I never noticed that before. Jesus was squatted down – kind of kneeling – in front of an adulteress." She continued reading aloud.

[10] Jesus stood up and said to her, "Woman, where are they? Has no one condemned you?" [11] She said, "No one, Lord." And Jesus said, "Neither do I condemn you;"

That's as far as she went. Tears began trickling down her cheeks. "Neither do I condemn you," she repeated. The tears became a flood as she called out louder, "Neither do I condemn you." She slipped off the pew to her knees and then bowed her face to the floor, sobbing again and again, "Neither do I condemn you. Neither do I condemn you."

CHAPTER 34

MEETING JESUS

Mr. G and his crew of three returned from the garden around noon. All of them brushed the dirt off their clothes and left their work boots on the veranda before coming into what turned out to be an empty kitchen with an empty table. Mr. G tried to cover his initial response, but the others could see the annoyance on his face.

"Maybe she lost track of time," said Tony. "You said she was working on a school assignment this morning. Do you want me to go check on her?"

"Good idea," said Mr. G. "Or maybe she decided to take a walk. Sarah, go check the trail, and Jonathan, you help me get lunch on the table. I think Mrs. G left some sandwiches in the fridge."

Everyone scattered, and after washing their hands, Jonathan began setting the table while Mr. G tended to the food. In addition to being annoyed, he was worried. This wasn't the first time one of their new girls had disappeared. After the trauma of their old life began to fade a bit, some of them found the rules here a bit confining and simply left. One of them went back to her pimp, and Mrs. G ran into her at the police station from time to time. Another was found, dead of an overdose, a week or so after she ran away. A third just seemed to vanish. He prayed Tatia wasn't one of those.

In a couple of minutes, Tony reappeared with his report. "She's not in the school room, Mr. G. The computer has been turned off, and her paper is in the tray, waiting to be checked before she submits it."

"OK, thanks," said Mr. G. "Wash up, and put ice in the glasses. There's a pitcher of tea in the fridge."

Before he finished speaking, the back door slammed open, and a breathless Sarah rushed in. "Mr. G," she panted. "Tatia needs you."

"Where is she?" he asked, heading for the door.

"In the chapel. She's on the floor crying."

"Go ahead and eat," he said. "I'll be back." He was running across the grass before the words were out of his mouth. He reached the chapel and bounded through the door without touching the porch. He quickly took in the scene – the open envelope lying on the pew, the open Bible on the floor, the girl in a heap in front of the altar. He knelt beside her. "Tatia," he asked quietly, being careful not to touch her. "Are you hurt?"

Tatia was still face down, but she was no longer sobbing. He could hear the breathing spasms and the sniffling that come when a storm of weeping has passed, and in a minute, he heard her muffled reply.

"No, I'm..." She rose up slowly, and he saw the soggy note floating in a puddle of tears. She lifted her face and gazed into his eyes with a look of wonder. "...I'm not condemned."

The look in his eyes reflected the look in hers. "No, you're not," he agreed. "He took your condemnation on the cross."

Both of them lifted their eyes to the cross above the altar. "Tell me what to do," she whispered.

He wasn't sure if she was talking to him, but he responded. "Talk to Him, the same way you'd talk to me. Tell Him that you need Him and why. Ask Him to come into your life and to stay with you. Thank Him for what He's done for you."

As she poured out her heart, he whispered a prayer of thanks that he had been allowed to witness the rescue of one more of God's children.

CHAPTER 35
CELEBRATING A NEW BIRTH

By the time Tatia and Mr. G returned to the house, the others were clearing the remnants of their meal. Sarah was at the sink rinsing the few dishes when the door opened.

"We saved you some sandwiches and fruit," she said without looking up. Her comment was met with silence – even the boys had stopped their chatter and were staring toward the door. Sarah raised her head and, throwing her arms into the air, she let out a whoop of delight.

"You've met Him! I can see it on your face. It's just like in Acts 4 – I can tell that you've been with Jesus." She ran around the island and over to Tatia where she threw her arms around her and squeezed. Even the non-resident volunteers had been briefed on Tatia's aversion to being touched. Knowing she'd overstepped, Sarah quickly drew back. "I'm sorry! I know you don't like it when I do that, but I'm just so excited. Oh, you're my sister now. I could just...just...oh, get over it!" Then, she hugged her again.

Tony and Jonathan shook off their daze and joined the celebration. They respected Tatia's space, offering enthusiastic congratulations but limiting the physical touch to a warm handshake. Tatia received all the attention bashfully, like a blushing bride in a receiving line. The chaos was just dying down when the front door opened and the shoppers returned with their treasures. Mrs. G was the first to enter the kitchen, and she was almost rear-ended by two of the girls when she stopped suddenly. The five celebrants had fallen silent, forming a rough semi-circle with the still-glowing Tatia in the center.

"What's going on here?" asked Mrs. G. "I can almost see the canary feathers hanging out of your mouths."

Tatia was still holding the limp piece of paper, and she held it out toward Mrs. G. "What's that?" asked Mrs. G as she stared at the smeared note. Then, recognition hit, and she looked into Tatia's face with a question in her eyes. The answer she was looking for was as plain as it had been to Sarah. "Oh, Tatia," she cried. She opened her arms and Tatia ran into them.

Several of the girls had started up the stairs to compare purchases and model them for each other, but the two who came into the kitchen with Mrs. G squealed when they realized what had happened. "Tatia's been saved!" shouted one. "Tatia met Jesus!" yelled the other. The rest of the girls tumbled over one another getting down the stairs, and in seconds, Tatia was the center of more chaos.

"Okay, okay," said Mrs. G as the girls laughed and chattered through tears and smiles. "Back up and give the poor girl some breathing space. Besides, we have a birthday party to plan." The girls jumped up and down like children, clapping with delight. "Ashlie, you get out the cake pans, and Kensey, see if we have cake mixes and frosting in the pantry. Jillian, pull a couple of bags of chicken breasts out of the freezer. Mr. G, why don't you take your crew and see what you can find in the garden to go with chicken. Everybody else, check the birthday cabinet for decorations."

As everyone scattered to their various tasks, Tatia stood in the middle of the room with a confused look on her face. "But Mrs. G, it's not my birthday. That was a month ago."

Mrs. G smiled tenderly at her and placed her hand gently on Tatia's still damp cheek. "Oh, but this is different, sweetie. It's your spiritual birthday. For the rest of your life, you'll celebrate this date as the day you were born again."

CHAPTER 36
INVITATION TO CAMP

Tatia closed the door of the chapel behind her and started toward the house, still lost in her memories even though she knew she had things to do before leaving for camp the following day. Her thoughts were interrupted by the sound that let her know she had another text from Jesse. She pulled her phone out of her pocket and sat down on the bench by the cross and mailbox.

2 more gas stops before I make it to Jerry's. Pick you up at 5:00 am. Maybe I can get all the road grime off me and the bike before then.

Tatia smiled and shook her head. She had asked Jesse what he had planned, but he was really good at keeping a secret. Whatever it was, she was looking forward to seeing him, and she texted him back to tell him so. She had seen him at camp every year since Mrs. G had taken her in, and every year she remembered the first time she had gone to camp as a staff assistant.

A few days after her experience in the chapel, Mrs. G asked Tatia to come into her office for a few minutes after dinner.

"Madison," she said to the easygoing girl who was wiping the table with a damp cloth, "would you mind covering Tatia's clean-up duties while we talk?"

"Of course not," she replied. "I owe her for last week anyway. She covered for me when I was cramming for my final." Even though it was mid-summer, most of the girls were eager to catch up on missed years of school and so continued with their studies year round.

Tatia felt a small flutter of nervousness as she followed Mrs. G into her office and took a seat. She loved the older woman and she knew the feeling was returned, but she was not yet secure enough to completely overcome the fear that her new family would disappear like her original one did.

"Is everything okay?" she asked anxiously.

"Oh, yes," said Mrs. G. "I'm sorry if I scared you. I wanted to talk to you about camp. The second summer session is coming up early next month. Jillian and Madison are staying here with Mrs. Gardener who is coming in to help them take care of the ministry.

The rest of the girls are going with Mr. G and me as teen helpers. How would you like to go with us?"

Tatia relaxed and smiled, but her face quickly fell into an expression of disappointment. "But I'm not old enough, am I? I thought teen helpers had to be sixteen."

"That's what the rules say, but there are always exceptions. I don't think they would allow you to stay in the dorm with the other girls or help carry out some of their regular duties, but I was thinking that maybe you could stay in one of the staff rooms with me and another staffer. Imagination Station has become such a popular activity, that we've added several more sessions. If you're willing, and if I can get approval, I'd like you to act as my staff assistant for the week."

"Oh, yes," said Tatia excitedly. "I'd love that. Imagination Station was one of my favorite parts of camp." Then, her eyes clouded as an unpleasant thought crossed her mind. She unconsciously covered her tattoo with her hand and asked, "I don't have to go swimming, do I?"

"No, Tatia. You don't have to do anything that makes you uncomfortable."

Her face immediately brightened. "Then count me in!"

CHAPTER 37
MEETING JESSE — AGAIN

The next morning, Mrs. G spent several hours working in her office. Tatia tried to focus on cleaning the kitchen and joining in the good-natured chatter that always accompanied house-cleaning day, but she continually found herself wiping the island and staring at the closed door. She hoped Mrs. G was talking with the camp director, asking permission for her to come to camp, but life had taught her that hope was usually futile, at least for her. She tried to remind herself of all the good things that had happened in the last few weeks, but it was difficult to forget the disappointments of the last decade.

After she completed her chores, she grabbed one of the three laptops that were available for general use. Some of the girls had their own computers, but each one was required to kick in half the cost from the money they earned from working in the ministry office. The pay was good, but Tatia wanted a computer and a tablet and hadn't saved enough for either one yet. She settled into a comfy spot with a convenient floor plug in case she out-lasted the battery charge. She also had a good view of Mrs. G's office.

"Hey, Tatia," said Madison as she passed through the great room on her way to the back yard. "It's a great day out there — too great to spend inside. Come on out and work on your tan."

"Thanks, Madison, but I'm going to work on this research paper for a while. My tutor went over it with me yesterday, and I want to work on her suggestions while they're still fresh."

"Okay. Just remember, though — all work and no play!"

Tatia smiled as the other girl breezed out the door, leaving a faint scent of sunscreen behind her. Turning her attention back to the screen, she blocked out her surroundings and focused on the task before her. She was surprised an hour or so later when she looked up and realized Mrs. G was standing in front of her calling her name.

"That must be a really interesting research paper you're working on."

"I'm sorry," Tatia said, her cheeks flushing in embarrassment. "I didn't hear you come out of your office."

"Don't be. I love to see you girls engrossed in your studies."

Tatia looked at the time and quickly closed her computer. "Oh, I lost track of time. I'm late starting lunch."

"Don't worry about it. I was a little caught up in my work, too. It won't take us long to throw a salad together. After lunch we need to fill out your paperwork for camp."

"Camp?" Tatia squealed as she jumped up from the couch, almost spilling the computer onto the floor. "I get to go?"

"Yes, you get to go."

Tatia grabbed Mrs. G around the neck. "Thank you, thank you!"

Mrs. G was so shocked by the uncharacteristic display that she could only stand with her mouth open. Tatia was too excited to notice or to even realize what she had done. Mrs. G watched her with love and tears in her eyes as the girl skipped into the kitchen, humming the camp theme song like the typical, carefree girl she should have been all along.

The next few weeks passed quickly. Tatia went to the two-day training session all camp staffers were required to attend. She was blown away by what the workers went through to provide a safe place for a bunch of kids to spend a week having fun. She was excited at the prospect of reliving a time that had been the best experience of her life – this time from a completely different perspective.

Before she knew it, it was time to pack, and then it was time to leave. The other girls left with Mr. G around sun-up and drove straight to camp where they, along with all the other teen helpers, would set up activity centers, unload trailers containing sports and outdoor game equipment, and generally ready the camp for the invasion of hundreds of excited kids on Monday afternoon. Since Tatia was to serve as Mrs. G's staff assistant, they left two hours later and headed east.

Tatia was almost vibrating with nervousness and excitement as they drove out of the gate. She had only been out of the compound a few times since arriving, so she felt exposed, as if Eric would be waiting around the next curve in the road to force her back into the hellish life she had endured for so long. At the same time, she was eager to see the world as the new creature the Bible said she had become. During the entire three-hour drive, she alternated between a non-stop string of questions about her responsibilities and an introspective silence as she reconnected with camp memories she had kept locked away along with the mementos in her treasure box.

Mrs. G encouraged her to eat something from the bag of fruit and other healthy snacks they had brought. "We have a lot of work to do before dinner."

Tatia took a couple of bites of a protein bar, but it fell into her lap, forgotten as she began to recognize landmarks that told her they were nearing their destination. By the time she saw the sign and the road that led to the camp, she had her nose within millimeters of the window, straining for the first glimpse of a building, a playing field, anything that was a part of camp. Finally, she saw the path that led from the main buildings to the dorm that had felt like home where she had spent four nights in a wooden bunk bed that had felt like hers. Then she saw the cafeteria, the chapel, the pool, and the pond with the zip line and the slide. She felt the car come to a stop, and she heard Mrs. G open her door.

"We're here. First thing I want to do is go check out the dining room to see if they've made any changes since last year." She stood just outside the car, stretching out the kinks from the non-stop drive. When she realized Tatia hadn't moved, she leaned in the door. "Tatia, are you awake? Grab an armload and follow me over."

Tatia had been watching the groups of teens scattered across the grounds, sorting bats and balls and nets, carrying cases of water, and putting together sets for the Chapel stage. She pulled herself back when Mrs. G spoke. She opened her door and climbed out. "Sorry! It's just that it brings back so many memories – the last good memories I have until you came for me."

"Well, let's get busy and make some more good memories. Shall we?"

"Sounds good to me!"

Mrs. G opened the back of the SUV and pulled out a box of painted rocks and a bag full of postcards she had written to the campers in the last few weeks. Tatia grabbed several shopping bags full of accessories the girls had picked up at the thrift store on their last trip into town. Just as she cleared the tailgate with her load, the bottom of one of the bags gave way.

"Oh, no!" she wailed as she knelt to retrieve two purses, a pair of shoes that matched one of the purses, and several pairs of earrings that had escaped behind the rear tire. She jumped and almost bumped her head on the tailgate when a voice behind her spoke.

"Why don't you let me help with that?"

Tatia looked up into a familiar pair of twinkling gray eyes that were still full of life and joy. She sat back on her heels and grinned.

"Jesse, isn't it?"

He looked surprised and pleased. "You remembered. I'm flattered."

She chuckled. "Before you get carried away, remember that you have on a name tag."

He looked down at his tag and blushed a little. "So I do." He knelt down and picked up the jewelry that was out of her reach. He put them into one of the intact bags and then sat back. "You have me at a disadvantage. I remember the face but not the name – and you don't have a name tag."

"It's okay. It's been three years, and I've changed a lot. I'm Tatia."

Jesse held out his hand, and Tatia took it hesitantly. He held on to her hand as he stood to his feet and pulled her along with him.

"You've changed some, too," she said.

"Better looking?" he quipped.

She ignored his comment and pointed to the inside of his left arm which was covered from elbow to wrist with a tattoo of a Celtic tree of life. "New ink."

"Oh, that," he said with a grin. "Yeah, I have several new tats. It goes with being in the business."

"Jesse," yelled a boy a little older than Tatia. "They need you over in the chapel to help set up the stage."

"Okay, Joey. Thanks. Can you help Mrs. G and her new assistant, Tatia?"

"Sure, Jesse."

"It was good to see you again, Tatia. Later."

CHAPTER 38

NO CONDEMNATION

Tatia did see him later. It seemed like everywhere she looked, she saw him – but she turned her head when he looked her way, and she switched paths to avoid running into him. She had really liked him that first week at camp, and she had thought about him often since then, thinking about how things might have been different. Now that he was close, though, she steered clear of him, ashamed of what she had been and afraid he would hate her if he knew.

The night of the big birthday party, she had no responsibilities, so she volunteered to help with the climbing wall. It was on the opposite side of the party area from the face painting booth, so she felt like she would be safe from an accidental encounter with Jesse.

She hadn't counted on the enthusiasm of The Group, the name she had given to four ten-year-old girls who had decided she was their favorite teen staffer. They squealed whenever they saw her and ran over, fighting to be able to hold her hand like players fighting for the last chair in musical chairs. The party was winding down when she found herself surrounded by The Group, all talking and jumping up and down, revved up with excitement, snowcones, and cotton candy. Finally, Abby yelled and pointed.

"You haven't had your face painted."

The rest of the girls began to chant, "Face paint, face paint, face paint." They grabbed her hands, two on each one, and began to tug. Tatia looked at the counselor who was supervising the wall, hoping for some support in her protests that she had to stay and work.

"Don't look at me," he said with a shrug. "They're the bosses. After all, it's their birthday."

"Okay, you win!" she said, pulling her hands away and drawing the girls into a group hug. She had discovered in the last few days that physical contact with the younger campers didn't bother her the way hugs from those her age and older did. When they broke, the campers aligned themselves, two on each side, and the five giggling girls worked their way across the party grounds toward the canopy covering the painting artists. Tatia still had hope, and she tried to steer the girls toward one of the other artists.

"Nooooo!" protested Abby. "You have to go to Jesse! He's the best."

"And the cutest," added another girl, bringing on a fresh storm of giggles.

Tatia was carried along on the delightful enthusiasm of her entourage until suddenly they fell silent and motionless, standing in awe in front of the older man of their dreams. She realized she had no place to run and no place to hide.

"They insisted that I come get my face painted," she stammered. His smile was easy and welcoming, and she wondered why she had been so worried.

"I'm glad they did," he said, motioning her into the chair in front of him. "I thought you were avoiding me."

She hoped the gathering dusk covered the evidence of her embarrassment as she felt the warmth in her cheeks. "Not at all," she said, avoiding eye contact. "Mrs. G has just kept me really busy."

"I can imagine," he said. "Now, do you want the same thing? Blue and silver butterfly?"

"You remembered!"

"It all came back to me once you reminded me of your name."

He began to concentrate on his work, and Tatia concentrated on holding still. The Group soon lost interest and waved good-bye. "We're going to the slide bounce house. We'll see you at the dance." Tatia smiled as they skipped away giggling. She knew the gang of sixteen- and seventeen-year-old boys who were supervising the bounce house was the real attraction, but it was, after all, their birthday.

"You've learned to sit still since last time," he said, breaking into her thoughts. "I didn't have to repair a single mistake. What do you think?" He passed her the hand mirror that lay on his table.

"It looks great," she said as she admired his handiwork. "Just like last time."

"Speaking of last time, I remember that you admired one of my tats, and I painted one like it on your arm."

She moved her gaze from the mirror to his face, and her eyes filled with horror as she realized what he was thinking. Before she could put down the mirror, he reached over and slid the long sleeve of her T-shirt up to her elbow.

"Did you ever get a real..." He stopped in mid-sentence as his eyes fell on the exposed tattoo. His mouth was still open as if the unspoken words were still waiting to tumble out. He looked at Tatia with a combination of pain, horror, and sadness. "Oh, Tatia," he whispered. "I'm so s..."

Again, he didn't finish what he was saying. Tatia dropped the mirror, and it hit the corner of the table, shattering in a rain of glass shards around her ankles. She jumped to her feet with tears smearing the fresh paint on her cheek, and she ran.

Mrs. G saw her leave the posted bounds of the party area and followed her. As Tatia reached the darker part of the parking lot outside the reach of the lights, she slowed and bent over with her hands on her knees. Mrs. G could see her shoulders shaking and hear her sobbing as she caught up with her.

"Tatia, sweetheart, what's wrong?"

"I...I don't feel well. I just want to go to bed. Can I go to the room now?"

"You know the rules. I can't let you go to the room alone. Besides, everyone is supposed to go to the dance."

Tatia groaned, but she stood up and accepted the tissue Mrs. G had pulled out of her ever present tote bag. Even with the tissues blocking part of her view, Mrs. G could see the misery in Tatia's face.

"I don't think anyone will miss us during these last few minutes of the party. Let's take a walk."

Tatia followed her down the walkway between the dining hall and a long, thin staff dorm and then down the hill that led to the pond on the western border of the campground. Mrs. G sat down on the grass and patted the ground beside her. Tatia sat down, close enough to talk but far enough away to discourage consoling hugs. Mrs. G sat in silence for a few minutes to see if Tatia would open up, but when she didn't, the older woman asked.

"Now, what's this all about? What has you so upset?"

Tatia said nothing, but Mrs. G was aware of someone walking up behind them.

"It's me, Mrs. G," said Jesse. "I crossed the line. Tatia, I'm really sorry."

Mrs. G's face flushed and you could see her maternal protective instincts kick in – but before the angry words were out of her mouth, she heard Tatia speak weakly.

"You must hate me."

Mrs. G looked at Tatia and, seeing her left hand covering her right forearm, she suddenly had an idea of what had happened. She clamped her mouth shut and looked away to remove herself somewhat and allow the pair to interact without interference. She prayed silently that Tatia would not be devastated yet again, just when she was beginning to come out of her shell.

"Tatia, no! I could never hate you. I hate whoever did this to you. Besides, who am I to judge or condemn? I'm certainly not perfect, and I don't have any stones to throw."

Jesse had eased around beside Tatia so he could see the side of her face. She turned her head toward him but didn't raise her eyes to his.

"No condemnation," she said, almost to herself.

"No condemnation. None!" He held his hands out toward her, palms forward. "Look!" he said, so emphatically that she looked at his hands. "No stones, not one."

The anguish in her face began to drain away, and she looked back out at the water. With a sigh, she said, "I read and really understood that story for the first time a few weeks ago. It's my favorite."

Jesse sank down, squatting on his heels and playing with a dandelion that raised a ball of white fuzz between his knees. After a few minutes of companionable silence, he looked around and found a yellow flower that had not gone to seed. He picked it and held it out across the distance between them.

"Can you forgive me?" he asked.

She remembered when Eric gave her a yellow flower in front of the library, and she was struck by the irony. She took the flower and cut her eyes up to him with a small smile that was still tinged with sadness. "Yes. If He doesn't condemn me, how can I condemn someone who's being..."

"...being a jerk?" he finished her sentence.

Her smile took on an impish quality. "I was going to say being insensitive, but yeah."

"Thanks," he said with a chuckle.

Mrs. G brushed a tear from her cheek and whispered a quick prayer of thanks before turning back to the two friends. "It looks like everyone is moving to the next phase of the party. Come on. We don't want to miss the big birthday dance."

CHAPTER 39

SAYING SO LONG, NOT GOOD-BYE

The rest of the week was a blur of activity. Tatia ran into Jesse from time to time throughout the day, but there wasn't time for much more than a smile and a wave. Both of them were popular with the campers, and even when they weren't busy, they were surrounded by needy kids who were vying for their attention. Once or twice they chatted for a minute or two at the staff meeting and work time after the kids were in bed, but there was not time for anything meaningful.

Friday after lunch it was time to say good-bye, and it was both chaotic and traumatic. Campers and staff gathered in the main parking lot amid piles of baggage and idling buses that provided a rhythmic background for the noise of saying good-bye. Everyone wore camp T-shirts, and markers magically appeared. Children shared hugs and signed each other's shirts, shy girls finally worked up the courage to speak to the cute boy they had noticed on the first day, and tears were shed as the inevitability of returning to the real world loomed outside the camp boundaries.

Tatia had just signed the shirt of a little girl she had seen around camp but didn't really know when she saw Jesse walking in her direction. He was wearing a black do-rag with orange flames and black leather biker boots with big silver buckles on the outsides. She knew he had created quite a stir among the staff when he arrived on his motorcycle in a cloud of dust and the roar of pipes. All week the campers had begged unsuccessfully for rides or at least to hear him rev the engine. The promise had been made by those with the authority to make such promises that, on the last day, Jesse would leave before the buses pulled out so they could watch.

The time had arrived, and he looked like the Pied Piper with a herd of campers trailing behind him. However, he was oblivious to his entourage – his focus was only on Tatia. He stopped in front of her just as a tiny boy ran up and grabbed her legs, burying his face against her knees, looking for a safe place to hide from the chaos around him. Jesse watched as she knelt and reassured him, signing his shirt before steering him toward the correct bus. She stood and looked up into Jesse's face with a smile.

"Show time, huh?"

"Yeah, but I need one more signature on my shirt before I go," he said as he pulled a marker out of his pocket. She grinned and surveyed his shirt.

"There doesn't seem to be any space left."

"Not true. I saved this spot just for you," he said, pointing to the blank spot just above the camp logo. Tatia felt her cheeks color a little as she scrawled her name on his chest. "If you added your email address," he continued, "we could keep in touch instead of waiting another year or longer."

She was surprised, both by his request and by the flutter it caused in her own chest. She thought those feelings had died years ago, and she wasn't sure she was glad to find out she had been wrong. "I, uh," she stammered. "I couldn't unless Mrs. G said it was okay."

"She already did. She said I could write you on two conditions."

"Which are?"

"You agree and that she claims auditing rights from time to time."

She laughed, the tension broken. "Yep. Sounds like Mrs. G." As if she had heard her name, Mrs. G walked into Tatia's line of sight over Jesse's right shoulder. Tatia looked at her with a question in her eyes, and she replied with a smile and a slight nod. Tatia smiled back and added her email address, making sure it was more legible than her signature.

"Great! Now, little lady," he said in a bad John Wayne imitation, "I gotta ride." He raised two fingers to the brim of an invisible Stetson and winked at her in a way that brought back the flutter.

She grinned and replied in an exaggerated southern drawl, "Y'all come back real soon, Sugah."

Laughing, he turned and jogged toward the wide trail that led to the staff parking lot. By the time he reached the path, the word had spread that Jesse was heading for his bike and the already deafening noise level ratcheted up a decibel or two.

Detailed instructions for his big exit had been given at lunch to keep the spectators safe. Staff members began to direct traffic, and children lined up along either side of the path and around the perimeter of the main parking lot. A few of the teen boys cleared away any baggage that had not yet been loaded onto the buses. When the route was totally clear, the camp director raised both hands in the air, and the chant began.

"Jesse, Jesse, Jesse," beginning at an almost conversational level but quickly swelling in intensity until the parking lot sounded like a rock and roll venue before the headliner came on stage. The noise almost drowned out the rumble of Jesse's Screaming Eagle pipes as he fired up his Heritage Softail and racked the pipes. He put the bike in gear and, as the engine settled into the familiar Harley chug, he headed toward the path. He rolled slowly into sight, looking every bit like an outlaw biker. He had exchanged his camp T-shirt for a black tank top that showed off the tattoos that now covered most of both well-muscled shoulders. He had also donned a pair of black fingerless leather gloves and a pair of black wrap-around sunglasses.

The organized chant disintegrated into individual screams and shouts as he rolled the big bike down the path and around the parking lot. Then, he stopped in front of Tatia, and the crowd fell silent. He took off his sunglasses and looked around the circle at the kids, waving and making eye contact with as many of them as possible. When his gaze returned to Tatia, his eyes lingered on hers for a few seconds before he put his sunglasses back on, revved his engines, and rolled toward the entrance. He gathered speed as he approached the gate, and as he passed through it, he rolled on the throttle and scattered gravel as he sped toward the highway.

The kids were screaming again, hopping up and down and waving wildly – all except The Group who had at some point materialized next to Tatia. Staring up into her face, one of them said in a voice filled with awe, "You signed his shirt."

Another one piped up, "Your face is all red. You like him, don't you?"

Tatia couldn't deny her burning cheeks or the pounding of her heart. "Yeah," she said, gathering the girls close. "I guess I do."

CHAPTER 40
FAMILY REUNION

Tatia sighed and stood up from the bench in front of the chapel. "Yeah," she said with a self-conscious smile. "I guess I still do."

Then, she hurried back to the house where she went upstairs to her room and set to work in earnest to finish her welcome signs and organize her dorm decorations and the other materials she would need for the week. The laser-like focus that served her so well in her career helped her finish and pack all the bits and pieces that she hoped would create magic for two little girls – just in time, too. As she tied the bow on the last gift bag, pandemonium broke out downstairs. The doorbell rang, and the sound of many voices and lots of laughter drifted up the stairs. Tatia was doing a final check of her own luggage when she heard a familiar voice above the others.

"Tatia, get your skinny butt down here and say hello to me!"

"Ashlie, is that you?" she shouted back.

"Who else, girlfriend?" The voice was coming closer.

Tatia ran for the stairs, and the two young women met halfway. Ashlie was one of the few people who could comfortably hug Tatia, and they embraced, squealed, and giggled like a couple of teenagers. Arm-in-arm they went downstairs and joined the group of alumni from what they affectionately called the Grochowsky Rescue Academy. The rest of the day was filled with catching up on lives that, although they were now diverse and spread across the country, had started with similar hardships and the shared experience of grace and love in the family created by Mr. and Mrs. G. More welcome signs were created, dinner came and went, and the evening wound down as memories, challenges, and victories were shared. Finally, Mrs. G appeared with the large Bible that always meant it was time to gather for a family devotional before bedtime.

"Mr. G left for camp earlier today to supervise the set up, so I'm leading the Bible study tonight."

She opened the large book to Matthew 25:40 and read:

And the King shall answer and say unto them, Verily I say unto you, Inasmuch as ye have done it unto one of the least of these my brethren, ye have done it unto me.

She closed the Bible and looked around the room at each woman gathered around her as tears pooled against her lower lashes and threatened to spill over. "I love you all so much. I look into your beautiful faces tonight, and I see the hurt, rebellious, frightened children you were when you came into my life. At that time, you truly were the least of these – the ones who had fallen through the cracks in our flawed system, the ones who had been written off as lost causes, but exactly the ones who Jesus came to seek and to save. And now," her voice cracked and she took a moment to compose herself. "Now you are all successful, happy children of the King, ready to go into the world this next week to minister to another group of children who, through no fault of their own, have become the least of these. May the Lord bless you and guide you so that, at the end of the week, you will be exhausted, having poured all you had to give into these little lives. Tatia, will you please open our time of prayer? After anyone who wants to voice a prayer has done so, I will close."

For the next half hour or so, the sisters-in-love lifted up the camp, the staff, and the campers in prayer. They asked for wisdom, strength, stamina, and all the things they would need to make it through the next week.

When the final "Amen" was said, the women continued to sit and visit quietly for a few minutes, and then they began to drift upstairs to bed. Tatia lagged behind until only she and Mrs. G were left downstairs.

"I think I'll go out on the veranda and look at the stars for a few minutes. Would you like to join me?" asked Mrs. G.

"I'd like that," said Tatia. "I probably won't sleep much tonight anyway."

The temperature in Texas doesn't go down much in August, so it was still hot and muggy. However, thanks to several ceiling fans that spun lazily and kept the air stirring, it was bearable. Mrs. G and Tatia rocked side-by-side for a few minutes in comfortable silence, and Tatia marveled at the millions of stars that are visible away from the city lights. Then, Mrs. G spoke.

"Are you ready for a hectic week?" she asked.

"Oh, yes! I look forward to my time at camp all year. I spend so much time immersed in the big picture that it's good to have some one-on-one time with some of the girls and just maybe to prevent them from getting caught up in what I did." She chuckled before going on. "Besides, it's nice to be out of touch for a few days."

"You don't have to be completely out of touch, you know. You can check in after the kids are in bed."

"I know, but don't let them know that at the office."

It was Mrs. G's turn to chuckle. "So, are you going to spend any time with Jesse besides at camp?"

"Oh, I forgot to tell you. He's coming to pick me up early tomorrow morning. He won't tell me what he has cooked up, but whatever it is, I'm sure he'll do it with flair," Tatia said with a grin.

"He's very special to you, isn't he?" said Mrs. G.

"Yes, he is. You always said you had first right of refusal on any of the guys we dated. So, what do you think?"

"He'll do. It was plain to see from the first time he saw you at camp that year you were fifteen that he's head-over-heels in love with you." Tatia was glad it was dark so Mrs. G couldn't see her blush. "In spite of the way he feels, he's respectful of your feelings, and as far as I can tell, he hasn't tried to rush you into anything you're not ready for. He also loves the Lord, and I love this new ministry he's into. Yes, I think he'll do."

"You're right about not rushing me. He is the most patient and understanding man I've ever known. Most of them are so busy thinking about what they want that they aren't even aware of the needs of anyone else. I don't deserve him."

"You're wrong. He is exactly the kind of man you deserve." She stood up and stretched. "Now, this old lady is going to bed – and before I go, I'm going to invade your space just a little bit." She leaned over Tatia's chair, placed her hand on the younger woman's cheek, and kissed her on the forehead. "I love you."

Tatia placed her hand on Mrs. G's and looked up into her eyes. "To the moon and back."

CHAPTER 41
THE NEXT STEP

Tatia stayed on the veranda after Mrs. G went inside, but knowing 5:00 a.m. would come sooner than she was ready, she followed in a few minutes. She was pulling a bottle of water out of the refrigerator when Mrs. G came out of her office.

"Oh, Tatia. I'm glad you're still down here. I hate to drop this in the middle of our party, but you really need to see this."

"What is it?" asked Tatia, looking worried.

"It's a letter from the Parole Division," said Mrs. G, handing Tatia a sheet of paper on which she recognized the State Seal of Texas.

"It's Eric, isn't it?"

"Yes. After the trial, I filed a victim impact statement as your guardian requesting to be notified when he came up for parole."

"It seems too soon. I didn't expect this for another five years or so."

"I know. I did a little checking, and apparently he has been taking advantage of every work and self-improvement program available to him. He's built up a lot of good time credit, so they're bringing him up for consideration early. I've written a letter about the after-effects of what he did, but a first-person account from you should carry a lot of weight. I'm sorry I didn't give it to you earlier."

"Don't be sorry. This is the perfect time. The festivities are over for the evening, and I can get a letter written and out of the way in plenty of time to get a good night's rest. Thank you for filing for me." She gave Mrs. G a quick hug and headed upstairs.

An hour later, Tatia sat on her bed staring at a blank screen on her laptop. She wrote legal letters for a living, and she had expected to dash off a few sentences and be finished – but when she tried to put into a few words why Eric should not be released on parole, all she could think about was her second meeting with Elizabeth Delaney.

The Cameron County District Attorney asked Tatia why she thought Eric should be found guilty of all the charges against him, and all she could think of was that he had hurt a lot of people and that he had ruined a lot of lives.

"Yes, he has," replied the DA, "but we need to go into more detail. Are you up to answering some questions for me?"

Tatia said she was, and shortly after that meeting, Eric was indicted on two first-degree felonies and one second-degree felony. A trial date was set for later in the year, and Tatia returned to Refuge where she continued to rebuild her life.

One morning about three months before the trial, Mrs. G called Tatia into her office. Tatia had come to trust her foster mother completely, so she experienced none of the uneasiness she had felt earlier in their relationship. She sat down across the desk from Mrs. G and noticed the serious look on her face as she stared at a piece of paper in front of her.

"What's the matter?" asked Tatia, still not too concerned.

"It's Eric's trial," she sighed. "I knew this would probably happen, but I hoped it wouldn't be this soon."

She looked up and saw the fear that had crept into Tatia's eyes. She hurried on, "Oh, I'm sorry. It's not that bad – it's just that you're doing so well, I hate to bring it all up again. But here it is," she said indicating the paper in front of her. "It's a letter from Joseph Pittman, Eric's lawyer, asking to depose you."

"What does that mean?" asked Tatia cautiously.

"It's a little like the meeting you had with Elizabeth. It will be in a conference room rather than a courtroom. You'll be sworn in and Mr. Pittman will ask you questions, and then Elizabeth will probably question you, too. A court reporter will record the proceedings – what you say can be used in court as evidence or to discredit your testimony if the two accounts don't agree. That doesn't sound too bad, does it?"

Tatia had been staring at the letter as if it was a snake, coiled to strike at any moment. "Will Eric be there?"

"He has a right to be there, but because of your age, I will petition that the deposition be taken by video. If that petition is granted, and I think it will be, he will have to watch the movie."

Tatia visibly relaxed. "You're right. That doesn't sound too bad."

CHAPTER 42

THE DEPOSITION

Tatia's sleep was troubled with bad dreams the night before the deposition. Even though the judge had agreed to a video deposition and all parties had agreed to dispense with some of the formalities, she was still scared. She was thankful she wouldn't have to face Eric, but seeing Joseph would be almost as bad. He had always been nice to her, but now she was on the other side, so she didn't know what to expect.

Mrs. G had told her to dress like she would for any trip into town, so she pulled out her favorite jeans and a pink long-sleeved pullover with a scooped neckline. She was thankful that it was unseasonably cool so she didn't look so out of place with her arms covered. After her shower, she pulled her hair back into a ponytail that would dry into soft, natural curls. She applied just a touch of mascara, blush, and lipstick and put on the small silver cross earrings Mr. and Mrs. G had bought for her on a recent shopping trip. She looked in the mirror, whispered a prayer, and went downstairs.

The breakfast table was unusually quiet that day as each girl wondered if she would have the courage to do what Tatia was doing. More eggs and bacon stayed on the plates than were eaten, and after the dishes were done, everyone hung around the kitchen waiting to see her off. Mrs. G returned to the kitchen after brushing her teeth, looked around the room, and shook her head.

"What is going on here? You all look as if we're going to a funeral or something. This is no big deal. Tatia is just going to answer a few questions, and we'll be back before you know it. Now, I believe you ladies have better things to do than sit around here with long faces, so say what you need to say and get to work!"

That broke the spell. There was a flurry of self-conscious laughter, high fives, and good luck wishes. After the group scattered, Tatia looked at Mrs. G with a grateful smile.

"Thanks! They were kinda getting on my nerves."

Mrs. G laughed, and the two headed out to the car. The two-hour drive was made mostly in silence while Tatia pondered what memories she might be required to dredge up and Mrs. G prayed for the foster daughter she had come to love so much. When they arrived at the courthouse, they breezed through security and walked quickly toward the conference room that had been reserved for the deposition. Mrs. G greeted many acquaintances along the way, and Tatia tried to maintain as low a profile as possible.

They were the first to arrive, and Tatia was relieved at how normal the room looked. An oval table dominated the room, and it was surrounded by six comfortable-looking chairs. A narrow table against the wall opposite the door was the only other piece of furniture in the room.

"Why don't you take a seat at that end of the table," instructed Mrs. G. "The camera will probably be set up at the other end, and the rest of us will be along the sides."

"You'll sit next to me, right?"

"If everyone agrees to that I will. If not, I'll only be one seat away."

Just then, the door swung open, and the court reporter came in and surveyed the room. "This room is always a little cramped, but it will have to do," she said to no one in particular. She grabbed the chair at the opposite end of the table from Tatia and rolled it into a corner. "The cameraman doesn't need to sit down anyway. I'll be right back," she said, seeming to notice the other occupants of the room for the first time.

In the next few minutes, the court reporter returned with a small table and her machine, the cameraman arrived with his equipment, and the district attorney came in with her briefcase. Ms. Delaney also carried a tote bag filled with bottles of water which she set in the center of the table. Mrs. G handed one to Tatia who immediate opened it and took a long drink.

"Thanks. My mouth is dry already."

The last to arrive was Eric's attorney. "Good morning," he said, scanning the room. "It looks as if everyone arrived ahead of me." He took an empty chair on the far side of the table. "I'm ready if everyone else is." Both the cameraman and the reporter gave a thumbs up, and the others nodded. "Then let's get started."

The next few minutes were spent introducing everyone and establishing their credentials for the record. A note was also made that all participants agreed to an informal proceeding and that no one objected to Mrs. G's presence. Then, Tatia swore to tell the truth, and Joseph Pittman began to ask his questions.

She felt a momentary panic when she first looked at him. The encouraging look that had always been there for her before had been replaced by an accusatory glare, as if she were the one who had done something wrong. Mrs. G saw her eyes widen and heard the shaky breath she drew in. She laid what she hoped would be a comforting hand on Tatia's arm and felt the girl relax a bit.

Pittman began by asking how Tatia had met Eric, and she relaxed further as she recounted how he had suddenly appeared in her life. His insinuating questions tried to make it sound as if she had pursued Eric, but her straightforward answers soon put an end to that line of questioning.

Next, Pittman probed further into the nature of their relationship – how Eric treated her in the beginning, how he provided for her when she was with him, and how long she stayed with him. The way he worded his questions again made it seem like everything was her fault, and Tatia wanted to defend herself. However, Mrs. G had instructed her to answer only what was asked and not to elaborate further.

His last questions were about her relationship with Cindy and about the nature of Cindy's relationship with Eric. Tatia struggled to keep her composure as she told about how Eric often took his anger out on Cindy, especially when she stood up to him.

"Miss Robins," he asked finally, "early on the morning of July 1 of this year, Mr. Hall allegedly beat Miss Landers severely. Were you a witness to that event?"

"No, sir."

"Where were you at the time?"

"I was in jail."

Pittman smirked with satisfaction and turned to the DA. "I'd like to hear your questions if you don't mind, Ms. Delaney."

Tatia thought Ms. Delaney looked like she wanted to throw a caustic comment back at Mr. Pittman, but she resisted. Instead she turned to Tatia and smiled kindly at her.

"How are you, Tatia? Do you need a break before I begin?"

"No, Ms. Delaney. I'm fine."

"OK, good. I just have a few follow-up questions for you. First, how old were you when you met Eric?"

"I was eleven – in the fifth grade."

"And did he know how old you were?"

"Yes, ma'am."

"How do you know that?"

"I told him – several times," she said with a small laugh. "I talked a lot about my upcoming birthday when I would be twelve – almost a teenager."

"Mr. Pittman asked about the gifts Eric gave you. Did you ever ask him for anything?"

"No, ma'am. In fact, I told him he shouldn't spend his money on me."

The questions went on with each one getting more difficult for Tatia – what kinds of things did he give you, did he expect anything in return, what happened on your twelfth birthday, how did your relationship change after that, why she stayed with him for three years. Unlike Mr. Pittman, the DA asked questions that allowed Tatia to explain the reality of what she had been through. She noticed that Mr. Pittman was scribbling notes and looking more unhappy with each answer she gave. She hoped that was a good sign.

She was surprised when Ms. Delaney said, "Thank you, Tatia. That's all I have for now. Mr. Pittman, do you have any further questions?"

He sat for a moment, staring down at his notepad. Finally, he looked up and said, "Are you offering any deals?"

CHAPTER 43
NO DEALS

Tatia didn't understand what was happening, but before she knew it, she and Mrs. G had said good-bye to Ms. Delaney and were on their way out of the courthouse. Once they were outside, she broke the silence.

"Is that it? Are we finished?" she asked.

"Yes, we are, at least for now," Mrs. G was quiet for a minute before continuing. "Tatia, many young women have refused to do what you just did, and that's one of the reasons men like Eric continue to do what they do. I'm really proud of you."

"Thanks," she said at the same moment her stomach growled loudly. She grinned sheepishly. "I guess I should have eaten my breakfast. Could we maybe get a burger or something before we head back home?"

"I have a better idea," said Mrs. G. "There's a little place around the corner that I think you'll enjoy – and I doubt you'll run into any old friends there."

The restaurant was called Ellie's Tea Room, and Tatia thought it was wonderful. The country décor reminded her of the kitchen at the Refuge, and it was much too feminine to attract many male diners. The menu included soups, salad, and sandwiches that were a refreshing change from fast food offerings of burgers and fries. She followed Mrs. G's lead and ordered a three-salad plate that included chicken salad, a cup of mixed fresh fruit, and a broccoli salad that was better than just about anything she had ever eaten. She also had a glass of mango iced tea that almost replaced decaf mocha as her favorite drink.

While they ate, the two continued to relax with small talk about shoes, make-up, and nail polish, but while they were finishing a dessert of angel food cake with a pineapple fluff topping, Tatia grew serious. "What did Mr. Pittman mean when he asked if Ms. Delaney was offering any deals?"

"He was talking about a process called plea bargaining. Sometimes, if a defendant agrees to plead guilty, the State will lower the charges to an offense that carries a lesser penalty. Does that make sense?"

"I think so."

"Let me give you an example. Texas law divides murder charges into capital murder, murder, and manslaughter. Murder, which is what Eric is charged with, carries a penalty of five to ninety-nine years. Manslaughter, which means the accused didn't intend to kill the victim, carries a penalty of two to twenty years. This is just a guess, but for a guilty plea, Elizabeth might offer manslaughter with the maximum sentence."

"Why would they let him off so lightly?"

"It would guarantee that he will serve some time for his crime, it would save the expense of a trial, and it would save you the trauma of testifying in open court."

"Do you think Eric will accept a deal like that?"

"Again, it's only a guess on my part, but I don't think so. I think his attorney will recommend it, but based on what you've told me about Eric, I don't think he'll go for it. He's arrogant enough to think he's above the law. He probably also thinks he can charm a jury into acquitting him altogether. If not and he's convicted, he still has a chance to talk his way into a lighter punishment in the penalty phase."

"Really? How does that happen?"

"Well, if a person is found guilty in a trial, he has to go through another process similar to the trial so the jury can decide what his punishment will be. If a person who is accused of murder can convince a jury that he was acting in the heat of passion, he might get two to twenty instead of five to ninety-nine."

"It's really complicated, isn't it?"

"Yes, that's why it took me two tries to pass the bar exam."

Tatia giggled and turned her attention back to her dessert.

A few days later, Mrs. G received a phone call that proved she was a good judge of character. After she spoke with Elizabeth Delaney for a few minutes, she once again called Tatia into her office.

"I hate being right in this case, but Eric rejected all offers of a deal. He'll be going to trial as scheduled, and you'll receive a subpoena to testify for the prosecution."

"What charges did they settle on?" she asked.

"Murder, aggravated statutory sexual assault, and human trafficking."

Tatia let out a big sigh and said, "OK. I guess I'd better start praying for some of that strength you keep saying you see in me."

CHAPTER 44
AN UNWELCOME ENCOUNTER

In early December, Tatia was sitting alone in the small conference room where she had given her deposition. She had only been there for a few hours, but it seemed as if she had been sitting in the same chair, staring at the same walls forever.

As the time for the trial had drawn closer, Mrs. G had explained that, in Texas, victims were allowed in the courtroom except when they were scheduled to testify.

"There is precedent to protest that rule if you want to sit in on the trial," said Mrs. G. "What do you think?"

Tatia was quiet for a few minutes, thinking about what it would be like to sit for days listening to the horror she had lived through discussed for the world to hear. "I don't think I want to hear it. You can tell me what I need to know."

"Not really. The reason for having you excluded is so your testimony won't be affected by the testimony of other witnesses."

"That's okay," said Tatia. "I don't really need to know anyway, do I?"

Both of them had laughed, but without any real amusement.

Tatia continued. "It's going to be hard enough to sit up there and talk about all of it with all those people looking at me, especially...him."

Mrs. G agreed, so she had driven alone into Cameron every morning for the last two weeks while Tatia stayed behind and tried to maintain a normal routine. During her time with Eric, she had developed an incredible ability to compartmentalize, and that helped her focus on her school work and her other responsibilities while ignoring what was going on a couple of hours away. Now, though, the jury had been chosen, opening statements had been made, the first witnesses had testified, and here she was, waiting to be called to the stand.

Tatia passed the time electronically – working on her schoolwork via the Internet, reading her most recent ebook purchase, and texting. Ashlie texted her almost hourly, sending jokes, silly selfies, and Bible verses in an attempt to help pass the time and buoy her spirits. The other girls texted, too, but only once or twice since she had left that morning. The messages she looked forward to the most, though, were the ones from Jesse.

In the months since camp, something unexpected had happened. A few days after returning home, she had received her first email from Jesse. It was a chatty, humorous message from a nice guy who, since he was almost a thousand miles away, raised none of the defensive feelings she felt when she was around other men. She waited a day or two before responding, and then she was careful to maintain the same light-hearted, casual tone of his message.

The correspondence between the two had continued regularly after that, increasing in frequency and regularity until they were interacting electronically every day and sometimes several times a day. Phone numbers were eventually exchanged, and texting became part of their routine. At first, they rarely actually spoke to each other, but as the trial neared, she often felt the need for a real conversation.

Mrs. G was comforting and patient, but Tatia sometimes felt as if she was taking more than her share of time. After all, there were other girls who needed Mrs. G's attention, as well as a ministry that was sometimes an administrative nightmare. Tatia discovered that, even if he was busy, Jesse always found a few seconds to respond to her texts with a few words and a promise to call or text later. He always kept his promises, and more importantly, he always seemed glad to hear from her. Theirs was an easy-going relationship that was so open she felt the defensive wall she had built around herself crumbling. She felt like she could tell him anything, and he seemed to feel the same way about her.

As the calendar counted down the days until the trial, Tatia could think about little else, and she relied more and more on her conversations with Jesse. He didn't let her become bogged down, though. He would listen to her for a while and then distract her with tales of the professors in the college classes he was taking and of the customers in the tattoo parlor where he continued to pursue what he felt was his real calling. Once she had laughed herself silly and he could hear the strength coming back into her voice, he would ask questions that led her to find her own answers and calm her own fears.

She was finishing a text to Jesse, thanking him again for his support, when the door opened and Mrs. G walked in. Tatia was so engrossed in the small world in the palm of her hand that the intrusion of the outside world startled her, and she almost dropped the phone. She laughed self-consciously when she looked up and saw Mrs. G standing there. Then, the half-smile immediately fell away as reality invaded the sanctuary of the conference room.

Her eyes were wide as she asked, "Is it time?"

"Almost – but first the judge called a two-hour recess for lunch. Are you hungry?"

"Not much, but a glass of mango iced tea sounds really good." She stopped and looked around the small, crowded room. "And I really want to get out of here for a few minutes."

"Sounds good to me," said Mrs. G. "Drop anything you don't want to leave here into my tote bag, and let's go."

Tatia let out a genuine laugh and held up a tote bag Mrs. G had loaned her for the trial. "I have my own, remember?"

"So you do," said Mrs. G with a wry smile. "Well, fill it and let's move."

So far, Tatia had not seen Eric. Mrs. G had made a point of arriving early and settling Tatia into her little nest well before the defendant arrived. Eric had made bail, and her guardian wanted to avoid any possibility of a chance encounter that would upset the composure Tatia needed to get through her coming ordeal. Still, her precautions weren't enough.

As the two strolled companionably down the hall, Tatia talked about her outfit. "I'm glad you suggested that I wear this today. It's one of my favorites, and I feel confident in it." She was wearing a sky blue draped cardigan over a simple black dress accessorized with a silver chain necklace and her cross ear studs.

"You look beautiful, dear," said Mrs. G, giving Tatia a quick hug.

"Yes, she looks beautiful," said a male voice behind them. "Very much like a girl named Kaitlyn Golden I used to know."

Tatia froze, not because of the unexpected display of affection, but because she recognized Eric's voice. Mrs. G made a sharp about-face that would have made a drill sergeant proud.

"Mr. Hall," she snapped. "It is not appropriate for you to be speaking to or about my daughter." A surprised Tatia looked at Mrs. G who was turning her attention to the man walking beside Eric. "Mr. Pittman, I suggest you control your client, or I will ask Judge Wellman to do so for you."

She spun back around, grabbed Tatia by the elbow, and hurried down the hall toward the door. "I'm so sorry, Tatia," she said. "Are you okay?"

Tatia took a deep breath and exhaled slowly before she answered. "I'm fine. I refuse to allow him to take anything else away from me, even if it's only the enjoyment of a glass of iced tea."

A few minutes later, they were at Ellie's, settled at a quiet table in the corner where they were not likely to be seen from the street. They each ordered the three-salad plate, although Tatia doubted she'd be able to eat much of it. She was sipping her tea absently when Mrs. G broke the silence.

"Penny for your thoughts."

Tatia looked up and stared seriously into Mrs. G's face. "You called me your daughter."

Understanding dawned in Mrs. G's eyes. "I did, didn't I? That's because Mr. G and I think of you as our daughter, and our dream is to make it official one day."

"You never said anything."

"That's because we didn't want you to feel pressured. If it happens, we want it to be your idea – when you're ready."

"Why me? Why not Ashlie or any of the others?"

"We've mentioned it to every girl we've fostered, but so far, none of them have brought it up again. And just so you know, we've never felt as strongly about it with anyone as we do with you."

Tatia sat quietly for a few minutes before looking up with a half smile on her face. "Once this trial is over, I think I'll be ready."

Tatia smiled in spite of the cursor that continued to blink impatiently on the blank screen. She let her mind drift to the last time she had appeared before Judge Wellman. That day he was acting for the Family Court, and it was the day she officially became Tatia Robins-Grochowsky. At her new mother's suggestion, she continued to use her birth name for professional purposes, but from that day forward, all the girls at the Refuge called her Ms. G.

CHAPTER 45

TATIA'S STORY

By the time the waitress brought the food, Tatia had regained her appetite. The next hour flew by as she and Mrs. G talked about the process and implications of adoption. When the waitress returned for the third time to ask if she could bring them anything else, Mrs. G leaned back in her chair and sighed.

"No," she said, "we have to go. Just the check please."

Tatia's face fell, the joy and most of the color draining away. "I wish I didn't have to do this. I really don't want to tell my story," she said.

"I know," replied Mrs. G. "But Eric needs to pay for what he's done."

"But it's so ugly."

"Yes, and that's why it needs to be told," she said as she put enough cash to cover the bill and a tip in the black folder the waitress had put on the corner of the table. "Now, grab your stuff and let's head back. We have time to visit the ladies room and freshen up before court reconvenes."

Tatia almost collided with the district attorney in the hall outside the restroom.

"Tatia," said Ms. Delaney, "just the person I wanted to see. You too, Deborah," she added, widening her gaze to include Mrs. G. She began walking toward the courtroom, assuming Tatia and Mrs. G would follow her. "I'll be calling you to the stand as soon as Judge Wellman gives me the go ahead. You can leave your things in my office – they'll be safe there. Why don't you wait outside in the hall, just in case Pittman pulls something unexpected. It shouldn't be more than a few minutes. Are you okay with that?"

"Sure, I guess," said Tatia. "Would it be okay if Mama…I mean Mrs. G stays out here with me until I go in?"

Mrs. G took Tatia's hand protectively and answered for the DA. "Of course, I'll stay with you. When they call you, I'll walk in with you and then take my seat."

Tatia looked at her gratefully and blinked rapidly to keep the tears from spilling out. Ms. Delaney watched with interest and spoke softly, almost to herself.

"Hmmm. A change in the dynamics of the relationship." Then she smiled broadly and said, "Okay, then. I'll see you shortly."

A few minutes later, Tatia and Mrs. G were sitting close together on an uncomfortable bench across from the door of the courtroom. They were still holding hands, and they were talking quietly.

"I don't know if I can do this," said Tatia.

"Of course you can. You've told me your story, and you've told Deborah. Just focus on one of us and you'll be fine."

"Jesus will be with me always, even here. Right?"

"Yes, especially here."

"And I have this," said Tatia, pulling something out of her pocket and holding it out in her palm. Mrs. G laughed as she recognized the stone she had give Tatia at camp – the one with the word *Strength* painted on it.

As they laughed together, the big double doors across the hall swung open, and the bailiff called out formally, "Calling Julie Smith to the stand."

Tatia looked around for someone else who might be waiting to be called. Then she realized Julie Smith was the pseudonym she would be using in court because of the privacy afforded a minor at trial. She knew the media was aware that her real name was not being used and also that they were prohibited from taking pictures of her or using any pictures they might dig up on the Internet or elsewhere. She stood up slowly with her head down. Then, she put her hand in her pocket and touched the stone, inhaled slowly, and spoke steadily, "I'm ready."

She followed the bailiff down the center aisle, hardly aware when Mrs. G left her or of the curious stares that were directed toward her. She was, however, aware of Eric's eyes boring into her, but she ignored him and kept her eyes focused straight ahead on Judge Wellman. She walked through the well in front of his bench and into the witness box without incident. Her voice cracked slightly when she said "I do" in reply to the recitation of the oath, but after taking a sip from the bottle of water the bailiff handed her, she repeated herself in a clear, strong voice. Then Ms. Delaney was standing in front of her.

"Hi, Julie. You doing okay?" she asked in a friendly, conversational voice.

"I'm fine. Thank you." She smiled a little to herself. Her real name still seemed strange to her after being called Kaitlyn for so long – and now she was answering to yet another name.

"Good. I don't want you to be nervous. I'm going to ask you some questions, and I want you to just answer in your own words. Okay?"

"Yes, ma'am."

"The court has already covered the fact that you're using a pseudonym today, so we'll skip that question and move on."

"Where do you live, Julie?"

"I live at Refuge which is owned and operated by Mr. and Mrs. Grochowsky."

"What kind of place is Refuge?"

Tatia looked at Mrs. G who nodded at her with an encouraging smile. Tatia gave her a small smile in return and answered. "It's a halfway house for girls...for girls like me who have been the victim of human trafficking."

"How long have you been at Refuge?"

"Since July 1 of this year."

"Was that when you first met the Grochowskys?"

"No, I met Mrs. G at camp when I was eleven. She gave me her card in case I ever needed her. Last July I needed her."

"Why was that, Julie?"

"I was in jail for prostitution."

There was an audible gasp from the courtroom, but Tatia ignored it as she listened for the next question. "How did that happen? What I mean is how did you become a prostitute?" She was so matter-of-fact with her questions that it was easy for Tatia to answer the same way.

"I was forced into it by Eric Hall."

The courtroom erupted into a confusion of exclamations and questions. Tatia wondered why everyone was surprised. She assumed Delaney would have mentioned her slate of witnesses in her opening statement. Maybe it was because she didn't look the part. Whatever the reason, Judge Wellman was not pleased, and he displayed his displeasure by banging his gavel again and again. When some semblance of order was finally restored, he glared around the room and barked, "I will have none of that in my courtroom. If there is a repeat of this display, I will clear the room."

Satisfied that his message had been received, he looked back at Delaney. "You may continue."

"Thank you, Your Honor. Julie, do you see Eric Hall in this courtroom?"

For the first time, Tatia looked around the room. She knew where Eric was sitting, but she was in no hurry to look at him. She began with the jury, looking at each one, trying to imagine what they were thinking at this moment. Then, she looked at the assistant DA and the clerk at the prosecution table before finally moving her gaze to the defense table.

"He's right over there," she said, nodding toward him.

"Just to be clear, can you please point him out."

She pointed toward the defense table. "There. The one between Mr. Pittman and the lady at the other end of the table."

"Let the record show that the witness has indicated the defendant," said the judge.

"Now that we've heard the end of the story," said Ms. Delaney, "let's go back and fill in some of the back story."

For the next few minutes, Tatia answered questions about her early years. Those years seemed like another lifetime, so she was able to tell her story with relatively little emotion, as if it were a story she had read instead of one she had lived. When she told about finding her mother's cold body on the living room sofa, she was startled to hear sniffles from the jury box. She looked in their direction and saw that two of the women were openly wiping their eyes with tissues, and several other people were obviously moved by her story.

"Julie, are you okay, or do you need a break?" asked Ms. Delaney, drawing her witness back to the task at hand.

"Oh, no," answered Tatia quickly. "I'm fine. Sorry."

"You're doing great, Julie. You just tell me if you need a break."

"I will. Thank you."

"Now, tell me what happened after your mother died." Gently, she led Tatia through the time she spent with her grandmother, her introduction into the foster system, and a brief overview of her experiences in it. At one point, Mr. Pittman stood and voiced an objection.

"Your honor," he said in a rather bored voice, "I'm sure we are all very sympathetic to the hard life Ms. Smith has led. However, I fail to see the relevance to the charges my client is facing and to the charges she herself has leveled at him."

The judge looked at Ms. Delaney and raised an eyebrow questioningly. "Your Honor," she said, answering the unspoken question, "I am laying the foundation for my client's relationship with the defendant, and I assure you that her life story is very relevant."

"I will allow it for now, Ms. Delaney," said Judge Wellman, "subject to your ability to show relevance – soon!"

"Yes, Your Honor. Thank you."

Mr. Pittman sat down with a disgusted look on his face and leaned over for a whispered conversation with his client. Tatia glanced toward the defense table just as Eric looked up at her. His eyes looked black, and she saw the flash of anger that had, at one point in her life, foreshadowed a severe beating to come.

"Julie, let's move forward a bit. Does the name Josie Clark mean anything to you?"

"Yes. She was my last foster placement – well, the last one before Mr. and Mrs. G."

"What was the situation there?"

"There were six of us kids. I was the oldest."

"And how old were you?"

"Eleven."

"What was your role in the house?"

Tatia looked confused. "I'm not sure what you're asking."

"Let me ask it a different way. What kind of chores did you have while you were there?"

"Oh, right. I watched the little kids, changed diapers for the ones who weren't potty trained, helped the older ones with homework, helped with baths and bedtime, that kind of stuff."

"Did you do the cooking?"

"Sometimes. Josie usually put a roast or a chicken in the Crockpot on the weekend, but I made dinner during the week. I cleaned up the kitchen regardless of who cooked."

"Did you have any free time – maybe on the weekends?"

"Not much. I helped with cleaning and laundry then.

"I think that gives us enough background for now. When did you meet Eric Hall?"

"I think it was in March of that year."

"The year you were still eleven. Right?"

"Yes."

The DA took her through their friendship and her birthday dinner. By the time they reached the part of her story where she was sprawled on the stained carpet in the motel room, Tatia was crying. Tears were dripping onto her lap the same way they had dripped onto the carpet that night, but she continued to speak softly but clearly.

"After he threw me to the floor, he grabbed me by the shoulders and jerked me to my feet. He got right in my face, and I could smell the liquor on his breath. He backed me up against the edge of the bed, and then he went back to talking about his friend.

"'After he kisses you, he'll want to touch you like this,' he said.

He grabbed my breasts. He was really rough, and when I tried to push his hands away, he...wrapped his fingers around my wrists and squeezed really hard." Her voice broke at this point, and she buried her face in her hands as if trying to shut out the scene she was describing.

"Julie," said Ms. Delaney gently, "do you want to stop for a minute?"

Tatia drew in a shaky breath and slowly lowered her hands. She looked toward Mrs. G who was sitting ramrod straight with tears running down her own face.

"No, let me tell it. When I cried out from the pain, he let go of my wrists. 'You're not being very nice,' he said. 'My friend will want to touch you.' He started to unzip my dress, and he said, 'He'll want to know what you look like under this beautiful dress that I bought you.'"

Tatia stifled a sob and closed her eyes for a moment before continuing. "I struggled to get away, but Eric was too strong. He pushed me back onto the bed. Then he grabbed the bottom of my dress in both hands, and ripped it all the way up – and then he did it."

Tatia's words hung in the silence for a few moments. Then, Ms. Delaney said, almost apologetically, "Julie, I need you to tell us what he did."

Tatia had carefully avoided looking at Eric since she had pointed him out, but now she lifted her head, squared her shoulders, and turned toward him. Looking him straight in the eye, she described exactly how he had raped her.

CHAPTER 46
CINDY'S STORY

When Tatia finished the story of that night, she was emotionally and physically exhausted, and so was Ms. Delaney. "Your Honor," she said, "I'd like to request a short recess before we continue with Ms. Smith's testimony."

Judge Wellman looked at his watch and over at Tatia. "I think we all need a break, and since it is 5:00 o'clock, we'll recess until 9:00 a.m. tomorrow." He gave the usual reminders to the jury, and as soon as he left the scene, the courtroom erupted in chaos. Reporters scrambled toward the door to try and make the evening news or to file their stories for the early edition the next day, spectators engaged in emotional discussions with their neighbors, and Eric added to the confusion with an angry rant about the inequities of the legal system and the incompetence of his lawyer.

Tatia sat unmoving in the witness box, staring at nothing, until Mrs. G reached out and touched her on the shoulder. "Tatia? Honey, it's time to go."

Tatia looked at her blankly for a moment, then shook her head as if to clear the memories she had just relived from her head. "Yeah, okay," she said, slowly rising from the chair and stepping down into Mrs. G's embrace.

"We can get a room here for the night if you're too tired to make that long drive."

"No," Tatia replied fiercely. "I want to be in my own room, even if it's only for a few hours."

"Deborah," said Ms. Delaney from the prosecutor's table as she snapped her briefcase closed. "Don't take her out into the hall. The vultures will be waiting out there, regardless of what the judge said about privacy. We'll slip out through the jury room. I think we can make it to my office without being seen. You can pick up Tatia's things and go out through the station. Maybe you can avoid most of the reporters that way."

They made it to their car with only one encounter, and Mrs. G dispatched that unfortunate reporter with what could only be described as a low growl and a murderous look. Tatia fell into her seat, leaned it back, curled into a fetal position inside her seat belt, and was asleep before Mrs. G backed out of the parking space. She woke up briefly when the car came to a stop in front of the house. Without a word, she climbed the stairs, draped her jacket and dress across the chest, crawled into bed, and slept until morning when Mrs. G knocked softly on her door.

"Tatia, we need to leave in an hour. That should give you time to get ready and eat something before we leave."

She knew there was no point in arguing, so an hour later, Tatia buckled into her seat after having eaten some peach yogurt and a piece of toast. She sat quietly, trying not to think about anything all the way to the courthouse. She wasn't very successful. She repeatedly rehearsed her testimony, trying to figure out a way of telling about the last few years of her life that didn't sound completely sordid. She wasn't successful with that either.

She spent the morning simply answering Ms. Delaney's questions as truthfully as possible. She told why she ran away from Josie's house and how the trip Eric promised her turned out to be a tour of truck stops and motels between Cameron and Las Vegas. She explained how Eric's business was structured and her part in it.

"I'm very familiar with the structure," she said, "because when I wasn't entertaining clients, Eric allowed Cindy to teach me how to do some of the accounting. I learned to enter data in the spreadsheets that tracked the productivity of each of the girls, and I actually helped her set up a scheduling spreadsheet so we didn't have girls with a lot of downtime or double book any of them."

The most difficult part of her testimony was talking about Cindy, and Eric's abuse of her.

"Tell me what you observed about the relationship between Cindy and Eric."

Pittman was on his feet immediately, something he had been doing regularly throughout Tatia's testimony. "Objection! Calls for hearsay and opinion."

"Exception, Your Honor," replied Delaney. "What Miss Landers told Miss Smith about her relationship with Mr. Hall is relevant to his state of mind on the night in question."

"Objection is overruled," said Judge Wellman, "but I will caution you, Ms. Smith, to confine your answers to only what Miss Landers actually told you and not what you think their relationship was like."

"Yes, Sir."

"Do you need me to repeat the question?" asked Ms. Delaney.

"No. The first time I met Cindy – the night of my birthday – when Eric called her to come in and help me with my make-up, he was rude to her. When she talked back to him, he got really mad. Later, after...you know...he called her back in to help me clean up. She sassed him again, and he raised his fist, but she got out of the way before he could hit her. I saw a big bruise on her leg, and she said he did it."

She went on, telling about the many times Cindy showed up with bruises, welts, and cuts. Tatia became skilled in the administration of first aid, but sometimes that was not enough. Sometimes there were broken bones, and once there was a ruptured spleen that required a trip to the emergency room.

When Tatia stopped, Ms. Delaney said, "Let's talk about the night Cindy died. Were you with her?"

"No, she was back at our apartment taking calls and watching the computer so she could set up last-minute appointments."

"So you didn't see what happened between her and Eric that night?"

"No."

Delaney walked back over to the prosecution table and consulted her notes before continuing. "Does the name Kevin Adams mean anything to you?"

Tatia smiled a little. "Yes. He arrested me twice – the first time I was brought in and that night."

"You mean the night Cindy died?"

"Yes."

"In Officer Adams' arrest report, he noted that when he brought you out of your room and you saw what was going on, you said, 'This whole thing was a set-up. Eric is gonna kill her! Oh, Cindy.' Why did you say that?"

"Eric was over at our apartment about two weeks before that night. He was looking through the weekend guide, and he saw an ad for the gun show and started talking about it. Cindy told him that she couldn't find rooms in the motels we usually used. The only place she could find was the place where we ended up, and Eric was really mad."

"Why was he angry?"

"He didn't like us all to be in one place in case of a raid – just like what happened. Instead of one or two of us getting picked up, we all got caught in the sweep. I knew he'd beat her up, but I didn't really think he'd kill her." At this, Tatia began to weep softly.

"Objection!" shouted Pittman.

"Sustained. The jury will ignore the last part of the witness's answer."

"Thank you, Julie," said the DA. Her usually strong voice was soft, and she sounded dangerously close to breaking into tears herself. She knew Tatia's words had hit their target in spite of the judge's admonition. "You did very well. Your Honor, I have no further questions of Ms. Smith at this time."

Judge Wellman called a lunch recess, and once again, Mrs. G led Tatia through the back hallways to Ms. Delaney's office. "Ashlie packed a lunch for us so we won't have to fight through the crowds and the press," she said.

Tatia didn't really want to eat, but Mrs. G insisted, so she nibbled at the tiny sandwiches and fruit salad her friend had prepared for them. She turned on her phone and was shocked at how many text messages and emails were waiting for her. Then, she remembered that she hadn't powered up her phone since she had been called to the stand almost twenty-four hours before. She smiled when she saw a dozen texts from Jesse, and she laughed out loud at some of his cyberspace antics. She showed Mrs. G some of his crazy selfies, and they shared the relief of laughter. Mrs. G was especially relieved to see some color come into Tatia's cheeks for the first time since she had stepped into the courtroom.

The ninety-minute break passed too quickly, but by the time Mrs. G told her to freshen up and get ready to return to the trial, Tatia was relaxed and had eaten about half her lunch. She had replied to all her friends and had received more messages of love and support, and Mrs. G was no longer worried about her. After both women visited the ladies room and checked their make-up, they held hands and said a quick prayer. Then, Tatia raised her head high and marched back to the witness stand.

CHAPTER 47
CROSS-EXAMINATION

"Well, Ms. Smith," said Mr. Pittman after the judge had gaveled court back into session, "you've spun quite a tale for us these last two days."

Tatia was still relaxed from lunch, so she simply sat with her hands folded in her lap, staring him in the eyes with a half smile on her face. He blinked first.

"Do you have nothing to say?"

"Oh, I'm sorry," she said. "I must have missed your question." She heard snickers from both the jury and the audience, but she managed to keep a straight face.

"Mr. Pittman," said Judge Wellman, "I hope you have a more interesting strategy than to bait the witness." He glared at the audience to quell the additional giggles his comment evoked.

Pittman nodded his head slightly, just enough to acknowledge that the judge had spoken, and turned his attention back to the witness. "Ms. Smith, the defense concedes that you have had a very difficult life, and we are extremely sympathetic. However, I hope you will not be offended if we skip the early years and begin with the time when Mr. Hall came into your life."

Tatia wasn't sure if it was because she was familiar with Pittman and his superficial shows of concern, or if he really sounded as sarcastic and uncaring as she thought he did. Either way, she didn't think he was making any points with the jury with his approach to her.

"Before we get into that, though, let me ask you something about your education. In school or at home, were you taught to be cautious of strangers and what to do if a stranger approached you?"

"Yes."

"What kind of things were you taught?"

"If a stranger approaches you, tell a trusted adult. Don't take anything from a stranger. Don't go anywhere with a stranger. Things like that."

"So, when Mr. Hall allegedly approached you, why didn't you tell someone?"

"He didn't really approach me at first. The first time I saw him, he just asked directions to a gas station. For two or three weeks after that, I would just see him driving by when I was walking home, and he would wave. I would have felt silly telling a teacher or the counselor that a guy waved at me."

"I can understand that," said Pittman. He was trying to sound more sympathetic at this point and was almost succeeding. "You said the first time you saw him when he wasn't in his car was outside the library. Right?"

"Yes."

"Why didn't you tell someone then?"

"He didn't seem like a stranger by then. He was always so polite and so non-threatening that it never occurred to tell anyone."

"So he was a nice guy, huh? Did it ever occur to you to change your route home?"

Tatia laughed. "Have you ever been to Springdale? There are only two main roads. There aren't any alternate routes."

Pittman laughed with her. "You've got a good point there. How about riding the bus? Weren't you supposed to be riding the bus anyway?"

"Yes, but facing the girls from school was more threatening to me than a seemingly harmless guy I didn't know that well."

"So you continued to walk the same route home from school every day and to encourage – one might even say entice – this nice, harmless young man into a relationship."

"No, I didn't do that."

"Did you tell him to stop coming to see you?"

"No, I didn't do that either."

"So, Ms. Smith, why did you continue to see Mr. Hall?"

"He was nice to me, and he was fun."

"Isn't it true that he bought you gifts?"

"Yes," she said defensively, thinking she may have said too much. Mrs. G had told her to only give details if they were asked for.

"What kind of gifts – jewelry, perfume, electronics?"

"Not at first. The first thing he gave me was a flower he picked out of the library lawn. I think it was a dandelion. Once he gave me a pink gel pen, and another time a pink T-shirt of my favorite band."

"How about a cell phone?"

"Just before school was out for the summer, he gave me a prepaid cell phone so we could keep in touch."

"So, why didn't he just call you on your home phone?"

"Josie didn't have a land line. All she had was a cell phone."

"And you didn't want him to call on her cell phone because..."

"Because she didn't know about Eric."

"So, you were deceiving the woman who gave you a home?"

"You make it sound so awful. It's just that she wouldn't have liked him."

"Why not?"

"Mainly because he was older."

"So, when you began to actually date, how did you manage to get out of the house?"

"I wouldn't call it dating. We just went for ice cream, or I would ride over to Cameron with him while he ran errands."

"And Josie approved of this?"

"No. She didn't know."

Pittman just raised one eyebrow and stared at her until she continued.

"I would tell her I was going to the mall with friends or to a birthday party or something like that."

"So, you not only kept things from your foster mother, but you also outright lied to her."

Tatia's lip began to quiver and she looked at Mrs. G for help. She simply nodded her head slightly and smiled encouragingly, and that was what Tatia needed to calm her enough to answer.

"Yes, I did."

"So you lied and deceived in order to carry on a relationship with this nice, harmless, fun, generous young man?"

"Objection. Asked and answered."

"Sustained."

"Once he allegedly began asking you to 'be nice' to his friends, why did you continue to see him? Did he kidnap you or chain you to the bed?'

"No, but he threatened to tell Josie what I had done. He said I'd end up in juvenile detention. Then, he said he'd be forced to go after Macy, one of my younger sisters."

"What about after you left Josie and went full time in your new profession? Did he lock you in your room or otherwise detain you?"

"No, but one time, I tried to stand up to him. I told him I wasn't going to do it anymore and that I was leaving. He threw me to the floor, pulled off his belt, and beat me so badly I couldn't work for several days. My back was full of welts, and I couldn't stand anything to touch it. I couldn't even lie on my back."

Pittman let her last statement hang in the silence that suddenly fell over the courtroom. When she realized what she had said, the color began rise from her neck into her face, and she hung her head in shame.

"Yes," drawled Pittman dryly. "I can see why that would be a problem for someone in your profession."

Tatia was wondering if she could slide from her chair and hide on the floor of the witness box when the silence was broken by a fit of coughing that sounded familiar to her. She raised her head just far enough to see the anger on Mrs. G's face and the determination in her eyes. She locked her gaze on Tatia and mouthed *NO CONDEMNATION* with such emphasis that she could almost hear it. Then, she pointed her finger at Tatia and lifted her own head high until Tatia mirrored her actions, straightening her posture and lifting her head off her chest. She slipped her hand into the pocket of her jacket, wrapping her fingers around her stone, and Mrs. G saw a spark of determination ignite in her girl's eyes. She almost laughed out loud in triumph when she heard Tatia's response.

"Yes, Mr. Pittman. I'm sure you understand. After all, you've worked for Mr. Hall longer than I did."

It took Judge Wellman at least five minutes to return order to the court.

CHAPTER 48
THE TRUTH

By the time the gallery was quiet enough to meet Wellman's standards, the defense attorney's face and neck had returned to his normal olive complexion. However, along with the angry flush, any pretense of the easy-going attitude he had put on before the commotion had faded away. Standing behind the defense table where he had retreated to gather what was left of his dignity, he asked a few final questions.

"You spent a great deal of time describing various injuries Ms. Landers suffered. Were you ever present when any of these injuries occurred?"

"No, Eric was always careful..."

Pittman interrupted her with a follow up. "So you cannot testify that Mr. Hall was responsible for any of these injuries."

"Not except for..."

"Were you with Ms. Hall the night she died?"

"No, not after I left for work."

"So you cannot testify that Mr. Hall was responsible for her injuries that night."

"No."

"Ms. Smith," he said, moving out from behind the shelter of the table and advancing slowly on the witness stand. "As I said at the beginning of our conversation this afternoon, you have spun quite a tale in this courtroom. In your own words, you lied to your foster mother on a number of occasions, you deceived her in order to sneak out and spend time with a nice, harmless young man you picked up on the street..."

Ms. Delaney jumped to her feet. "Objection, Your Honor. Counsel is badgering the witness."

Wellman sustained the objection, but Pittman would not be deterred.

"...you accepted many gifts from him – including a diamond necklace – before he allegedly forced you into a physical relationship and a life on the streets..."

"Objection!"

"Sustained!"

"...and you have been in and out of jail often enough..."

"Mr. Pittman..."

"Why should we believe a word you've said?"

"...one more word and I'll hold you in contempt!"

"My apologies, Your Honor," said Pittman in a tone that was anything but apologetic. "I withdraw the question. I'm finished with this witness." He spun on his heel and marched back to his chair.

"Don't push me, counselor," growled Judge Wellman.

"No, Your Honor," said Pittman with a look of total innocence on his face.

"Does the prosecution have further questions?"

"Yes, Your Honor."

The DA flipped through some papers in front of her to give her witness a few minutes to collect herself after Pittman's attack. When she saw Tatia's teeth unclench a little, she put on a relaxed smile and approached the witness box.

"Julie, you have already done a good job of explaining to the jury why you lied and deceived your foster mother. You've testified about how you came to 'a life on the streets,' as Mr. Pittman so eloquently phrased it. I don't think there is any reason to rehash any of that. I would, however, like to give you a chance to answer Mr. Pittman's question – why should we believe you today?"

Tatia relaxed, a genuine smile lit her face, and she began to speak in a quiet, calm voice. "That's easy, Ms. Delany. Before I stepped into this witness box, I put my hand on the Bible and promised God that I would tell the truth. That's what I did. I sat in front of a room full of strangers and told things that I have never told anyone but Mama G." She exchanged loving glances with her guardian before she continued. "I would never have shared those things if they were not true and if I didn't believe with all my heart that Eric Hall must pay for what he's done."

CHAPTER 49

THE DEFENSE RESTS

After Tatia's testimony, the prosecution rested, and court was adjourned for the day. After dinner that night, Tatia opted out of movie night with the rest of the girls. Instead, she talked to Jesse for a few minutes and then put on her walking shoes and took a few quick laps around the track. As she finished a mile, she noticed that Mrs. G was sitting in one of the rockers on the veranda, sipping a glass of iced tea.

"That looks good," she shouted from the track, slowing her pace.

"I brought an extra," answered Mrs. G, pointing to a second glass on the table beside her. "Join me?"

Tatia veered off the path and settled into the rocking chair on the other side of the little table. She took a big mouthful of the tea and let it trickle down her throat slowly before letting out a big sigh.

"Glad it's over?" asked Mrs. G.

"You have no idea!"

"I guess no one really could unless they had lived your life. I do know that I couldn't be prouder of you." She reached over and laid her hand on top of Tatia's. Realizing what she had just done, she drew her hand back slightly. "I'm sorry. Is this okay?"

Tatia smiled and turned her hand over and grasped Mrs. G's. "Yes. I know you love me, and I know you don't have any ulterior motives. It's nice."

They sat like that for a few minutes, and then Tatia broke the silence. "So what happens next?"

"Tomorrow Pittman will present his case. I can't imagine how he will defend everything Eric has done – probably with a string of his girls who will say how wonderful he is, what a liar you are, that he never forced you into anything, and that he never hurt anyone, especially Cindy."

"Do you think he will testify?"

"I wouldn't put him on the stand if I were his attorney. He can't sit through five minutes of testimony without rolling his eyes, scoffing under his breath, or sneering. I can't imagine how he could add anything positive, but I can imagine all kinds of damage he could do."

"Are you going?"

"Yes. Now that you've finished your testimony, you can sit in the courtroom with me if you want to."

"I'd really rather not. I'd like to spend a normal day at home. I owe the ministry some hours, and I'm behind on a couple of my study goals. I might even sit out here in the clean, fresh air and do some reading. Do you mind terribly?"

"Not at all. In fact, that's exactly what I'd recommend."

The next morning, Tatia had just finished drying her hair when there was a knock on her bedroom door. "Come in."

Mrs. G opened the door and stuck her head in. "I'm leaving. I was a little concerned when I didn't see you downstairs in the breakfast prep chaos, so I wanted to be sure you're okay before I leave."

Tatia shook her head and smiled. "You're not going to turn into a worry wart, are you, just because I called you Mama a couple of times?"

"No," Mrs. G said a little defensively. "It's just that you've had a pretty rough few days."

"I'm fine. Really. I just stayed in bed for a few extra minutes after I woke up. Guess I'd better get down there, though. I have lots of KP duty to make up."

"Don't worry about that. Everyone has been glad to cover for you."

"Yeah, we'll see. Let me slip on some shoes, and I'll walk you to the door."

They made it down the stairs without mentioning the trial even once. At the door, Tatia surprised Mrs. G with a brief hug.

"Drive carefully," said Tatia as Mrs. G walked down the sidewalk. "Mama G," Tatia called out as the older woman opened the car door. She stopped and looked up. "Thanks," said Tatia, blowing her a kiss.

She stood on the porch and waved until the car was out of sight around the curve of the driveway, and then she went into the kitchen and enjoyed breakfast with her sisters-in-love for the first time in much too long. After the food was gone and Tatia had satisfied everyone's curiosity about the trial, she ran them all out of the kitchen.

"Shoo! You have all covered for me the last few days. Now, go do whatever you need to do this morning while I pay my debts." The girls scattered without too much protest, and she was left with the remains of breakfast for ten to clean up. As she stacked the dishes and carried them to the sink, she began to hum, and soon, she was singing under her breath – *a big, big house with lots and lots of room, a big, big table with lots and lots of food.*

Once the kitchen was in order and lunch preparation was done, she gathered study material and found a comfortable spot on the veranda where she buried herself in literature, history, and government. Around noon, the noise inside broke her concentration, and she knew it was time for a lunch break. By the time she made it into the kitchen, the garden crew was streaming in to wash up and Felicia and Kensey were pulling out the meat, cheese, and vegetable trays as well as the bowl of fruit that Tatia had arranged earlier. She had already placed the plates, bread, and chips on the counter, so once the ice was in the glasses and the tea was poured, the sandwich buffet was ready.

The time around the table was another welcome chance to share stories and laughter, and Tatia began to leave the darkness she had revisited all week in the past as she settled back into what had become her new normal. Mr. G interrupted the relaxed mood when he announced that it was time for the outdoor gang to get back to mulching flower beds in preparation for the coming winter. One by one, the girls reluctantly rose from the table and carried their dishes to the sink before resuming their various chores and studies – all except Madison who shooed everyone out of the kitchen.

"My turn in the sink," she announced. When Tatia tried to protest, she scowled. "You, young lady, have a mound of work the bookkeeper piled up in your absence. Now, go git 'er done!"

"Yes, ma'am," giggled Tatia with a mock salute.

She spent the rest of the afternoon sorting papers, entering data, reconciling statements, and otherwise bringing order to the mess. She was so engrossed in her work that she was surprised when she heard the sound of the front door opening followed by the sound of Mrs. G's voice.

"Yoohoo! I'm home!"

Tatia filed the last few pieces of paper, shut down her computer, and hurried into the great room where Mrs. G sat, drinking a glass of iced tea. Her shoes were lying in a pile next to her tote bag and her feet were propped on an ottoman.

"Are your feet hurting?" Tatia asked.

"Yes. I should have known better than to wear those new shoes."

"Hey, let me rub your feet while you tell me what happened today." Without waiting for a response, she sat down on the ottoman and took Mrs. G's feet into her lap. As she began to manipulate the tense toes and tired insteps, Mrs. G closed her eyes and almost purred with pleasure.

"Where did you learn to do that?" she asked.

"Cindy taught me. She said if you could get a client to let you rub his feet first, and if he enjoyed it enough, he might forget what he was there for until his time was up. Then, he'd be too embarrassed to raise a fuss. Of course, that only worked once per client."

Mrs. G laughed until tears were running down her cheeks. "Thanks, Tatia. I needed that. Maybe one day you should consider writing about the lighter side of prostitution."

"Yeah. Well, that would be a really short book."

Tatia hands dropped into her lap, and the smile faded from Mrs. G's face. "You're probably right. I'm really glad you didn't go to court with me. If I didn't know better, I'd think Pittman was on the veranda last night listening to our conversation. Anyway, he finished his case today."

"Does the case go to the jury now?"

"Not yet. Monday Elizabeth and Pittman will give their closing arguments. Then it goes to the jury. If you're serious about studying law, you might want to go listen to that."

"Maybe. I'll have to think about it."

CHAPTER 50
NEW EVIDENCE

Saturday was laundry day for Tatia. Her regular day on the rotating schedule the girls had worked out was Wednesday, but she had missed it that week. Saturday was Stephanie's day, but she said Tatia could have her day as long as she could throw a little bit of underwear in. Tatia usually enjoyed doing her laundry, but this time, she couldn't stop thinking about the trial and whether to go hear the closing arguments on Monday.

Absently, she folded, hung, pressed, and put away clothes. Her last task was to replace the freshly laundered sheets on her bed. She decided to add a little bit of cover since the nights were getting a little chilly. She opened the trunk at the foot of her bed and was picking up a pale blue thermal blanket when her eyes fell on a box next to the linens. At first, she was puzzled – then she remembered.

A couple of months after Cindy died, the police had released the apartment, and Tatia and Mrs. G had gone over to retrieve any of her things that might be left. As Tatia had suspected, all her personal electronics, along with the television and extensive sound system, were gone. In addition, Eric had apparently taken out his rage on inanimate items as well as on Cindy, and most of the pictures, mirrors, and other decorative items were smashed.

In Tatia's room, the drawers and closets had been emptied onto the bed or the floor and the contents picked through. Even her books had been pulled off the shelf and flung around the room as if someone thought she was hiding a secret stash of money in the pages. She picked up a paperback that looked to be intact, but when she flipped it open, she saw that about half the pages had been torn out of the center of the book.

"At least my e-books will still be in the cloud when I get my new tablet."

"Sure," said Mrs. G. "All of this can be replaced. In fact, most of it already has been. Why don't we just concentrate on any keepsakes you want to take with you. We have a volunteer crew that has dealt with this kind of thing before. They'll come in, pack up everything that can be donated, and throw away everything else."

At the mention of keepsakes, Tatia ran to the closet and felt around on the shelf until her hand touched the box. "I think it's still there, but it's been pushed back, and I can't reach it."

"What is it? Maybe I can reach it."

By stretching and jumping a little, Mrs. G was able to catch hold of the camp memory box. She held it out to Tatia and asked, "Is this what you were looking for?"

"Yes," replied Tatia tearfully, hugging the box to her chest. "Thank you."

She made a cursory search of the debris that had been her life and shrugged. "I don't see anything else I need. Let's look in Cindy's room before we go."

Mrs. G followed behind her as she picked her way through the mess in the living area and on to the bedroom on the other side of the small apartment. The mess there was even worse, but she suspected that messiness was the natural state of the room. Tatia walked around, touching an item here and there, picking up others and putting them back down. She picked up a frame that was lying face down on the night stand. Mrs. G could see that it was a picture of Tatia and a large, dark-haired girl with laughing hazel eyes.

"Oh, Cindy," sobbed Tatia as she brushed the remaining shards of glass onto the floor. She turned to Mrs. G and asked, "Do you think we can find a piece of glass for this?"

"Absolutely! Even if we have to have it custom cut. I see what looks like some empty boxes in the corner of the closet. Let's put anything you want to take in one of them."

Tatia laughed through her tears, "I'm sure there are several in there. Cindy never threw anything away."

While Mrs. G found a box that would work, Tatia wandered into the bathroom. All the cabinets and drawers stood open and the contents were in piles on the counter and the floor. She knelt on the floor in front of the empty cabinet under the sink and began pressing different spots on the floor. Mrs. G walked in a watched for a minute or two.

"What are you looking for?"

Without looking up, Tatia answered. "Cindy once showed me a hole she made here so she could hide her stash from Eric. I'm trying to remember how she opened it. Just curious if she left anything important in there."

Just then, the corner of a board popped up about half an inch.

"That must be the spot," she said as she caught hold of the rough edge and lifted the top off Cindy's hiding place.

"How did she do that?" asked Mrs. G.

"I don't know exactly. The last year or so, her relationship with Eric got more hostile, and it seemed like her main mission in life was to defy him. The more he tried to make her stop doing drugs, the more determined she was to take everything she could get her hands on. See," she said, piling a small pharmacy on the floor.

"Hmmm," said Mrs. G. "I'd better see if I can find a plastic bag for all of that. We'll stop by the police station on our way out and let them dispose of it."

While she was gone, Tatia felt around in the hole and pulled out a few more items – a small photo album, a stack of greeting cards, and a spiral notebook. Tatia put them in the box Mrs. G had left on the bed along with the few things she had collected. Finally, she grabbed a faded sweatshirt that still smelled like Cindy and stuffed it into the box before closing it.

Four months later, the box still had not been opened. With her Saturday to-do list finished, Tatia decided the time had come. She settled down in the middle of her bed with the box in front of her and opened the lid. The faint scent of Cindy's favorite bath and beauty products drifted up from the sweatshirt, and Tatia slipped it on over her T-shirt. Next, she found the framed picture and laid it on the bed where she could see it.

She wanted to look at the photo album next, but the cards were on top of it. She picked up the stack and heard the faint tinkle of metal as if something had fallen out of one of the envelopes. Curious, she removed the other items from the box. She saw a flash of silver and pulled out the heart-shaped locket she hadn't seen since her twelfth birthday. She remembered that night, after her first client had left, she sat in the plastic chair and removed the necklace that, a few hours before, had seemed so special. She had placed it back in the velvet box and dropped it, along with the card Eric had given her, into the trash can. Cindy must have retrieved it when she came back into the room to get her blue nightie.

Tatia flipped through the stack to see if Cindy had saved the card, too. She had. Cindy never threw anything away. She wondered what she had done with the velvet box. She slipped the necklace into the envelope with the card and set it aside before picking up the photo album. She flipped through it quickly, but most of the pictures were of Cindy and Eric when she was younger and slimmer. There was a joy in her eyes and a softness in his that she had never seen. She put it aside, too.

Finally, she picked up the journal and sat back against the headboard to read the thoughts Cindy had saved. She hadn't known her best friend and roommate kept a journal, so she looked forward to learning what lay behind the sassy, sarcastic front she put on. She was disappointed that only a few pages had been used. The journal began several months before Tatia came into her life, but there were long periods of time between entries.

Cindy's first few attempts were on a par with a pre-teen who started every entry with *Dear Diary*, but she seemed to find her voice quickly. She wrote of her sadness at the growing distance between her and Eric and at her part in a business that exploited young, vulnerable girls.

In one of the later entries, she mentioned her growing affection for her new roommate who she referred to as "Little sis." After reading this, Tatia had to grab a box of tissues from the bathroom.

When she returned to the bed, she flipped over to the next entry which was also the last. Her mouth fell open when she read what was written there. She re-read the brief account several times. Then, she grabbed the envelope with the card and locket along with the journal and ran downstairs to find Mrs. G.

CHAPTER 51
THE VERDICT IS IN

Monday morning, Tatia and Mrs. G were once again on the road to Cameron. Even though they had discussed the situation endlessly since Saturday, Tatia wanted to go over it again.

"So, after the closing arguments by both sides, the case will go to the jury. Right?" she asked.

"Right," answered Mrs. G who was ready to answer the same questions as often as necessary to put Tatia at ease.

"Tell me again why Ms. Delaney isn't going to ask the judge to let me testify about what we found before she makes her closing argument."

"I scanned and emailed copies of the card and the journal to her. After reading them, she decided to save them. Introducing the new evidence at trial might give the defense grounds for immediate appeal and reversal. She's confident that we'll get a conviction on all three counts with what we've already presented. Evidence that wouldn't be allowed in the guilt-innocence phase can be presented during punishment, and she thinks this new information will be a great help in getting a more severe sentence."

"And that comes after the jury reaches a verdict?"

"Yes. It will be like a continuation of the trial. The jury was qualified on the punishment phase in the beginning, so we can just move ahead with no break."

"And I'll testify then."

"Well, either that or give a victim impact statement. That's the same as testifying except that Elizabeth won't ask you questions. We'll decide that when we meet with her later today."

Tatia was quiet for a while, lost in her thoughts about the legal system. As they entered the city limits of Cameron and approached the courthouse, she finally spoke.

"I have another question – if that's okay," she said, cutting her eyes over at Mrs. G.

"I will answer your questions all day, any day. I love it when you girls are eager to learn."

"Okay. Eric is charged with two first-degree felonies, each with a possibility of five to ninety-nine years, and one second degree felony with a possibility of two to twenty years. Right?"

"That's correct."

"If they find him guilty of all three and, just to make it easy, gets twenty years on each count, how would that work?"

"Good question! He could be sentenced to serve the three terms consecutively for a total of sixty years, or they might be served concurrently for a total of twenty years."

"How about parole?"

Mrs. G laughed. "Either you've been studying up, or you've been watching a lot of Court TV. He will be eligible for parole – the general rule is after he has served half his time. It could be sooner than that if he accumulates what's called 'good time' for being a model prisoner."

Tatia mulled over what she had heard before she spoke again.

"When I become a lawyer, I want to be a prosecutor like Ms. Delaney. I want to make sure people who do the things Eric has done don't get away with a ridiculous sentence like five years."

Mrs. G smiled. "I think you'll be an excellent prosecutor. I don't think I'd want to go up against you in a trial."

Tatia was still smiling when she walked into the courtroom. Now that her part in the proceedings was over, her curiosity was piqued, and she was a little excited about seeing what went on when she wasn't the center of attention. She was also curious to hear the DA review the evidence that was given by other witnesses and to learn how Mr. Pittman would try to defend what Eric did.

Mrs. G had been worried that Tatia might be upset by hearing the recitation of her history, but she was so absorbed by the process that she didn't seem to be personally affected. The only time she reacted was when Ms. Delaney talked about Tatia's medical history during the period of time when she was with Eric. She turned to Mrs. G with an incredulous look on her face.

"She showed them my x-rays?" she whispered.

Mrs. G patted her knee while continuing to stare straight ahead. "It's okay. You have cute bones."

Tatia snickered loudly enough that several people, including Eric, looked back to see who thought a murder trial was a laughing matter. By biting her cheek, Mrs. G managed to keep a straight face while Tatia struggled to control her giggles. When she finally looked up, she realized Eric was still staring at her – leering was more like it – and when he caught her eye, he winked before turning back around.

Tatia ignored the chill she felt under his gaze as she tuned back in to what was going on in the well where Ms. Delaney was addressing the jury, appealing to those who were parents or grandparents of girls Tatia's age. Tatia thought she saw several jurors fighting tears, and others were glaring at Eric. She was glad Delaney was on her side.

When it was Mr. Pittman's turn to speak, Tatia was equally glad he was no longer her attorney. His superior attitude seemed offensive to Tatia, and his arguments seemed weak. He reminded the jurors of the string of witnesses who extolled the virtues of the defendant and impugned the character of the prosecution's star witness. He reiterated that there were no eye witnesses to any of the crimes with which Eric had been charged. He closed with an appeal for mercy for his client, but based on the looks on the jurors' faces, she didn't think they bought it.

After Judge Wellman instructed the jury and released them to their deliberations, Tatia and Mrs. G ran the gauntlet of cameras and microphones to escape the courthouse. They were just getting settled at their favorite table with their favorite tea when Elizabeth Delaney joined them for an early lunch and a planning session.

The first big decision to be made was what to eat – should they have the brunch quiche or fight the slight chill in the air with a bowl of creamy baked potato soup? It ended in a split decision with Elizabeth ordering the quiche and the other two going for the soup. They did, however, come to an agreement on the salad. The kitchen had not yet run out of the strawberry gelatin salad with the pretzel crust, so that's what they all ordered.

Although they avoided talking about the trial itself, the mealtime conversation was lively with talk of Tatia's ambitions to study law and advice from the two experienced attorneys about what she should study and where. By the time they agreed to share a bowl of peach cobbler with vanilla ice cream, the young woman's future was laid out in a way that had her head spinning with the possibilities. Then, reality intruded.

"You're Julie, aren't you?" asked an older woman who had been sitting at the next table. "You're that girl that's testifying in that trial. I'm sorry to interrupt, but I just wanted to tell you how much I admire you for your courage. I have a granddaughter who is five years old, and people like you are making Cameron a safer place for her to grow up. Thank you so much."

Tatia was too shocked to respond, but Mrs. G spoke up. "We're very proud of her, too. Thank you for your kind words."

Even though the woman's words were kind, and the waitress let them know she had paid for their lunch, the intrusion had spoiled the mood.

"I guess it's time to get back to the office and plan our strategy for the punishment phase," said Elizabeth. "Who knows? We might just get a quick verdict."

That didn't happen, though. Elizabeth and Deborah discussed strategies with input from Tatia now and then. By five o'clock, it had been decided that the DA would ask questions to guide the testimony and Tatia would make a short statement at the end. As Tatia's eyes began to droop, Deborah brought the meeting to a close.

"Elizabeth, if you're comfortable with what we've laid out, I'm going to take our star witness home. If anything happens tonight, you can text me."

They were halfway home when Mrs. G's phone announced the arrival of a text. "Tatia, why don't you read that out loud. Maybe it's good news."

"It's from Ms. Delaney. *Verdict is in. Guilty on all counts. See you in court at 9:00 am!*"

CHAPTER 52

CINDY SPEAKS

Tatia felt both nervous and excited as she and Mrs. G neared the courthouse the next morning. While she was anxious about her testimony, she was confident that Ms. Delaney would lead her through what she needed to say, and she couldn't imagine any questions Mr. Pittman could ask her that would be any more difficult than those she had already answered. Most of the butterflies she felt were caused by the anticipation of seeing the proceedings from the beginning.

She and Mrs. G sat in the row behind the bar that separated the spectators from the participants. They took the first two seats so Tatia wouldn't have to crawl over anyone when she was called to the stand. Even though she had stood in this same courtroom several times, she was amazed at what she had missed as she focused on her problems. This time, though, she was so busy asking questions about every detail of the courtroom and the people who were already in their places that she was not even aware when Eric walked down the aisle and took his place between Mr. Pittman and his assistant. She wasn't aware of the slight shuffle in his step and the lack of confidence in his posture, and she also missed the glare he shot her way.

When the opening ritual was finished, Tatia scooted forward a little in her seat, not wanting to miss a word or a gesture. She listened intently as the DA gave a brief outline of the part of the trial they were entering. She hit the highlights of the evidence that had brought them this far, and then she made the statement that made everyone, especially Mr. Pittman, sit up, lean forward, and pay closer attention.

"Ladies and gentlemen of the jury, today you will hear new evidence that surfaced too late to be included in the guilt-innocence phase. Mr. Pittman will object, saying our new evidence is inadmissible; however, I'm sure he will be reminded that any information about the defendant is admissible when considering punishment.

"He will attempt to justify his client's behavior by saying that Mr. Hall didn't know Ms. Smith was so young. We will show you evidence from Mr. Hall's own hand that this is a lie.

"Mr. Pittman will claim there is no evidence to show that force was involved in the relationship between Mr. Hall and Ms. Smith. He will claim that she chose the sordid life she has lived for the last three years. But you will hear evidence from Ms. Landers herself that he compelled by threat and by force not only Ms. Smith but also a host of other young women into a life of prostitution.

"He will plead for a lighter sentence because he beat Ms. Landers in the heat of passion. Again, you will hear evidence from Ms. Landers that, if not actively planned, her death was not a spur-of-the-moment event.

"Finally, you will hear a statement from Ms. Smith outlining how the actions of Mr. Hall have impacted her life and will continue to impact her life for years to come – if not forever."

Delaney wrapped up her opening statement with a few points about the parameters of deciding punishments for multiple crimes, but Tatia was too busy going over her statement in her mind to pay much attention. She perked her ears and listened for a few minutes when Pittman began to speak, but she could tell right away that his opening was a recap of what he said in his closing the day before. She sank back into her thoughts and was surprised when she heard her name and felt Mrs. G's hand on her arm.

"It's time, Tatia. Go tell them what's on your heart."

Tatia turned and gave her a smile full of more bravado than she felt. Then she stood and walked toward the witness box.

"Ms. Smith," said Judge Wellman as she stepped up to take her seat, "you do understand that you are still under oath."

"Yes, Your Honor."

She sat and smiled at the jury, looking each one in the eye as Ms. Delaney had told her to do. Most of them smiled back, except for a stone-faced man in the back row and a woman in the front who looked as if she had already been crying. Tatia made a mental note not to look at her while she was testifying.

Ms. Delaney approached the witness box and, standing just close enough to create a visual bond between herself and Tatia, she turned so the jury could see both of their faces. "Julie, I mentioned in my opening that we have some new information to share with the jury. You're the one who found that information. Isn't that right?"

"Yes, ma'am."

"Would you tell the jury what you found and how you came across it?"

For the next few minutes, Tatia explained why she and Mrs. G had visited her old apartment and what they did there. When she began to talk about Cindy's hiding place, Ms. Delaney interrupted her for a moment.

"Julie, why did you want to look in that hiding place? What did you expect to find there?

"Oh," said Tatia, choosing her words, "I guess I was curious – you know – to see if whoever had made such a mess had found any drugs Cindy might have left."

"And what did you find?"

"Nobody, including the police I guess, had found it, because it was still intact and there was a stash of stuff in there."

"What kind of stuff?"

"There was some marijuana, some uppers, and some downers."

"What did you do with all those controlled substances?"

"I gave them to Mrs. G, and we dropped them by the police station when we left the apartment."

"Did you find anything else?"

After Tatia described what she had found and the box she used to pack everything, Delaney wrinkled her eyebrows in thought and asked a follow up question.

"So, if you found these items at the end of August, why are we just now hearing about them?"

Tatia explained how she put the box away and only came across it on Saturday. She described what was in the photo album, and then Delaney asked about the cards.

"Well, I don't know if I mentioned it, but Cindy hated to throw anything away. The night of my twelfth birthday, after..." At this point, Tatia paused and took a deep, shaky breath before going on. "After what happened, I took off the necklace and threw it away, along with the birthday card Eric had given me. When I was taking things out of the box, the necklace fell out of the stack. Cindy had apparently fished it out of the trash and dropped it and the card back into the envelope."

Ms. Delaney walked over to the prosecutors' table and picked up an envelope. She handed copies of the envelope and its contents to Mr. Pittman and another set to the bailiff. The bailiff passed his set to the Judge who looked at it curiously and then turned his attention back to the DA. Pittman scowled at his copies for a few minutes and then began a whispered conference with his client while Delaney passed the original envelope to the witness.

"Julie, take a look at this and tell me if you recognize this envelope."

"Yes, ma'am. It's the birthday card he gave me."

"How do you know that?"

"I recognize his writing, and it has the heart he drew with our initials in it."

The DA turned to the Judge and said, "Your Honor, we have marked this envelope and its contents as State's Exhibit H and offer it into evidence."

Judge Wellman looked at the defense table to see if there was an objection. Pittman glanced up from his conference long enough to say, "We object, Your Honor, based on relevance."

"Your Honor," responded Delaney, "this exhibit will speak to the defendant's claim that he didn't know how old the victim was at the time of the rape."

Before the Judge could respond, Pittman was on his feet. "We also object, Your Honor, based on authenticity."

The Judge looked at him with his signature raised eyebrow and spoke dryly. "Do you have any more objections, or is it okay with you if I respond now?"

"Sorry, Your Honor."

"Ms. Delaney, if you can provide proper proof of authenticity, I am prepared to allow the testimony with the understanding that you will show relevance."

"Thank you, Your Honor," she said as she hurriedly took three sheets of paper from her assistant and distributed them. "This is a report from John Weatherly, a recognized expert in handwriting analysis. He compared the handwriting on Exhibit H with Mr. Hall's handwriting on the pre-trial paperwork, and in his opinion, there is no doubt that Mr. Hall wrote the inscription inside the card. We have marked his report as Exhibit G and offer it into evidence. May I also add that Mr. Weatherly is available to testify with about thirty-minutes notice if necessary."

"I don't believe that will be necessary," said Judge Wellman, looking pointedly at Pittman. "Unless, of course, the defense objects."

Pittman accepted his defeat, but not gracefully. "No objection," he groused, immediately returning to his conversation with his client.

"Exhibits are provisionally accepted into evidence. Proceed."

"Thank you, your Honor. Julie, would you please remove the

card and read the inscription written at the bottom?"

Tatia had been so interested in watching the process going on around her, that she had almost forgotten what came next. She looked blankly at Ms. Delaney for a moment. Then, she cleared her throat and leaned toward the microphone before she began to read.

Dear [Julie], I have waited for this night from the moment I first saw you. Happy, happy birthday to the most beautiful 12-year-old I know. Love, Eric

"Thank you. Is there a date?"

Tatia looked back at the card. "Yes, ma'am. At the top he wrote *June 30, 2013*."

Delaney turned expectantly toward the Judge. He, in turn, instructed the clerk. "Mark both exhibits as evidence."

She struggled to keep her broad smile from turning into a gloating sneer as she turned back toward the counsel tables. The assistant DA was ready with Cindy's notebook and the requisite copies. The DA did the legal dance that was necessary before she could present the next portion of Tatia's story. After the Judge had completed the last steps, Delaney handed the notebook to Tatia. She led her through a recap of where she found it, and then she moved on to what was written in it.

"You'll notice two colored tabs along the right edge. Would you please open to the first one and read the date at the top of the page?"

"June 30, 2013."

"Can you remind the jury of the significance of that date?"

Tatia looked toward the jury and noticed the man in the back row. His face still looked as if it had been carved from stone, but the flush that had crept up his neck and into his ears betrayed the emotion behind it. The lady in front used a rumpled tissue to dab at her already red eyes. Tatia watched the panel as she answered.

"It was my twelfth birthday."

"Continue reading what Cindy wrote about that day."

It seemed to Tatia as if most of the jury sat up straighter and leaned forward slightly, a sign of focus and a desire to hear what Cindy had to tell them from the grave. Tatia began to read.

Well, Eric broke in a new one tonight – a 12-year-old for crying out loud! This may be the youngest and the prettiest one yet. She has big blue eyes, blonde hair, and so innocent! If Eric could just keep his pants zipped, he could have charged big bucks for the first time with her. Of course, I had to clean up the mess afterward. I almost lost it when she looked at me with those big eyes and asked what she was supposed to do when her first client got there. I hate being part of forcing another kid into this life, but what's a girl to do? Even if I could leave, which I can't without him killing me or making me wish I was dead, where would I go? I got nobody and I got no skills except this one. Poor kid. I didn't have the heart to tell her that it's all downhill from here.

Tatia raised her eyes from the page. "That's the end of that day." She was aware of movement in the jury box, and she glanced over to see the teary woman passing a tissue to the woman next to her. She turned her attention back to Delaney. "Do you want me to go on?"

"No, that's perfect right there. Now, turn to the next marked section and read the date."

"June 30, 2016. That was my fifteenth birthday. It was also the day Cindy died. Do you want me to read this one, too?"

"Yes, please."

Eric was so mad when he called on the phone – not mad like usual like he'll slap me around a little and then get over it kind of mad but like I'm really scared this time. I don't know how I missed the date on that gun show but it's too late now. When he found out I had to book all the girls in the same place, I thought he was gonna tear the place apart and me with it. Before he took off he whispered right in my ear and said I'd better pray that things don't go bad, because if they do, it will be the last mistake I ever make. Now things have gone really bad. He's on his way, and I'm praying. I think he means it this time.

Tatia swallowed hard against the wave of emotion that rose into her throat while she read Cindy's last entry in her journal. She carefully avoided looking at the jury, knowing the ladies on the front row would draw her into their tears if she caught a glimpse of them. Delaney saw her distress, so she handed the journal to the bailiff to be marked into evidence and slowly returned to the counsel table. After she checked her notes, she turned, leaned casually against the table, and smiled at Tatia. Tatia smiled back, grateful for the extra time to compose herself.

"Thank you for your testimony, Julie. That's all the questions I have for now, but I believe you have a statement you want to read to the jury." With that, Ms. Delaney took her seat behind the table.

"Yes, ma'am," she said, a little breathlessly. "You and Mrs. G told me that..."

Judge Wellman interrupted, "Ms. Smith, can you speak up a bit please."

Tatia looked up at him nervously. "Yes, Your Honor. Sorry." She leaned forward and spoke strongly into the microphone. "Ms. Delaney and Mrs. G told me that I had the right to make a statement outlining how my life has been affected by what Eric Hall did to me." She glanced down at the sheet of notes she had taken from the pocket of her jacket, but she had gone over what she wanted to say so many times in her mind, that she didn't look at it again.

"It's hard to put into words how much he has taken from me. First, he robbed me of my innocence. He took my virginity when I didn't really know what that meant.

"I've had nightmares most of my life, but they're worse now. I rarely sleep more than a few hours before I wake up screaming, crying, or hyperventilating.

"I've never been a touchy-feely person, but now I don't like to be touched by anyone or even be really close to anyone, especially men." She looked at Mrs. G and smiled. "Of course, I'm comfortable with Mrs. Grochowsky, but I'm still a little uneasy around Mr. G.

"Physically, I have a number of scars, mostly on my back. When he beat us, he was careful to do it where the marks didn't show much. He dislocated my shoulder a couple of times, and I still have limited range of motion. My physical therapist says I'm improving slowly, but she says it will probably never be completely normal. The good thing is that I can now predict the weather because it aches when the weather changes."

Her last comment was met with some quiet chuckles as some in the gallery enjoyed a moment of comic relief. The respite didn't last long, though.

"The worst thing Eric did was to take Cindy away from me. She was like a big sister. She protected me when she could and comforted me when she couldn't. She taught me skills on the computer that I'm now using in my work in Mrs. G's ministry center. She was my best friend, and now she's gone."

Tatia's chin trembled a bit as she talked about Cindy. She looked down briefly while she composed herself before going on.

"My mother took me to church when I was little, but no one else had taken me until I went to live with Mr. and Mrs. G. We go every Sunday and most Wednesday nights, and we have Bible studies every night. I have become a follower of Jesus, and I know that I have been forgiven for the things I've done. I also know that Jesus taught that we must forgive those who hurt us. I'm not quite there yet, but I'm working on it. Even if I reach the point where I can forgive

Eric Hall, though, that doesn't mean that he does not have to suffer the consequences of his actions. All it means is that I accept that it is not my job to administer those consequences."

At this point, Tatia turned and looked at the jury, once again making eye contact with each one. Tears were streaming down her face, but her voice remained steady. "That's your job. That's why I'm asking you, when you retire to consider what sentence to give Eric Hall, that you make the punishment fit not only the crimes themselves but also the lasting impact they have had on my life and on many others who are not here today to speak for themselves,."

CHAPTER 53

TATIA'S TATTOO

When Tatia finished her statement, there was dead silence in the courtroom until Judge Wellman cleared his throat gruffly and looked at his watch. "Court is recessed for lunch. Be back at 1:15." He banged his gavel and was out of the courtroom before the bailiff could give the *all rise* order.

Tatia stepped down from the stand, and Ms. Delaney met her in the middle of the well. She was congratulating her witness on how well she had done when Mrs. G appeared and threw her arms around Tatia.

"I am so proud of you!" she exclaimed.

Tatia willingly accepted her hug, leaning in as if to draw strength from her. "Was my statement okay?"

"Sweetheart, it was perfect. I'm glad you insisted on writing it by yourself with no input from me or Elizabeth."

"Thanks. I just hope I can make it through the cross-examination. Mr. Pittman was making a lot of notes while I was up there."

Elizabeth excused herself, saying she needed to go over her closing arguments during the break. The reporters, most of whom had faced Mrs. G's wrath at least once during the trial, were busy filing stories based on Tatia's testimony and statement, so their stroll to the tea room was unhindered except for a few people who wanted to offer congratulations. The lunch recess passed quickly, and shortly after the judge returned to the bench, Tatia was back on the stand facing Joseph Pittman.

He had apparently decided against attacking the birthday card and journal the prosecution had presented. Instead, he went straight to Tatia's victim impact statement.

"Ms. Smith, in your statement you laid the responsibility for your nightmares and your relationship difficulties at the feet of Mr. Hall. Is that correct?"

"Yes, sir."

"In your earlier testimonies – the part where you discussed possible reasons why you stayed in the foster system rather than being adopted – you described yourself as..." He stopped to refer to his notes. "Ah. Here it is. You described yourself as 'an emotionally unavailable little girl.' You said that you rarely made eye contact and that you resisted efforts to get close to you. You also said that you had frequent night terrors and recurring nightmares. Is that correct?"

"Yes, sir," she said. She sensed where he was going, and she looked at Mrs. G with a trace of fear in her eyes. Mrs. G gave her a big smile and a thumbs up.

"So, would it be fair to say that your relationship and sleep difficulties began before you ever met Mr. Hall?"

"I guess so, but..."

"How did you sleep last night?"

"What?" she said, looking confused.

"Did you wake up screaming during the night?"

"No."

"So, is it possible that your sleep difficulties are getting better?"

"Well, I..."

"And you said you are able to accept physical affection from Mrs. G, didn't you?

"Yes."

"So, your relationship problems don't seem to be permanent either." He hurried on before Tatia had a chance to respond. "In your statement..."

"Your Honor," interrupted the DA. "If Mr. Pittman is going to ask questions and answer them himself, perhaps we should let Ms. Smith return to her seat and let him take the stand."

"Ms. Delaney, I know the rules are a bit more relaxed in the punishment phase, but we are still in a court of law. In the future, if you have an objection, state it in the prescribed manner." He continued before she had a chance to respond. "In this case, however, I tend to agree. Mr. Pittman, if you have a question, allow time for the witness to answer. If not, save your theatrics for closing arguments."

"Yes, Your Honor," responded both attorneys.

"Ms. Smith," continued Pittman, "in your statement you mentioned your shoulder pain, and I believe you stated that your therapist said you are improving. Is that correct?"

"Yes, slowly."

"Slowly, yes. Did your therapist say that you would never be completely well?"

"Not exactly. No."

"So there is the possibility that a resilient, healthy young woman like you might soon have a completely normal shoulder. Correct?"

"I suppose it's possible." With each answer, her confident posture slipped a little further, and her voice became softer until it was barely above a whisper.

"Ms. Smith," said the Judge, "you need to speak up so the jury and the court reporter can hear you."

Without looking up, she leaned toward the microphone and repeated herself at a slightly higher volume.

"Regarding your friend Cindy," continued Pittman, "I am very sorry for your loss. This isn't the first time you've dealt with this kind of loss, is it?"

"No."

"And do you feel those losses as acutely as you did when they first happened? I don't mean that you've forgotten your parents or that you don't still miss them but rather that it's not a constant pain that is with you every minute of every day."

"If you put it that way, I guess I'd have to say no." Guilty tears began to trickle down her cheeks.

"You closed your statement with a plea that," he looked down at his notes, "'the punishment fit not only the crimes themselves but also the lasting impact they have had on my life.' You just testified that you sometimes sleep through the night and that you have a close relationship with Mrs. Grochowsky. You also said your physical therapist says you are improving and might possibly regain full use of your shoulder."

Mrs. G watched Tatia who had sunk so low in her chair that she was barely visible to the gallery. The mama bear in her was enraged as she saw her cub threatened. She knew she had to control herself, but inside, she was praying as hard as she could and shouting at her daughter-to-be to sit up straight and to stand her ground. As if she could hear the thoughts coming her way, Tatia angrily swiped at the tears on her face and lifted her head. Mrs. G could see the muscles in her jaw tensing as she ground her teeth together.

"No!" she said, too quietly to be heard.

Pittman was so taken with his own rhetoric that he didn't notice the change in the witness he was trying to discredit, so he charged ahead with his prepared argument. "You also agreed that time can heal the loss of a loved one, even the loss of one's parents."

"No!" she said loudly enough that he could hear her.

He glanced at her in surprise, his rhythm momentarily broken, but he recovered quickly and continued. "With all this in mind, wouldn't you agree that some compassion, some leniency, is in order in setting the punishment for Mr. Hall?"

"No!" said Tatia strongly and directly into the microphone.

Pittman had been playing to the jury, so her outburst startled him. Before he could rein in his reaction, he did a double-take and said, "What?"

She stared him straight in the eye and spoke slowly and carefully. "I said no! I don't agree. His actions have had lasting effects."

As she spoke, she took hold of her right cuff with her left hand and began to roll up her sleeve. As Mrs. G saw what she was doing, she gasped and clinched her fists so tightly that her nails bit into her palms.

"Don't tell me the impact on Cindy wasn't lasting," continued Tatia, gathering momentum and volume with every word. "I have permanent scars, emotional and physical scars that will never go away. And I have this!"

She thrust her tattooed arm, now bare to the elbow, toward Pittman like a weapon. She heard several gasps from the jury, and the teary woman burst into uncontrollable sobs. Before the attorney could find his voice, the stone-faced juror blurted out, "By golly, that looks like a bar code!"

Tatia turned slowly toward him. "Yes, it's a bar code like you see on a piece of meat you buy in the grocery store. He marked me like the piece of meat he turned me into!" She turned back to Pittman, piercing him with a look that caused him to take a step back. "He marked all of us like so much merchandise!"

Finally, she turned her wrath on the defendant. "No, I don't agree that Eric Hall deserves compassion or leniency!"

CHAPTER 54

THE SENTENCE

Tatia smiled at the still-blank screen on her computer, as she remembered the chaos her flare-up had caused. Pittman immediately tried to dismiss her from the witness stand while Delaney screamed above the noise that she had questions on redirect. Judge Wellman banged his gavel and threatened to clear the courtroom as the jury and the spectators reacted with every emotion humanly possible and reporters scrambled out into the hall to film on-the-scene reports. Tatia further agitated the pandemonium by holding her arm toward the gallery so photographers with telephoto lenses could get a good shot, and Mrs. G stood and applauded the entire incident.

When Wellman began threatening to hold the entire population of the room in contempt, peace was finally restored, and Ms. Delaney approached the stand.

"Julie, that was a very brave thing you did."

Tatia didn't seem quite sure whether to feel regret or pride, but she managed a smile and a polite "Thank you."

"I know I promised you we wouldn't talk about your tattoo, but now that you've broached the subject, may I ask a few questions about it?"

"Sure."

"Thank you. As we all can see, that tattoo looks like a bar code. Does it work like a bar code in the store? What I mean is, can it be scanned?"

"No, but it can be used for identification. Eric put them on all his girls – a lot of pimps do." It was the first time she had used the word in court, and she saw several people in the gallery wince. "The first few numbers identify us as Eric's girls, and the last few are individual identifiers."

"I'm still not sure I understand. How are the numbers used?"

"First of all, in his accounting system, he used the numbers instead of the names in an attempt to mask what was really going on. Second, if a girl ended up out of her regular area – like if she ran away or something and another pimp found her – there's a website on the dark web where he could use the numbers to track back to where she belonged. Out of 'professional courtesy,' her pimp would be called and asked what should be done with her."

"Were any of Eric's girls ever tracked like that?"

"Once, a couple of years before I was recruited."

"What happened?"

"I don't know exactly. Cindy said all she knew was that no one ever saw or heard from her again."

After that, the prosecution rested their case, and the defense decided there was nothing a hundred witnesses could do to undo what the jury had seen and heard. The closing arguments were virtual re-runs of the ones given in the guilt-innocence phase, and Tatia was so exhausted after her ordeal that she almost dozed off.

Once the jury had retired to decide the fate of Eric Hall, Tatia trailed behind Mrs. G in almost as much of a daze as she had the first time she had followed her out of the courthouse. She was oblivious to the lights and microphones that were shoved at her as she clung to Mrs. G's arm and buried her face against the older woman's shoulder like a toddler clinging to her mother's skirts. She shut out all the questions and comments and focused only on the comforting refrain of "No comment" in the one voice she completely trusted. She felt protected by the air of power that seemed to surround her guardian. Then, she felt an invasion – someone was pressing close on her unprotected side and hissing directly into her ear.

"You think you've won, but this isn't over."

Tatia jerked her head up and swiveled it around just in time to see a man who looked like Eric disappear into the crowd. Mrs. G felt her sudden movements and hesitated just long enough to ask Tatia if she was okay.

"Fine," she said, not sure that her tired brain hadn't manufactured the entire incident. Still, the encounter disturbed her enough that she stayed awake all the way home, replaying the last few days and especially those last few words, trying to figure out how things could go wrong at this point. She did break the silence long enough to ask Mrs. G if they had to return to Cameron the next day.

"No. I told Elizabeth to text us with the sentence, and aside from that, I didn't want to hear from her for a while. No offense meant or taken, of course."

Tatia chuckled distractedly. "Of course not."

She enjoyed a leisurely dinner, an evening of meaningless banter and chit-chat, and when bedtime came, she slept the sleep of the exhausted. The next day, she immersed herself in school and office work. Later that evening, when the long-awaited text arrived, she and her family celebrated the sentence with sparkling grape juice purchased especially for the occasion.

In a show of uncharacteristic assertiveness, Mr. G insisted on making the toast. "Here's to twenty years on the charge of human trafficking, thirty years for aggravated-statutory sexual assault, and forty years for murder – the first conviction of many more to come in Cameron County. Thank you, Tatia."

Ten years later, as Tatia stared at the empty screen, she was still warmed by the emotion behind Mr. G's words and chilled by the venom behind the words that Eric had whispered in her ear. At last, she put her fingers on the keyboard and told the justice system once again why Eric Hall should remain behind bars where his actions could not have a lasting impact on more innocent victims.

SUNDAY

CHAPTER 55
JESSE'S SURPRISE

After she printed and prepared her letter for mailing, she reread the last few texts Jesse had sent her while she was remembering the trial. She sent him a quick response, telling him she was looking forward to seeing him shortly. Surprised at how much she meant that, she took a quick shower and crawled into bed, hoping for untroubled sleep. She never slept very well the night before camp, though; she was too eager to meet her girls and too busy praying for them and for all the other campers and staff. Tonight was no exception, and once she finally closed her eyes, she was troubled by dreams of Eric, out of jail and coming after her.

She awoke a few hours later feeling tired but excited. Still wearing the tank top and house pants she had slept in, she pulled on Cindy's old sweatshirt that was now more patches than shirt. She also slipped on the pillowy Dallas Cowboys house shoes that Jesse had given her a couple of years ago – the ones that were so big and ridiculous that she only wore them when she was at Refuge and then left them behind when she went home. Her outfit was probably too warm for the summer heat, even at this time of the morning, but at least she would be protected from the Texas-sized mosquitoes. She crept quietly down the stairs and out onto the porch where she stood leaning on the railing and watching the wide Texas sky where millions of stars winked at her.

She didn't realize how long she had been standing there until she heard the familiar sound of a Harley approaching, first on the county road and then on the driveway. Jesse was one of the few non-staffers Mrs. G trusted with the gate code.

Tatia's hands went automatically to her hair, and she was glad she had taken a shower the night before and had brushed her hair and her teeth before coming downstairs. Her right hand unconsciously reached over and tugged at the sleeve of her sweatshirt. In spite of the fact that Jesse – and most of the western world – had seen her tattoo, she still preferred to cover her own personal "mark of the beast."

She was expecting Jesse's black Heritage, so she was shocked when he appeared on a fire-engine red Electra Glide Ultra Classic.

It was tricked out with fairings that shielded his arms and legs from flying rocks, vicious bugs, and other airborne road hazards. What really interested her was the luxurious passenger seat as well as the hard-sided trunk and saddlebags.

Jesse was wearing a red half-helmet instead of a full-face, so even in the dim glow cast by the security light next to the driveway, Tatia could see that he was grinning from ear to ear. He pulled up in front of the gate, killed the engine, put down the kickstand, and dismounted. Tatia strolled out and leaned on the gate wearing a grin that matched his.

"Does everyone but me have a new ride?" she teased.

"How do you like it?" he beamed.

"Well, it's not understated. People will definitely see you coming."

"My thoughts exactly. I thought it would make my passenger, who will be sitting in the ultra-comfy two-up seat with extra soft padding and armrests, feel more secure knowing that we are extremely visible as well as radically audible."

"Jesse, you are as crazy as ever," she laughed.

He loved hearing her laugh. There had been times when he thought she would never smile, much less laugh, again. She walked out the gate and ran her hand over the passenger seat.

"I have to admit, it looks more comfortable than that banana seat you had on the other bike."

"Well," he said, leering at her in a playful way, "you can't take a test ride dressed like that. Go put on your jeans and boots, and let's go!"

"I'm not getting on that thing without a helmet."

He marched around the bike in a stilted manner, opened the trunk, and pulled out a red helmet that matched his exactly. He bowed at the waist, and with a comical flourish, he presented the helmet to her. "Your *chapeau, mademoiselle*."

With equal formality, she curtsied and accepted the helmet. "How can I resist such a presentation? Thank you, kind sir."

They continued to smile into each other's eyes, and she felt the same flutter in her chest she always felt when she first saw him after a long separation. She became flustered, and looked down at the helmet. "Here," she said, shoving it toward him. "Put this on my seat, and I'll be back in a couple of minutes."

She trotted toward the door, but stopped at the edge of the porch and turned back toward him. "I'm glad to see you, Jesse. I've missed you."

"Yeah, Tatia. Me, too."

She smiled, and then dashed through the door and up the stairs.

As she disappeared around the curve, Mrs. G came walking down the entryway wearing her robe and slippers. She glanced up the stairs with a loving smile, and then she fixed a scowl on her face before she threw the door open.

"When you said you were coming early," she growled, "I didn't know you were going to wake up the whole house in the middle of the night."

Jesse had pulled a cleaning rag out of the trunk and was wiping bugs off the windshield. He looked up and tried to hide his grin behind an appropriately penitent look. "Yes, ma'am. I'm sorry, ma'am. I asked the dealer for a quiet one, but this was all they had."

She laughed and shook her head. "I'll just bet you did. Now get up here and give me a hug."

"As you wish!" he said. He vaulted the gate, trotted up the walk, and swept her into a bear hug, swinging her around and setting her back on the porch. "I thought hugs weren't allowed around here," he said with a wink.

"Only from the ones with issues," she said with a sigh. "I hope you won't give up on her, Jesse. She really cares about you."

"Mrs. G," he said seriously, "I'll wait as long as it takes – and if what we have is all there is, that will be enough."

"You're a good man, Jesse"

The door burst open, and a bunch of yawning young women straggled out. There were hugs from those who had known Jesse for years, introductions to the few who didn't know him, admiration of the new bike, and requests for rides. Suddenly, a shrill whistle pierced the cacophony.

"Ladies," said Tatia in a commanding voice. She stood on the porch, dressed in black boots, black jeans, and a black long-sleeved Harley T-shirt Jesse had given her the previous summer. A pair of black, wrap-around sunglasses and a stern look completed the image. With her hands on her hips and her feet firmly planted shoulder-width apart, all she lacked was a cape to complete the super hero look. "Get away from my ride and unhand my driver," she said as she descended the steps and strode down the walk.

The girls broke into gales of laughter and backed away from the bike, bowing and scraping in mock fear as she passed. She turned back toward the house and gave the royal wave, raising her hand and giving it a slight twist as if screwing in a light bulb. The girls screamed and waved as if she really were a princess.

As soon as he saw her come out the door, Jesse had mounted the bike, pulled it into an upright position, and raised the kickstand. With a wide grin, he announced, "Your majesty, your chariot awaits." She picked up the cherry red helmet, the one splash of color in her outfit, and fastened the strap under her chin. Then, in one graceful move, she stepped onto the footboard, swung her other leg up and over the back of the seat, and settled in. She put her hands on the armrests and wiggled around a bit as if finding just the right spot.

"Hey," she said, "this really is comfortable!"

"Told ya!" he said, still grinning. He waved at Mrs. G who held up her wrist and tapped her watch.

"We're leaving for camp at 11:00," she said.

"Yes, ma'am, I'll have her back in plenty of time," he shouted back. Then, before she could reply, he fired up the Harley with a roar – and the crowd went wild. He made a full circle around the driveway before heading toward the gate, racking the pipes up to an ear-splitting volume, and the girls screamed wildly and waved until the bike was out of sight.

Even though the sky was beginning to lighten, the sun was still not up and there was a bit of an unseasonal chill in the pre-dawn air. When he stopped to wait for the gate to swing open, Jesse shouted over the rumble of his idling engine, "Are you warm enough? If not, I have a sweat jacket in the trunk."

"I'm good," she said, "but thanks for checking." Tatia had ridden with Jesse a few times, often enough to know that he was an excellent rider with enough common sense to respect the power of his machine. She was also touched by his concern for her comfort and her safety, and she knew their morning ride would be a good one.

She was enjoying the fresh smell of the morning air and the feel of the breeze in her face when she became aware that Jesse had not turned toward town like she had expected him to. Instead he had turned toward the lake, and as far as she knew, there was no place in that direction to get breakfast. She totally trusted him, but she wondered once again what he had in mind.

She didn't have long to wait. A minute later Jesse turned the big bike onto the access road to the public boat ramp and then maneuvered it into one of several empty parking spaces. He glanced over at the horizon where the first arc of the sun was just beginning to show.

"Great!" he said. "We haven't missed it." He put down the kickstand, pulled off his helmet, and hung it by the strap from the handlebar. He hurried around to the left saddlebag where he pulled out a thermos. Then, he opened the trunk and pulled out a blanket which he pitched to Tatia.

"Go spread that out, and I'll bring breakfast."

As she watched his hurried preparations, a curious smile tugged at the corners of her mouth. She knew he would reveal himself soon enough, though, so she found a relatively flat spot that was almost free of rocks and afforded a great view of the sunrise. She was on her hands and knees smoothing the wrinkles out of the blanket when Jesse walked up with the thermos and a picnic basket. He watched her for a minute and wanted nothing more than to pull her to her feet and hold her in his arms. Instead, he sat down on the blanket and patted the blanket beside him.

"Have a seat. The show's about to start."

A few clouds had gathered on the horizon, obscuring the sun but scattering the colors into a spectacular sunrise. Jesse opened the basket and removed two thermal mugs and then filled them with steaming coffee from the thermos. "French vanilla creamer, just like you like it."

Tatia took a sip, closed her eyes, and sighed. "Perfect! Nothing like the first sip of coffee."

He pulled a small round basket out of the larger one. Several dish towels wrapped it, and when he removed them, a warm, delicious smell distracted her attention from the sunrise. "What do you have in there?" she asked leaning over to take a look. She saw two varieties of bite-sized quiches and a dozen small chocolate covered cream puffs. "I don't believe it! Did you bake these?"

"I did!" he said proudly. "Straight out of the freezer and into the oven. And just in case you're worried about your weight, I brought fruit." He produced a plastic container of mixed melon, grapes, and pineapple with the deli tag still attached.

"Jesse, you're amazing!" she said, reaching out and covering his hand with hers.

A jolt like an electrical shock traveled up his arm when her hand touched his, but he forced himself to sit still, holding his breath, afraid of spoiling the moment. Tatia was equally shocked when she realized what she had done. She sat for an awkward moment staring at her hand, enjoying the feel of his hand under hers, but uncomfortable at the same time. Slowly, she pulled her hand back and raised her eyes to his. "I mean it. You're a very special man."

"So are you," he said. There was a split second of shocked silence before they both burst out laughing, and the momentary tension was broken. They enjoyed their breakfast, catching up on the news since their last FaceTime session and sharing plans for camp. Finally, she sat back and said, "I can't eat another bite. It was all delicious and a wonderful surprise."

"Surprise? This wasn't your surprise," he said, grinning mysteriously.

"Well, this and that," she said pointing toward the bike.

"Ha! That's not it either. Are you ready for the real surprise?"

"I can't imagine anything that would be better than this, but sure. Bring it on."

He walked over to the bike and retrieved a small cardboard folder from the saddlebag. He returned to the blanket and set the folder down between them. He took a deep breath and began.

"You know I've been doing cover-up tats for gang members."

"Uh-huh."

"Well, lately I've had requests from girls who have other kinds of tattoos – marks from a particular pimp or stable – and most of them are barcodes."

Tatia drew back almost imperceptibly. She crossed her arms in front of her and unconsciously placed her hand over her own tattoo which was already covered by her sleeve.

Jesse went on. "At first, I did cover ups for all of them, but some of the girls were still tormented, knowing what was under the beautiful picture. I did some research and found this new removal system that uses a combination of light and magnets to break up the ink and remove it."

"Kind of like a laser?" she asked in a flat voice.

"Yeah, but less invasive. While I've been helping these girls, I've been thinking about you." He glanced at her arm, and she tucked it a little closer to her body. "We've never talked about it, but you know I saw it. Anyway, this is the surprise."

He flipped open the folder and revealed a transparency with a small rendering of Mrs. G's house. Above it was a rough piece of wood bearing the legend "My Father's House."

Tatia stared at it for a minute or two. "It's beautiful," she said. "But I'm not sure I understand what it's for."

"I'll show you, if it's okay," he said, reaching for her hand. She flinched, and he stopped with his fingers resting on her wrist. "Do you trust me?" he asked quietly. She nodded as a tear escaped from the corner of her eye and rolled down her cheek. Slowly she relaxed her arm until the back of her hand lay in his palm. He gently stretched her arm out until their nested hands rested on his knee. Then, he wrapped his other hand around the edge of her sleeve and began to push it up toward her elbow. She grabbed his hand with her free one.

"Don't!" she whispered.

He stopped and gazed into her eyes. "I will never do anything you don't want me to do. And I will never intentionally hurt you."

They sat with their eyes locked in an embrace until her hand began to relax again. Then, still gazing into his eyes, she gently covered his hand with hers and, using both their hands, she pushed her sleeve up until her barcode was exposed. He didn't move until he felt her relax completely. Then, he removed the transparency from the folder and carefully laid it over the barcode. When it was perfectly aligned, he looked up at her. She was staring out at the water, and her tears were flowing freely.

"What do you think?" he asked.

She dashed the tears away with her free hand, and with great effort, she forced herself to look at the arm she had avoided for years. Her eyes widened in wonder, and then she began to sob. "It's perfect," she managed to choke out.

"Of course," he said, "I could remove it if you prefer. You know, if it would bother you knowing it was still there."

"No," she said as her sobs began to subside. "I want it there. I want to remember what Jesus saved me from."

They sat quietly for a few minutes until Jesse began to chuckle. "What's so funny?" she asked.

"We'll have to work out the when and the where, but regardless, this is going to involve quite a bit of touching," he said.

A little smile flitted across her lips. Then she sighed, still staring at her hand which was resting on his.

"Jesse, I don't know why you keep coming back. You give so much and get so little."

"Look at me." She slowly raised her eyes and looked into his totally serious face. "Tatia, I..." He swallowed the word he wanted to say and continued. "I care for you more than I can say. I want you to be a part of my life, no matter what that looks like. I will always be here for you, and whatever you have to give will be enough."

She continued to gaze into his eyes as, very deliberately, she rotated her hand in his until their palms were touching. As his fingers curled protectively over hers, they shared the tender healing of a deep friendship with the promise of so much more. At that moment, the Texas sun burst up through the clouds, and a new day dawned.

EPILOGUE
SIX MONTHS LATER...

Mrs. G sat in her chair staring at the cursor blinking on a blank screen. Kensey, who was now the full-time IT manager for the ministry, was waiting for her weekly words of inspiration column so she could post it on the website, but her mind was as blank as the screen. She picked up her notebook and began flipping through the pages, hoping a random note she had jotted down during her morning quiet times would spark an idea. She was about to give up hope when Tatia's ringtone sounded on her phone.

"Tatia!" she said with a smile in her voice. "You called at just the right moment to save me from a bad case of writer's block."

"Glad to be of service," Tatia laughed. "What are you working on? Anything exciting?"

"Not yet, but God's Word is always exciting. I just need to settle on a Scripture and the rest will come. Now, tell me what's going on in your life. That's always inspiring."

"What's on your schedule for the third Saturday in April?"

"Just a minute – let me check." Tatia could hear the rustle of pages as Mrs. G flipped through her calendar. "It's clear at the moment. Do you want to plan a meeting or something?"

"No, a wedding."

"A wedding?" said Mrs. G, her voice rising with excitement. "You mean...?"

"Yes, Jesse and I are getting married."

"Oh, Tatia, that's wonderful news! I've been praying."

"I know. And God has heard you."

"We're going to have to get busy. We don't have much time to plan a wedding."

"It shouldn't be a problem. We want to keep it simple. You and Mr. G and maybe a couple of other witnesses in the chapel."

"Okay. We can do that. Can we have a party in the house afterward?"

"Sure, as long as you don't get too extravagant."

"Who, me?" Tatia could hear the grin in her voice. "Do you want to send me a guest list, or will you leave that up to me?"

"You can do it. We just want a few friends from Refuge and from camp. You know – the ones we've been closest to."

They chatted for another ten minutes or so about colors, cake, and other details. Then, when the conversation slowed a bit, Mrs. G asked a question.

"Tatia, I don't mean to get too personal, but I have to ask. You've known Jesse for a long time, and I've never seen a more loving friendship than the one you share, but have you thought this through? I mean, are you really ready for marriage – for all the aspects of marriage?"

Tatia laughed. "Yes, Mama G. Jesse and I have been seeing a counselor together for several months, and all three of us agree that I'm ready. It may take a little time and adjustment, but I have never known a more patient man than Jesse. We will be fine."

"I know you will. I'm just being a nosy old woman."

"No, you're not. You just want what's best for me, and I love you for that. And I love you for all your good advice and for your prayers. Keep it up!"

"You can count on that."

After a few more minutes, the conversation ended. As soon as she disconnected, Mrs. G bowed her head. "Father, thank You for this new family You are bringing together. And thank You for this big house You've blessed us with. I have a feeling we're going to need lots and lots of room."

Two years later...

Tatia's ringtone sounded, and Mrs. G distractedly hit the speaker button.

"Tatia? What's up?"

"We want to come for Christmas this year, and I wanted to get our reservations in early."

Mrs. G turned away from her computer screen and gave Tatia her full attention. "Oh, sweetheart! You know I always have a room available for you two."

"Oh, and Mama, this year make it a room for three."

"Three?"

"Yes, and we'll need a crib."

It was the first time she had ever heard Mama G scream.

COMING SOON!

FALLEN ANGEL SALVAGE

BY LINDA BRENDLE

FALLEN ANGEL SALVAGE

"Mommy, did I get any more cards today?"

It was the day before Joy's birthday, and she had received more mail in the last week than she had in the previous nine years. She loved the emails and e-cards her mom and dad shared with her, but she loved the cards that came in the mail even more. They felt more like they belonged just to her. Tatia sorted through the small stack of envelopes and handed two of them to her daughter.

"It looks like there's one from Alicia at school and another one from Mama and Papa G. How many is that from them anyway?"

"Seven! One every day for a whole week! What about that one. Is it for me?" she asked pointing to the plain white envelope Tatia was staring at curiously.

"No, it's addressed to me, and it doesn't have a return address."

"Probably a bill," said Joy, and she took her cards to the couch to read them.

Tatia opened the envelope and pulled out a single sheet of notebook paper. On it was taped a small article from the Cameron Morning Telegraph dated the previous Sunday.

Cameron, TX. After serving twenty years of three concurrent sentences for murder, aggravated statutory sexual assault, and human trafficking, Eric Hall was paroled from the Texas State Penitentiary at Huntsville this week. His was the first of several convictions that resulted after a very brave young woman, later identified in her book Groomed for the Streets *as Tatia Robins, testified against him. These convictions freed Cameron from the human trafficking trade that had plagued our city for years.*

Below the article was a short, hand-written message:

I wonder if Joy is as brave as her mother.

ABOUT THE AUTHOR

Linda first began to write during her years as a caregiver. After two memoirs, *A Long and Winding Road* and *Mom's Long Good-Bye*, she ventured into the world of fiction. *Tatia's Tattoo* will be followed soon by *Fallen Angel Salvage*, the continuing story of Tatia, her family, and Eric ten years later.

In semi-retirement from the business world, Linda holds a part-time job as secretary for her church and an on-line position as an accounting specialist for BookPros. She also writes a column for the weekly newspaper in the tiny East Texas town where she and her husband David live with their feral cat Kitty.

Blog www.lifeaftercaregiving.wordpress.com
Email lindabrendle@yahoo.com

Photo courtesy of Constance Ashley, Photographer, www.constanceashley.com